'A fantastic and intense book that grips you right from the very first line.'

—We Love This Book

'McGowan's pacey, direct style ensures that the twists come thick and fast.'

—*The Irish Times*

'A riveting police thriller.'

—*Woman* (Pick of the Week)

'Taut plotting and assured writing.'

—*Good Housekeeping*

'A gripping yarn you will be unable to put down.'

—*Sun*

'A brilliant portrait of a fractured society and a mystery full of heart-stopping twists. Compelling, clever and entertaining.'

—Jane Casey

'A keeps-you-guessing mystery.'

—Alex Marwood

'A brilliant crime novel . . . gripping.'

—*Company*

'A compelling and flawless thriller . . . there is nothing not to like.'

—Sharon Bolton

'Ireland's answer to Ruth Rendell.'

—Ken Bruen

THE PUSH

ALSO BY CLAIRE McGOWAN

The Fall
What You Did
The Other Wife

Paula Maguire series

The Lost
The Dead Ground
The Silent Dead
A Savage Hunger
Blood Tide
The Killing House

Writing as Eva Woods

The Thirty List
The Ex Factor
How to be Happy
The Lives We Touch
The Man I Can't Forget

THE
PUSH

CLAIRE McGOWAN

THOMAS & MERCER

Text copyright © 2020 by Claire McGowan
All rights reserved.

Published by Thomas & Mercer, Seattle

www.apub.com

Amazon, the Amazon logo, and Thomas & Mercer are trademarks of Amazon.com, Inc., or its affiliates.

ISBN-13: 9781542019996
ISBN-10: 1542019990

Cover design by Heike Schüssler

Printed in the United States of America

THE
PUSH

Prologue

The babies all look the same. They lie in a circle on a patterned rug, heads in, legs fanning out like a star. They will grow up to be so different; some rich some poor, some happy some sad, some hearty some sickly. Their lives will be determined by the jobs of their parents, the street where they live, their skin colour, their gender. But for now they are the same, despite the different skin tones and disparity in the cost of their clothes. Chubby blank canvasses, for the world to stamp its print on.

It is Monica's idea to take the picture, of course. Her clamouring Instagram followers need to be fed. She calls it a *flat lay*, only with children instead of books and cups of coffee and flowers. Some of the group don't want their babies in the shot – Hazel raises an objection, *we didn't want his picture online yet*, and Aaron surprises everyone with his dislike of social media, and at his age too! But Monica rides roughshod over them all, and so the babies in their blue and pink and yellow are arranged and the shot is taken, and Instagrammed and Facebooked and hashtagged, out there forever in the world, the children at two weeks old appearing in more digital impressions than recent ancestors would have in their lifetimes.

The picture was taken at 2.35 p.m., the timestamp helpfully showed. The police would later have the task of trawling through every image taken that day, which was a lot. By 3.02 p.m., the murder had taken place, though of course it would be some time before they could even prove that's what it was.

Alison

'There were twelve adults here?' said Alison to the PC guarding the crime scene. It was a boiling-hot day, just her luck to catch on-call duty during a heatwave. She'd grumbled about it as she headed to the car from her flat, her skin a slick of suncream and the sky denim-blue, but part of her was pleased, despite the sweat pooling behind her knees. This was a big one. A death at a barbecue in this suburban corner of South-east London. A fall from a high, glass-sided balcony. A multi-million-pound house with blood spatter all over the rockery, and a dozen suspects screaming and complaining and having hysterics at various locations in the house and garden. Not to mention the babies.

The babies. Alison was trying hard not to look at them, but they made themselves known, howling little bundles of pure need. She counted four dotted around the house, held tightly in arms. Some kind of antenatal group reunion. There'd been six couples in the group, she had gathered. Shouldn't there have been six babies for six couples? She made a mental note to find out. She could hardly take witness statements from the babies, however, which was a shame, as she wasn't getting much sense out of the adults either.

If you counted the teenager, thirteen adults had been here for the barbecue. Alison's mam, a Catholic from Cork, would consider that unlucky – one year at Christmas Alison's brother Liam had been made to eat his dinner in the kitchen, to avoid having thirteen at the table. And it was true it hadn't ended well here. Someone was dead, on a Saturday afternoon in June, a perfect sunny day, at a barbecue, a reunion of a baby group. It should have been a happy event. Alison didn't often get called out to houses like this.

The house was massive – five bedrooms – ultra-modern with marble and glass everywhere. The back garden was overhung by the balcony, which looked on to a collection of rocks and plants tumbling down a hill to the lawn, which in turn backed on to a park and even had a gate leading out to it. Bright green grass. Hot blue sky. A smell of recently cooked meat, and clumps of people standing about wild-eyed and shocked. Alison was doing sums in her head – a million quid at least, for the size, for the location. Most likely more.

She took a breath. *What do I do with this?* It was overwhelming for a moment, all these hysterical people who couldn't seem to answer a straight question, many of them crying, babies grousing, the heat, the dead body on the rocks. Then sudden cloud drifted over the garden, and instantly it changed everything, the flowers now less jewelled, the food less appetising, the people paler and more shocked. Even the dead body, crumpled on the rocks, suddenly looked smaller. More manageable. The blood less scarlet. As the heat dissipated from her head, Alison felt more in charge. She straightened up, adjusted her sweaty polyester suit. 'Right,' she said, to the constable guarding the body, who looked very young and unsure indeed. 'Who owns this place? I'll speak to them first.'

Jax – ten weeks earlier

I used to be proud of my body. I wasn't obsessive about it, I still ate cake and roast dinners, and lay on the sofa on Sunday afternoons watching old *Poirot* re-runs and posting M&M's into my mouth. But it was reliable. I rarely got sick, I could hike up Munros and swim across lakes and survive an advanced spin class with Leslie, who'd made more people cry than *Toy Story 3*. That was before.

But since getting pregnant, I seemed to have lost control of it. It would arbitrarily start to leak or weep or flush red or demand to pee, despite being literally on the way out of the loo. Maybe it was overwhelmed coping with what my GP called 'a geriatric first-time pregnancy'. I didn't feel geriatric. Before this, I still wore miniskirts and went to festivals. Until meeting Aaron I had stayed up all night at least once a month. I got IDed in Sainsbury's often enough to carry my driving licence in my wallet. But despite all these things, despite the years I'd held time at bay, I really was thirty-eight, and my body was showing me this by slowly crumbling around me with each new day of my pregnancy.

The morning of the first group meeting, Aaron found me on the bathroom floor, weeping. 'What's happened now?' He hunkered down beside me.

I hiccupped. 'Can't get my shoes on.' I had overbalanced and almost fallen trying to tie the laces.

'Come here, I'll help you.' He was so good. He'd grown up helping foster siblings, younger kids in the care homes, and now me, his geriatric pregnant girlfriend. 'Babe, it's OK.' I let him prop me on the side of the bath, not as easy as it used to be when I wasn't enormous.

'Do we have to go?' I bleated, pathetically, as he eased my feet into my Converse.

'We've paid for it now. And it'll be good, come on. Meet other people in the same boat, yeah?' It was true we had paid for it, and money was tight at the moment. The flyer had come through the door one day, a stock photo of happy pregnant ladies and their partners, standing around some medicine balls. *Antenatal group. Meet other new parents and learn what to do!* That sounded good to me. I had no idea what to do. But all the same, now it was time, I felt afraid. Nervous, in some way I didn't understand. Like I was about to take a test, one I hadn't studied for and wasn't at all sure I would pass.

Aaron had a way about him, gentle but steadfast, that could get me to do almost anything. Soon I had my shoes on and was in the car heading to the community centre where the antenatal group was held.

I'd never liked groups. Even at school I was the rebel who'd refuse to join in with the shared Home Economics project, making a pair of curtains or whatever (why?). My mother had always despaired of that. Changing my name from the decorous *Jacqueline* to the ladette *Jax*. Running out on my wedding to my ex, rich and terminally dull Chris, and then getting pregnant at thirty-eight with a guy fourteen years my junior. But I didn't care. Offending my mother meant I was on the right track, that I'd escaped my middle-class fate of listening to *The Archers* and getting really into gardening.

When I walked into the community centre, I could tell right away that this, the baby group, was not my kind of thing. A group of men and women sat in a semicircle on plastic chairs, in a dingy hall with parquet flooring and high, dirty windows. There was a trestle table with some paper cups and a tea urn, a Tupperware container of professional-looking cupcakes, which someone had clearly brought with them. No one was talking, like people in a new and unsure social situation. I hung back, hands on my bump. Aaron indicated two free seats and I shuffled towards them, not making eye contact. A quick glance around told me there were two clearly not-pregnant women in the group, and I wondered why – gay couples? Hysterical pregnancy that everyone was too polite to mention?

'Hello there,' said another woman, brightly. She was forty or past it, wearing a lot of diamonds. Her voice was authoritative, as if she might be the group leader, but she was pregnant and seemed to be with the man beside her, a Riviera type in cream slacks, fingering what I hoped what his phone through his trouser pocket. 'I'm Monica. We're just waiting for the facilitator.'

'Jax,' I muttered, sitting down, or rather collapsing, which was what I did these days. Aaron, politer, shook hands, and there was some murmur about setting up an email group to keep in touch. I could see them register us, how young he was, how old I was, perhaps wondering briefly if I'd brought my grown-up son as my birth partner. But then, everyone had something. No one's life was simple. I didn't have to make any small talk, thank God, because the door opened then and the facilitator came in, clinking jewellery and swishing a long print skirt, and she was so slim and tanned and beautiful I immediately felt like a cow. She even had a toe ring. I hadn't been able to reach my toes for months. Her eyes, bright blue, swept over us all. Her voice was husky, sexy.

'I'm Nina. Welcome, everyone, to your exciting journey.' Three seconds in and someone had already used the word *journey* in a non-transport sense. I was going to hate this.

◆　◆　◆

It was amazing how different we all were. All we had in common was we lived in the same part of South-east London, Beckenham-Penge-Crystal Palace, and we were all having babies. Well. In a manner of speaking.

The youngest person there, even younger than Aaron, was Kelly, who was twenty-two. That seemed an almost indecently young age to be pregnant nowadays, but I reminded myself that was how old my mother had been when she'd had me, already married for a year. Did we just grow up more slowly these days? The oldest mum was Monica, the lady with the diamonds, resplendent in her flowered Boden smock. She was forty-four, she told me proudly. It wasn't IVF, she was at pains to point out. *All natural!* 'This is Ed, my beloved.' Ed looked like a boiled ham that had wandered down Jermyn Street.

Then there was Cathy, who looked a few years younger than me, and Hazel, her partner. Wife, maybe. Hazel kept her hand on Cathy's bump all the time, as if an alarm might go off were she to remove it. I wondered how they'd done it, wondered if they were thinking the same about me, if I'd needed IVF at my age, why Aaron was even with me when he was so young and so ridiculously handsome. There was Aisha, pretty underneath a headscarf, who I guessed was about thirty, with her handsome husband who wore what looked like a paramedic's uniform. And then there was Anita.

Ah yes, Anita. Around forty, I guessed, and not obviously pregnant. She was sort of a faded version of Monica, rich but in a kind of hemp and tote-bag way, all nervy, darting little glances at our swollen bellies. It was so weird, this many pregnant women together. Like a milking parlour at a dairy farm. All those extra people who were in the room and yet not.

Nina, the leader, looked round at us, her eyes startling in her tanned face. Something a little piercing behind them. I was aware that I'd sat up straight, wanting her to like me. 'So. Let's all tell the stories of how we came to be here.' I tried to catch Aaron's eye – what did she want, positions? – but he was staring at her, determined to take it all in. Bless him. So worried he wouldn't do the right thing, like whoever his parents had been.

I squeezed his hand, then realised everyone was staring at me. 'Oh! I'm Jax, Jacqueline, and this is my partner Aaron, er . . . it's our first.'

'Both of you?' asked Nina, and I flushed because I realised she meant I was so much older than him that I might already have kids. I could have kids in their twenties, really. 'Yeah.' I turned my eyes to Anita, willing Nina to move on.

'Oh hello,' Anita twittered. 'I'm Anita, this is Jeremy.' Jeremy was a rumpled tweedy type, with longish greying hair and a fashionable scarf. He appeared distracted and didn't look up when she said his name. 'Obviously we're, I mean, I'm not pregnant – we're using an adoption agency. In America.'

'So . . . you won't be around the baby till it's born?' This was Monica, hands on her own smug bump.

'Um, no. They don't encourage contact. They think it just . . . complicates the issue.'

'Goodness,' laughed Monica. 'It's taking a lot on trust, isn't it? I'm not sure *I* could do it.' I decided I might hate Monica.

Nina was taking notes; I wondered what she'd written about me. 'How far along are you, Monica?'

Monica paused. 'Isn't it a group for people eight weeks off? I'm eight weeks off.'

'Right.'

'Although they can't always tell for sure. Isn't that right?'

'Sometimes,' was all Nina said.

Next was Cathy. Hazel spoke for them both, hand never moving from the bump, explaining that they'd used a donor from Denmark and conceived via home insemination. Nina: 'Cathy, you're also eight weeks off your due date?'

'Um, yes.'

A short silence while Nina wrote that down. 'In your situation of course, it's quite certain when you conceived.'

'Um . . . right.'

Nina made another note, then her gaze moved on to Kelly, who was sitting beside an empty seat. She mumbled that her partner Ryan had to work today, but was 'dead excited about being a dad'. She looked so young, and I realised she could be my daughter at a push. How depressing. There was also Rahul and Aisha, and they looked unsure when called on and spoke over each other.

'This is Ai—'

'I'm Aisha – oh, sorry. You go.'

'Sorry. I'm Rahul. It's our first. Er. Yeah.'

Then there was Nina. I felt a surge when I looked at her, almost like when I'd met Aaron two years before. I knew I could either hate her or worship her. She could have been any age from twenty-five to forty-five. The toe rings. The artful curly hair, the tattoos on her taut brown arms. My own tattoos had begun to sag and discolour as I stretched, exactly as my mother had warned me they would. 'So,' Nina said, once we'd all introduced ourselves. Her eyes seemed to bore into mine, though it must have been an illusion. 'Let's begin.'

Six couples, twelve people in the room. Thirteen if you included the absent Ryan. Unlucky for some.

◆ ◆ ◆

Monica was the kind of woman I sometimes wished I could be. She packed the Tupperware container of cupcakes – empty now of course, Aaron had eaten three – into a cotton tote printed with *I Shop Local*. 'So lucky to have such a diverse group,' she trilled to me. Monica had already told us several times that she was forty-four. Forty-four and pregnant. I'd thought I was getting on a bit. And yet she looked great. The rest of her was trim, her ankles unswollen, her face unpuffy, her breasts unsaggy, as far as I could see anyway without staring. I could tell she'd had her hair cut and coloured recently and her flashy rings still fitted her fingers. Aaron had half-heartedly proposed to me when I got pregnant, but I'd have felt too stupid standing in a big white dress next to my child-groom. Anyway, he couldn't afford a ring. If I wanted diamonds, I'd have to buy them myself.

Monica leaned in – expensive perfume – and said, 'So. Where did you find *him*?' I turned, saw her nod at Aaron, who was chatting to Kelly. *They're closer in age*, I thought with a pang. If Kelly looked too young to have a baby, did that make Aaron too young to be a dad?

'Oh. Well, we just met, you know. In a bar.' That was the official story, even if the truth wasn't quite that.

'Lovely.' I blinked at her naked admiration of him. Was this the way men talked about their trophy wives? 'How old is he? Twenty-one?'

'Twenty-four.'

She cackled, digging me in the side. 'Good on you, girl! Isn't it funny, Ed's son from his first marriage is twenty-four.' I glared at her, and despite the undeniable deliciousness of her cupcakes, decided I did hate her after all. She didn't seem to notice the glare – how I envied that, the ability to not see real slights, let alone not imagine fake ones. 'Must dash, I have prenatal yoga and then a spot of acu, have you tried it? I've got a wonderful lady if you want the number, byeee.' She beckoned to Ed, who I hadn't heard speak yet but already knew I wouldn't like – I didn't trust men who wore pastels – and they went out, and Kelly followed them, zipping a hoody up to her acned chin. She looked about fifteen. I saw Aaron was now talking to Nina the facilitator, and as I watched, she squeezed his upper arm, which I knew from experience was firm and muscled, and although it was probably just an encouraging gesture, something about it made my heart lurch, and I crossed the room to them a little too fast. 'We should go. Don't forget your jacket.'

He looked surprised at my tone. 'OK, babe. Nina was just recommending me some parenting books.'

'It's wonderful he's so involved,' said Nina in her husky voice, as if Aaron was some precocious child. 'Not all young fathers are the same.'

'Yes, well, I was two by the time my dad was his age,' I said, taking the car keys from my bag.

She saw this. 'It's hard to drive at this stage of pregnancy. Dad should think about doing it, if possible.'

'Hmm, yeah, shame Dad doesn't know how.' It embarrassed me that he didn't have a licence, though lots of people didn't drive these days, especially in London. It made him seem even younger, I felt. My mother always commented on it whenever we saw her.

Nina was watching me. 'Jax, may I give you a piece of advice?' Aaron had moved just out of earshot to get his jacket from the chair.

I wanted to say no, but why else was I here? 'What?'

'It's hard for the younger guys. Especially when there's . . . an age gap. Look after him too, yes?'

Before I could think of anything to say, Aaron was back, his arm around my shoulders. 'Thank you, that was great! See you next week!' He was so polite. I just gaped at her. Was she supposed to say things like that to me?

Nina let us go with a sort of namaste gesture, and I saw that she, like Monica, had the kind of unaffected confidence no one could pierce. I was jealous of that. Aaron might have been young, but I was the one who so often felt like a sulky teenager, stuck forever with my mother's criticisms echoing in my head.

◆　◆　◆

I still couldn't believe I was joining this new group. *Mothers*. My friends had started to drop off into it, sidle off quietly to the other side of the curtain, ever since I was in my early twenties. Some of my school friends had teenagers, grown from tiny babies in what seemed like months, to semi-adults with massive feet and sulky faces. Time was speeding up. When I met Aaron I was thirty-six, and it was like I'd woken up one day and realised – *oh my God. This maybe isn't going to happen, this whole motherhood thing.* I wasn't the kind of person who'd been desperate for a baby, for marriage and nurseries and soft plush bears – I was more MDMA and festivals and tantric sex workshops just for fun. I was afraid I'd miss something if I settled down. But when I turned thirty-six I realised – I did want that. Or rather, I didn't want to never have that, and if I didn't do it soon there was a good chance it wouldn't happen at all. I tried to imagine being in my forties, knowing it was too late. If I'd be peaceful, still enjoying my life and my disposable income, never having to wipe up anyone's vomit (unless it was a particularly hard-core night out), being able to pick up and travel as the whim took me. That could be a lovely life. The trouble was I just didn't know. I didn't know if I'd regret it, and that tormented me.

It tormented me so much that I went speed dating. I let my friend Mariel, who'd been divorced for three years and was similarly panicking about the future, drag me along to an over-thirties meet-up in some smelly City bar that reeked of bleach and spilled beer, and I felt my heart sink when we walked in. The men had a hopeless, hunted look in their eyes, sweat patches blooming under their arms. Not one was under forty. Mariel all the same threw herself at a soft-bodied, hard-faced banker with a Rolex, tinkling laughter at his sexist jokes. I went through the motions, smiling and chatting to each man – several hadn't even turned up so there was just empty air in their slots – and filling in my thoughts on a little scrap of paper. Each time I ticked: *Just friends. Just friends.* I had no intention of being friends with any of them. As Mariel resolutely failed to let me catch her eye, I drifted to the bar, determined to drink till I felt less hopeless. I didn't feel old. I'd always imagined there was still love and passion out there for me, and yes, a baby too when I felt ready. Maybe I was wrong.

'Rough night?' I hadn't looked properly at the barman as I ordered my gin and tonic, but I did then. He was very cute, mixed race with blue eyes and close-cropped hair. But so young. So very, very young.

'Do these things ever work? Do people hit it off that way?' He shrugged, placing the drink in front of me. I watched the shift of muscles in his shoulders, the long, lean span of his back. He was delicate. A boy, really. 'You probably don't know. I guess your generation does it all over the phone.'

He looked me right in the eyes then, and I gasped a little, corny as it sounds, the air punched from my lungs. 'Personally, I like to meet people analogue-style. Offline.'

'Oh? And how do you do that?'

He shrugged again, ironically. 'I work in a bar. I meet people all the time.'

'I bet you do. I bet pissed-up middle-aged women are always trying to grope you. Hen dos pulling off your trousers.'

He blushed. 'A bit like that sometimes, yeah.'

'And you? What kind of girls do you like?' Nineteen-year olds, I was thinking.

'I like women,' he said, wiping the bar with practised swipes. 'Older. Mature, you know.'

I wanted to call Mariel over and laugh (though she was by now practically wearing the banker as a scarf). The barman was hitting on me! Maybe he thought I'd be easy, a desperate older woman who couldn't score with the sad divorcés here, or that I had money. That I'd finance his band or stand-up comedy career. Little did he know I worked for a charity and barely 'earned my age', as we had once been earnestly encouraged to benchmark ourselves against others. I laughed. 'I bet that line works a treat as well. Bye.'

I took my drink away and nursed it for a while in Mariel's eye line, until she reluctantly came over, trailing laughter at the hilarious jokes of Simon, who, it would later turn out, wasn't divorced at all, or at least not to the knowledge of the wife and children he very much still had. 'I want to go. This was a bust.'

'It wasn't so bad.' She looked back at Simon, as if she could shape this unpromising man-clay into something workable. Into love, into hope.

'Come on, Mar. You can do so much better than that suit.'

She drained her white wine. 'Can I?' Disappointment seemed to radiate off her in waves, and I was worried I'd catch it.

I went home disconsolate and lay awake wondering where the middle ground was between twenty-something pick-up artists and older men cheating on their wives. But the next day after work, I found myself walking past the same bar, and thinking about the young barman with the blue eyes, the simple unaffected way he'd spoken to me. Something genuine about it, not awkward-flirty or just plain awkward like the single men I met at my age. I could call in for a drink, couldn't I? I was an independent woman in my thirties with no one to go home to; what was to stop me popping in for a small cocktail or a glass of Merlot? So I went in, on one of those small whims that change your life, and there was Aaron working again. The smile he gave me made me ashamed of my cynicism, that a young man couldn't treat me with respect and admiration without me throwing it back in his face. 'You came back,' he said.

'Yeah,' I said. That was it. Sometimes it is very simple, if you can just get out of your own way.

Afterwards, Mariel loved to tell the story of how I went speed dating and picked up the young barman instead. I didn't love it as much. In fact, I didn't really see her much nowadays.

Alison

She stared at the little stick, fighting a desperate urge to pee on it.

Tom's voice came through the door. 'It's too soon, mate, I told you.' He always called her *mate*, just like he had when that was all they were, friends, partners, colleagues. She wasn't sure how she felt about it.

'I'm not doing it!' It was far too soon, he was right. It would only be negative, even if she was, technically, pregnant. Alison peed – not on the stick – flushed, washed her hands, using the towel to push down the cuticles on her hands as her mother had taught her. She needed a manicure, but the chances of finding the time for one were up there with spotting Sasquatch on Beckenham High Street.

She opened the door to find Tom hovering. 'You've got to chill, mate.'

'I am chill,' she said, in a very non-chill voice. 'But . . . what if we can't . . . ?'

'Then we get the IVF.'

'And if that doesn't work? We only get one free round.'

'Try again, I guess.'

'Just lob five grand at it, like?'

He shrugged. That was always his attitude – do the thing to fix a problem or accept it as it was. Men. So infuriatingly practical. 'How's the case, then?'

She was grateful to change the subject. 'Jealous, are you? What's it you're stuck with, petrol fraud?' It had been a long day at the site of the death, a suburban house in Beckenham, going over forensics and taking initial eye-witness statements, and she was sweaty and tired but despite all this, fired up. It was a good one.

He scowled. 'It's so boring. And everything stinks of petrol now. Tell me about your exciting one.'

They moved into the kitchen, where dinner was cooking. She stirred the pot. It was still a surprise to find herself living like this, domestically coupled up, buying cushions and making Nigella meals, and with Tom Khan of all people, once her irritating partner when she worked in Sevenoaks, barely even a friend. Everything had changed when Alison got the offer of a promotion, but with the Met in Bromley instead of Kent, and when she announced it Tom had declared himself in a surprisingly romantic way and now they were a thing. A couple. He was still working in Sevenoaks, and they lived somewhere between the two, clinging on to the very outer edges of London, which every day extended to surround and engulf them. 'Well, there's ten possible suspects. If you don't count the babies.'

His face changed. 'There's babies?'

She stirred, not meeting his eyes. 'Well, yeah, did I not say? It was some antenatal group meet-up. Babies sort of come with the territory. I think that's the only reason they know each other.' It was strange, the diverse make-up of the group, social, racial, and age. Where else would you find such different people socialising like that? Tom turned down the dial on the hob; she swatted his hand. 'Stop back-seat cooking!'

'Yeah, yeah. Are you going to be alright with that?'

'What?'

'Babies. You know.'

'I can be around babies. I'm not some crazy barren woman.' She wished she hadn't said the word, even in jest, because it made it more real. *Barren. Barren.* She was only thirty-six, not even that old. Some of those women there were years older than her, she was sure. She had time, whatever her mother said. But it didn't feel like that. It felt monumentally unfair that even though human lives were stretching, that she could expect to live to a hundred, her fertile years were still so short. Whereas Tom's would go on and on.

'It's going to be OK.'

'You don't know that. There's only a twenty per cent chance it'll work, even with IVF. That's pretty crap, isn't it?'

'I got twenty per cent on a maths test once,' he reflected, fiddling with the hob again.

'And? Did you pass?'

'Ha. Nope.'

'And they still let you do the job. Her Majesty's finest.'

He went to set the table. 'Who's your new me, then?'

'That Diana Mendes – she's come down from North London. Young but good, I hear.' Alison had yet to work with her new partner, which was just another thing to worry about.

The cutlery drawer rattled. 'So what happened then? One of the yummy mummies snapped and pushed them over the edge?'

'I've no idea. Things were very confused. I've had ten different versions of the story so far. Most of them insisted it was an accident. A fall, a slip, no foul play, honest officer.'

'What did Colette say?'

Alison's boss was inclined to the accident angle, which meant less officer power for the case, less urgency, less budget. 'She thinks probably that, yeah.'

'But?'

He knew her so well. 'She wasn't at the scene, was she? It was *weird*, Tom. They were all, I dunno. Off their heads. Different stories. Jumpy as hell.'

'Maybe you would be, if someone just died at your party.'

'It was more than that. I'm gonna look into it, for as long as she lets me.' They'd had to let the witnesses go home overnight, but she would be calling on them all, starting tomorrow. At least until Colette pulled her off it to work on something that was definitely a crime.

Tom leaned against the counter. 'Because?' He was listening avidly, and she was glad of this, that they'd always have something to talk about together, namely the grisly things that people did to each other, the lies that they told.

'You ask me, the balcony sides are way too high to fall over accidentally. I think there must have been a push. I just have no idea who from.'

'They can do forensic modelling of that sort of thing.'

'If she gives me the budget.' It was confusing enough trying to figure out where everyone had been at the party, and exactly when the fall had occurred. All they had was the phone records, but two separate 999 calls had been made three minutes apart, which was suspicious in itself. 'You should see this house though.' She sighed, looking round at their one-bedroom flat, which could charitably be called cosy. Tiny was also a word that would fit. Cramped. 'Five bedrooms. Rockery. Glass all round, hot tub, garden studio. Not that the rockery'll be much good after forensics dig it all up.' It also currently had bits of a person smeared over it, but she didn't want to dwell on that while cooking spaghetti bolognaise. 'This is done.' She turned off the pans, fished out a colander for the pasta. As she did she caught sight of the calendar on the wall. Two days from now, a big red x was marked. The earliest day she was allowed to test, to see if it had happened this month, by some crazy chance, unlike every other month for a year. If it hadn't, it would have to be IVF most likely. And if that didn't work, if it vanished inside her like a ghost baby? Then what? Another, and another, until they had nothing left? When did you call it quits, admit you weren't going to be a parent? It might not be so bad. More money, lovely holidays, pelvic floor tone, unsaggy boobs . . . She thought of the babies today, their chubby little wrists and vulnerable heads, their helplessness. The idea of having her own seemed so far away. Two days. That was all she had to wait, but it felt like forever.

Jax – ten weeks earlier

At work, I was the opposite of how I was with my mother. Firm, authoritative, but never cruel. At least, I tried not to be. After all the self-help books I'd read, I was aware of how easily a bullied person could begin to bully another, just to assert some power, a sense of self. I strode in the Monday after the first group meeting, my bump carried high in front of me in my wrap dress. I'd given up heels when I got pregnant, with much relief – approaching forty, my body just didn't forgive me for pushing it too hard. Coffee, an unexpected spin class, carrying a bag on my shoulder – all these things could ruin me for a week.

My assistant, Dorothy, rushed out from her desk to meet me. Despite her name, Dorothy was twenty-two years old. She wore large clear-rimmed glasses and seemed to live in jumpsuits, which meant I spent more time than I should wondering how she peed. 'Problems?' I said, without breaking stride. I actually liked managing people. I tried to guide them, build their careers. There were fundraisers loyal to me spread across many of the charities in our interest area (vulnerable children and teens). I'd had half an eye on applying for a CEO post in a different charity, before I got pregnant. Funny how it just happened: a cell divided, and all your careful plans for the future were derailed. Maybe that was why my generation found pregnancy and motherhood so hard. In the past, people knew not to make plans. They knew that life was something that happened to you, not something you directed yourself.

'Um, no, all cool.' I'd tried to get Dorothy to speak more professionally, but behind the *ums* and *literally* and *all the feels*, she actually knew what she was doing, so I'd overlooked it. One day I'd coach her on how to hide all that in job interviews, how to fit yourself into the mould they expected, so later on you could unfurl yourself and smash it all wide open. I put my bag down in my office, rolled my wheely chair to the desk, and wondered if I could ask her to make me a tea. Assistants didn't seem to do that sort of thing any more.

'Where are we with the mailing?' I was keen to get our annual fundraising mail-out done before I went off. Although print mailings were old-fashioned, so were many of our donors, and it was our biggest single source of revenue each year. When I needed inspiration for my work, I usually flicked through *Protect*, our supporter magazine, thinking about the good things the money I raised could do. Training for teachers and youth workers, programmes for abused kids, even a halfway house for when they came out of care, something that would have helped Aaron a lot when he was a kid. Some days it felt like I was trying to prove it to the universe. *See, I'm a good person.* Despite the evidence against.

'The printers said, like, you could sign off the proofs this week.'

'Good. Chase them up if they're dragging their feet.' She was still hovering in the doorway. 'All OK?' I asked again.

'Um, well, there was just one kinda weird thing. A message through the info at email this morning. I forwarded it to you.' We got a lot of strange spam through there, requests for money, anguished cries for help, and so on. I sighed. I didn't need this today.

'You can send that kind of thing to Sharon, or just bin it if it's spam,' I explained patiently. Semi-patiently. I thought young

23

people were supposed to be digitally literate. Sharon was our CEO, not very good at it – if I'd wanted, I could have had her job within six months, but I had better things in mind than this middling child-protection charity.

Dorothy twisted her hands. 'It's about you, Jax.'

What? 'Alright. I'll take a look.' Finally, she left, but I could see her head at the desk outside my door, bobbing anxiously. I clicked on my email. I hated my desktop computer – I'd lobbied for years for ergonomic keyboards and proper chairs, but Sharon was of the old-school 'save the budget' approach. She didn't see that you had to balance it off against potential lawsuits from employees with RSI.

The email Dorothy forwarded had come from a bot-like address, a string of meaningless numbers and letters. It read, JACQUELINE CULVILLE IS A CHILD MOLESTER. *She got with her 'boyfriend' before he was 16. Pass it on.*

I sat and stared at it for a moment, my whole body turning cold like a wave was passing over it. What the hell? I'd met Aaron two years ago. Admittedly, he'd been twenty-two then. Admittedly, I was fourteen years older than him, something that in a man might be thought sleazy. But there was a world of difference between twenty-two and not-quite-sixteen. Wasn't there?

My finger hovered on the mouse, shaking slightly. Nasty spam, lies and rubbish. *Jacqueline*, it said, which I never called myself – only my mother called me that. I'd been Jax since university, trying to reinvent myself as someone cool and edgy. So whoever had sent this didn't know me well. I ran through names in my head – someone I'd fired, some service user with a baffling grudge? A lot of the people we worked with were unstable, not always able to see who was trying to help them and who wasn't. I told myself firmly it was nothing, blind malice, likely from someone hurting and confused. But I worked for a charity that did child protection. The merest whiff of scandal here had to be rooted out. But someone must have sent this. Someone had been watching me, and knew my partner was young, and had sat down and written this and sent it to a general inbox, that anyone could read. That meant someone must have it in for me. A jealous ex of Aaron's? I wasn't aware that he had any serious exes.

I should tell Sharon, I knew. We had to be spotless here, above any suspicion whatsoever. We'd laugh about it probably. Sharon's husband was so old he was dead – he'd had a heart attack last year. My partner was too young to hire a car by himself in some places. Maybe she wouldn't laugh as much as I thought. I breathed deeply, feeling how much this had shaken me, feeling angry that a mere string of words could do that, and I pressed delete.

I didn't tell Aaron about the email. He worried, and I could see when I came home that he already had something on his mind. When you were with someone much younger than you, money was almost unavoidable as an issue. Aaron had been working in a variety of temp jobs since quitting the bar – he wanted to spend his evenings with me, he said, and especially when the baby came he didn't want to be out hauling barrels until 2 a.m. I knew he hated the new job he'd found in an insurance office, the petty squabbles over who'd used whose margarine, the monotony of every day being the same, having to be indoors all the time. He did it for me. He was studying bookkeeping on the side, with a view to becoming an accountant, something I couldn't feel excited about and I didn't think he could either.

And me, in my turn, I worried about how little money he made in the entry-level admin job, the cost of his season ticket and suits and lunches. I'd be supporting three of us soon. That gave me another stab of anxiety over the stupid email – what if I lost my job? Who would send such a thing? But I squished it firmly down, carrying on chopping the pak choi for dinner, with Minou my Persian cross twining about my legs, hoping for titbits. Aaron knew nothing about cooking when I met him, not even how to peel a potato. In the foster homes where he grew up, they taught them to make things in microwaves and with kettles. Often, that was all they had access to in the tiny bedsits and studios the kids were kicked out to at seventeen.

'What's up?' I said.

He set down his man satchel, which I'd bought him for Christmas. It had the unfortunate effect of making him look like a schoolboy. 'Oh, nothing.' I'd learned with him that you had to ask several times to find out what he was thinking. In the homes, you didn't last long if you were vulnerable.

'Nothing?'

He sighed. 'I heard back from the adoption people today.'

'Oh?' I slid the leaves into the wok. Stir-fry felt too easy, too lazy – I could just imagine what my mother would say – but Aaron was bowled over the first time I knocked one up. *So tasty! Amazing!* It broke my heart a little, the things that impressed him. Going to the theatre. Flying. Vegetables.

Aaron had been searching for his birth mother for the past year or so. It was something he'd always wanted to do but didn't know where to start or how to even begin to feel about it. I think it was meeting me that gave him the push, the capacity to kick it off. I had researched it for him, found the right forms. We didn't even know his mother's name, which made it harder, or what Aaron had been called at birth. I think he felt it more urgently now our baby was coming, the need to search. 'They're still looking. Can't find anything so far, maybe the records went missing or something.'

'Oh. That's a bit rubbish.' Although I had helped him, I didn't know how I felt about this whole thing. Did I really want some mother-in-law coming into my life, upending everything? My own mother was enough to handle. Aaron had turned out amazing considering his upbringing, but there were dark depths I knew nothing about, moods that sprang up out of nowhere. I needed him as stable as possible now, because who knew what would happen to me when I gave birth?

My mother's voice told me I should have been leaning on him, now that I was so heavily pregnant, that if I didn't fully trust him we shouldn't be having this baby together. Since the support group, it had been joined by Nina's voice telling me to take care of Aaron, that it was a struggle for age-gap relationships. I ignored both as best I could.

Aaron hunched by the sink, and he looked even younger when he did that, a sulky angsty teenager, so I put my hand to his back and gently straightened him out. Minou, who wasn't his biggest fan – he had usurped her – slunk away. 'They'll find her, love. It just takes time. Anyway, it gives you a bit of space to adjust to it.'

His gaze snapped up, hard and blue. 'What's that supposed to mean?'

'Just that it might be tough, seeing her again.'

'Why?'

'Because . . . well, she gave you away.'

He toyed with an apple from the fruit bowl, rolling it along the counter. I wanted to ask him to stop but I struggled every day not to turn into my mother. 'She won't have had a choice. They'll have made her.' Aaron had convinced himself of this fact, that his mother had desperately tried to hold on to him. It was true he had lived at home with her until he was two, unusually old. It had made it harder for him to be adopted, which meant a life ping-ponging between children's homes and foster care. I worried that, when she did resurface, his mum would be hard-faced, tattooed, a drunk, a drug addict, not the sweet helpless girl of his imagination.

I didn't want to think about why my boyfriend, abandoned by his mother, was with me, so much older than him. He put the apple back, visibly pulled himself out of the mood. He came and put his arms around me from behind, and I sank into his warmth and strength. 'Sorry, babe. How was your day?'

I should tell him about the weird email, I knew. But something stopped me – some long-ago shame, memories I didn't want to dredge up. Fear of disturbing the calm we'd found, waiting for our baby to arrive. Nina's unasked-for advice. 'Oh, it was OK. Bit of a slog, you know. Sharon getting on my nerves.'

'You'll be out of it soon.' He massaged my neck as I finished cooking, and I wondered why the words sent a shiver down from where his hands were. That was what I was afraid of, being out of it. What would happen to my career if I stepped aside for a year, on reduced pay? And if I wasn't working, who was going to hold this tiny family together? Could I rely on Aaron to keep things running?

'Go and sit down,' I said, forcing a smile. 'It's almost ready.' As he moved out of the kitchen, I turned my gaze to the apple he'd been playing with. As I'd thought, it was bruised now. Spoiled.

Alison

Monica Dunwood, the owner of the house where the death had taken place, was very, very nervous. Alison had learned over the years that this wasn't a sign of guilt, not necessarily. She'd interviewed men about a missing wife or girlfriend who it turned out was lying murdered upstairs, and they hadn't turned a hair. She'd seen parents who knew very well that their child was dead do begging press conferences urging their 'abductor' to bring them back. Equally, some people were so distressed by the very idea of the police that they went totally to pieces, babbling about every transgression from going two miles over the speed limit to once smoking a spliff in college.

'Mrs Dunwood . . .' The woman was at the living-room window, peering out on to the street.

'Sorry. Sorry. Your car, I just – is it marked? You know, the neighbours, I wouldn't want them to ask questions.'

'You had a violent death on your property, Mrs Dunwood, I think that ship has sailed,' said Alison crisply.

Diana Mendes, Alison's new partner, frowned. 'The car isn't marked, ma'am. Why don't you sit down? Would you like a cup of tea, perhaps?' So she was good cop in this situation, forcing Alison into bad cop, and that suited her just fine in her current mood. During the hours that had passed since she'd eyed up that pregnancy-testing stick, her breasts had begun to ache, a sure sign her period was coming, like a squall of bad weather. She was telling herself it could also be a pregnancy sign, but didn't even believe her own lies.

Monica turned, distracted. 'Oh no, I don't drink caffeine.' She was that nervy without coffee? Alison would have appreciated a cup of tea herself, but apparently none was on offer.

Diana nodded. 'Please tell us, in your own words, what happened yesterday.'

'Oh, it's awful, just awful. I never could have imagined – in my house!' That stirred an echo for Alison, something she had once read or seen, but she couldn't think what. 'And my rockery's ruined. Five grand, that cost. Who's going to pay for it?'

Diana's sympathetic expression sagged a little. 'You'll have to take that up with your insurer.' Diana was a small and neat woman somewhere near thirty, with shiny black hair pulled into a bun, clear olive skin and quick, dark eyes. She reminded Alison of that US congresswoman, Alexandria something. Young and vital. Alison hadn't realised she was actually old until quite recently, when she'd seen on her medical file that she was considered geriatric in baby-making terms. Jesus wept.

'But it's destroyed! And it was practically brand new! We only moved in six months ago!'

That struck Alison. Was that an odd time to move, while pregnant? Or did it make sense to find a bigger place while you could? She caught sight of a wedding picture on the mantelpiece, noticed that Monica's hair was the same as it currently was, dark with a Claudia Winkleman fringe, so it must have been taken recently. A shotgun wedding, perhaps, if those still existed. 'How long have you been married, Mrs Dunwood?'

Was that a slight hesitation? 'A year or so. Why does that matter? I have officers in my garden, people in white suits tracking over my upstairs landing . . .'

'Yes, well, could we talk about the death?' They weren't using the word *murder*. Not yet. Not until they could get more of an idea who'd been where that day. Alison was getting the impression Diana also thought it was an accident, but still. She was going to ask questions for as long as she was allowed.

Finally, Monica sat down, perched on the edge of her grey sofa as if about to take flight any moment. She brushed at invisible crumbs on the cushion. Alison passed her a piece of paper. 'Can you confirm this is everyone who was here yesterday?'

She scanned over it, biting her lip. 'That's right. The adults, the five couples plus Kelly and . . . the other one.' She didn't seem able to say the name. 'Eleven apart from . . . you know. But no, that's not right. Chloe was here too. Thirteen! Oh God, unlucky.'

Alison raised her eyebrows at Diana, whose face remained still. 'Who's Chloe?' She was having trouble keeping track of all these people.

'My daughter, of course. My other daughter, I mean. From my first marriage.'

The teenager, then. Why did some people have children coming out of every pore, and she had none? 'And how old is Chloe?'

'Fifteen. She's at Beeches.' Alison looked blank. 'You don't know Beeches? Oh, you must not have children then, you'd know otherwise.' Alison stared very hard at an ugly ceramic lamp, thinking how easy it would be to swing it against the wall and smash it. 'It's *very* exclusive. Chloe's doing *very* well there, such a shame she's been ill, lost a whole term, but we're making sure she doesn't fall behind.'

Diana was taking neat notes. 'What was she ill with?'

'Glandular fever, poor thing.' That used to be called the kissing disease, when Alison was young. She wondered what this Chloe was like, how it would be having a mother like Monica.

'Is Chloe about today?'

'No, she's at drama club. Very important to keep up with hobbies, ahead of UCAS applications.'

'Alright, so your family is you, Chloe, your husband . . .'

'Ed, Ed Dunwood. He's a very successful trader, you know.'

'Right, Ed, and the new baby.'

'Isabella.' Monica smoothed her dress over her legs. She'd had a recent gel manicure, and her highlights looked fresh. Weren't new mothers supposed to be dishevelled? 'There were four babies here as well, if we're being completionist about it. And the twelve adults.'

'Thirteen if you count your daughter,' said Alison, just to get a reaction, and Monica twitched. Weird. Was she superstitious? Alison's mother was, of course, but she was Irish, it was to be expected. Salt flung over the shoulder, magpies counted, sign of the cross when passing a church or ambulance. Alison wouldn't have imagined it here, in this middle-class haven.

'Right.'

'Could you tell us a bit about the antenatal group?' said Diana. 'How did you hear about it, for example?'

'Oh. I saw a flyer somewhere, in a cafe I believe.'

'There weren't other groups about?' Alison had been wondering about this. Wouldn't someone like Monica, with all her money, want to go to a more prestigious group, an expensive, accredited one? With people more like her?

Monica smoothed her dress again. 'Personally, I think it's nice to meet a variety of people. It was such a lovely *diverse* group.'

'What can you tell us about Chloe's father?' Diana was diligently writing all this down.

Monica's mouth puckered. 'What relevance does that have?'

'We have to investigate any possible conflict, anyone with a motive for violence.' With so many people present, that was going to take a while.

She sniffed. 'He doesn't have much motive for anything, Thomas. Lives in Hong Kong with some much younger *Chinese* girl. Pregnant, apparently, though I suppose they can just get a nanny out there, no need for him to even think about changing a nappy. Of course, he's forgotten all about the child he already has. Poor Chloe.'

Alison crossed him off the list. It was pretty tenuous anyway – she imagined from this brief meeting with Monica that the man was more than happy to get away from his ex-wife, never mind being jealous enough to come here and cause trouble. 'What was your relationship like with the victim?' she said. Diana frowned at her; perhaps *victim* was not the right word, if no crime had been committed.

'Well, it was fine, I mean we didn't really know each other, any of us. Just through the group. That's all.' Alison waited a few moments, something she found to be very effective with nervous people. 'Just a terrible accident. We'd had the balcony steam-cleaned the week before – I do hope it wasn't slippery, or anything like that.'

Alison was about to ask another question, but she heard footsteps in the hallway and a middle-aged man came in, very red in the face to match his trousers. 'Who's that blocking the drive?' Loud, entitled voice.

'Police,' said Alison, giving him her best Bolton stare. 'Mr Dunwood? We'll need to talk to you too.'

She was gratified to see his expression change. 'Oh, er, of course, no problem. Did Monica offer you a drink? Tea, water?'

'She didn't,' said Alison pointedly. 'I'd love a tea in fact. Milk, no sugar.'

Diana was frowning again – these younger officers didn't drink tea at the houses of suspects, thinking it compromised them in some way, but Alison was parched and hot and more than likely not pregnant, and she was going to take her small comforts where she could get them. 'So, Mrs Dunwood. Please tell us in your own words everything you can remember.'

The day of – Monica

7.58 a.m.

It had to be perfect.

Perfect, it seemed to Monica, was a fairly clear concept. It meant spotless, like a properly cleaned kitchen. It meant flawless, like an expensive diamond. It meant above reproach, which was something she strived to be, every day. Unfortunately, her latest cleaner, Marisol, did not seem to share the same vision. It was almost eight on the morning of the party, and Monica was standing by the sofa in the living room, which she had lifted up by one end to show the dust underneath. She was briefly proud of her upper-body strength. 'Not good enough, do you understand? *No es bueno.*' Marisol, a stoical woman from Ecuador, looked confused.

'I'll talk to her.' Chloe had come into the room, walking silently in her bare feet. Monica hated that. Not just the footprints of sweat left on her marble floors, but the fact that she never quite knew where her daughter was. Chloe let off a string of Spanish to the cleaner, and Monica was briefly shocked at how good she was, especially given she'd missed a term of school.

'Did you explain?'

'Mum, you pay her for two hours a week. It's not enough time to clean this massive place. And hello, it's less than minimum wage.'

Monica sighed. Yes, she could afford to pay more for cleaning, but that wasn't the point. She offered market rate, and still the results weren't what she wanted. 'Well, just tell her it needs to be perfect for the party later.'

Chloe sighed deeply. 'You're really going ahead with this? Are you kidding me?'

'Why shouldn't we have a party?' It seemed obvious to Monica – a chance to celebrate the end of the group, the arrival of the babies. Or most of them, at least.

'Er, because of everything that's going on? You really want people round here, watching?'

'We have to act normal if this is going to work.' And having parties was normal for Monica. Every time she had something done to the house, or bought a new plant or rug or picture, it didn't feel real until someone had come round to admire it. And the antenatal group was a whole new group of people to dazzle and wow with her new five-bedroom house and spacious garden, her art collection, her rich husband.

And her daughter. Well, Chloe didn't quite fit into the perfect vision either. She'd have to be carefully managed, or perhaps even kept out of sight. Monica turned to the gilt mirror on the wall (antique, French, eighteenth century) and examined her body. High and full and firm, her stomach flat again. Everything looked fine. It hadn't been much fun looking fat again, of course, wearing maternity clothes for the first time in fifteen years, but at least this new baby was a chance to start over. Get it right this time, with the right husband, not the corrupting influence of Chloe's father, who was best forgotten. Monica did not allow herself to think about him, as with many things.

Walking through the house, she whisked small specks of dust from furniture, stooped without difficulty to pick up a thread from the floor. Her mind went to the antenatal group, the odd mix of people who'd be descending on her soon. Anita and Jeremy clearly had money – Monica had been on the waiting list for that handbag for a month – but Anita seemed so nervy and timid, and no wonder. Buying your baby from America must be so shameful. Then there was little Kelly, a scared scrap not much older than Chloe, her boyfriend not even around. Chavvy, of course. She hadn't been invited, for the best since she'd lower the tone – not to mention the unfortunate thing that had happened to her. Although it would be fun to see how dazzled she'd be by this place, the new rockery, the glassed-in balcony. At least the boyfriend wouldn't come and wear his jeans round his bum, like they all seemed to nowadays.

Then there were the lesbians. She didn't have a problem with that sort of thing, but they were so very *open* about it now. In Monica's day there were polite euphemisms, like her aunt with the spinster friend she went on coach trips with. The pregnant lesbian, Cathy, was surprisingly pretty for one, with long shiny hair. Feminine. The other, well, Monica didn't get it. Did they want to be men, was that it? Couldn't they do that nowadays, if that's what they wanted? She wondered how they had managed the pregnancy, and thought vaguely of turkey basters and beakers, felt queasy. Surely if you chose that kind of lifestyle, you sacrificed having children. The poor thing would be mocked at school for having no dad, two mothers. It wasn't fair really.

Then the Asian couple. She hadn't spoken much, probably he dominated her at home, poor thing. She'd heard that some Muslim women couldn't see male doctors, even in an emergency. Perhaps they'd gone private for the birth.

The fifth couple were also odd – the woman much older than the man, well, the boy really. He was a handsome lad, but he was tongue-tied and awkward like everyone under thirty nowadays. The woman, who called herself something aggressive, like a toilet cleaner, was nothing special to look at. *Jax*. Clearly, she'd had a difficult pregnancy, oozing and loosening all over, red in the face and swollen. How had she attracted such a handsome boy? Money, that must be it.

What a strange assortment. Did no one do things the right way any more, a man and a woman of the same age or ideally the man a little older, who got pregnant as nature intended? *That was the trouble*, she thought to herself, crumpling a dead petal from the floral display in the hallway (delivered fresh every five days). Nobody did anything properly any more. Corners cut all over the place.

Jax – ten weeks earlier

On Wednesdays, I left work at four – thank you, flexitime – and I went to visit my mother in Orpington. I didn't know why, since neither of us got much out of it, but it was what you did. Aaron had offered to go with me at the start, but I loved him too much to put him through it. And I couldn't stand the way her eyes followed him round the room, as if he might nick one of her Royal Doulton figurines.

I parked outside, my heart sinking at the familiar shape of the house, the fake bay windows and scrubbed-clean red brick. I might as well have been fifteen again, trailing to the door with a heavy heart, waiting to hear what I'd done wrong now. *I am thirty-eight*, I told myself. *I'm having my own baby. I have a house, a good job, a man who loves me.*

The nasty email had followed me all week, and each morning I'd been anxiously tensed for another. I'd told Dorothy to send anything strange straight to me, but there was nothing. It must have been just one of those random horrible things.

Even the sound of Mum's doorbell annoyed me. I could feel her irritation too as she tap-tapped to the door. She always wore high heels, even though there was no one else at home. 'Did you have to park so near the hedge?'

'It's OK, I didn't clip it.'

'I know what you're like. World's worst driver!'

Of course I was. A bad driver, a bad student, a bad daughter. 'How are you, Mum?' I dragged after her into the kitchen, an expanse of clean marble. She was so slim, so tiny she could fit into size-eight jeans. I was a whale beside her. I looked around; there was nowhere to sit except for some uncomfortable high stools at the breakfast bar. I'd never get on to one of those. On the wall, prominently displayed, was a picture of my father. He looked frozen, stopped in time. He'd died when I was twelve, heart attack at work, right at the culmination of the war between me and my mother that had been building since I was seven, leaving me alone with her, in this house.

Goosebumps stippled me, and I had to remind myself again that I was thirty-eight, pregnant, independent. I could stop visiting her any time. But I wouldn't, because she was my mother and I'd already lost one parent and I had no siblings. Sometimes I imagined them, my ghostly allies. She'd lost three that I knew of before me, to stillbirth or very late miscarriage. I had to remember that. I had to make allowances.

She was talking. 'Oh, it's been such a nightmare. Next door are having building work done. You know the ones. Foreign.'

'They're not foreign, Mum, they're British.' What she meant was they were Asian. I changed the subject. 'We had our first antenatal class at the weekend.'

That amused her, as I knew it would. 'I never heard the like, really. Paying to be told common sense! What kind of things do they teach you – don't leave the baby alone with knives?'

'Well, it's kind of what to expect at birth, how to look after the baby, that sort of thing.'

'Load of rubbish. We never had anyone tell us how to do it, and we were fine.' The irony of this took my breath away for a moment. I suppose in the eighties, you were doing a good job as a parent if your child had all its limbs intact and most of its blood inside its body. There was no awareness of the emotional damage you could do to a baby, like a bomb thrown into a kindergarten. 'And what are the other people like?'

'Mum, can we sit on the sofa? I can't get up on these stools.'

She raised her eyebrows (threaded weekly). 'Really, Jacqueline, there's no need to stop exercising just because you're pregnant. You don't want to gain even more weight, not at your age.'

I gritted my teeth. 'Even so.' Reluctantly, she showed me to the living room as she began to twitter around with cups and saucers. I was strictly on the decaf, no caffeine that might harm the baby, no matter how tired I felt.

'So go on then, who else is on your course? All ancient, I imagine?' She was avid for the gossip. 'I don't know what it is with these women now, leaving it so late.'

'One woman is forty-four, yeah.' Mum loved nothing more than an example of a woman doing a terrible job as a mother. Again, the irony seemed to escape her.

'Oh. You're not the oldest, then.'

Thanks, Mum! 'No. There's a twenty-two-year-old though. Quite a range.'

She sniffed. 'Common, then. Where is this group? Can't you go to a nice one?'

'Well, it's a mix, isn't it, that's kind of the point.' I quite liked that, the fact that we had nothing in common except our babies. Not that we all had babies. 'There's one woman adopting, from America.' I felt a bit guilty throwing poor Anita under the bus, but it would take the heat off me.

Mum practically hooted. 'She's not even pregnant?'

'No, her baby's over there, with this other woman.'

'It'll end in tears, mark my words. What's to stop this American woman holding on to the baby?'

41

'I don't know. Would someone do that?'

Another hoot. 'You're too naive, Jacqueline.'

There was a short silence, during which she looked like she might sit down, but then darted to the kitchen to get a cloth and wipe up a small drop of tea I'd spilled pouring it from the pot (which had leaked since 1998 but which she wouldn't replace). 'Do be careful.'

'Aaron's doing well at his new job,' I volunteered. Mum never asked after Aaron, but I kept on plugging away. Sometimes I felt like his PR woman.

'I suppose he's the youngest father there.'

'There's another young one, but he didn't come yesterday.'

'No surprise there. She'll be on her own with that child, mark my words. What does a man in his twenties want with babies?'

I sipped my weak tea, wondering if she thought of these things to hurt me, or if she was just very good at it. 'Aaron's really committed. He's got all the books and everything.'

'Yes. Well.'

I knew better than to rise to her bait, but sometimes she just pushed me too far. 'What?'

'Oh, darling. You know I don't like to interfere.'

'Don't interfere then.'

'It's just . . . Darling, he's very young. You have to be prepared that he might not stick about, when the baby comes. All the dirty nappies and screaming – he'll want to be out with friends, won't he?'

I counted to ten, held the tea in my mouth until it burned. 'I really don't think he will. He's not like other twenty-four-year-olds. He had to grow up fast.'

She sat down opposite, taking a dainty sip from her coffee. 'I just don't want to see you hurt, Jacqueline. That's all. I don't say these things to cause trouble.'

Sure you don't. It was a struggle to bite my tongue, change the subject. 'Mmm. So how's the book group?'

'Oh goodness, you won't believe this, but Louise actually suggested we read a *chick-lit* novel this time? I said, Louise, I think you'll find this is a club for serious readers. If you want to read trash do it on your own time.' I wondered if Mum would have been kicked out of the book group long ago if they weren't all so scared of her, and she didn't have the biggest living room. I let her catty commentary wash over me, wondering if things might get better when the baby came, when I was a mother myself. Or if they would just be a new person for her to terrorise. The thought of the email rose in my solar plexus again. She must never find out about it.

Jax – nine weeks earlier

The next time we went to the antenatal group, Anita had baked. Gluten-free vegan Bakewell tarts, each individual one glistening and perfect. I wanted to groan at the way women did this, forced ourselves to do extra work, make things nice for everyone. Men wouldn't even notice if we stopped; we did it for and to ourselves. I also knew that I would eventually end up baking something myself, resenting every second, just because I'd feel bad otherwise. I saw Kelly's eyes flicking nervously to the tea table as well. There had been a flurry of group emails over the week, about hospitals and sleeping positions and antacids and nurseries, so much so that I'd already muted them. Who had the time to read all that?

When Nina swept in, almost late again, she looked at the tarts as if they were foreign and blinked. She was so slim, she must never eat pastry. I highly doubted if Anita or Monica did either, but maybe the point was not to eat the thing. It was to make other people eat the thing.

Today we were learning baby first aid, which I was glad about, but which also made me anxious, thinking of all the things that could go wrong. Things we didn't even know to be afraid of when I was a kid. Grapes. Blind pulls. Cots. Nina had a baby doll with an unsettling blue gaze, and she placed it on a mat in the centre of our circle. I noticed that Kelly's partner wasn't here again today, and nor was Jeremy. 'Work crisis,' explained Anita with her nervy little laugh that made me grit my teeth. The kind of woman who was afraid to take up space in the world. I knew Jeremy was a lecturer, an academic, and wondered what constituted an emergency in that world.

Nina held the baby up, turning it round so it looked at each of us with its merciless glare. 'Imagine the scene. You leave your baby alone for a second while you answer the door. In its high chair, maybe, or on the floor.' Monica tutted, as if she would never do such a thing. 'You come back, he's turning blue. Jax. What do you do?'

I started. Why me? 'Um . . .'

'Quick! Your baby is dying!' I knew it was just role playing, and my baby was safe inside me, but those weren't the kind of words you wanted to hear when you were pregnant, all the same. I got up, shaky, and knelt down with difficulty on the mat where Nina had deposited the baby. It was the same colour as before – a sort of waxy beige – but I imagined it blue, choking, staring up at me. *Save me, Mummy.* Oh God. What did I do? I knew nothing about baby first aid, that was why I was here. Tentatively, I put my hands on its chest. It felt rubbery, nothing like a real baby.

'Full CPR can kill a child,' said Nina crisply. 'Their ribs can't take the pressure.'

'Then what . . .'

'Try two fingers. Gentle.' I massaged the fake baby, feeling both stupid and like a murderer. 'That's better. Unfortunately, your baby didn't need CPR – it was choking on a grape.'

'Who'd give a baby a grape?' exclaimed Monica. Me, apparently, the baby dunce. I'd killed him. My baby was dead.

'Would anyone else like to try?' Nina took the fake, dead baby, who could apparently come back to life, and held it out. 'Rahul?'

He came forward, took the baby and immediately held it upside down under his arm. He mimed putting a finger in its mouth. 'You feel inside, see if you can pull out the thing that's stuck, then if not slap their back gently like this.' He showed us. The fake baby juddered.

Nina angled her head. 'Very good. You've had training?'

'I'm a paramedic,' he said shyly, as everyone clapped. 'Kind of cheating.'

'That's very lucky.' She cast a glance at me, as if to say, and *good luck to* your *baby, Jax.* 'It's so important that parents know these things. A child can choke to death in seconds, drown in an inch of bathwater. We have to be vigilant. We have to be watching all the time. That's what becoming a parent means – from now on, you're responsible.'

Beside me, Aaron was taking notes on a little pad he'd bought in WH Smith. Why didn't I know these things? How did I get to almost forty without knowing how to save the life of another human being? Surely there was nothing more important.

We went round the circle, practising the move Rahul had done so smoothly, and everyone had a go. Kelly held the baby as if it were a bomb that might go off. Monica slapped it so enthusiastically it would probably die of shaken-baby syndrome. Hazel, who it turned out was a personal trainer, also knew how to do CPR, though Cathy was less sure. Aisha did it in a quietly competent way – she was a physiotherapist, she said, and I wondered if she'd met Rahul at the hospital. Aaron was good too – he'd either been watching closely, or he'd learned some first aid before, maybe when working at the bar, maybe in the homes. How did I not even know this about him?

Nina did not give me another chance, and I was too embarrassed to ask. 'Very good,' she said to everyone else, and I cravenly wanted her to say it to me too. I told myself it wasn't a competition, that I was here to learn so I could be the best mum possible, but all the same I felt like I was failing already.

Alison

'Obviously, we didn't expect Kelly to turn up to the barbecue.'

Alison was sitting in the kitchen of Hazel Jones and Cathy Hargreaves. Their little boy, Arthur, was strapped to Cathy's chest in a complicated fabric sling as she made herbal tea. 'We're a caffeine-free household,' Hazel had informed her firmly, and Alison had reluctantly agreed to a mint tea. She and Diana were working apart that day, with Diana chasing up forensics from the body and the crime scene. Monica would be furious at all the activity on her balcony, no doubt. Alison had to admit she felt more at ease without the other woman watching her interviews, judging her probably. Making her feel old and past it. 'Why did you not expect Kelly?' she asked.

Hazel widened her eyes, a gesture she had that seemed to indicate incredulity at someone else's stupidity. In this case, Alison's. 'Didn't you know? Kelly lost her baby. Stillborn at eight months.'

'It was so awful,' said Cathy, sounding genuinely distressed. 'Poor Kelly, she's so young, and that boyfriend of hers was no help at all. They've split up now, I think.'

'If you ask me, she's better off.'

'Hazel!' Cathy looked shocked.

'Well, she is. Think how he was at the group, that day, kicking off. Now she's not tied to that twat for the rest of her life. She can study, make something of herself. Plenty of time to have children later.'

'Do they know what caused her loss?' Alison would of course be talking to Kelly herself, but she'd like to go in armed with knowledge, so she didn't put her foot in it. She filed away the reference to an incident that had happened at the group – that could be relevant.

'I'm not sure. An infection of some kind, maybe.' Cathy set their cups on the table, and Alison caught a glimpse of Arthur's soft baby head between her breasts. Was he comfortable like that? Could he breathe? Was it like an adult having their face stuck in the pantry all day?

'So, what, she stopped coming to the group after that?'

'Well, of course she did.' Hazel reached over Alison to take a mug, blew on it aggressively. 'All those smug mums. Wouldn't you?' It jolted Alison, the exact thing she'd been thinking, coming from this woman she'd assumed she'd have nothing in common with. Then Hazel ruined it by waving her cup and saying, 'We make our own teabags, you see. We're a zero-waste household.'

'Not even nappies?'

Hazel opened her eyes wide again. 'Especially not nappies. Landfills are absolutely choked with them! We're doing terry cloth and washing them.'

'*I'm* washing them,' said Cathy, sitting down. She hadn't made tea for herself. She looked exhausted. 'Hazel's not found much time to do it.'

A brief moment of tension went between them, their eyes locked in some kind of silent argument. 'I'm working,' Hazel said, looking at Cathy still.

Alison felt she had to step in. 'You didn't get maternity leave, Hazel?'

'No I didn't – how discriminatory is that? I might sue.'

'You're self-employed,' said Cathy, in a quiet voice. Hazel glared at her.

Alison took a sip of her drink – mint-flavoured hot water. What was the point? She eyed the couple over the rim of the cup, which was lumpy and looked handmade. She was here to examine these two, run her fingers over their lives searching for bumps or cracks. Hazel was toned, fit, tattoos on bare wiry arms in a vest. Her hair had been shaved up into an undercut, in a way that Alison had to admit looked tough and sexy. She moved all the time with restless energy, tapping her fingers and eyeing the room as if looking for something to improve. She was a personal trainer, she'd said, staring at Alison's doughy middle.

Cathy was younger – eight years younger. All the same, her long brown hair was greying at the roots, and she seemed slow and tired. Understandable when she'd just had a baby. She winced when she sat down, hinting at unknown horrors in the undercarriage department. She worked for the council that ran the leisure centre Hazel trained at; this was how they'd met. Alison said, 'I'm sorry I have to ask this, but you used a donor? I mean, what kind of donor?' Of course they'd used a donor, duh. They'd hardly done it themselves. Tom would have ribbed her mercilessly for that. 'I just need to check everyone's . . . associations.'

'Overseas,' said Hazel, even as Cathy was opening her mouth to answer. 'Denmark, that's where most of it comes from in the UK.'

'And . . . was it IVF or . . .' She was trying not to say the words *turkey baster*.

'Home insemination. Cathy popped up to the bathroom and did it.' Hazel did not seem remotely embarrassed, and why should she be? Alison would have to get over her own qualms if she and Tom were going to embark on fertility treatment, which seemed to

49

involve talking to total strangers about the state of your cervix on a regular basis. 'Lucky for us it worked first time.'

'And you chose Cathy to be pregnant because . . . ?'

The eyes went wide again. 'I'm older, obviously. And I had some . . . issues.'

'Hazel has PCOS,' said Cathy, speaking for the first time in several minutes. 'Polycystic ovaries. She tried with a previous partner, but it didn't work.' Hazel looked annoyed.

Hastily, Alison nodded. 'Right, right. So the donor . . . there's no contact with him, nothing like that?'

'No contact. We don't even know his name.' It was Hazel speaking, of course, but Alison watched Cathy. She didn't look up, just fiddled with the sling around the baby's head. He appeared to be fast asleep.

'And your previous partner, Hazel . . . ?' She felt she was grasping at straws here. So far, she hadn't heard anything to suggest the fall wasn't just an accident, except for the insistent feeling in her gut. Police intuition. Although, as Colette had told her tartly the day before, the budget did not stretch to cover feelings.

'Oh no, we're all good friends. Her new partner is pregnant too, actually.'

Very amicable. 'And how did you hear about the group?' Alison was still intrigued about the make-up of this group, how different they all were. Maybe all antenatal groups were like this. She wouldn't know.

They looked at each other vaguely. 'In the library, I think it was,' said Hazel. 'Seemed affordable, so we thought, why not.'

'I see.'

Cathy leaned forward. 'DS Hegarty – how come you're asking all this? I mean, it was just an accident, wasn't it? A fall.'

'We haven't ruled anything out yet. It would help if you could tell me your exact movements leading up to the . . . incident.'

They exchanged glances. Getting their stories straight? Cathy said, 'I was changing Arthur in the downstairs loo. It was a messy one, so I was in there a while, and when I came out people were screaming and it – it had already happened.' Alison tried to recall the layout of Monica's house – the downstairs bathroom was under the stairs. 'Did you see who'd been up there?'

Cathy bit her lip. 'I don't know. People had come running to see what was going on, you know.'

'And you, Hazel?'

Hazel furrowed her brow. 'I'm trying to remember. It all happened so fast. I was in the garden, I think, doing the barbecue. Ed, that's Monica's husband, didn't have the faintest idea how to get it going, everyone was starving.' That did not surprise Alison in the slightest, either Ed's failure or that Hazel had taken over. 'Aisha and Rahul, they were nearby. When it happened, I went inside to see what was going on, check on Cathy and Arthur. I think I passed Ed and Monica in the kitchen.'

'So you saw it happen?'

'Not really. I was poking the coals. Then there was this kind of – a shadow, I guess, a shadow went over the garden. There was a scream. Then the noise.' For the first time, she looked unsure. 'It was the most terrible noise when it – happened. The rockery.'

'Did you see anyone on the balcony? Anyone else, I mean?'

'No. I was looking at the barbecue. I didn't see anything.'

'And how was your relationship with the deceased?'

Hazel shrugged. 'We only knew people from the group really. Just those eight sessions.'

'And was there any conflict within the group?'

A pause. This time Cathy spoke, jiggling the baby. 'It was all very friendly,' she said, and Alison couldn't read her tone. 'A really nice group, though we were all quite different. Very supportive.'

This time Hazel was looking away, drinking her vile tea.

'What about Kelly's partner? You mentioned an incident at the group.'

'Oh, no, that was nothing really. We hardly saw him except for that one time. He wasn't even at the barbecue, I think they've split up.'

Alison sighed. 'Alright. Thank you for your time.' It was the same thing she'd got from Monica and Ed Dunwood – they maintained they'd been in the kitchen when it happened, trying to save some kind of dessert that was melting because someone had left the fridge open. They hadn't seen it happen, and neither apparently had Cathy and Hazel, despite Cathy being right downstairs and Hazel in the garden in eye-shot of the balcony. How could it be that there were so many people in one house, and yet nobody had seen a thing?

The day of – Cathy

Kelly had come. No one could believe Kelly had come. Cathy and Hazel had arrived just before her, somewhat late because Hazel had come back from the shops that morning with the wrong kind of flowers. 'What does it matter?' she'd asked, brow furrowed in annoyance.

It would matter a lot to someone like Monica. They had to be the kind from a florist, wrapped in brown paper and tied up with twine, not supermarket daisies covered in plastic. Hazel was grouchy because she'd had to get up at eight – the weekends were the only time she didn't have to start work at six – but since Cathy had slept for maybe forty-five minutes all night, she wasn't very sympathetic. She'd never known tiredness like it. It wasn't just yawning, spacing out, drooping eyes, jerking awake on the sofa realising you'd fallen asleep with your head lolling forward. It was more like a kind of madness. As she walked the dim rooms at night, Arthur a heavy weight in her arms, sniffling and huffing, she wondered what might happen if she never slept again. Like, ever. How quickly would you lose it? Go insane?

Sometimes, she took Arthur into the bedroom and held him close to Hazel's face as he cried. She never woke up.

That day when they finally arrived, Monica swept them in, casting an eye over the flowers Cathy had brought. She nodded her approval. 'Lovely. From the nice place on the high street?' Cathy felt her shoulders relax. Why was she so worried what these mothers thought of her? Maybe it was just a symptom of a larger worry, the anxiety that had engulfed her ever since she'd seen the line on the pregnancy test and done a little creative accounting with her cycle.

'Oh dear, you look exhausted. Arthur giving you a bad time? Isabella sleeps right through, it's amazing! We're so lucky.' Monica didn't look tired at all. Her skin was radiant, eyes clear, and she wore a white sundress. White! At a party for babies! At a barbecue, with ketchup on every surface! Cathy drank it in, humbled, knowing she could never be as perfect.

Monica had just said, 'I think that's everyone now, you're the last but you've made it *eventually*,' when the doorbell rang. She frowned. 'I don't know who that can be.'

Cathy peered into the sunlit hallway, through the sunburst windows on either side of the door. 'Oh my God,' she said, dismayed. 'It's *Kelly*.'

'Kelly?'

'Did you invite her?' said Hazel, coming back in from the garden, a beer already in hand.

'No, well, I mean not specifically, I just sent a reminder to the email group.'

'You didn't take her off the list?' Hazel's tone was judgemental.

Monica answered, snippily, 'Well, no, I don't have the time to trawl through taking people off willy-nilly, do I.'

'Oh my God. Has she been getting all our messages about the births?' Cathy winced. Kelly had, understandably, gone quiet since the terrible news about her baby. The little boy had died inside her, his heart stopped. Cathy couldn't bear to think of it, literally couldn't bear it. Her stomach would clench and her palms sweat and her breath narrow. How could you survive such a thing, carrying a baby inside you for months only to lose it anyway? Kelly would've had to give birth to the poor little thing, this far along. And she was so young, just twenty-two.

Monica rolled her eyes. 'She hasn't brought that awful Ryan, I hope.'

'No, it's just her.' Oh yes, Ryan. Cathy still had horrible flashbacks to that day at group, the violence suddenly exploding in their midst, the fear of realising she could not protect herself if something happened, could not protect her baby. She didn't imagine Ryan would be around much longer, if he hadn't already gone. Poor Kelly.

Hazel and Monica just stood there. Hazel took another gulp of her beer. Cathy said, 'Well, shall I let her in?'

Monica pursed her lips. 'I suppose we'll have to. I do hope there'll be enough salad.'

Salad! Bloody salad. She wished she didn't admire Monica despite her awfulness, didn't long for her approval. Imagine being that sure of yourself. Cathy moved to the door. Through the glass, Kelly was tiny and hunched. When the door opened, there she was. Cathy tried not to react to how awful she looked – bruised dark eyes, green-grey skin, shivering despite the heat. She wore a denim jacket and tracksuit bottoms. 'Oh, Kel. I'm so sorry,' she said, feeling the inadequacy of the words.

'Is it OK I'm here? I just wanted . . . I wanted to see them. The babies.'

Cathy realised she should have gone to visit her. Never mind that they barely knew each other, they were in the trenches together, and this could have happened to any of them. 'Oh, you poor thing.' She stepped forward to hug her, bring her in, but Kelly flinched away. Cathy realised she had Arthur against her in the sling. She was so used to it now that he felt like part of her body. Kelly stared at him. Hungry. Like the way a starving dog eyes a treat.

Cathy might have done something, maybe, with that revelation, something that could have stopped what happened next. But as Kelly stepped into the hall, arms folded around herself, Cathy's phone vibrated where she kept it tucked into the sling. Hazel would object if she knew, would say the radiation was bad for Arthur, even though there was no evidence of that, but Cathy was too afraid to let it out of her sight. And sure enough, it was him. Dan. *Please. We need to talk.* Heart stuttering, she tucked it away again, and followed Kelly back into the kitchen. She wasn't going to answer the message, of course. It was hopeless, dangerous, stupid. But all the same she found she was already crafting a response in her head.

Jax – nine weeks earlier

That night, after the CPR class, I was shaken awake by a dream so vivid I felt like someone was holding me down in the bed. I woke up gasping, terrified. There was a baby, and it had turned blue, and I was calling an ambulance but it wasn't coming, my phone didn't have reception and I couldn't make my fingers work the buttons, and the baby was floppy, and I rubbed its chest but I couldn't make contact somehow, and it was dying, the baby was dying and it was my fault.

I sat up in bed in the dark, pulling the dream's remnants from me like cobwebs. Beside me, Aaron breathed peacefully. He had slept in such awful places over the years, rooms full of screaming kids, under the stairs, even outside in the garden a few times when a foster dad was trying to punish him, that his rest was rarely disturbed. A coffee-flavoured chocolate could keep me up till 3 a.m.

I went for my phone, knowing that I shouldn't be charging it in the bedroom, that it disrupted my sleep and possibly would harm the baby. Since I was already being bad, I let myself slip into old dangerous habits. I had a look at Chris's page, happy with his wife and two adorable girls, and I wondered if I should have stayed with him after all, if that four-bedroom house and those holidays to Mauritius could have been mine. Stupid. I hadn't been happy with him, that was why I'd left. Aaron, for all his youth and poverty, loved me in a way Chris never had. He saw me. He listened.

Then, slipping even further into bad habits, I searched for *him*. He wasn't on Facebook – it had all happened just before it became widespread – but he had the remnants of an old profile on Bebo. That, in itself, should have been a warning sign. Of course, we weren't friends online, never had been anything like that, but a certain amount was public, and it hadn't been taken down. I wondered if he could access social media where he was. Most likely not. Surely not, even in this supposedly lax country. He posed in black and white up a mountain, his back to the camera, his face half turned. I hated that I still knew how to find it so easily, that his name flowed from my fingertips. If I'd never met him, how different would my life have been? Would I have settled down earlier, had this baby years ago? Even clicking on this old profile made me jumpy, as if it might draw him back into my life. He couldn't know I'd been looking at it, could he?

It was dangerous, being awake while your partner slept peacefully. You started to feel alone. You started to feel they could never understand you, in your troubled insomnia. I would need to pee in a second too, but the room was cold and I put off getting up. I let things rattle around my head like peas. Nina's contemptuous look when I didn't save the fake baby. The weird email at work. My mother, just waiting for me to mess up. And I was facing a deadline that would not move – in seven weeks or thereabouts, I would go into labour. And I was terrified, both of that and what came after. How would my almost-forty body recover from the birth? Would Aaron ever fancy me again?

He never did. He just wants your money.

I didn't even have that much money, just this small house that I'd bought with my father's legacy. I shut down the stupid voice and clicked idly on to Facebook again. I saw a red mark, meaning I'd had a notification since I last looked two seconds ago. An account called 'Ann Onymous' had posted on my timeline. Big screaming capital letters. JAX CULVILLE IS A PAEDOPHILE.

Oh my God. Oh my God. The sick helpless feeling of the dream was back, and I heard myself gasp. Aaron murmured in his sleep, throwing an arm over his face. He couldn't see this. I didn't even want it between us, the ugly word, the end of the spectrum of 'jokes' people made about us. *Cradle-snatcher.*

Hands shaking, I clicked on it and made it go away. Luckily, my settings meant no one would have seen it yet. Then I clicked on the profile, the stupid fake name. The icon was a single rose, colourised against a black and white background. There was no info, and the person had made no other posts. The profile was brand new. What the hell was this? Someone had it in for me, but who? I ran my mind over my life. Who had I hurt, enough that they would do this to me? I'd dated lots of guys in my single years, of course, and some of them I had probably hurt without meaning to, just as I had been hurt. All part of the contact sport known as dating, which injured more people than rugby. Would anyone come out of the woodwork after all this time, and say such terrible things? Or was it as I'd thought first, a disgruntled service user? But I had only ever done my best to help them, the troubled kids we worked with.

Before Aaron I had never dated anyone younger. Even in my teens, I'd been too much of a good girl to have any boyfriends. My mother would not have allowed it. And I worked in a charity that protected children from abuse! Of course, that didn't mean much – I thought of the recent scandals around Oxfam and Save the Children. That couldn't happen to us. We were too small, we wouldn't survive. They would likely have to fire me if anything got out, wash their hands of me as thoroughly as possible to save the charity. I'd lose everything I'd built up all these years, my chance to be a CEO. And it wasn't *true*. The unfairness of it made me gasp again. Who was this? Who could possibly hate me enough to do this, and when I was heavily pregnant too?

The answer came to me as if it had always been there. The name I had pushed out of my mind when making lists of who would want to hurt me. The person I had genuinely wronged, who made me feel clammy all over with guilt if ever I thought about her, which I tried not to do.

His wife.

When Aaron got up the next day, he found me dozing in the living room with the cat draped over me, body bent out of shape, eyes dry and restless. I'd spent most of the night refreshing Facebook, terrified something else would appear, although I'd updated my privacy settings to draconian levels and blocked the anonymous account. I wished I had taken a screenshot to prove it was real, apart from anything else. I would have to tell Sharon. Oh God. Of all the things.

'You OK, babe?' He was frowning, worried. He looked so sweet in his shirt and tie. I'd had to take him to buy a real one, show him how to knot it. 'Did you not sleep?'

'Bad dreams. About the stupid baby class.'

He stroked my lank hair back from my forehead. 'Oh hey, how could you know what to do when you never learned before?'

'Poor baby with a dummy mummy.' I was trying to joke but my tone was as exhausted as I felt.

'Maybe you should stay home today.'

'No, no, I'm not on leave for another month.' Having covered the pregnancies and child-related emergencies of work colleagues for seventeen years now, I was determined to inconvenience no one with mine. Certainly not before the baby was even born.

He cleared his throat. 'Got some news just there now.' He held up his phone.

'Yeah?' *Not something else bad, please.*

'They finally found my adoption details – I can see my birth records, if I want.'

I should have been pleased for him. But all I could feel was a weight of dread in my chest, that things had taken a wrong turn somehow, and I didn't know how to find my way back. 'That's great, babe.'

'You'll come with me?' He looked so vulnerable as he said it, so young.

'Of course I will.' I forced a smile, but I couldn't help thinking that this was another step away from peace, towards the chaos I feared so much.

That morning at work, I was no earthly use to anyone. Dorothy had to tell me three times to answer my phone to one of our biggest donors. I could see her looking at me, thinking *poor cow, the baby is eating her brain.* Was that what happened? I'd read that they formed their bones from yours, leaching you out like a husk. I felt so helpless – I'd always been able to rely on myself, and now I'd have to lean on Aaron, who could barely take care of himself. I turned the messages over and over in my head, no idea what to do.

I had to tell Sharon. But I was afraid. I told myself I'd wait till the mailing was over and done with. It would have gone out that morning, so donations should start coming in later today.

After lunch – I forced myself to eat a salad from Tupperware at my desk, which was wilting in the heat of the plastic – Sharon called me in. It was when she liked to strike, to catch people at their lowest ebb. She had my mother's instinct for that. I resented everything about the process, having to drag my lumbering self to Sharon's office, the fact that she didn't ask me to sit down right away so I stood there as she peered over her glasses and typed two-fingered at her computer.

'Jax.'

'You wanted to see me?'

'I thought we ought to have a little chat.' The words *little chat* were so innocuous. They should mean a cosy catch-up over tea and cake, but in a work context they meant, *you are in serious trouble.*

My breath hitched. 'I need to sit down, Sharon.'

Her eyes flicked to me. 'Of course.'

We adjourned to the softer chairs to the side of her desk. The coffee table was marked with rings and stacked with copies of our in-house magazine, *Protect*. A simple word that packed an emotional punch. There were things I wanted to protect. My child. My relationship. My job. Lately it felt like everything was at risk. As I lowered myself into the chair, I realised I wouldn't be able to get out again without help. 'What is it?' My heart was pounding, and I felt as nauseated as I had at the start of my pregnancy.

She smoothed out her skirt. Sharon was very much of the Birkenstocks and tie-dye school of charity CEOs, but that didn't mean she was soft. 'The mailing went out as planned?'

'I believe so, yes.'

Sharon slid two pieces of paper across the table to me. One was an envelope, with her own name on it – she liked to be part of the mailing, to check it was all up to scratch. The other was the letter that went inside it. 'Can you look at that for me, please?'

I leaned over, with difficulty. It looked fine to me. I opened my mouth to say so, then I saw it. The name on the letter was not the same as on the envelope.

A flush of dread rinsed through me. How – what . . . ?

The names had been transposed. 'Is it . . . ?'

'It's every one, yes. I already spoke to the printer.'

This was a disaster. Every single mail-out had been addressed to the wrong person. In theory people might still open the letter and donate, but our supporters were old-fashioned and easily riled. A slip-up like this could cost us thousands. 'I . . . don't know how this happened.'

'You signed it off with the printer. They showed me your signature on the proofs and the mailing list. You didn't notice the columns were off?'

'I . . .' A long moment went by. My first instinct was that this wasn't my fault, it couldn't be. I had been doing mail-outs for years. I would never make such a stupid mistake. But was that true? Was the pregnancy indeed addling my brain?

'There's another problem too.'

My stomach dropped, and suddenly I hated her for drawing it out, for the arbitrary power the structure of work gave her over me. What was to stop me standing up, saying *screw you, Sharon, and no one's worn Birkenstocks since the eighties*? Security, that was what. Status. The fact that my partner still qualified for youth training schemes. 'Oh?'

'This was in the post this morning.' She slid something over the coffee table to me, and I saw it was a plain notecard with some square writing on it. *Did you know that your head of fundraising, Jax Culville, likes young boys? Do you really think you should be employing someone like that?* The neatness of the writing added to the chill it gave me. This wasn't some mad person. And now they were calling me Jax.

Sharon went on, 'Dorothy tells me there was an email too.' *Damn you, Dorothy, have you no loyalty?* 'You're supposed to report things like that to me, aren't you?'

'Um . . . it made no sense. It was like a spam thing, I thought.'

'This is pretty clear, I would say.' She tapped the card with one ragged fingernail.

My head hurt. 'Sharon, what can I say? This is clearly rubbish.'

'Your partner is younger than you, isn't he?'

'He's twenty-four.'

'And you met him . . . ?'

I stared at her. 'Two years ago. Do you need help with the maths?' Oh dear. I had just been very rude to my boss, and worse, I got the impression I'd played right into her hands. She sat back.

'You know we have to investigate any allegations made.'

'It's not an allegation! It's just . . . some crazy person, mouthing off. They don't even say what they mean, who these boys are I'm supposed to have . . .' I couldn't finish the sentence, I was so suddenly afraid. The situation seemed to be slipping through my hands.

'Can you think of anyone who would have a grudge against you?'

'No,' I said, but that was a lie. I could. But would she really do this? I didn't know enough about her to say for sure, the woman whose life I had ruined.

'I think we better look into this. Keep everything above board.'

'Good.' My voice shook. 'I welcome the chance to clear my name.'

'Of course, you can't be in work while that goes on.'

A pause. Checkmate. 'But . . . we have the big donor gala next week.'

'We can manage.' It was the keynote event of the year. A dinner for all our donors, a hundred quid a ticket, an auction and raffle and lots of other ways to raise funds. Our target for the evening was thirty grand, and I had planned every moment of it. Sharon was earnest and cared about the cause, but our rich donors wouldn't take too well to her aggressively recycled frocks.

'You really think so?'

'I don't see we have much choice. Why don't you start your maternity leave early?' She cast a pointed look at my belly.

Oh, really Sharon, fuck you. I got up, steadying myself against the back of the chair. 'I'll go now then, if that's how you feel.' Screw them. I'd do some shopping, have a rest, watch telly. But something was nagging me. 'Will I still get paid?' I hated having to ask. I'd have loved to be able to march out, Bridget Jones style, and tell Sharon what I really thought of her. But I had a family to support now.

She nodded. 'You'll get your maternity pay as planned, just earlier.' That meant an extra month of full pay I would have to do without. And I couldn't rely on Aaron to make up the difference. 'We'll speak soon, Jax.' I got the feeling she was really enjoying this.

The house was quiet in the daytime, and time felt all wrong, like I'd slept in or had an unexpected sick day. Minou greeted me disdainfully, making it clear the sofa was her domain during the day. I put down my bag and jacket and wandered disconsolately through the rooms. Aaron was at his own office, where he was the most junior person, the one who did the photocopying and coffee runs. I let the thought cross my mind – how it would feel to be with an older man, one who was a CEO, perhaps, who would say things like *you know you don't need to work, darling* or *just quit, that Sharon's a cow and you're too good for that place.* Hair just touched with silver, credit card glazed in gold. The kind of man who would buy me lingerie and take me on unexpected mini-breaks.

I hadn't told Aaron I was home from work. I needed to explain it first, find a possible reason for what was going on. The printers had been in touch, very apologetic but keen to point out I'd signed off the mailing list spreadsheet. Clearly, the address and name columns had been transposed by one cell. A tiny change, and easy to do, but catastrophic. Had it been that way when I checked it? I was sure it couldn't have. But not sure enough. Was this my mistake? Or was it the same as the messages – someone else's revenge? I had lied to Sharon, because in fact I had a good idea who might be behind this. Who might want to ruin my life.

I had met Mark Jarvis in my first proper job, at a very large children's charity, the kind that's synonymous with do-gooding. Its image is brave toddlers with shaved heads from cancer, scared teenagers with bruised eyes. They are crusaders, saviours. They will do a lot to preserve that image.

Mark was on the board, an ex-City hedge-fund manager who was richer than I could ever dream of. At the time I was twenty-three, living in a house share in Camden with four other girls. The mould in the one shower looked like a Jackson Pollock painting. Mark liked to come into the office once a week or so, to have a meeting with our then CEO, sign documents, that kind of thing. I remember when he spotted me. He was crossing the floor of the open-plan office, striding with the wide gait of a man who is busy, who has many calls on his time. His day job, which he'd wound down after already making more money than he knew what to do with. His wife, who had her own charity work, plus her busy Botox schedule. His gym routine, his season tickets to rugby and football, a man of the people despite his wealth. Expensive suit worn without a tie. Receding hair well-cut enough that it didn't matter. He was forty-four years old. He came to my desk. 'Hello! You must be new.'

I was cowed, of course. Technically he was my boss, my boss's boss. 'Hello. I'm Jax.'

His eyebrows went up. 'Goodness. What kind of name is that?'

'Short for Jacqueline.' My mother absolutely hated it, and under his gaze I felt my resolve to be Jax, not Jacqueline, crumble.

'Oh, I see. How are you settling in?'

'Fine. I love it.' That was pushing it – I could already see how many inefficiencies there were in the way the charity worked, how they'd failed to integrate the internet or stop wasting vast sums on glossy brochures, which would all get thrown away. How much time was frittered away by people working at quarter speed. I was filing it all away, because I already knew I would run a fundraising department before I was thirty, and I would do it better than this. I felt that if people gave you money to help at-risk kids, and you wasted it, that should be a crime. I was gung-ho at that age. I believed that if you weren't part of the solution, you were part of the problem.

He leaned on my desk. I got a whiff of his aftershave, something expensive and overpowering. 'We should schedule some induction time, Jax, so I can bring you up to speed on the board. Perhaps we could even have lunch?'

I was new to working life at that point. It was the early 2000s, before Mc Too, when boozy lunches and post-work drinks were still just about the norm. And I was twenty-three and he was my boss. How did I know what was appropriate? 'Sure,' I chirped. 'That would be lovely.'

This was the start of it. He hadn't told me who he was. He just assumed I would know, and I envied that, I wanted it for myself. I didn't want to bask in his power. I wanted my own power. That was what he never realised.

On my own now in the house that I shared with my partner, who would have been in primary school when this happened, I wondered. It wouldn't be him, of course. He hardly had access to the internet where he was, and they must check his outgoing mail. It must be her, then. The wife. Claudia.

I pulled my laptop towards me and googled Claudia Jarvis. There was nothing about her. Of course, there was plenty about him, for all his lawyers sent out cease-and-desist letters. The internet held on to things better than any collective memory. I skipped over those articles; I already knew what they said and didn't wish to relive it. Nothing about her, except in connection with his story. I couldn't believe it. There were people with that name, of course, but none of them was her. I tried *Claudia Jarvis husband*. I tried *Claudia Jarvis socialite, philanthropist, model*. Nothing. Back when I'd known Mark, Claudia had been high profile, the kind of person who'd pop up on the *Evening Standard* social pages eating tiny canapés, or more than likely not eating them, in order to keep wearing the kind of backless dresses you couldn't pair with a bra. Now it was as if she'd disappeared off the face of the universe.

I clicked on my own Facebook profile, switching to 'view as' to get a sense of what someone who wasn't friends with me could see. I had always been careful not to put up too much about my life, like where I lived, or even the fact that I was pregnant. But that didn't stop other people. There it was, a picture one of Aaron's colleagues had put up when we'd gone for drinks with them a month back, and tagged me in against my will. My ripe pregnant belly swelling for all to see. She had typed Aaron's name in the caption, hoping to tag him too I suppose, but Aaron didn't go on Facebook, one of the things I liked about him. In the picture I stood uncomfortable, this random girl's arm around me for the 'selfie', her skin glowing, neat blonde bob. I'd suspected she fancied Aaron and was trying to neutralise me by being nice, and I wanted to tell her I was too old and pregnant and tired to care. But if someone wished me ill, if someone was trawling social media waiting for a gap to open up in my life, here it was.

Alison

Next to visit were the third couple who'd been at the barbecue that day. Aisha and Rahul Farooq. The door was opened by a young, pretty Asian woman in a headscarf, with a North London accent. 'Hello. Come in, please.' She was a physiotherapist, Alison knew, her husband a paramedic. Just like her and Tom, trying to make a life on public-sector salaries, trying to offer help to people who increasingly threw it back in your face.

Seeing a neat line of shoes by the door, Alison grunted her way out of her ugly courts. It was hot, and her feet had swollen. Not through pregnancy, sadly. Probably they never would. A baby's cry rose from the next room, and the woman disappeared, coming back with a wrapped bundle in her arms. She gazed at him with devotion. 'This is Hari.'

'Cute.' They all kind of looked the same to Alison at that age. Was that a bad sign? Should she be more doting if she was going to have her own? 'Is your husband here?'

Aisha bit her lip. 'He should be. His work, I don't always know . . . If something comes up, he has to stay.'

Alison sighed. She had enough to do without traipsing back here. 'Well, you and I better talk now.'

'Oh, I don't know if I should . . .' Alison gazed at her steadily – why the reluctance? Did she have something to hide? 'Alright then.'

'So, talk me through the events of the barbecue.' They were in the living room now, Alison drinking a PG Tips. She had already asked Aisha her routine questions, discovered she'd met her husband just over a year ago, married quickly, got pregnant quickly. *Easy.* They too had seen a flyer for the group, in the leisure centre, Aisha thought. They had chosen it because it was so much cheaper than the others.

Still nursing the child, Aisha now screwed her eyes up. 'We got there just after one that day, I think. We were late because Hari spit up on his Babygro, and we had to go back. Rahul was worried – he thought maybe saying one o'clock meant we had to get there at one, like a dinner party, but I thought it was more like you could arrive any time you wanted. Then we got there and Monica was a bit funny with us.'

'Funny how?'

'She said something about, oh isn't it strange how different cultures work, I did hope everyone would be here at one, when we weren't even the last ones! And Rahul got annoyed.'

Alison leaned forward, interested. 'What does he do when he's annoyed?'

'He . . . He goes quiet,' said Aisha, looking down at her son. 'He goes really quiet.'

The day of – Aisha

They drove all the way to Monica's house without speaking a word. This was often the way between them, and Aisha didn't know if he was happy with it, if he thought this was how a husband and wife should be together. 'It'll be strange,' she said, as they turned out of their street. It was hard to think of the house, a small brick terrace, as home, instead of her parents' place. She'd lived here for so short a time. But then it felt as if her entire life had changed in the blink of an eye. She'd been married to Rahul for a year. She'd lived in this house the same amount of time. She had known him for a year and three months. The speed of it had burned her, at the same time as it lifted her up with the romance of it, the excitement of how completely life could change in a short time. She had a baby now, with a man who was still a virtual stranger. And he was good with the baby. He did everything he was supposed to, he'd come to all the antenatal group sessions, he changed and bathed Hari and got up at night even though he was still doing shift work. It was just her that he never talked to.

It took him a long time to answer. 'What will?'

'Seeing all the babies together. Here in the world, you know. Little people.'

He glanced at her. She waited, having given him an opening, but he didn't say any more, and suddenly it rose up in her, the idea of going home later, back inside their neat little house, with the scent diffusers and large TV and framed wedding photos, and it was overwhelming. The silence of it, after the noise and arguments and cooking smells of her parents' house, she and her four siblings all falling over each other. Aisha had always wanted a home of her own, a husband and child. She'd been delighted when her parents had suggested a few introductions. When they'd produced Rahul, the son of her dad's wholesaler, a paramedic – practically a doctor! – and she'd seen him standing shyly in her mum's living room, eating dip, she'd felt so lucky. Her sister Jasmina had nudged her as she hung over the stairs. 'He's well fit, Ais, you lucky cow. Maybe I'll get Dad to find me a guy too.'

He was fit. He had a good job. He was kind, considerate. He washed his own dishes, made his own breakfast. But he didn't talk. Every conversation between them seemed to bloom and quickly die, like some fragile short-lived flower. Aisha had hoped the antenatal group would be a rich source of conversation, speculating about the other couples, the ones whose baby was inside some other woman in America. The older woman and the handsome young man. The two women together, and she wondered what her mother would say about that. That Monica, how awful she was, how she'd bored Aisha's ear off about a trip she'd made to Pakistan, when Aisha had never even been there. That young girl Kelly, where her boyfriend was, if he'd ever turn up to help her, poor thing. She looked permanently terrified.

When they arrived at the barbecue, Rahul held the car door for her to get out, and she lumbered into the back, unstrapping the baby from his seat, before taking in the house. All the glass, the neat lawn around it, the driveway with a BMW and a Jaguar parked. 'So big!' she exclaimed. 'What do you think it's worth, a place like this?'

He had his phone out, the rectangle of glass and metal that held his attention approximately a hundred times more than she did. 'Don't know.'

Aisha sighed. She had a small baby. She was stuck in her life, in her neat silent house with this neat silent man, and she couldn't go on like this forever. Something had to be done.

◆　◆　◆

Sausages, pork skewers, hot dogs. Aisha nudged Rahul. They were temporarily alone in the garden, everyone else having scattered. Monica's husband had shown them the food table, then made some noise about getting more charcoal. It was the most she'd ever heard him say in a sentence. That was a while ago, at least ten minutes, and they were still alone out here. She said to Rahul, 'Look. Pork pork pork.'

'Does it matter?' he said irritably. 'I'm not hungry anyway, it's too hot.'

Aisha had spent the night breastfeeding a starving baby. She was very hungry. 'Get the stuff from the car, will you?' She'd brought a small Tupperware of leftovers from their meal the night before, anticipating this issue. Nothing seemed to be cooked, in any case, and she could tell by looking that the barbecue wasn't anywhere near ready. Maybe there was salad, but hungry as she was, she couldn't get excited at the idea of lettuce.

'You're not going to eat that?' Rahul looked pained.

'Well, yeah, I have to eat something.'

He glanced around them furtively. 'It's sort of rude, I just think, to get our own food out.'

Aisha counted to ten but lost her temper at three. 'What are you going to do, be hungry all day?'

'I don't know.'

'Give me the car keys.' She held out her hand. 'I'll go, if you won't.'

He sighed. 'Alright, I'll get it in a minute. Don't make a fuss, OK?' His mantra. Don't make a fuss. Hide in plain sight. Pretend everything's fine. But it wasn't, was it? It wasn't fine at all. She just didn't know what was wrong.

'Is there anything to drink at least?' She was also extremely thirsty, given that all the liquid in her body was being sucked out by a small demon-like creature hour after hour. Funny how she loved him all the same, would lay her life down for him without a second thought. The way she had wanted to feel about Rahul, in fact. *But you don't, do you?*

Rahul scanned the drinks table. Beer, wine, Prosecco. 'Nothing soft either.'

'I brought some fizzy drinks. What happened to those?' She'd handed them over to Monica when they arrived, seen a little pull in Monica's face, even though it was posh lemonade, from Waitrose. Aisha found herself wondering what she'd done wrong, feeling annoyed because she knew it was nothing, not really. Monica was just one of those people who wasn't happy unless she could judge someone.

He shrugged. 'She must have put them in the fridge.'

'I need something to drink, Rahul.' In his sling on her front, Hari was stirring. He would want to be fed soon, and she'd have to find somewhere quiet to do it. Luckily, she was among other new mums here. Cathy had arrived after them, and her little boy Arthur was howling somewhere in the house; Hadley was in a bouncy chair up near the patio doors. Isabella, of course, didn't ever seem to cry. Monica would not have allowed it. She was upstairs apparently having her nap. Four babies. It should have been six, of course. Poor Kelly, she had lost hers. And Anita and Jeremy . . . well. Who knew what was going on there? There was certainly no sign of the baby from the States.

She said, 'I'm taking him to feed. Please get me something. Water, even.'

Rahul hunched one shoulder, which might have been a yes. He looked worse than ever, his skin grey and sweating in the heat. What was the *matter* with him?

On her way in she passed Aaron, coming out to check on Hadley perhaps. 'Hi,' said Aisha shyly. He was very good-looking, she couldn't help but notice. She'd seen a man from Afghanistan once at a family wedding who had ice-blue eyes and dark skin, and Aaron reminded her of him.

He looked exhausted too, dark circles under those striking eyes. 'Oh, hi. How are you?'

'Pretty good. Coping, anyway.'

'It's hard. We don't get much sleep.' He picked his little girl up, holding her against his shoulder. 'She's just the best though. I mean . . . this is the first time I ever had anyone I knew was my family. Blood family, like. You know what I mean? Like . . . she's *mine*.'

She nodded. She felt the same. Just then, Jax came out into the garden too. She still looked pregnant, her middle swollen up, her skin sagging and pale. Was it her age? Aisha wondered, with a pang of sympathy. She herself seemed to have 'bounced back', as they said in those magazines she sometimes sneaked a look at in the doctor's waiting room.

'Is she alright?' Jax said to Aaron.

'Think so.'

'I keep trying to feed her,' Jax said to Aisha, with a wobbly voice. 'And she just doesn't want it. Are you managing?'

'Well, yeah.' It was so simple for Aisha, so natural, she couldn't imagine anyone struggling with it. Poor Jax. 'I'm just going to feed him now.'

'Lucky you,' said Jax, taking her own baby, who immediately started to cry, screwing up her little red face.

Aisha moved through the kitchen, where Monica was fussing with a salad, Hazel lecturing her on something called HIIT. She saw with surprise that Kelly had come, poor Kelly. 'Hello, sweetheart,' she murmured, pressing her arm. Kelly looked terrible, white and green at the same time, dressed all wrong for the weather. 'I just need to feed him then I'll be back.' She passed by the living room where Cathy paced with the baby in a matching sling to Aisha's. She smiled hello; Cathy smiled back. Cathy looked harassed, her hair wild. Her phone was in her hand.

Upstairs was quieter, cooler. Ed was coming down the staircase, the sound of a loo flushing following him. Aisha blushed. 'Is it OK if I feed him somewhere?'

'Oh! Yes, yes, of course. Any of those rooms.' He waved a hand at a vast array of doors. Aisha thought of their little house, washing drying in the living room and all up the stairs. It was no way to live. And yet people did, they lived like this their entire lives.

Isabella's room door was ajar, and a teenage girl Aisha had not seen before was bent over the crib, watching the baby's still sleeping face, one hand clenched in a fist above the tiny head. The girl jumped when she saw Aisha looking in. 'Oh!'

'Sorry. I'm looking for a place to feed?' It was so embarrassing, having to do this intimate act in public, but it was either that or stay home all the time.

'Oh. Well, there's a spare room in there.' The girl indicated one of the closed rooms.

'Thanks.' She felt rude. 'I'm Aisha. From Monica's antenatal group?'

The girl made a snorting noise. 'Sure. *Her* group.'

'Is this your baby sister?' There was a resemblance between Monica and the teenage girl that made Aisha sure she was her daughter.

A strange movement went over the girl's face, and she stared down again at the sleeping baby. 'That's what I've been told, yeah.'

How strange. Had Monica mentioned she had another daughter? From a previous marriage, it must be. If so, Aisha couldn't remember the girl's name, or maybe she hadn't been told it, and she really needed to feed now, as Hari was rooting around desperately near her chest, and her breasts were beginning to ache. But as she shut the door on the pristine spare bedroom – taut clean duvet with shiny bits, fringed lamps, wall-to-floor mirrored wardrobes – she somehow felt uneasy about leaving the teenager alone with the baby.

Jax – nine weeks earlier

Aaron was nervous, I could tell. He gripped the sides of the office chair he was sitting in, knuckles turning white, and his knee jiggled to a rhythm only he could hear. I placed a hand on his leg to calm him, but I was nervous too. A woman was going to come into the room any minute and maybe tell us who he was, the history of him, the secrets that lurked in his DNA. And there was nothing we could do to change it. I was worried. This, on top of the baby coming, of the pressure of me not working, it tipped the balance too far. I felt I too was holding on tight to empty air, trying to steady us. I'd told Aaron I'd decided to go on leave early, and it was a lie. I had lied to him, about something huge too. I told myself I was trying to protect him, at this difficult time. Or maybe I couldn't bear him to find out the truth about me, all those things in my past I had never admitted to him.

The door clicked and the archivist, Magda, came in. She wasn't a social worker but rather someone the council had employed to deal with these requests. Inviting us in for a chat, I felt, did not bode well.

'Mr and Mrs Cole?'

'No,' I said automatically. Puzzled, she looked down at the file in her hands, as if she was in the wrong room. 'I mean, we're not married.'

'Oh.' I saw her notice how much older I was than him, the subtle double take that I chippily imagined men with younger partners did not get. It didn't help that Aaron was dressed like a teenager today, in too-loose jeans and a hoody, slouching low in his seat. 'Well, I have the information you wanted.'

Aaron's hand groped for mine; his skin was cold. I didn't know why I felt so sick, as if waiting for test results at a doctor's. Whatever it was, it was in the past, and couldn't hurt us. Could it? 'Your mother was a teenager at the time of your birth – fifteen years old.' Aaron nodded. I told myself it wasn't unusual in many parts of the country. 'Her name was Georgina, Georgina Partington-Smith. She was white.'

Georgina. That didn't sound like a council-estate name. I revised my assumptions, felt ashamed of them. Magda passed over something, a birth certificate. Aaron snatched it up, poring over the photocopied paper like it was his actual mother's face. 'You were taken into care at your family's request at the age of two.' She looked up at him. 'You weren't adopted subsequently?'

He cleared his throat. 'No. Fostered a few times.'

'Your father we don't know much about, I'm afraid. She didn't name him on the birth register.'

'He was . . . black?' I felt Aaron's embarrassment at having to ask this, at not even knowing the story of his own life, the stamp of which he carried on his skin. We didn't even know for sure. His father could have been Asian, or Hispanic, or perhaps some past ancestor on either side had African or Caribbean DNA. We just didn't know.

'I'm sorry, I don't have that information.'

'So . . . where is she now? Georgina?' Aaron tried out the name.

Magda shook her head. I could feel her anxiety vibrating across the table, and wondered how often people exploded at her, in tears or in rage. 'I'm afraid I don't . . . have that information.' It seemed to be a set phrase. 'If the birth parent has agreed to contact in advance, we sometimes have their details on the system and can pass them on. But in this case we don't have anything. The care order was closed.'

'Meaning?' I spoke this time, seeing that Aaron was overwhelmed by the information, or rather the lack of it, that she'd given him.

'The family did not request ongoing contact.' She said it crisply, but she meant that his mother had not wanted to stay in touch with him. That unlike most children in care, he hadn't been wrested from her because she couldn't take care of him. He had been given up, because for whatever reason she didn't want him. I squeezed his hand again. It felt limp in mine; he tugged it away.

'So how do we find her?' Me again. I tried to smile at him, to reinforce the 'we', but he was staring at the dingy grey carpet.

'People sometimes hire private detectives to track relatives down. Of course, they may not want to be contacted. Psychologically this can be quite tough, can feel like a second rejection. Are you sure you want to do it?'

Aaron said nothing. It was down to me, the decision, because I would have to pay for it. I thought through the different possible outcomes. I imagined Aaron finding this woman, who would be my age or a little older, assuming she was still alive, and her still not wanting him, as she hadn't when she was a teenager. I thought of myself at that age, shepherded from school to ballet to clarinet to netball, never even speaking to a boy, let alone kissing one, and wondered how it would be to have a baby when you were still a child yourself. Could I blame her, for giving Aaron up? My own baby kicked me, as if to remind me how hard that must have been. I tried to feel pity for her, this unknown woman. Maybe she'd married, had more children. Maybe no one knew about her first pregnancy. If we came to find her, would we upend her life, ruin her peace?

I reached for his hand again, forced him to give it to me. 'We're sure,' I said, looking nervy Magda directly in the face, casting the die, starting something I could not predict the ending of.

◆　◆　◆

It's funny how your peace of mind can vanish overnight, like a storm whipping up on a cloudless day, and tearing the sky to shreds. The messages had unsettled me, the mistake with the mailing, my virtual suspension from work, even if we weren't calling it that. Aaron's quest to find his mother had rattled me too. Sleep had already been elusive, what with the equivalent of three hot-water bottles strapped to me and kicking me from the inside, but it got even worse now. Three nights in a row I watched as dawn lightened the window, the cheeping of morning birds an irritating reminder that I hadn't slept and that Aaron would be up in two hours, making enough noise to wake an army. I lay and listened to the drone of planes overhead and thought about my life, the decisions I'd made, good and bad, that had led me here. Claudia Jarvis had dropped off the face of the earth. If it wasn't her who sent those messages, who else might have it in for me? The only other person I could think of was my ex, Chris.

I hadn't spoken to Chris in ten years, since I left him in . . . let's say less-than-ideal circumstances. I idly stalked his Facebook feed from time to time, of course, and sometimes I wondered irrationally if he was posting things for my benefit, to show me what an amazing life he had. He'd married someone else within a year of me leaving him, at dizzying speed, and they had two little girls. With great trepidation, I clicked on the message box and started to draft one. *Hi! Long time no talk huh. I got a slightly weird message the other day, couldn't tell who the sender was. Don't suppose you know anything about that? I'm asking everyone I can think of!*

Which was a lie. I pressed send, a pocket of cold deep in my stomach telling me I was making a mistake. What would Aaron say, for a start, at me randomly contacting my ex? I wouldn't say he was jealous, not exactly, but he was sensitive to my feelings for him, on days when I felt bored or irritated, as happens in every relationship. It wasn't surprising, given how little attachment he'd had from anyone in his childhood. Telling him what was going on would only upset him. I wondered why I felt so protective of him and didn't want to examine that thought further. He was my partner, not my child, but I worried about him, what instability lay just beneath, stirred up by all this business with his mother.

Chris replied later that day. *This is a surprise! I don't know anything about that, no.*

I wrote back. *OK. Just wracking my brains really.*

He was typing something – the moving dots gave me a jolt. Chris, a ghost from my past, was on the other end. So easy just to reach out and bring him back into my life. Too easy, maybe. *Perhaps I can help. Do you want to have lunch or something?*

My heart began to race. *Lunch?*

Yeah. Be nice to catch up.

I thought about it. What good could come of seeing my ex, a man I had badly hurt? A man I had rejected? Why did I need this, when I was close to having another man's child? But all the same I was bored and restless and worried, and enforced maternity leave wasn't helping matters. And Aaron would scarcely talk to me ever since we'd got the news about his birth mother, keeping it all inside, festering. As I typed in, *Sure, I'm pretty free right now*, I already knew I wouldn't be telling him about Chris.

◆ ◆ ◆

The next day I went into London to meet him. He still worked at the same management consultancy firm near London Bridge, ten years on. Taking the train at that time was strange, empty and quiet, not having to fight my way on or stand pointedly beside people until they gave me a seat, which didn't always happen, even at eight months pregnant. I watched the train pass Canary Wharf, the skyscrapers tearing a white sky, and thought of the years I'd lived with Chris there, near Crossharbour, in a flat he paid for as easily as a pack of tissues. Not like Aaron.

It hadn't occurred to me that Chris didn't know I was pregnant. But why would he? He didn't stalk my Facebook feed as assiduously as I did his, in all likelihood, and that made me feel tired and ashamed. In any case I hadn't posted much about my pregnancy, cautious of being too vulnerable. When I walked into the chain restaurant (a classically boring Chris choice), I saw his face change. What was the expression? Shock? A little chagrin? 'Wow! I had no idea.'

'Oh, yes, almost due now.' I hugged him awkwardly. He had lost weight but aged, his face lined, his hair grey. He wore a nondescript but expensive suit and tie, and he looked like any City worker, a well-paid cog in a wheel. I saw he wore a signet ring on a little finger, something I would have mocked him for, back when his body was mine to touch and comment on. Back when he was part of my life. It was so strange how little I knew him now, this man who had once meant so much to me.

'I didn't even know you'd got married.'

Was that a dig? I sat down, with difficulty. 'Probably because I didn't.'

'Oh?' His head cocked, as if seeing a chance to win the break-up. 'Still not your thing then?'

'It wasn't . . . not my thing, exactly.'

'Just not with me.' He laughed. 'Hence why you left me at the altar!'

'It wasn't at the altar, Chris.'

'As good as. A month before. Cost the same.'

'I know. It was a very difficult choice, and I was very sorry to hurt you, but looks like you're really happy now?'

He softened. 'I was lucky to meet Alicia, yes. She values home-making, family – makes it a lot easier for me to do what I do.'

I surmised from this that Alicia was the stay-at-home-in-the-suburbs wife he'd wanted, one of the many reasons I'd cut my losses and run from my expensive wedding, at the age of twenty-eight. My mother had almost died of rage and shame. *You really think you'll meet someone else, at your age? That's it for you, Jacqueline. You'll never have children. I'll never be a grandmother now.* At least I had proven her wrong about that. 'And two kids! You've been busy.'

He got out his phone and showed me two insipid blonde children, in matching pink striped dresses. I had in fact already seen the picture on his Facebook, but didn't say so. 'Iris and Emily.'

Sounded like two great-aunts in a nursing home. 'Lovely.'

'And you – what does, eh, your partner do?' The most important question for a man like Chris. *What does he do?* I tried to think how to answer this. 'At the moment he's working in insurance.' I was ashamed of myself for that, making Aaron's job sound better than it was.

'Oh yes? I do a lot of business with insurers, which one?'

'Er . . . Dependent.' Technically that was true, but he just worked in a regional branch of it, doing admin.

'I wonder if he knows Colin Richards? I could put some business his way, perhaps.'

'Um . . . I don't know. He's just started.' I looked down at my menu. Nothing on it appealed to me, since I couldn't eat shellfish or soft cheese or rare meat. 'And Alicia?'

'Oh, she's at home with the girls. Wouldn't have it any other way.' The pride in his voice made something crack in me. I hadn't wanted this life, a rich husband out at work twelve hours a day, while I wrangled kids in the countryside and had to ask him for the cash to buy groceries. But had I wanted the opposite? Being entirely responsible for our family's finances, lying awake worrying about money? And not just money, but our emotional even keel? Keeping the boat of our family afloat?

'Shall we order?' I changed the subject, opting for some dispiriting pasta that cost ten pounds. Aaron and I rarely ate out, because when he saw the prices, even in chain places, he went quiet and anxious and it ruined my enjoyment. Our second date had been at a Nando's.

Chris had the steak very rare, in a manly gesture, and told me at great length about the low-carb diet he was on, the secret of his weight loss. I wondered how I had ever shared my life with this man, had sex with him, come within a month of being his wife. In the end, I hadn't wanted to be anyone's wife. That was what swung it. I told myself I still didn't. So why had the comment about me being married stung me so?

We traded small talk for a while – his job, mine, neither of us really listening but just saying things politely in order – and when the food arrived, my pasta already cold, I said, 'So you really can't think of anyone who'd send a weird message about me? It was sort of . . . nasty. I'm really wracking my brains.' I couldn't bear to tell him what it actually said.

He chewed his steak, showing red blood and flesh between his teeth. My stomach turned over. 'I was thinking. What about that man? You know the one. What was his name – Jarvis?'

I winced. Chris was one of the few people I'd told about the whole business, since I'd met him not long after. In fact, I doubted I ever would have got together with Chris if I hadn't been so broken by everything that happened. 'I thought of that. But . . . he's not around, is he? He'd hardly be able to get online.'

Casually, as if he had no idea of the bomb he was throwing into my world, Chris said, 'Oh, but he's out now. I was talking to a former partner of his the other day at golf. He got out in March.'

I set down my fork. Chris frowned. 'You OK? You didn't know?'

I hadn't known. Of course. I didn't know why I hadn't thought of it before. It had been years, of course he was out by now. 'Excuse me, Chris,' I said, and I waddled as fast as I could to the ladies. *Don't puke don't puke.* Before pregnancy I'd had a strong stomach. I was rarely sick, even after slamming tequilas all night. I stood there in the cubicle, the floor littered with tissues and damp footprints, and I breathed as hard as I could until I knew I wouldn't throw up. Mark Jarvis was out of prison, and no one had told me. He was free and out, and fully aware that it was me who'd ruined his life. Oh my God.

◆ ◆ ◆

When I got home, Aaron was already there. I glanced at the wall clock we'd bought in Dunelm, a cheap fake-brass one. It was later than I'd thought. Everything moved so slowly, at this stage of pregnancy. 'Where were you?' he said. Glancing into the kitchen, I saw he'd made a stab at dinner, pasta and a bought jar of sauce. The last thing I wanted was more pasta, but this to Aaron was as advanced as cooking got.

'I went into town. I was going out of my mind stuck here. Thought I'd look at some baby stuff.'

'You didn't buy anything?' I had no bags with me, true.

'I can't carry them. I'll buy online.' I moved past him. I didn't want to tell him I'd seen Chris, because I couldn't bear any hassle right now, but if he asked, I wasn't going to lie. I wouldn't be that person.

'Babe . . . are you alright?' I turned, and he was looking at me with care in his eyes. 'I'm sorry I've been so in my head. This adoption stuff . . . it's really getting to me.'

I stood with my hand on the banisters. 'I know. But you have to try and talk to me about it, OK?'

He nodded. 'And you. You have to talk to me as well.'

'What do you mean?' I said it too snappily.

'Just . . . why've you suddenly taken off work? You said you wanted to go till the end, and then you said you just wanted a rest, but you go into town right away?'

'I didn't realise you were checking up on me.' That wasn't fair.

'I wasn't,' he said mildly. 'I just want to help. Let me help, babe?'

But how could he help? I couldn't bear to tell him any of this, see his opinion of me change, maybe bring my mother's predictions true, send him out the door. If anyone needed help it was him. 'Alright. I'm sorry.'

'Don't forget we have baby group tomorrow.'

'I know. I'm going to lie down now though, I'm exhausted.'

'I made dinner.'

'Thanks. I'll have some later, maybe.' I hefted myself up the stairs, and could feel his worried gaze on me, but I didn't turn around.

Alison

Going back to the station at the end of the day, Alison became the victim of a drive-by bollocking, finding her boss, Colette Milton, standing by the blind-shrouded window of her office. She beckoned to Alison, who, with a sinking heart, went in. Colette was in her early fifties, had come up during the sexism-and-cigarettes years of the force and triumphed, a high-heeled foot on the necks of her red-faced, over-lunched male contemporaries. She wore a silk blouse and suit skirt, a rope of pearls round her neck, all the better to throttle you with.

Colette rarely bothered with small talk. 'Alison. I've had a complaint from one of these barbecue women.'

Surprise, surprise. 'Which one?'

'The house owner – Monica Dunwood.'

Again, surprise, surprise. 'We followed regs.'

'She's a tricky one – the kind who can dig up a long-lost uncle on the police complaints commission. Says officers have been tramping all over her house, leaving it a mess. Try to smooth her over.'

'Someone died there, ma'am. Forensics had to get in.' Typically, they did not clean up crime scenes. Even if your nearest and dearest had bled to death in your living room, it was up to you to deal with it.

'Yes, yes. See if you can spare some uniform to go and brush the floor, make her a cup of tea.'

'She's a suspect in—'

'In what, Alison? Because from all I've seen it was an accident, a fall. Since when do we devote days of police time to accidents?'

Only one day so far, but Alison didn't say that. 'I think there's more to it.'

'Based on . . . ? I've seen the autopsy report. There's nothing to suggest foul play. A slip, a fall, happens all the time, especially when there's booze involved. You know that.'

'I just . . . think that's not the full story. Please, can I have a few more days to look into it? I haven't even interviewed all the witnesses yet, not properly.'

Colette sighed. 'Till the end of the week. Then if you haven't found anything, it's an accident and you move on to something else, understood?'

'Alright.' She'd just have to find proof by then, that this death was not accidental. Even though everyone insisted it was.

'And go easy on them. They are new mothers.'

Alison counted to ten. Glanced at the framed photo on Colette's desk, her rich lawyer husband and her two polished children at the graduation of one of them. Why did having a baby make Monica Dunwood worthy of special treatment? What kind of person complained about the floors, when someone had died at their house? 'I'll see what I can do.'

Outside, Diana was waiting, her dark hair smoothed into a bun, her make-up fresh even after working all day. 'How did you get on?'

Alison summed it up. The first three couples hadn't revealed much. Monica and Ed claimed to have been in the kitchen at the time of the fall, oblivious. Hazel and Cathy said they hadn't seen it happen, only the aftermath. Aisha had claimed to be down at the barbecue with her husband, and also with Hazel, who had gone running into the house when they first heard screams. No, she hadn't seen who was on the balcony or exactly what happened. Same thing they'd all said so far. The husband, Rahul, had not made an appearance, and Alison needed to track him down, as well as Monica's teenage daughter, Chloe Evans. She might well know something, if she was fifteen. Diana nodded slowly as Alison finished. 'So . . . it's not conclusive?'

'They're all saying accident.'

'And they all said the group was harmonious, no fights or anything like that?'

'That's one of the things that makes me think they're lying. There must have been *some* tension, in a group that size, all so different.'

'Hmm.'

Alison was irritated by the *hmm*. Was her partner just playing along, humouring Alison as the more senior officer, but convinced like everyone else it was an accident? 'Look, it's hard to explain. It's little things you notice, after years of doing this. I don't mean to be patronising, saying that. But . . . Hazel and Cathy, there's tension there. They were speaking very carefully, waiting for each other. Rahul Farooq, he didn't even show up to the interview. Monica Dunwood – well, she's insane, you saw that. All she cares about is her bloody rockery. A woman like that's going to cause trouble wherever she goes, and yet everyone says the group's all peace and light, holding hands in a birthing circle? No one ever spoke a cross word to the victim? No, I don't buy it.' Diana was looking at her curiously. Alison caught her breath. 'Anything from forensics? I heard the autopsy came in.'

Diana flipped open a stapled wad of paper. 'As we thought, late thirties, excellent health, great teeth and muscle tone – oh, she'd had a child at some earlier point.'

Alison filed that away – where was the child? How old? They would need to find out.

'Forensics, it's going to be a while, sadly, since it's not high priority. Various people's DNA on the balcony, proves nothing really since they were all milling about the place all day. One thing – there were hairs caught in the victim's bracelet.'

'Oh? What kind?'

'Dark. Long. Could be her own, but there's a lot of them.'

Alison thought over the women at the party. 'Can they cross-match them to the attendees?'

'Yes, I'll send a tech round to get samples from them all, but again, it's not going to be right away.' Still, that was good – if the victim had indeed been pushed over as Alison suspected, there was a good chance she'd struggled with her assailant, and getting hairs trapped in her bracelet made sense. 'Any skin under her nails?'

'Nails were cut short. So, nothing there.'

'Shame.' All the same, the hair was something, and Alison was glad, because so far she had no sense at all of what had taken place that day. Usually, murderers were deeply disturbed by what they'd done, and any police officer with experience would pick up on that in preliminary interviews. But in this case, she had no gut feeling for it. Each person was acting guilty in a different way.

The day of – Chloe

She couldn't believe this was actually happening, that her mother would do this to her. Only weeks after the birth, and Monica was throwing open their house, inviting people round to poke and pry and find out all their secrets. Women who'd just had babies. They'd know, wouldn't they? How could they not know?

She'd gone back to bed after her earlier run-in with her mother, and had been dozing, as she had for most of the previous month, when her mother marched into her room. She didn't knock, never had. She threw open the curtains, which were in a floral print that Chloe hated. Sunlight streamed in like an interrogation lamp. 'I can't believe you went back to bed. Up we get! T minus two hours!'

Chloe blinked herself awake, like some hibernating animal. Her body hurt all over, her eyes, her head, even her toes, weirdly. 'I can't.'

'Well, you have to. Just put in an appearance, smile and look nice, then you can skulk up here if that's what you want.'

'But . . . what am I going to wear? Nothing fits and it's going to be boiling.'

Her mother paused, as if she hadn't considered that. 'Don't you have something baggy?'

'I don't know.' She pulled the duvet around her, though it was stifling in the room. Trying to hide her body, what it had become. Her mother was rooting through her wardrobe.

'God, what a mess. Why must you dress like a devil worshipper? You'll have to wear something of mine, though I'm not sure it'll fit you, you're so big now.' Chloe registered the hit, let it sink in. Her mother was just like this. Her own body was still remarkably slim and toned, probably because all she did since marrying Ed was go to the gym and nutritionist and acupuncturist. So many people were paid to put their hands on her mother's body, something Chloe had not voluntarily done since she was a child. She shuddered at the thought.

Monica marched out again, banging the door, her high heels rattling on the marble staircase. Chloe hated this house, it was so different to the nice red-brick one they'd lived in until recently, the one she'd shared with her mother and her dad too, who had at least acted as a buffer to her mother's madness. There was no softness in this house, just glass and chrome and marble, huge windows letting anyone look in, which was ironic, given all they were hiding. No wonder Ed practically lived at the office, paying for this place and her mother's gym-going personal-training lifestyle, not to mention the private school Chloe hated and was, as her mother kept telling her, failing to make the most of. She missed her old life. She missed her dad, but he was a twat now apparently, with a pregnant girlfriend in her twenties, so that was sad too. He hadn't even contacted her in months, which made things easier in a way, because she didn't have to lie to him, but also gave her an ache right at the bottom of her stomach and behind her eyes.

She crept along the bright white walls of the hallway, passing the baby's room. It was all done up in an explosion of pink, something Chloe would never have chosen. She sidled in. The baby was asleep, her eyes crumpled up, her tiny fists against her head. Chloe felt oddly detached from her, barely related at all. Poor little thing.

Chloe was going to be out of this place in three years, but the baby had another eighteen to get through. Was it fair, to leave her like this, at the mercy of Monica? She stretched out a hand, not sure what she was going to do.

'Chloe!' Monica was standing in the doorway, holding some massive flowered dress. 'Leave her alone, I've just got her to sleep.'

'I just . . .'

'Put this on. The caterers will be here in a minute and you're not even dressed.'

'I . . .'

'Everything has to be perfect today, you understand? Perfect.'

It was a word Chloe had heard often during her childhood. Keep up appearances. Don't let the cracks show. In the years when her father had left, moved to Hong Kong with his job, and they'd had no money because her dad needed to pay for his new flat as well, and her mother wouldn't get a job, they still had to pretend it was all good, keep up music lessons and dancing and drama school. She'd wanted to shout at her mother – *why? Who is this all for?* Anyway, then Monica had found Ed and basically dragged him to the altar and now she was back on top, since Ed was actually richer than Chloe's dad. And now there was the baby.

Monica had called her Isabella, an old-fashioned name that Chloe would never have picked. She'd have wanted something lovely like Rain, or Summer, or cool and edgy like Trixie or Jamie. But she didn't get a say in it. She'd known that right from the start.

Chloe went back to her room, where her mother had thrust the dress on to her unmade bed. It would make her look forty, but she put it on, and brushed her hair and rubbed some make-up over her wan face. She wondered what Sam was doing. Her mother had taken her phone away, of course, and Chloe wondered if she'd ever get it back. If he'd like to know what she was up to. If he was thinking of her at all.

Jax – eight weeks earlier

I stood on the back doorstep, shivering in my dressing gown. It was an old one, towelling, with bits of toothpaste crusted round the neck. Why didn't I own any nice things? I was shouting, 'Minou! Minou!' I rattled the cat's metal dish, which usually brought her elegantly loping from wherever she was hiding. But today, nothing.

'You'll catch cold, babe,' said Aaron, coming into the kitchen in his weekend clothes of jeans and a hoody. I wished he would wear something else, anything to make him look more grown-up, but didn't want to turn into a nagging older woman. I had been awake most of the night, worrying about what I'd learned from Chris. Mark Jarvis was out. He could be anywhere. Was it him, sending the messages? I would have to contact him to find out, and I couldn't have stood that, even if I'd known how. I'd searched for the anonymous Facebook account in the middle of the night, but hadn't been able to find it again. It was as if I'd imagined it.

'The bloody cat's gone.'

'Oh?' Aaron, who'd never grown up with pets, was suspicious of Minou, and it ran both ways. She wasn't above landing on his shoulders from a high bookcase and sinking her claws in. 'Cats do that though, don't they?'

'I guess. She never has before.'

'I'm sure she'll turn up. Come on, babe, we'll be late.'

I groaned at the thought of the antenatal group. I supposed it was useful, and would come in handy once the baby arrived, but I couldn't help but feel judged by that group of mums-to-be, who all seemed to know more than me, and most of all by slim, blue-eyed Nina.

◆　◆　◆

That day we were learning about breastfeeding – what to eat, or rather, what not to eat, a tediously long list. I saw that Anita had turned up to the session, though she wouldn't need to know any of this, and Jeremy hadn't, perhaps thinking it wasn't worth his time. Anita said he was 'at a conference', being the kind of woman who'd feel she had to make excuses. No Ryan again, either, and I was beginning to think we'd never meet him. Kelly held her head high, chin jutting, making no excuses for him, and I admired her for that. She had brought some cupcakes today from Lidl, and I felt my heart breaking for her, so young, trying to swim in this sea that held sharks like Monica, who I noticed pointedly turning her nose up at them.

Nina was giving us a long, long list of things we weren't allowed to do. Drink, of course. Smoke, take drugs. She gave me a hard stare at that, I felt, or perhaps I was just being paranoid. Certainly, I'd indulged in the odd pill or spliff at times, but not since meeting Aaron and of course, not since getting pregnant. Besides, I had my mother on my case, monitoring sugar and caffeine levels. Nina went on. 'Coffee, even too much tea, seafood, soft cheese, cured meats like chorizo, nuts such as peanuts . . . and not too much sugar, of course.' She seemed to glance at the trestle table where the cupcakes were, and Kelly bit her lip.

I didn't know what made me speak up. Some rebellious streak, or the fact that I was reminded a bit too much of Mum. 'I actually read the guidelines had been relaxed a bit. Like you could have a glass of wine sometimes if you wanted. Don't they do that in France?'

You would have thought I'd dropped a bomb into the room. Everyone stared at me, Cathy and Hazel with horror, even Kelly with confusion, Monica with barely concealed judgement. I saw Aisha's eyebrows twitch – of course, she probably didn't drink anyway. Nina's eyes were wide, unblinking. 'It's up to you, Jax. Most people feel that if there's even a slight chance of harm to the baby, then it's not worth the risk for a glass of wine now and then.'

Oh God. Cowed, I lowered my gaze. 'No, no, I'm not drinking myself, of course. I just . . . I read something.'

Anita spoke up then, perhaps to save me, and I was grateful. 'I had a question, actually, Nina, about diet. Jeremy and I are vegan, and I won't have my own milk to feed the baby when she comes. Is it safe for babies to follow a vegan diet?'

Nina was about to answer, when Monica cut in with a loud sigh. 'Honestly, when did we all become so picky? There's people starving, and we fuss over gluten and nuts and dairy and everything. It wouldn't be right to feed a child on tofu and beansprouts!'

Anita opened her mouth, then shut it again. Ed chipped in, 'Nothing wrong with a good steak, gives you energy.'

Hazel weighed in. 'I researched this for my dissertation. Actually animal protein from meat is really important in brain development. I agree, it's cruel to deprive a child of that.'

Cathy, it seemed, did not agree. 'I don't think it needs to be animal protein, as long as it's protein.' Hazel frowned at her. Aisha looked troubled. Rahul, as always, said nothing, his eyes flicking down to the phone he held under the chair in what he probably thought was a subtle manner, but which wasn't.

Aaron coughed, and since he rarely spoke, everyone stopped and listened. 'There was this kid in a home I lived in – four or so. Only ate chips and beans since he was weaned, so kind of vegan I guess. Anyway, his bones and teeth hadn't grown – he looked like a little baby still. So.' He sat back, embarrassed.

Nina chimed in now. 'Very interesting discussion, everyone. Aaron is right that a vegan diet in very young babies, if not carefully planned, can lead to malnutrition and loss of bone density. Anita, if this woman is entrusting you with her child, I would think you'd want to take care of it as best you can.'

There was a short, tense silence. Had she really just said that?

'I can give her milk, of course, that's fine. We don't – we wouldn't impose it on her.' Anita looked miserable, and I tried to catch her eye as a fellow Bad-Mother-To-Be, but she was staring at the floor. 'I just . . . wondered.'

'Well, you have your answer. It's not fair to the child, in my view.'

'Right. Of course.'

'Now,' said Nina, producing a sheaf of papers from her mirrored bag. 'For this week, I have some homework for you.'

God. This was more like school every day. I was thirty-eight, I didn't feel anyone should compel me to do homework. But Aaron was taking notes, anxious that if he failed somehow, they'd take the baby away, or put a mark on a file somewhere that said we were bad parents. For all I knew that could be true – maybe Nina was keeping tabs on us all. As we shuffled out that day, I saw that Anita was crying, and I was fairly sure she felt the same as I did. Judged, and found wanting.

◆ ◆ ◆

I read the homework for antenatal class three times before it sank in, sitting at the kitchen table. Was she serious? How deeply offensive was this, especially given where we lived, which wasn't exactly 2.4 children suburban England? *Draw your family tree to three generations on both sides, so that your baby will have an idea of its heritage.* 'We don't have to do it,' I said hurriedly, as a slow frown spread over Aaron's face. 'It doesn't matter.'

'It does matter, or else Nina wouldn't say to do it.' His face had grown tight. How could he help it? There was my side of the family, my mother and father, my kind Auntie Julie, who lived in Wales, her husband, my cousins, and there was my weird Uncle Alistair, Mum's brother, who lived in Singapore and wasn't to be spoken of in company. Maybe not the most illustrious bunch, but I knew who they were, I knew their names and what had become of them. I knew the names of my grandparents and great-grandparents, and Granny Culville was even still alive in a beautiful house in Surrey I might inherit one day, not that I wished her gone. Aaron knew nothing. He didn't even know what race his father was.

'We know something now,' I said, touching his hand on the table. 'We can put Georgina Partington-Smith.' Our attempts to google her had led to nothing, so we were still left with a blank.

'Not much, is it.' His face twisted. 'Just a name. Doesn't tell us anything. I don't want this baby to be like me, Jax. Not knowing anything. Not knowing who they are.'

'But they will know,' I said soothingly. 'They'll know me, and you . . .'

'And what good will that do them?' he snapped. 'Some mongrel dad, a foster kid, a no one from nowhere.' He slammed his fist down on the table, making the sheet of homework paper jump.

Silence, in which I registered my own shock. Aaron had snapped at me. He'd been violent. 'Babe . . .'

'It's easy for you. You had a dad, you've got a mum, and all you do is complain about her.'

'Because, you know how she is. She's . . . difficult.' I bent with difficulty to pick the paper up off the floor.

'At least you have her. Not to mention the ponies and tennis lessons and private school.' I didn't recognise this tone he was using, so sneering. 'What did I have? Fucking fags put out on my arms. Sleeping in the garden. Kicked out at seventeen with ten quid a week.'

'I know. I know, baby, it wasn't fair.'

'I just wish . . .' And then his hand went over his face and his shoulders were shaking, and I saw to my horror that he was crying. I'd never seen him cry before. It filled me with sympathy, and sadness, and a nasty dart of fear. He couldn't fall apart on me, not now. 'I just wish I understood. How do you keep a baby, a little boy, how do you keep him till he's two then give him away? How do you do that? What if . . . What if I feel like that? About ours?'

'You won't,' I muttered, but my voice lacked conviction. I stroked his tense shoulders, but he shied away. We knew nothing about why he'd been given up at that age, when he would almost but not quite remember his mother. Who knew what horrors had prompted it? 'Listen, babe, maybe we shouldn't do it yet. The whole private-detective thing. Not now anyway, with the baby coming.'

He stared at me. 'You think I won't like what I find.'

'I think that's a possibility. And . . . money's a bit tight right now.'

He thumbed the tears from his eyes, angry. 'Your money, you mean. You don't want to pay for it. And why should you?'

'That's not what I—'

Aaron stood up, gulping down his tears. 'I'm going out.'

'Out where? It's nine o'clock!' I gaped at him.

'Just out, OK? I'm twenty-four years old! I need to go out sometimes.' And he was gone, slamming the door, and it was just as my mother had predicted. It was one thing being with an older woman when she was cool, did pills and went to festivals at the weekend. It was another being stuck in every night with an exhausted woman more than half your age, and a screaming baby. Maybe this was the beginning of it.

I could not allow my mother to be right. As silence fell again, I took out my phone and began to google private detectives.

Alison

The doctor did not make eye contact with them once during the appointment. He had spent several minutes writing what looked like notes on a yellow Post-it, but when he turned it round she saw he had in fact drawn a female reproductive system, with several large sperm worming their way towards it. They were each as big as the uterus, and for a moment she wondered what that would be like, and shuddered.

Tom nudged her and she realised she had drifted off. The room was so quiet and sterile, the doctor so offhand, it was hardly surprising she would need to dissociate her mind. She said, 'So there's something wrong with both of us. We knew that already.' Another nudge. It was easy to get impatient at the process, having to tell the same story over and over to different people, as if they couldn't read the notes or didn't share them with each other, the months of waiting between each appointment, her age creeping up each time. She was constantly doing maths in her head. *If this takes six months I'll be thirty-seven. Cut-off for NHS treatment is thirty-nine.* Her period had started that morning, the desperate hope she'd covered herself in evaporating, the truth settling in. It hadn't worked this time either. It never worked.

'Broadly speaking, yes. Your ovulation is disordered, due to polycystic ovaries, and your partner has low motility.' As Tom had put it, his sperm were lazy bastards, and her hormones were all over the shop.

'So . . . what can we do?'

'We'll get Mr Khan on some supplements, then test again in a few months. And for you I'd like to do a laparoscopy, take a look at your uterus, see if the tubes are open. If not, IVF is your best option.'

She reeled back, as if she'd been slapped in the face. She'd expected a load more steps before that, having heard IVF horror stories of hormones, bloating, marriages ripped apart. Sex lives destroyed – it was already hard trying to time things right, whether you were in the mood or not. 'So soon?' Not that it would be soon, it could still take months.

The doctor shrugged. 'The odds are not great without it.'

'So . . . there's no hope?'

He cleared his throat. 'There's always a chance, of course!'

But not a good chance. Maybe like winning the EuroMillions Lottery, which nevertheless Tom insisted on playing each time, and that said everything about their relative positions on the positivity and negativity spectrum. 'Alright.'

That was it. An appointment they'd waited months for, only to be told everything she'd already known from googling their test results. She felt a certain solidarity with NHS staff, herself being also a public servant trying to do her best in the face of crippling cuts, but would it kill them to smile? Give you some reassurance? See you at the time you'd been told to arrive? It was an hour and a half past it now, and she'd be late for her meeting with Kelly Anderson, another attendee of the party at what her colleagues were already calling the Grand Designs Murder House. Not that it was officially a murder, of course. If it was, Alison would have been part of a whole team, would have had a budget for quick forensics, the works. All the same, she had a strong feeling that each of the couples she'd met so far had been hiding something. Lying to her. A terrible accident, honest. No conflict in the group. Very supportive and helpful. Hardly knew each other, or the victim.

They stood in the rain for a moment outside the hospital, as Tom looked for the car keys in his rucksack. Inside the car it was fuggy, stale from his breakfast cheese pasty.

'Shit,' he said, staring out the windscreen. 'That was brutal.'

'Well. We knew it wouldn't be good.'

'I know. He just seemed so . . . hopeless about the whole thing.'

'Yeah.' She could almost feel it around them, like a fog, but one with muscles, pushing them apart. The questions, the wondering. *Is it you? Is it me?* At least it was both of them. Was that good? Or just more problems to overcome? She didn't know.

He started the car. It didn't matter that they'd just had devastating news, they still had jobs to go to. Someone was still dead, smashed all over a five-grand rockery. 'You'll be alright? Around all those mad mums?'

'I'll have to be.' Maybe it would add an extra edge to her questioning. Stop her being softened by their bewildered sleep-deprived eyes, their traumatised bodies and the tiny helpless lives they held in their arms. Because even if no one else believed her, Alison was sure of it – one of them had helped the deceased over the glass edge of the balcony, to her death below.

Tom drove her all the way to the station, though he'd be late for his own meeting on the fraud case. 'I need to take care of you.'

She missed working with him, a side effect of having him in her bed instead. Diana was good, but she was a bit too chillily efficient. Every form filed on time, no hunches entertained. No pasties eaten in the car, not that this was a bad thing. 'Can you get rid of that?' she said, stepping from his Focus, indicating the greasy paper bag. 'The whole car stinks like Greggs.'

'And that's bad because . . . ?'

'Please. It makes me feel sick.'

'Alright.' He threw her a worried look out the window. 'You're really OK?'

'Yeah, yeah.' She set her shoulders, walked to the door. Nothing was any different, she told herself. She would do her job like it was any other day.

Jax – eight weeks earlier

My mother was watching Aaron closely. 'Would you like a teaspoon, dear?'

Aaron looked up at me, panicked. His method was usually to drink the tea with the bag still in it, getting it as strong as possible. A legacy perhaps of a lifetime eking out the cheapest products there were. He reused the bags too, something that sent my mother into paroxysms. *I think we can stretch to another, Aaron!* 'Um . . . sure.'

She jumped up, and he was passed a silver spoon, tiny in his large hands. 'Umm . . .' There was nowhere to put the bag now. 'Do you have a plate maybe or . . .'

My mother refused to understand for a long moment. 'Oh! Well, why don't I just take it?' She stood there with a rubber-gloved hand outstretched, waiting for the bag. Defeated, Aaron plopped it on, like a dead frog, and she spirited it away like toxic waste. Mum only drank coffee, as she reminded us constantly, making a big fuss of finding an old box of teabags in the cupboard when we went round. I, pregnant, was not allowed caffeine at all and instead had to have no-sugar lemon squash. It made me realise how unbearable my mother was without the narcotics of wine or gin or at least caffeine and sugar. I reached for a piece of the Victoria sponge she'd baked that morning after her power walk, and she raised her eyebrows. 'Ought you to, darling? You don't want to gain more weight. I was on a strict diet before you came.'

I resolved never to mention to the baby what I'd gone through for him or her. Not the scans, not the vomiting every day for weeks, not the look on Sharon's face when I told her I needed a year off, not the tears and agony that awaited me. Not nine months of no booze, cheese, chorizo, or even tea.

Aaron and I had been on our best behaviour with each other since the night he'd stormed out and not come back until gone midnight, reeking of beer. The next day he'd been tearfully apologetic. *How could I shout at you like that, when you're pregnant? I'm so sorry, babe.* I hadn't brought it up since, but the worry was there. He was off-kilter and so was I. Nina's comment about our ages had lodged in my head, a small splinter, not to mention my mother's many digs over the years. I had brought him today in a show of solidarity, a tableau I was acting to show how fine we were. For Mum. For myself, too.

'Aaron, tell Mum how the job's going.'

He looked like a rabbit caught in headlights. 'Um, yeah, it's OK.'

'Any word of promotion?' trilled my mother.

'Not yet. You have to, like, be there a year or so.'

I saw her mouth pucker at his syntax. 'That's a shame. The money would be useful, wouldn't it, with the baby. Given that Jacqueline won't be on her full salary for some time.' She had picked up on the fact that there was something strange about my early mat leave, though I'd done my best to explain it away. She always knew, somehow, when I wanted to hide things.

'Yeah. No, yeah, it would be.' We lapsed into silence. I saw that Aaron's teabag had left a drip on the marble floor, which no doubt she would later find and store away to bring up some time. *Don't splash it all over the place like last time, dear!*

I wished we hadn't come. I needed to be on top of my game to handle my mother, and all this, Aaron's mysterious mother, our fight, Mark being out of prison, the messages, the pregnancy, even poor missing Minou, who still had not come home, it was making me weak. I no longer had the strength.

◆　◆　◆

Telling my mother about Aaron was one of the hardest things I'd ever had to do. Our relationship, never easy, had been in tatters since I'd called my wedding off, followed by eight years of being single. Every time we met, she would bring up her friends from book club who had grandkids, sighing, 'Oh, I suppose that will never happen for me.' For her! As if that was the only purpose of my body, and indeed of me.

That day, we'd had the usual ritual of cake and tea, her not eating anything, urging it on me then keeping careful note of what I had so as to bring it up later. 'Mum,' I said, as nervous as a teenager, when she started her usual round of *Which Grandkid.* 'I've actually met someone.'

She stopped at the sink, rubber gloves clasped. 'Really?'

'Really.'

'Someone nice?'

'Well, I think he's nice. Very nice in fact.' No one had ever been as nice to me as Aaron was, something that made me sad. Why had I put up with such treatment? Even dull Chris wasn't nice as such, just too boring to be horrible in an imaginative way. Even he had put me down, joined in with my mother's jibes about my weight and my underpaid career.

'Good job?'

'Well, he's sort of in the food industry right now.'

She frowned, then brightened. 'He owns a restaurant?'

'Not . . . exactly.' I sighed. There was no point unless I told the truth. She would find out soon, after all. Aaron was not going anywhere. 'He works in a bar.'

'What?'

'He's young. Twenty-four.'

'*What?*'

I ploughed on. 'He's a care-leaver. In foster care for years. He's done really well for himself, in fact.'

The news was so shocking that Mum actually sat down. 'Jacqueline, what's the matter with you? I wanted you to meet someone nice, with prospects, a good job! Someone who can take care of you, give you babies! I know you want babies, darling, and time's ticking on, it might already be too late, and here you are wasting your time with some toy-boy barman?'

I'd drained my tea, the last drop I would be allowed in her house for some time. 'Well, that's the thing, Mum. He *can* give me babies.'

'*What?*'

'I'm pregnant. You're going to be a granny!'

It was the one time in my life I'd ever seen my mother speechless, and to be honest it was almost worth the weeks of tantrums that followed, just for that.

◆ ◆ ◆

Minou had not come back from wherever she was, and the house was quiet without her. I wanted to put posters out around the neighbourhood, but I could hardly walk the length of a street and Aaron obviously felt I was overreacting. 'She's just gone off hunting. She'll be back.' I wasn't so sure, and I missed her warm self-satisfied purr, the silky drape of her over my lap. On top of that, Sharon was dodging my calls about the investigation into the messages, and

I was afraid she'd take this chance to manoeuvre me out forever. She'd always thought I was after her job. There had been no more Facebook messages, but still I felt wary, on high alert, jerking awake in my sleep, getting up for a glass of water and wandering through the house, the time and myself out of joint. From time to time I googled Mark, but there was nothing more online about him. The world had moved on, forgotten all about his case. But I hadn't.

Since I had nothing else to do all day, I had put out feelers to several private detectives I'd found on Google, and eventually settled on a woman, feeling she might understand the situation better. Her name was Denise Edwards, a retired detective with a forty-a-day voice who seemed entirely unperturbed by my request. Apparently tracing birth parents was a PI's bread and butter, which seemed sad. 'I can do that for you, yes my love. When was the last contact with her?'

'He went into care in I guess, 1997? When he was two.'

I heard her writing it down. 'Was there any further contact with the mother?'

'None. It was a closed order.' If she hadn't left her details with the adoption people, this Georgina, did that mean she wouldn't want to talk to him? I wouldn't tell him about Denise until I had good news, if I ever did have it. 'Does that make it harder?'

She coughed, a smoker's hack. 'Can do. Don't you worry, darling, most people are easy enough to find. Facebook and that, it's a gift you know.'

I was about to finish the call, but then I blurted out: 'Actually, Denise, could you trace someone else for me too?'

'Of course. Another birth parent? The dad?'

I hadn't even thought of trying to find Aaron's dad – the lack of a name on the birth certificate seemed to make that impossible.

'Er, no . . . just someone I lost touch with, and can't find online. A friend.'

Her voice betrayed no judgement, so maybe this was something people asked for all the time. 'And what are they called, my love?'

'Claudia Jarvis.' I was too afraid to look for her husband, was the truth. I waited for a reaction. But Denise seemed not to know the name, or if she did, was too discreet to mention it.

Alison

Kelly Anderson's flat was a sad place. Not just the shabbiness, or the smell of chips and cigarettes, the peeling MDF furniture and the pictures torn from magazines and Blu-Tacked to the walls. There was also actual sadness here, seeping out from the cheap foam sofa, and from every pore of Kelly, who sat on an uncomfortable-looking wooden chair while Alison and Diana had the two-seater. She noticed the furniture was pointing at a TV stand, but there was no TV on it, just a square of dirt where one had clearly sat until recently. 'First of all, I'm so sorry for your loss, Kelly.'

Kelly ran a hand through her lank hair. She wore a baggy hoody and tracksuit bottoms, and underneath was stick-thin except for her slightly swollen stomach, an echo of the child that had until recently been in there. 'Oh. Thanks. One of those things, isn't it.'

Alison felt an urge to share her own pain, bond over it somehow, the sisterhood of women to whom babies did not come easily, but it wouldn't have been professional. 'Well, I'm sorry. I gather you went to the barbecue anyway?'

She scowled. 'Why shouldn't I? I was part of the group, wasn't I?'

'Of course. I suppose I thought it might be . . . upsetting for you?'

She said nothing for a moment, looked off to the side at a space on the carpet where a piece of furniture had recently been, a bookcase or something like that. 'Can't go through my entire life avoiding babies, can I?'

'No, no, of course not.' Alison nodded to Diana to take over, with her cool indifference to motherhood. Her own sympathy for this girl, her identification with her as a fellow sufferer from lack-of-baby disease, was going to cloud her judgement, she could tell. Diana's tone was firmer.

'How well did you know the deceased?'

Kelly fiddled with some chipped polish on her nails. 'Not that well. I stopped going to the group, like, when I . . . when I lost the baby.'

'Of course. You didn't notice any conflict, anyone who didn't get on with her?'

She shrugged. 'Dunno. She seemed nice. Wasn't it just an accident? Thought she just, like, fell.'

Diana did not look at Alison. 'Possibly. What can you tell us about that day, Kelly?'

Kelly grew more lively as she spoke about other people in the group. Her pale face was animated, some colour in it. 'Monica has a well-fancy house. It was all, you know, stuff from Waitrose, twelve-quid bottles of wine, that cheese that squeaks when you eat it. Everyone was there from the group. Jax and her fella – he's almost my age, he is – Anita, she's sweet, Jeremy, bit of a posho, Ed, City wanker, Aisha, I like her too, she sent me the sweetest card when I . . . after I came out of hospital. Her guy I don't know so well, he doesn't say much. Cathy's nice too. Hazel, not so much, bit of a bossy boots. Oh, and we found out Monica had this other kid she never mentioned, like fifteen or something.'

That was interesting. Diana glanced at Alison and back to Kelly. 'You didn't know she had an older daughter?'

'Nope, don't think she ever said. Which is weird cos she made sure we knew everything else about her, I mean *everything*. I practically knew what kind of pants she had on. Maybe she wanted to pretend she was younger or something, I dunno.'

'And what happened – how much were you there for?'

Kelly clenched her hands. 'I . . . not for the fall. I went home before that. Jeremy drove me.' Alison glanced at Diana – they had known already that Kelly wasn't at the scene when the first officers arrived. They were still hazy on the details of why.

'How come you left, Kelly?' Alison tried, gently.

'I . . . There was like a mix-up. Someone thought I . . . did something. But I didn't. I didn't do anything.'

Alison could see Diana wanted to press her, so gave her a look. *Careful.* They'd check with Jeremy of course, but everyone so far had agreed Kelly was gone when it happened, so she didn't want to distress her more than necessary. They'd find out from someone else what the 'mix-up' was. Although why had no one else mentioned it?

'So before you and Jeremy left, everyone from the group was there that day.'

'Yeah.'

Diana leaned forward. 'But that's not true, is it, Kelly? Ryan wasn't there.'

The scowl fell back down over her face. 'Ryan never really came to the group.'

Also not true. Alison said, 'We heard he came one time.'

Kelly acknowledged it. 'One time. Just for a bit, like.'

'And there was a kind of . . . altercation, is that right?'

She pursed her lips. 'Dunno what that means.'

Alison was fairly sure that she did. 'A fight. I heard Ryan turned up one day and there was a fight. Can you tell us about that, Kelly?'

◆ ◆ ◆

On the way out a while later, interview finished, Alison nudged Diana and pointed to a stain on the cream wall of the flat. Any police officer – any woman for that matter – knew what blood looked like when it was inexpertly washed off and dried. And there was definitely blood on Kelly Anderson's wall.

The day of – Kelly

Kelly stood outside Monica's house for a long time before she rang the bell. In her head she was talking herself into and out of it. Why shouldn't she go in? She'd been invited, even if they'd probably just forgotten she was on the email chain. She wanted to see everyone, even though she knew it would hurt like a knife, the babies that had survived, the happy mums. She wasn't really a mum, was she? But she kind of was. She didn't know how to describe herself now.

It had all gone wrong anyway because of the stupid group. First there was the homework. She'd read the assignment for the class four times and she still didn't get it. *Draw your family tree to three generations on both sides, so that your baby will have an idea of its heritage.* Why? The baby wouldn't have a clue what that meant, not for years, and anyway she wasn't totally sure about some of her heritage. Did she put on her grandma, who'd been married three times and also had a kid with the next-door neighbour, Kelly's Uncle Dave, but no one officially knew that, even though Dave looked exactly like the neighbour? What about her dad, who'd left before she was born, or her stepdad Pete, who'd been her actual dad in all the ways that mattered, but was now divorced from her mum and had two new kids with a woman called Eileen? She hesitated with her pen over the paper. 'Hon?'

Ryan was sprawled on the sofa, with the TV on some reality show, his eyes fixed on his phone. 'What?' There was an edge to his voice. He was working a lot at the minute, pulling double shifts at Sainsbury's, trying to save for the baby coming, because Kelly wouldn't get much maternity leave from her job at the swimming pool. They already followed her around with little yellow signs in case she might slip in a wet patch. She knew they'd want her out before too long.

'It's this homework for class. Family trees. I need yours.'

He made a noise of annoyance. 'I don't have time for this shit. What's it for anyway?'

She read him out the instructions.

'Like the baby can even understand that?'

'I know. But Nina said.' At school Kelly had always done all her homework, trying to meet the directions exactly, so she wouldn't get told off. Still she often got it wrong, sometimes because her mum hadn't bought the right ingredients to cook with or plastic to back her books with or socks for gym. It was a lot of extras, school, even when it was supposed to be free. And somehow Kelly always got blamed for what her mum hadn't done. She thought about ringing her to find out the rest of the family tree info, but she and her mum weren't really talking right now. Her mum had hoped she'd make something of herself, maybe become manager of the swimming pool, which was definitely possible as the current one, James, could barely add up, but then Kelly had gone and got herself pregnant at twenty-two. Her mum had hinted strongly that she 'didn't have to have it, you know', and Kelly knew that, she supported a woman's choice, of course she did, she'd taken three friends of hers to have abortions already. But this was her baby. And she couldn't explain why, but she wasn't going to do that. She just wasn't. Even if Ryan wasn't exactly . . .

'What are you hovering there for?' he snapped. 'I'm relaxing. I have to work again in an hour. This is just middle-class shit anyway, happy families where everyone has the same mum and dad and they stay married forever. I don't want them knowing all my family business.'

'OK.' She'd just make it up. They would never know, surely, even though that Nina had eyes that somehow seemed to see right through her. 'Sorry, hon.'

Are you scared of Ryan? her mum had once asked her, watching her run around after him at a family party, trying to find the right kind of beer and sausages done the way he liked, a little bit pink in the middle. Of course not, she'd said, laughing. But was it true? As she scuttled away to finish the family tree in their tiny bedroom, could she say that she honestly wouldn't feel her whole body relax the moment the door-slam told her he'd gone to work?

Then there was the row when Ryan turned up that day. Fair enough, he was drunk, but did Nina really need to kick him out like that? Kelly'd had to go running after him, drag him away from the Asian guy, who was talking to him outside the church hall, all intense and scary. He'd pushed Ryan's face into the wall and Nina had almost rung the police, though she didn't in the end. They'd gone home and not mentioned it after, but she'd felt Ryan simmering away, his anger, his humiliation. So maybe it was the row, or maybe it was just one of those things. Who knew?

No one could tell her why it happened. She was woken one night, a month off her due date, by the blood. She'd been dreaming something weird, that a pipe was leaking from the ceiling, or that a window was open above her and rain was dripping on her, making the bed wet. It took quite a few seconds to remember that they didn't have a skylight. It was just before dawn, already bright enough to see shapes in the room. She could hear birds outside, and the drone of planes above London. Something had woken her. What? The bed was wet. Not from a window, there wasn't one. She felt around, finding a wet patch underneath her. She lifted her hand into the pale dawn light. It was dark, sticky. It was blood.

A moment of total clearness, of complete and absolute terror. 'Ryan.'

He'd come in late from his shift, and he wouldn't want to be woken, not when he'd only been asleep for a few hours. She pulled her hand from his shoulder and went to the bathroom, bunching up her nightie between her legs trying not to leave a trail. Even so a drop of dark blood fell on to the hall carpet, and she thought about their deposit, how much it was. *It's OK*, she told herself. People still bled when they were pregnant, that was why so many didn't even seem to know they were up the duff. There was a whole TV programme about it, even. She'd be alright.

Under the harsh bathroom light – no window in there either – she could see how bad it was. Her legs were splashed and crusted in it, her nightie wet and see-through, and it was all over her hands, embedded in her nails and even some in her hair, turning the blonde a strange brown colour. Her eyes were wild and terrified in the mirror. *Is this happening? Am I losing it?*

Hospital. She had to get there. It wasn't far away. Ryan would have to drive her. She wadded up a towel and made her way back in. She wanted to lean on the walls for support but then the blood would be there too, handprints everywhere like a murder scene. Funny how on TV and in films blood always meant someone had been murdered, when really women saw blood all the time, with their periods, and . . . what this maybe was. She didn't want to say the word. She was too far along for a miscarriage. The baby could live now, if it came. A little glass cage and tubes and tiny woolly hats. It wouldn't be the worst thing in the world, get it over with now when the baby was still small, maybe avoid some of the worst pain.

She switched on the light, and it felt weird to have it on in the morning. 'Ryan.'

He woke up slowly, face screwing into a snarl. 'Jesus! Turn the fucking light off.'

'Ryan, I'm . . .' She didn't know how to say it. 'I'm bleeding.'

He blinked and looked at the bed. 'Jesus fucking Christ. What did you do?'

Later, she would think about that question. Wonder: what *did* she do? Was it the ham she'd had for dinner, or the cheese on her pizza, or the weed smoke she walked past on the high street, or the half glass of wine she'd let herself drink after work, despite what Nina had said about that? Or did she walk too far or stand up for too long or something? Get too upset about Ryan at the group that day? Nina had something to say about that as well. *Your baby is at risk.*

It could have been anything. At that moment though, she could only stare at the bed. It was the worst bit by far, a pool of dark black blood that had seeped through to the mattress. It wasn't theirs, they'd have to buy a new one. Security deposit gone. It was on Ryan too, a bloody tidemark on the white T-shirt he slept in. He tore it off, disgusted.

'You need to take me to hospital, please.'

'You'll get blood all over my car!' Was this really happening? He was worried about his car seats when she was maybe . . . *no I'm not it'll be OK* . . . when something was maybe really wrong?

'I'll sit on some towels. Please, Ryan. I'm scared.'

And then the wave of pain struck, like a fist hammering her from the inside out, and Kelly gasped and fell back against the hallway wall, so that when she came back the next day there would be a mark of her body there in blood, staining the old-fashioned cream paint, and there was no way to get it out and no, they never would get their deposit back. But by then it wouldn't really matter.

Ryan finally got up, moving with bad grace. 'Fucking disgusting,' he muttered, at the print of blood on his torso. 'I need a shower.'

She could hardly speak. 'There isn't time!' She'd always spoken softly to him, knowing he could easily be scared away, like a roosting bird. She didn't care any more. 'You stupid selfish bastard. I could be dying. The baby could be dying. Now shut up and fucking drive me to hospital.'

He went pale, licked his lips. It was like he didn't know her for a second. Then he nodded and pulled a hoody from the back of a chair, and took the car keys from the bedside table. His phone, his wallet. Kelly pointed. 'My phone. My bag. Get the stuff I'll need. Essentials. You can come back later.'

He scooped it all up, and then they hurried out of the flat – trying not to leak blood on to the lobby carpet – and into the half dawn, and it was like getting up early to go on holiday, except it wasn't like that at all, and as she sat with her head against the cool window, she knew nothing was going to be the same again.

◆ ◆ ◆

And it hadn't. She didn't want to think about after, the careful way the doctor told her, in a cold bright little room, that there was no hope at all, her baby was dead, and she could hold him for a little while but then they'd have to take him away. How Ryan had reacted, shouting and punching the wall and how, when she got home from the hospital, she'd called her mum and her mum's boyfriend Larry came round and changed the locks and had a word with Ryan and she hadn't seen him since. It hurt her head to think about it all, how it had gone so wrong. Was it the group, the homework, the way Ryan had been treated that day? Was it Nina and her advice? Because now she was alone, with no baby and no partner, and everyone else at this party, they would have both those things. It made you wonder. Was it anyone's fault, what had happened to her?

Eventually, she got too hot standing on the street. She walked up to Monica's house with the smart glass door and rang the bell. No one answered for a while, and then she saw someone coming towards the door. It was Cathy. And she had a baby strapped to her chest.

Jax – seven weeks earlier

The bus clanked and wheezed its way to the church hall, and I thought longingly of my old Golf, languishing in the garage. Like hospital for sick cars, or rather very, very old ones that might soon be taking the Dignitas option to the scrapyard in the sky. I'd turned the key in the ignition that morning to pop to the shops for milk, and nothing had happened. The garage had to come and tow it, an expense we didn't need. I fretted about money, doing sums in my head, thinking about the cost of buying a new car, or an old new one, while I was on maternity pay, or had possibly lost my job, depending on what happened (Sharon had still not been in touch). It said a lot that I didn't even factor Aaron's pay into my equations. He sat on the outside seat of the bus, his long legs stretched out, a hand on my thigh.

I had grown used to Aaron's silence. Unlike other men his age, unlike everyone else on the bus, he didn't look at his phone or listen to music, he just sat quietly. Aaron must have been the only twenty-four-year-old with a non-smart phone, a cheap Nokia one. Partly this was frugality, but mostly it was wanting to disappear, wanting quiet in his mind. There had been little of that growing up.

'Next stop, babe,' he said, stirring. As we got off – he held his body to protect me, shield me, and I wondered did he even know he was doing it – two yummy mummies got on, buggies and matching yellow Boden raincoats. I saw one glance at Aaron, then at me, and a trill of giggles followed us off. I was sure I heard the word *cradle*, but I walked on, heavy feet landing in puddles, a flush spreading over my face. It would always be this way, I knew. People would look at us and think I must be rich, or maybe it was a visa marriage, that there was something pathetic about me, believing a young man like this really loved me. Aaron would probably only get more attractive, as happened to many men, their eyes crinkling and hair silvering. What would people think of us when I was sixty and he was just in his early forties? *There goes that man with his mum, how nice?* Urgh. I had to stop thinking like that. It was just sexism, and anyway I wasn't even going to be an old mum; Monica and Anita were both older than me. Kelly was the one who stuck out now, only in her twenties. I wondered if her boyfriend would show up today.

We reached the hall, already familiar with the layout, walking down the cream and puce corridor. I wondered who would have brought baked goods today, and sure enough it was Aisha this time, with some sticky sweets rolled in coconut, bright-coloured and pretty. God, I really didn't want to have to start baking but it would clearly be my turn soon.

Monica swallowed a bit, grimaced. 'Oooh, a bit sweet for me.' Cathy had one too, though Hazel frowned and said we should all be watching our sugars.

'I agree,' said Nina, sweeping in with a jangle of bracelets and rings. Her skin was tanned, her glossy dark hair braided, her body slim and supple. I hated her. I wished she liked me more. 'Too much sugar isn't good for the baby.' Seeing Aisha's face fall, I made sure to take one, though it left my fingers sticky and I kept wiping them surreptitiously on my jeans. Looking about, I noticed that Kelly's supposed partner had not shown up again. I felt proud briefly, that Aaron, also a young dad, had made the effort. He was good. I had to trust him, like he said. But it was hard, after years on my own.

◆ ◆ ◆

It had become clear as time went on that our little group had nothing in common except for our pregnancies. There'd been disagreements over diet, childcare arrangements, birth plans, and of course the snippiness about veganism. That day, our fourth session, was the day Jeremy, of all people, threw us into turmoil. We were having 'free discussion', where we aired our thoughts and worries about childbirth. I had so many worries that I felt I couldn't voice them all or I'd be judged. When it was my turn, I just muttered something about 'following my birth plan'. As if you could plan for being blown up.

Nina smiled thinly. 'Good luck with that, Jax. It rarely goes to plan.'

'I sometimes wonder why people even have children.' Jeremy did not say much, so his comment landed in the circle like a brick. 'Nothing is more guaranteed to ruin your bank balance, your career, and your marriage. Your body too, for the woman.'

Cathy looked the most upset to start with. She was wearing a knitted jumper with a penguin on the front. 'But it's what you do – humanity would die out otherwise!'

He smiled abstractedly, untouched by the emotion his remark had stirred up. 'That's the thing though. The global population will reach ten billion in a few years – and think what a mess we've made with seven. Food and resources will be stripped. Animals will go extinct.' He pointed to Cathy's jumper. 'Those penguins you love, for example – they won't exist any more. Humanity may well die out if we *don't* stop having children.'

Anita was staring at the floor, embarrassed. Aisha shifted in her seat, worried, and Hazel made some comment under her breath. *For God's sake*, it sounded like.

Cathy scowled. 'But you're having one.'

Jeremy shrugged. 'Adoption. And I'm not immune to the drive to reproduce, none of us are. I just think it's interesting, is all. From a philosophical standpoint.'

Monica said, 'People will always have children. The undereducated most of all – it's our duty to keep intelligent genes going too.' I could have sworn she flicked a quick glance at Kelly here.

'Well, this is what my research is about. What stops people having children – work, life circumstances, worries about the planet – and what spurs them on. Social competition. Gender roles. Fear of old age, of loneliness.' Then suddenly he looked at me. 'You, Jax – you're in your late thirties, yes? What was it that stopped you having children before?'

All eyes on me. 'I . . . I was single I suppose. Didn't want to do it alone.'

'So, life circumstances. It's an equation – your fear of leaving it too late wasn't greater than your wish to be in a stable partnership first.' Jeremy crossed one leg over the other, becoming properly animated for the first time that I'd seen. 'Did you ever think of simply not having any?'

Had I? I must have, in those years when there was no man on the horizon, and my age ticked up every month. When I imagined my life, I had always assumed I would have children. It was just what you did, as Cathy said. Nothing happened without it. No inheritance. No continuance. No ongoing resentment. No man handing on misery to man.

Nina stepped in before I could answer, a frown on her lovely face. 'This is very interesting, but I feel we should move on now . . .'

It was then that we heard the commotion.

Someone was standing in the door of the meeting room, swaying vaguely as if drunk or, guessing at his piggy red eyes, high. A man, a few years younger than Aaron I'd guess, white, with a shaved head and grey tracksuit. So many young guys who lived near us seemed to dress exclusively like this and I didn't know why.

Kelly stood up, alarmed, scraping her chair. 'Ryan!'

So this was him. The elusive boyfriend. I saw Monica nudge Anita and whisper something. I saw Nina frown; she did not like being interrupted. 'Can I help you?' she said.

'That's my baby in her belly.' He started to walk over. 'Entitled to be here.'

'Ryan, is it? Kelly's partner? Of course you're welcome, Ryan, but we don't normally advise joining a group midway through.'

He glared at her, cross-eyed. 'You're the one, are you? Your stupid homework. Family tree. Not everyone has a bloody middle-class family, missus. You should know that.'

Privately, I agreed, but it was somehow shocking to see someone stand up to Nina. Not even Monica had ever dared go this far.

Kelly was looking terrified. Her hands were splayed over her bump, as if trying to hide it from him. 'Ry, hon, why don't you wait for me in a cafe, get a coffee or something, yeah? I'm almost done.'

'You don't want me here, that's it?' He hadn't sat down but was sort of pacing behind the seats. I was craning my neck to keep track of him, the way you would with a dangerous dog in the room.

Kelly's voice was weak. 'It's not that, hon, you know I wanted you here, but well . . .'

'What?'

'You're drunk, aren't you?' And more than that.

'You fucking *cunt*.' The word was vicious; I saw Anita's head snap back. I wondered had she ever heard it spoken aloud before. 'I got a right to be here.'

Aaron stirred beside me with some kind of primal memory of violence, a fear that gets into your every cell. Although he was a tall man, his urge was still to freeze, to make himself as small as possible, like the child he'd been. I'd seen this before when we encountered violence, as you do in London, drunken punch-ups outside pubs, harsh words on the bus. Aaron was scared. And suddenly I was too. All of us in the room, so pregnant, so vulnerable. I think it was then I realised I'd never be truly safe again.

Ed spoke up. 'Now listen, mate, this really isn't on.'

'Fuck off, you yellow-cords twat.' I almost gasped, with fear, with a wild terrified joy that someone was saying these things I had not dared to. Ed glanced in outrage at his mustard-coloured trousers.

Monica rose, her chest swelling like her bump in rage. 'How *dare* you speak to my husband that way!'

'You can fuck off an' all, Boden bitch.'

Monica turned puce. I looked at Aaron – *we have to do something* – but he was frozen still.

'Nina, Nina, we need to have him removed, is there security in this place?' That was Monica. I highly doubted a community hall hired by the hour had anyone we could call – we were on our own here. Without really realising it, I had begun to edge my chair away, hands over my belly. If there'd been a cupboard I would have hidden in it.

'Right.' Ed advanced on Ryan, rolling up the sleeves of his pink shirt. 'I'm not having this, chum. Jeremy, mate, give me a hand?'

Jeremy blinked. 'Me?'

Even I could see Jeremy was no fighter. But it didn't matter, because just then Rahul stepped forward, put Ryan in a restraint hold, and marched him out of the room.

Alison

She checked the address. Was this really it? The person who lived here had been in the same group as Kelly Anderson, with her tiny one-bed flat? She marvelled again at what a leveller it was, fertility, childbirth, babies. It didn't matter how much money you had; you couldn't always buy your way to a healthy child. 'Nice, isn't it,' she offered to Diana.

Diana wrinkled her lovely nose. 'These old places can be really damp.'

Anita and Jeremy Matheson-Coulter had a lovely house on the edge of Beckenham Place Park. Smaller than Monica's, maybe. Certainly more tasteful, in red brick with clematis on the front, a garden full of wild flowers and roses. Alison knew the husband was an academic, so it must be Anita's money, or else family money. She liked the house much better than that glass palace of Monica's – everyone would be looking in at you there, looking down your neck, as her mother would say. The door was opened by a thin, nervy woman, one hand clutched to her throat. 'Oh! Hello. You must be . . . Um, come in, come in.'

The place was very clean, like Monica's. That was a mark of class also, houses kept tidy by the unseen hands of other women paid to clean and melt away, as servants in the olden days had turned their faces to the wall when their masters passed by. Paid to be invisible. Alison and Diana were led into a very tidy living room, red leather chairs and dark wood, like a men's club. Framed on top of the (small) TV was an ultrasound picture. 'Is that . . . ?'

'Yes. Victoria.' Anita gave a small nervous laugh. 'At least, that's what we plan to call her. Planned. Honestly, I don't know what to say about it.'

Alison knew things hadn't quite worked out with their adoption – at any rate, there was no baby in this clean and tidy house. She was dying to ask for the details. 'I'm sorry. Shall we sit down?'

'I must make tea! Or would you like coffee, or a soft drink, or something else?'

Alison was tempted to ask for a G 'n' T, the day she'd had, but settled for tea.

'I have Earl Grey, or I think maybe there's some builder's . . . ?'

Alison suppressed a smile. 'Earl Grey would be lovely. DC Mendes?'

Diana looked disapproving. 'A glass of water would be nice, thank you.' Alison sighed. Times like this she really missed Tom, who'd once eaten an entire roast dinner at a witness's house.

The tea came in a leaf-tea pot, with some shortbread on a little floral plate. It looked home-made. This house was heartbreaking, everything done so well and so thoroughly, and yet empty all the same. 'Jeremy should be home soon. The trains, you know.'

'And do you work?'

'Oh yes, I'm a lawyer, but I took some adoption leave. That's what they class it as, not maternity. I suppose that makes sense.'

Alison waited as she poured the tea, offered milk, straightened everything on the tray. Sometimes people had to work their way up to telling a painful story.

Diana prompted, 'In your own time, Anita.'

'The adoption is proving harder than we thought,' Anita admitted, finally. 'We'd been told the baby was due two weeks ago, hence

130

why we joined the antenatal group. The flyer said it would cover baby care, not just the birth process, so we thought, why not. But then it all went quiet. The agency in America said the due date had been wrong, the mother was confused, it would be another while yet. But now I don't know. I can't even get through to them, and they're not replying to anything.' Her hands had gone white clasping each other.

'And you've paid for this service?'

'All the mother's medical bills, plus a big donation to the agency, yes.'

'So you were expecting to have a baby when you went to the barbecue?'

'Well, yes. There should have been six babies. Poor Kelly.' Two out of six babies not arriving. That seemed unusually bad odds.

'But you went anyway?'

'I wanted to see the others. And I thought the baby was on her way, a little delayed perhaps.' Alison thought how that would be, for Anita and for Kelly too, walking into a house full of babies, none of them yours. Having to smile and coo and pretend your heart wasn't breaking. It was all too easy to imagine, because she'd been to many a baby shower herself, a hideous American import. Soon it would be gender-reveal parties, and Alison did not know enough swear words to express what she thought of those.

Diana clearly didn't have much patience for this baby talk. 'So the day of the barbecue. Did you see the incident take place?' The murder, as Alison thought of it. But they couldn't call it that until they knew for sure, and still there was no concrete evidence, only some hairs in a bracelet and a feeling in her gut. The only person who'd clashed with any of the group was Ryan, Kelly Anderson's partner, and everyone said he hadn't even been at the barbecue.

'No. I was waiting for Jeremy to come back from driving Kelly home – I was in the side garden of the house, watching for his car.'

'He wasn't back before the . . . incident?'

Anita shook her head. 'Not quite. To be honest, I thought we might leave when he got back. After what happened with Kelly, it was a bit . . . It didn't feel like a party.'

Aha. Finally some answers. Alison said casually, 'Oh yes, we heard there was some issue with Kelly. Could you talk us through that, do you think?'

The day of – Anita

She knew rationally there weren't that many babies there. Only four, not the six there should have been. But all the same they seemed to be everywhere as she moved about Monica's (huge yet somehow tasteless) house. Arthur in the living room, being shushed by Cathy. Hadley alone in a bouncy chair outside, which worried Anita – what if she rolled out, what if an animal came along and bit her? Then there was Isabella, who had been brought down from her nap and was being passed around like a little doll in pink frills, and upstairs, when she went to wash her hands, Hari being fed by Aisha, a blissed-out zen look on both their faces. Anita wondered if she would ever experience it. Not the feeding, she'd never have that. But just a baby, to hold in her arms, to call her own.

Her baby was a girl. She was going to be called Victoria, after Anita's mother, who had died five years before. Before she died, she'd pressed a gold locket into Anita's hands, a family heirloom. 'For your daughter, my darling.' Anita's mother had not been that old – barely seventy – and Anita sometimes felt everything had gone downhill since she'd lost her, the one person who'd always been there for her. She'd been quite old before she realised not everyone's mothers were like this, loving and supportive and always,

always in your corner. Look at Jeremy's, a cold-voiced tartar who'd sent him to Harrow at seven and still never hugged him now. Any affection she had was reserved for her brood of Labradors.

Five years ago, Anita had been thirty-six. She and Jeremy had been talking about children for years, on and off, but something always came up. Her promotion. His elevation to department head, with the increase in hours it brought. Then moving house, going on holiday, possibly being exposed to the Zika virus in South America, which meant waiting six months just in case. Always something. Then trying, failing. Then finally going for tests, and the news – she was in premature ovarian failure. She would not be pregnant, not ever. That part of the female experience was cut off from her, and never had she felt it more than when walking into the antenatal group, the swelling ripeness of all those women.

It was funny how far you could slip into madness before you realised. First it had been years of trying – cough syrup, legs in the air, expensive vitamins for both of them, though she was sure Jeremy didn't remember to take his all the time. She didn't want to examine that too closely, her sense that Jeremy's enthusiasm, never great to begin with, was waning, the fact that he hadn't turned up to some of the group sessions. Then IVF – private, since the NHS thought their chances were too low to fund it. IUI. IVF. ICSI. A parade of acronyms. A womb-scratching procedure that made her howl with pain, like an animal. A Chinese medicine doctor who stuck pins in her feet and made her drink foul-smelling herbs brewed up in tea. Nothing.

So then you asked more questions. Could we cope with adoption? Even though there were no babies available in their borough, just older children who'd been through hell and whose birth families were still fighting to have them back? Could we try egg donation? A child that was not hers, but would be Jeremy's? You couldn't pay for it in the UK, which led them to America, a land where everything opened up with money, even the womb of a stranger. Eventually, when Jeremy's sperm count also came up as inadequate, they settled on adoption, which in the States you could arrange before the child was even born. The woman who was having Anita's baby was called Brandi, though she wasn't sure it was her real name. They'd been sent pictures of a homespun, slightly overweight girl in her twenties, smiling broadly with her hands on her bump. Was the picture even real, or just a stock image? Anita had spent so long staring at it, imagining the child inside the bump. Victoria.

That day, at the barbecue, Monica had come bustling into the kitchen where Anita stood, holding Isabella slightly away from her, as if the baby might soil the white dress she was wearing, which was a very strange choice for a barbecue. Anita was wearing a dress from Boden, striped pink and white, but it felt all wrong on her. A dress for someone soft and yielding, not someone with a phone in each pocket (it had pockets, yes) waiting for New York or Dubai to call with yet more work for her to do. Always more work, despite the leave she was supposedly on. 'There you are! So no baby?'

Anita forced a smile, which was getting harder and harder. 'Not yet, no.'

'Wasn't she due two weeks ago?'

'Yes. But these things can be wrong.' The idea was she and Jeremy would fly over when the birth seemed imminent. But it would take at least twelve hours to get there, and the silence from the US was deafening. Panic rose up in her again and she pushed it down, like someone cramming a jack back into a box. 'But look at Isabella! Hello, sweetheart.'

'Here you go.' Monica passed the baby over like a tray of canapés. 'I must get Ed on to that barbecue, or no one will eat!' Ed and Jeremy had disappeared off somewhere, and Anita was vaguely annoyed with him for leaving her like this in a sea of babies.

135

Now Anita stood alone in the kitchen, the baby in her arms. It felt so right. The squashy little helpless body, the tiny curved toes. The hands that had never held anything. *I could run with her. I could just go now.* She shook her head to clear the thought, then looked up to see a teenage girl lurking in the doorway, dressed bizarrely in a too-big floral dress. 'Hello.'

The girl said, 'She needs her neck supported more.'

'Oh.' Anita blushed. Even this girl – Monica's older daughter? Had she been mentioned before? – knew more about babies than she did.

The girl held out her arms. 'I'll take her.'

Anita handed her over. What else could she do? Maybe some women just weren't meant to be mothers. Maybe she'd never have had a child, even if she'd started at twenty-one the way people used to. Something fundamental in her body seemed just . . . not to work. *I'm sorry, Mummy,* she thought, adjusting her expensive dress, on which the baby had left a small trail of drool that didn't bother Anita in the slightest. *I tried. I really tried.*

Jax – seven weeks earlier

After Rahul pushed Ryan from the room and Kelly lumbered out after them, a stunned silence fell. Ed looked wrong-footed. 'I'd have sorted him,' he said plaintively. 'Bloody bad manners, scaring the ladies.'

Monica looked like she might blow her top. 'It's unacceptable, Nina. You have to do something. Nina!'

Our leader had been sitting in a sort of trance since Ryan kicked off. Now, she stirred herself. 'Everyone, please stay here. I'll handle this.' She got up and moved out, unhurried. The rest of us sat for a moment, looking at each other with pale scared faces. Myself, Cathy, Monica, Aisha were holding on to our bumps as if we could protect them that way. Stupid. Beside me, Aaron was also frozen. His eyes vacant.

I nudged him. 'Babe?'

He didn't move or answer. I found myself getting to my feet, with difficulty, and moving to the door. No one stopped me, as I had vaguely thought they might, and I didn't know what I was doing, although I'd had mediation training through work, and angry young men were something I had experience of. Except, of course, I hadn't been pregnant then.

The group were gathered at the end of the corridor. Rahul had Ryan against the wall, pressing his face into the chipped paint. He must be a lot stronger than he looked. Ryan was complaining, 'Oi, it hurts! It hurts!'

Kelly stood nearby, pale and panting. 'Please, stop it! You're hurting him, Rahul!'

Nina was also there, exuding a calm authority. 'Rahul, you can let him go now. He'll leave, won't you, Ryan?'

'Fuck's sake! Alright, I'll go. It's my fucking baby too, you know!'

Rahul had not moved. He seemed not to hear them. Ryan's face was turning white where it was pressed to the wall. 'Rahul!' Nina's voice snapped. 'Move aside.' Finally, he appeared to come back to himself, and all the tension left his arms, and he moved away from Ryan. 'Who has a phone?' demanded Nina. 'Rahul, give me yours. Watch him, but don't touch him.'

'What?' said Rahul, in a quiet puzzled voice.

Nina held her hand out. 'Your phone. I know it's in your pocket.'

With extreme hesitation, he handed it over, unlocked it. Nina keyed in three digits.

'What are you doing?' said Kelly miserably, as Ryan adjusted his collar, gasping for breath, muttering dire curses about Rahul.

Nina held the phone to her ear. 'Calling the police, of course.'

'What? No, he didn't mean any harm!'

'I have a room full of pregnant women in there, Kelly. Including you. I can't allow any danger to come near them.'

Ryan had gone pale. 'Please, missus, don't call them. I didn't mean nothing. Just – I had too much to drink, like, and I lost it. I'll go. I'll go.'

Nina looked between them, as if deciding. 'Ryan, you'll have to leave right now and never come back to this group.'

'He will. Won't you, Ry?'

'Fine! Jesus, I can see when I'm not welcome.'

'Ry!'

'Alright, I'm going!' And he went, kicking the door as he left. Kelly started to cry. Nina took her arm and led her back down the corridor.

'I should go after him . . .'

'You should not. In fact, I would strongly advise you to have nothing else to do with Ryan from now on. Your baby is at risk. You must see that.' I blinked as their voices drifted down to where I stood. Telling Kelly to leave her partner, while she was pregnant – that was a big deal for a baby-group leader to say, wasn't it?

Kelly said nothing, sniffling and downcast. As they approached me, Nina frowned. 'Jax, you shouldn't be out here. Come inside now.'

Behind her, Rahul trailed. 'Eh . . .'

'What?' she said, irritably. 'We need to get started again.'

'My phone . . .'

'Oh.' Nina looked down as if she'd forgotten she held it. She glanced at the screen for a moment, then handed it to him, no expression on her face. And we all went back inside the room.

◆　◆　◆

God, the days were so long. How had I never realised this? Before I'd met Aaron, I'd felt constantly busy. I dragged myself out of bed, then it was a rat race to get to work and the gym and eat well and see all my friends and have hobbies to talk about when I got round to having dates. There was never quite enough time. Now, I had so much time it was as though a giant hourglass had smashed and crushed me to the ground with sand. My mother came round sometimes, of course, bringing all the wrong things, like a mobile for the baby that would take hours to put together. The ingredients to a complicated pie, saying it would do me good to 'nest' a little.

The Monday after that dramatic baby-group session, Aaron left at eight, kissing me on the forehead. 'Promise you'll take it easy, babe? I'll do the cleaning when I get home.'

Which meant I'd have to sit and look at dirty dishes all day, or suddenly realise in the daylight how much dust there was on the bookshelves round the TV. By the time I got up, washed, and dressed in a stretchy tracksuit, then arranged myself on the sofa with a cup of tea, it was barely half nine.

I emailed my union rep, who was dealing with the outcome of the messages, and was told it was still 'under investigation'. *I hope you're enjoying mat leave*, she added rather pointedly. Probably, they felt my case was low priority, since I'd been about to take a year off anyway. I also texted the private detective, Denise, who didn't reply.

Daytime TV was rubbish. I felt too guilty, too much my mother's daughter, to binge Netflix all day, so I tried to read something improving from last year's Booker shortlist, but the lines seemed to blur and warp. Worsening eyesight was actually another side effect of pregnancy, but I thought this was instead more anxiety. Someone had tried to get me fired. To ruin my reputation both at work and beyond. My cat was missing, just as I most needed her soothing purr and way of half closing her eyes in drowsy tolerance of my strokes, and despite what Aaron said I couldn't help but feel this might be connected. I'd spent the previous morning designing a missing-cat poster, hunting through my phone for a picture of her that she'd actually sat still for, no easy feat. I would need Aaron to copy them for me, take them round the lampposts of the area.

So who could be doing all this? The only people I could think of were Mark Jarvis and his wife. I pulled my laptop towards me and balanced it on my bump, hoping that what they said about radiation wasn't true. This time, digging deep into the internet, I found an article that showed Mark had been released three months ago, as Chris had said. *Disgraced financier freed after fifteen years.* The photo was grainy, showing a middle-aged man in a tracksuit holding a clear plastic bag of possessions, shielding his face from the camera. Nothing at all like the suave businessman who'd taken me out for lunch all those years ago. If only I'd said no. How different might things be now?

◆ ◆ ◆

I should have said no. I knew that even then, I knew by the knot of my stomach that this wasn't right. But what else could I say? I was so new and so green and he was in charge, and he was older and handsome and well-dressed, plus I'd never been to a restaurant that nice. My mother didn't believe in eating out, since she hardly ate anything anyway. Daddy had always promised me we'd go somewhere special for my eighteenth birthday, but then he'd died and instead my mother had given me a diet book.

'I hope this is alright.' He stood up when I approached the restaurant he'd suggested I meet him at, pulling my chair out. Boys my age did not do this kind of thing, and I blushed, almost stumbling as I walked across to him. He was in a suit that looked expensive, though I knew nothing of such things, a dark-blue tie. I noticed his cufflinks looked like solid gold. And his smell was aftershave and leather and money. I was wearing a print dress from Primark on which the hem had already dropped, and last summer's sandals, which had left unpopped blisters on my heels. My toe polish was chipped and I was sweaty from the tube. I didn't belong here. But he didn't seem to care.

The waiter came, silent as a cat. 'Something to drink to start with?'

Mark smiled. 'I will if you will. A glass of fizz to celebrate your appointment?' I knew it wasn't right to drink at lunchtime on a work day, but again what could I say? I nodded and soon two cold glasses of champagne appeared. I'd had Cava at university but never the real thing and the taste hit me hard, rich and intoxicating. He knocked his glass against mine, 'Cheers, Jacqueline. To an exciting career.'

I murmured something back and glanced at my menu. It had no prices on it. I was so gauche that I wasn't even sure if he was going to pay or not, and began silently to panic, thinking of my overdraft. Charity work did not offer high salaries. I should have known that with men like Mark, you never pay. Not with money, anyway.

I jerked back from the laptop as a sound reached my ears. Not something I heard often, unless we had an Amazon delivery during the evening. The doorbell. Who would it be? We didn't have anything on order – we'd agreed to scale back the online purchases, both to help local businesses and our bank accounts – but it could be a meter reader, Jehovah's Witnesses, chuggers. Or worst of all – my mother again. None very palatable, but on the other hand if I didn't answer it, I wouldn't talk to a single other person until Aaron came home. I dragged myself up off the sofa, which was getting harder every day.

There was a blurred shape behind the glass of the door. It hadn't entirely occurred to me yet that I needed to be careful with this pregnancy, not just of falls and alcohol and soft cheese and prawns, but of other people too. Of those who might actually want to harm me. Nothing so far, not the emails, not the botched mailing, not the still-missing cat, had made me realise this. How stupid I was. I opened the door and saw a middle-aged woman, her face lined, her hair grey, gaunt under a vast shabby coat that nonetheless was a Burberry trench, costing around a grand new. It was Claudia Jarvis.

Alison

'How are you? Alright?' Becky put a sympathetic hand over hers, and Alison fought the urge to pull it away. She took another large gulp of her wine, shouting over the noise of the bar. Becky, a friend from university, always wanted to meet somewhere like All Bar One, which was cheap and near the station so she could rush back to her husband and kids.

'I'm fine! I said I wasn't going to go mad over it!' It was true she had said that, back when they were casually trying to get pregnant, just seeing what happened, a lie that so many people tell themselves. Within six months she was charting, taking her temperature every morning and typing it into an app, and diarising sex several weeks ahead, whether they felt like it or not. Within a year she was putting her legs in the air afterwards, gulping down bitter-tasting cough syrup, badgering Tom into vitamins and supplements that cost a fortune. Haunting the fertility forums, looking for miracle stories. Hoping. Paying £60 an hour for a woman to stick her full of needles and rub her feet. Despairing.

It ate away at you. She had said she wouldn't do IVF, didn't want to put herself through the injections and heartache and invasive tests, but that was when she still hoped it might happen the old-fashioned way. When it came down to it, it was very hard not to try just one more thing. She knew that was how couples waded deeper into debt, letting more and more strange things be done to their bodies. Look at Anita and Jeremy Matheson-Coulter, wiped out on the promise of a baby from America that was maybe never coming.

It had already taken its toll on her and Tom. On their sex life, on their sense of fun, on their relationship. And it had given nothing in return. She forced a smile. 'How are the little ones?' Becky had three now. Five, three, and less than one. Popping them out, getting pregnant every time her husband looked at her sideways, it seemed. How Alison envied that, to become pregnant easily, because you had sex when you felt like it, a baby born from desire and love, rather than careful counting and joyless thrusting, or inside a laboratory. She told herself it didn't matter, but she knew it did, to her at least.

Becky was telling a long story about a woman at work who had it in for her because she'd had to leave early three times the previous week. 'I mean, what was I meant to do, Maeve had a cold and then Finn got croup, and Hamish threw up in nursery and they won't keep them there if they're sick.' She only worked three days as it was, having once been head of her department in a large secondary school. So many of Alison's female friends had experienced the same. None of the men. Most of them didn't even take the shared parental leave they were entitled to, too worried about their careers, as if women hadn't had to deal with that for decades.

She sighed. 'And she complained about you, are you sure?'

'Well, someone did. The head gave me a right dressing-down, and Anna's always giving me the evils when I come in late or I leave marking at home because the kids are tearing the place apart. It's OK for her, she's not even married, just does what she likes.' Tears were glinting in Becky's eyes. 'It's so hard, Alison, honest, you have no idea.'

'You're right. No idea at all.' She could see her friend was upset, but her sympathy also went to this unknown Anna, having to pick up the slack yet getting paid the same, just because she was childless.

'Oh.' Becky looked stricken. 'I'm so sorry, love, I didn't mean it that way.'

'It's fine.'

'No, it's not, I've gone and put my foot in it now . . .' Which was worse – tactless friends complaining about their kids, or trying to make up for it with solicitous concern, as if Alison was that stereotype, a crazy infertile woman, desperate to snatch your baby from its pram? She didn't want anyone's random baby, that was the point. She wanted her own, her and Tom's. Why was that so hard?

'Never mind,' she said, sick of the conversation. 'Shall we get another bottle?'

Becky looked at her pointedly. 'Is that a good idea, love? I stopped drinking for six months before I fell pregnant with Hamish.'

Alison counted to ten. It didn't help. 'You know what, you're right. I might just call it a night.'

'Oh no!'

'Got a big case on at the moment.' That was true, anyway.

'Because of what I said? Al, I didn't mean it, I'm just venting. Am I not allowed to talk about my kids, is that it? Just in case it upsets you?' Becky's face was flushed. She was angry-sad, a lightweight now who was drunk on the two glasses of Merlot she'd had. Alison couldn't be bothered. She had no issue with pregnant women, with mothers, and yet the world seemed determined to pit her against them.

'It's fine.' She hugged Becky, trying to smooth over the bad feeling. 'I'll see you soon, OK?'

'Assuming I can get a babysitter again,' said Becky stiffly.

What about your husband? Alison wanted to scream. Carl didn't help out at all, she knew that; he worked till nine every night then took the train down to where they lived in Surrey. But that was Becky's choice. Wasn't it? Everyone made their choice, and they shouldn't complain about it after.

She wanted another drink though, and Tom was working late on the petrol fraud case. Overtime, to help pay for what could well be a failed IVF cycle. On impulse, she took out her phone and texted Diana Mendes. *I'm in town and I need some wine. Would you like to join me?*

Failing that, she was going to go to a bar and drink by herself. Might as well fulfil the childless-woman stereotypes while enjoying a good Chablis, after all.

The day of – Jax

So this was it then. Motherhood. I wasn't sure if I felt different on some elemental level, or if it was just physical pain and sleep deprivation. I'd only experienced anything like it on long-haul flights, crazed with jet lag and discomfort, but at least that had been one night only. This had so far been two weeks and counting. At nights I walked the floor, no longer sure what time it was or even what day it was. I'd lived so much of my life out of the moment, I realised. Plugged into my work, or a podcast, or a book, or a TV show or play. Now I was forced to be in every bloody howling minute of it. I hadn't had a proper shower in three days – that morning Aaron had held the baby outside the door while I frantically soaped my hair, which hadn't been rinsed properly and was flat and lifeless. Hadley had screamed the whole time, desperate sobs as if she'd been abandoned down a well. Aaron had no idea what to do with her. He looked like a teenage babysitter, equally uncomfortable. I hadn't read a line of a book, or watched more than five minutes of TV, or gone to the loo without agony either. Two weeks. It turned out that was a long time to live every single awful moment of your life.

And that wasn't counting the way things were with me and Aaron. I hadn't wanted to come to the barbecue today. I'd woken up – or rather, floated out of the half-doze which was all Hadley ever allowed me to have – with a sense that something bad was going to happen. 'What could happen?' Aaron had said. As if nothing bad had happened already, as if bad things hadn't been happening for months now. But he didn't believe me, did he? And that was the root of the problem.

'I don't know. Something.' But it was hard to tell if it was unusual dread or just the everyday kind, the sort I'd grown used to since being pregnant. Of another day without any sleep. Of not being able to sit down and eat a meal, or go to the loo, without the plaintive fox wail of the baby starting up.

'It'll be fine. Come on.' Aaron had even laid out clothes for me, a heartbreakingly poor choice of short shorts and a T-shirt I only wore to the gym. I'd been moved enough by that to get up, shower half-heartedly – my legs had not been shaved in months – and put on something more suitable, a long floral dress that made me feel like a three-piece suite. And we had driven to Monica's to play happy families, to put on a show, ignoring what was really going on.

Now I was in the kitchen at Monica's, dazedly floating in the cross-currents of conversation about nurseries. Monica seemed to feel a Montessori approach was 'dangerously lax', that your child would never get into a good school if you sent them there, and Cathy disagreed, her baby hoisted on her front, quiet and milk-drowsed. Hadley never seemed to get enough to eat, and I was wondering if I should stop, give up on breastfeeding altogether. I imagined what they'd all say if I was to announce that now. If they'd run me out of the place for being a bad mother. A failure at what the rest seemed to do as naturally as breathing. Monica, who'd clearly had a manicure and blow-dry, looked unbelievably slim and toned in a strappy white dress. A white dress! I wouldn't have worn that even before I got pregnant, not at my age. Not to a barbecue.

Monica was a sickener, she really was. Everything was so immaculate, the tableware sparkling, the lights hung up in the garden, the spread of salads and meat. Outside, Hazel had taken command of the barbecue, and Anita hovered by the food table, looking uncomfortable with Rahul, who I didn't think had spoken one word so far. An odd trio, with nothing to say to each other, clearly. I was dying to talk to someone about Anita's baby, how it hadn't arrived yet and what that might mean, but of my allies in the group, Cathy was busy arguing the toss with Monica about nursery education, and Aisha was . . . oh, there she was. She came into the room, smoothing down her long-sleeved top, having clearly just fed her own baby, who was drowsing in her arms. She looked troubled, biting her lip. I said, 'Did you see Aaron up there?'

Aisha blinked, as if snapping into the room. 'Hmm? Oh. No. I haven't seen him, sorry.'

Vaguely, I wondered where he was. I'd assumed he was with the baby, who was outside in her bouncy chair. Hadn't I said, *stay with her?* What if a bee came along and stung her? I knew I should move to check on her. But just for a second, I found I couldn't. For once no one was asking anything of me, to be fed or held or taken care of, and the idea of going out there and perhaps causing storms of howling froze me. Just for a moment. That's all it was. I would tell myself that a lot afterwards.

As I went out the back door, I saw Aaron at the bottom of the garden, along with Ed and Jeremy. I had a vague idea that Ed's shed or 'man cave' was down there. How ridiculous, a grown man with a playroom. Ed looked red-faced and somehow guilty, whereas Aaron and Jeremy both looked uneasy. 'Where's Hadley?' I said, irritated. Why was it always down to me?

'Is she not . . .' Aaron looked past me, trailing off, and I followed his gaze. I saw the bouncy chair I had placed the baby in, when was it, not more than fifteen minutes ago surely? Or was it more? I saw that it was now empty.

My reaction was oddly delayed. It was a bit like how my contractions had taken hold of me, slow at first, then tightening like a giant fist to utter agony, past the point where I felt I could bear it. In the same way, the terror was slow to arrive, pushing through the mist of my exhaustion and apathy. But then there it was. 'Aaron. *Where's the baby?*' Ed, Aaron, Jeremy. Hazel. Rahul, Anita. In the kitchen, Aisha, Cathy, Monica. I realised there was one more person who'd been at the party. Frantically, I ran the count again. Maybe the baby was there, she had just rolled out or someone else had her or . . . No. There was Arthur and there was Hari, both in their mothers' arms, and Isabella was upstairs, napping again. Hadley was not there. She just wasn't there. I didn't want to say it. I didn't want to let that feeling hit me, grab me in its fist. I didn't want to say, *the baby is gone. Kelly is gone and the baby is gone.* I wasn't ready to face that, the terror, the nauseous horrific reality of the empty chair.

But it was Hazel who said it in the end, coming over to take control of the situation, a pair of barbecue tongs in her hand. 'Has anyone seen Kelly?'

Jax – seven weeks earlier

I let Claudia in. Of course I did, what else? I was so shocked by her appearance that I worried it showed on my face, she who'd always been so stylish, so slender and polished. Still, I probably didn't look as good as I had at twenty-three either.

Her eyes roved everywhere, over me, my body, my house. 'You're pregnant.'

I could hardly lie. 'Yes. Due in five weeks.'

'Oh.' And between us was everything that had happened, swamping me with an overwhelming desire to apologise, but it hadn't been my fault. This was how I'd sustained myself all this time, held the terrible guilt at bay like a dam. *It wasn't my fault.*

'Can I get you . . . tea? Coffee?'

She shook her head, her hands in the pocket of her coat. I asked the most obvious question, which perhaps I should have asked first. 'What are you . . . How did you know where I lived?'

She gave me a quick look. 'It's not hard to find where people live. You're on the electoral roll, that's public. You haven't changed your name.'

'No.' Why would I? I hadn't done anything wrong, or so I told myself.

'I've had to do both those things. And move, three times. People still think I must have known. That I . . . let it happen.'

'I'm sorry to hear that.' I swallowed hard. We were both standing up in the living room, the sofa between us. What did she want?

'You were looking for me, I hear. Why?'

'Um . . .' How to explain. 'Some weird things were happening, and I just thought, I wondered, who might . . . want to do a thing like that to me.' It sounded so stupid now, just a few malicious messages, nothing concrete.

'I see. And you thought, because you ruined my life, it might be me.' I couldn't read her tone. Mostly, she sounded worn out. I didn't need to ask had she moved on, met someone else, had other children. I could see from her whole demeanour that she hadn't. Disappointment, that was what she radiated. A life that had suddenly and irretrievably lurched off the rails, all thanks to me. 'Well, it wasn't. I'd done my best to forget it all until you came snooping round.'

'I heard he got out.' Meaning Mark. I couldn't say his name out loud. I hadn't done anything with what Chris had told me, hadn't looked for him properly, because I was afraid. I knew I couldn't face him, even after all this time.

'Apparently so. I won't be seeing him.' She gave me that look again, and I saw the woman she used to be, poised, razor sharp, chair of multiple charity boards. In a different world, Claudia could have run a company herself. Her life would not have been so ruined by what her husband did. She would not have taken his name, probably, and would have been able to unyoke herself from him so much more easily. 'Believe it or not, Jax, I did accept it. What you said. They found the evidence, after all. I'm not a fantasist. I know he did it.'

'But you said . . .' I thought back to the day in court, her screaming at me across the gallery. *You lying bitch! This is all your fault!*

'I was upset. You can understand that, can't you? After what happened. And the thought that the man you love, that you think you know, could do such things. I mean, you understand that, don't you, Jax? After all, you were going to sleep with him too.'

I could have protested that I was young, railroaded into it, just being polite. Instead I said what I had tried not to before. 'I'm sorry.'

'Ah well. It's too late now. But I wanted you to know, none of this is me, whatever's been happening. I highly doubt it's him either. They watch him like a hawk. Waiting for him to do it again. Apparently, it's just a matter of time.' She shrugged, straightened her spine. I felt like coming to talk to me had helped her somehow, reminded her that she used to have poise and grace, that she wasn't defined by what Mark had done. 'I hope it all goes well with the baby.'

'Thank you.' I knew it must have cost her a lot to say that, considering what she'd lost. I shuffled behind her to the door, and watched until she disappeared from view at the end of the street. Claudia Jarvis, or whatever she called herself now. I wondered for the thousandth time if I had done the right thing back then.

I was shaking when I closed the door to Claudia. I had liked her, that was the worst thing. She seemed broken down, grown up in a way Mark never had to me. I wondered had she always been like that, and I'd made her into a grouch, a killjoy. What a stupid kid I'd been. I felt myself swept with a deep and shattering shame. *All your fault. All your fault.* But I hadn't meant for it to happen. I'd done the right thing – the only thing I could have done. Hadn't I? But as I sat back down on the sofa, which already had a soft hollow from where I'd been slumped, bits of crisps collecting in it, I found that I wasn't sure I had at all.

◆　◆　◆

After that first lunch, Mark began to stop by my desk most weeks. It got to be embarrassing – I could see my colleagues roll their eyes, and when Hillary the fundraising manager retired (not a moment too soon in my opinion, since she barely knew how to type, let alone use databases), he suggested I apply for her post. At twenty-three, this was quite a coup and I would have talked myself out of it, in classic female style, if not for his encouragement. On the day of the interview he was on the panel, as was standard, along with my boss, Veronica, the head of fundraising, who was good but in my opinion too taken up with her twin toddlers, and a service user, a girl called Nicky who'd come up through one of our programmes. Nicky didn't say much, picking at some old scars on her arm and asking her assigned questions in a halting South London accent. Veronica, whose phone went off in the middle of the interview with a text from her nanny, was distracted, barely listening to what I said.

Mark, who had coached me over lunch the day before, smiled encouragingly as I fed him back my smooth answers. I felt we could diversify our income profile ahead of the possible coming recession. I'd involve service users at every level. I'd offer an internship to a former beneficiary. I'd develop our high-value donor programme. Five minutes after the last candidate was seen – a middle-aged woman in a stained suit, who kept dropping papers from the binder she carried – Mark came to my desk and laid a hand on my arm. I felt goosebumps run up me. 'Congratulations, Fundraising Manager.' I had never known anything to be so easy before. He whispered, 'I have a few things to finish up, then how about a celebration drink?'

I looked at the clock. 'It's only three.'

'Never mind that. We'll say I have to brief you.' With a light squeeze of my arm he was gone. I looked up to see Karim, the database manager, watching me, and flushed with a shame I didn't quite understand.

◆ ◆ ◆

'Another?'

'I shouldn't really, I'm tipsy.' I was slight then, young, unused to drinking like Mark did, client dinners with £800 whisky and matchless wines, where he had to keep a clear head somehow. Three glasses of cheap sparkling wine and the world was swimming. I'd be fundraising manager. I'd call my mother later and tell her. Maybe I'd make it sound a bit more impressive than it was – she wouldn't understand it was a big step forward for me. She'd ask what the salary was, then echo it back to me, incredulous. *Darling, that seems like exploitation.* Plus, I was fairly sure I sensed a coldness among the other fundraising team members, the ones who hadn't been coached to a promotion, who'd been there longer. Susan had applied too, I thought, but I'd not seen her have an interview. Never mind all that. I was on my way. And this man, this suave grown-up man, seemed to like my company.

I hadn't interrogated it too closely. He was married – I'd glimpsed his wife at a donors' event, slender and glamorous in a white silk dress and diamonds, though old to my eyes. He wouldn't be interested in me if he was married. He was just helping me out. He reminded me of my father in some ways, the whisky, the suits, the fountain pen in the pocket. Veronica had once whispered to me that Mark and Claudia had no children, so sad, so that's why he worked with the charity. To help the other kids, the ones that had no chance in life. Maybe he saw me as a kid in some ways.

I was naive back then, but not that naive. What it had been was an excellent piece of self-deception. I'd taken note of his hand on my arm, his fingers on my lower back, steering me to a table. Now his leg brushing mine under the table. And the next question was a dead giveaway. 'So, Jax, is there a young chap in the picture? Some rocker with a beard?'

I laughed. 'Oh no. Boys my age, they're so . . . well, you have to mother them so much. I'm not up for that.'

'You'd rather have a real man.'

I took a sip of wine. 'Maybe.' My heart was racing. Something was happening. I didn't know what. But it would happen. And that suspended moment, right before it did, was my favourite. It still is.

That's when I saw her. A woman was crossing the room, her eyes roving among the half-drunk pub-goers in suits. Dark hair, anxious face, expensive camel coat. It was Claudia. His wife. 'Oh, there you are.'

Mark jumped right away from me. 'Darling! What are you doing here?'

'I went to the office to find you. They said you might be here.' She looked at me when she said it.

'We've just promoted Jacqueline here. We thought we'd celebrate.' I wanted to run. I understood that, even though I technically wasn't doing anything wrong, I still was. I wanted to apologise to her.

'Right. Well, I had a meeting nearby, I thought we could get a cab. I get so nervous on the Tube now, there's never any seats.' She turned slightly then, and I saw the swell under her coat. Mark's wife was pregnant. She must be at least forty, I thought.

'Of course.' He got up, a small boy caught misbehaving, and put his coat on. 'Sorry, Jax. You'll be OK getting home?'

'I'll get the Tube.' Taxis were for women like her, with handbags that cost more than my rent. Not for the likes of me, one step up from a student, for all my promotion. Although it was against my religion to leave alcohol behind, I waited until they'd left – Mark did not kiss me goodbye, and she said nothing to me – then got up, abandoning a full glass of Prosecco, and trailed off to the Underground. I wanted to cry suddenly, and for some reason I found myself blaming Claudia Jarvis, for the way she'd come in and pulled him out, taken him away from me. *Jealous old woman*, I thought to myself, standing up on the packed Tube. *Pregnant at her age. It's not right. Poor Mark.* I suppose it was then that my thoughts began to turn towards the idea – maybe Mark wasn't very happy. Maybe he needed someone younger. Someone like me.

Alison

Alison was standing in the office, looking at what was always portrayed on TV as a sophisticated whiteboard covered with clear, up-to-date pictures. This was more like a glorified cork board, and people were always stealing the pins so there were never enough to go around. She was looking at the pictures of the couples at the barbecue that day. This not being TV, they were not perfectly posed headshots, but rather whatever she could get off their Facebook, Twitter, and Instagram posts, plus all the images actually taken that day (Monica alone had snapped dozens). The house. The garden. The rockery, still pristine, the glass balcony above. No useful clues, sadly, so she'd turned to their social media instead. In this day and age it almost felt rude when people didn't have a readily accessible social-media presence, and apart from Aaron Cole, which was strange given his age, all the people at the party did. Almost all, anyway.

Jax Culville's feed was full of angry articles from the *Guardian*, with comments like *We must pay attention to this now*. Anita's was limited to the odd holiday picture, her standing beside Jeremy with a strained smile, as if she knew what she ought to be doing but her heart wasn't in it, and lots of posts about saving stray dogs. She had also made some tentative posts in adoption and fertility forums.

Jeremy's was all academic articles and links to his own occasional appearances on television.

Monica, with a fully curated Instagram linked to her Facebook and Twitter, could have shown Anita how to do it. She'd already uploaded pictures of her baby, who could barely lift her head up, with signs saying *one week old today* and *two weeks old today*. How long this would go on for was anyone's guess – *I am one thousand weeks old today!* Alison would not be that kind of mother. She would maybe not be any kind of mother, of course. One thing – she'd found wedding pictures from Monica and Ed's 'big day', which had been more extensively photographed than Harry and Meghan's, but the date clearly said it had taken place only six months ago, not a year. Why had Monica lied about something so small? Maybe she was just ashamed that she'd got pregnant before marriage, which seemed bizarre in a divorced forty-something. Daft cow. Alison still had to ring the ex-husband, Thomas Evans, but he was in Hong Kong and the time difference made it hard.

She was aware that she was irritable, probably from her encounter with Becky the night before, who'd sent her a whole string of messages on her way home which managed to be both apologetic and accusatory, or the fact that Diana hadn't even replied to her text, just greeted her that morning with a cool, 'Oh, sorry I didn't reply, I'd already gone to sleep.' And she hadn't wanted to go to a bar on her own in the end, so she'd drunk the rest of an old bottle of cheap rosé at home instead, and fallen asleep, so that when Tom came in from work she woke up stiff and cranky on the sofa. And these interviews, with these glowing new mothers, were not helping her mood. Why couldn't one of them tell her the truth? Someone must have seen *something*.

She moved on. Cathy's feed was recipes, baby pics, warm comments on other people's photos with lots of kisses, while Aisha did some of this too, and also posted in a lot of forums related to her physiotherapy job, and sometimes exchanged comments in another language that Alison assumed was Urdu. Facebook helpfully offered to translate these, and they were just the usual classic auntie messages like *lovely pic, hope u r enjoying ur holiday xx*. Hazel's was all run times from Strava and encouraging comments on people's Ironman pictures, her personal-training clients, Alison assumed.

Kelly Anderson was a prolific poster on Facebook, understandable given her age. Likewise, Ryan Samuels posted a lot about football, and was a fan of a site called LadBible. But he hadn't been at the barbecue that day. If only he had, Alison would actually have a motive, someone she knew had clashed with the victim. She'd checked with Sainsbury's though and he'd been at work in the warehouse all that day, even caught on CCTV unloading pallets on to shelves. Annoying.

Among the other men, Ed Dunwood posted articles from the *Economist* or got into heated arguments with strangers on neighbourhood groups over things like cricket or parking or access rights. Rahul Farooq posted a lot online, which Alison was surprised about, given how taciturn he was in real life. She also noticed he had 'liked' a few online gambling sites, and made a mental note of that little red flag. It was almost depressing, how easy these were to find, especially given that everyone now voluntarily shared all their innermost secrets with the internet, a hungry shark gobbling up their data, using it against them. Alison barely used Facebook now, and the only reason she hadn't deleted it was because her mother gave her grief about no longer being able to see her 'holiday snaps'. Tom was an enthusiastic poster and commenter, and like Ed Dunwood sometimes got in rows about things online, especially people criticising the police. If they had a baby, she'd talk to Tom about a no-screens policy, no pictures of the kid online till they were older. Not that it was likely to happen. God, she had to stop thinking this way! Didn't everyone say it made things worse to stress about them?

Scanning through all the social-media profiles, a few things stood out. She wanted to look further into Aaron Cole. Why would someone his age be so private? Then there was the fact that Monica's daughter Chloe Evans, who she still hadn't interviewed, had posted prolifically online until about six months ago, when all her accounts had gone quiet. She hadn't put up a single thing since then, which seemed odd to Alison. The girl had been ill, her mother said, but would that stop her going online? The other thing that struck her, looking over them, was that there was nothing online at all for Nina da Souza. She didn't even have a Facebook account, she didn't use email as far as Alison could see, and all the set-up for the group had been arranged via text, from a mobile number that was now out of service. It was so frustrating. If this was a murder case, she'd have been part of a team, and everyone would have been hauled in right away, before they had the chance to get their stories straight. So much time had already been lost, but she couldn't do much more with just herself and Diana. She was pretty sure Diana still leaned towards the accident angle in any case.

'Anything on the socials?' Diana herself came over then, looking as glossy and neat as always. Was the shine on her hair something innate, Alison wondered, or did she just have a really good shampoo?

'Maybe. I want to request further access to some of them.' She was distrustful of Ed, and also of Jeremy, but perhaps that was just a class thing, a chip on her shoulder. And if Kelly Anderson had left by the time the fall took place, Jeremy also wasn't there, since he'd driven her home. 'Funny thing about Nina da Souza, she has no online presence. I can't find her anywhere.'

'You think that's weird?'

'Nowadays, yeah.'

'Could be one of those off-grid people, you know. A low-techer. That would make sense, if she's a hippy-dippy doula type.'

'Yeah. But I'm thinking – what if it's a made-up name?'

Diana was less sure. 'She'd have had to do a DBS check to get that job, surely.'

'Not necessarily. I mean, think about it. She'd no ID on her, no wallet, no phone even.' Nina da Souza was a total mystery, in fact. They didn't even know where she lived yet. 'You found anything new?'

Diana shook her head. 'Still chasing up forensics on those hairs, they're so slow. You reckon it's significant, the thing with Kelly Anderson at the barbecue?'

Alison frowned. 'Can't see how. She'd left before anything happened.' But could two separate incidents really take place at the same quiet suburban party? How likely was that? 'That's it, nothing else?'

'Well, you know we talked about seeing if anyone had a record.'

Alison pounced on that. 'Did they?'

'Not exactly. Squeaky clean in fact, except for one.'

'Who's that?'

'On your desk there.'

Alison flipped open the file, made an emoji-face of surprise. 'Always the quiet ones, isn't it. Reckon it's relevant?'

'Honestly, no. But we should go and have a chat anyway.'

'Was that really all?' She'd hoped for something more. A violent offence of some kind, a little hint at the kind of person who might later push someone off a balcony.

'Yeah, as far as convictions go. But Jax Culville, she was a witness in a big case about fifteen years ago. In fact she blew the whistle on the whole thing in the first place.'

'What case was that?' Alison was leafing through the endless pile of paperwork on her desk. New regs. Parking instructions. Pass-agg reminders about washing-up.

'Mark Jarvis. Do you remember that one? He—'

'I remember,' Alison stopped her, a queasy feeling rising in her stomach. 'I was seconded to CEOP a few years after that.' An innocuous acronym for one of the hardest jobs there was – the Child Exploitation and Online Protection team.

Diana raised her neat eyebrows. 'Yikes. I've managed to avoid it so far.'

'Wise. So that was Jax? The girl who . . .'

'Yeah. Want to hear something else that's interesting? Mark Jarvis got out of prison three months ago. He's living in a halfway house in Ealing. Fancy a trip out there?'

Alison eyed her paperwork pile. 'Sure. It's not like I have anything else to do just now.'

Diana gave a faint smile in acknowledgment of the irony. 'Alright. You want to get some food in a bit? I'm on a late and I need to eat.'

Alison was taken aback. A social invitation, from the ice queen? Maybe she felt bad about blowing Alison off last night. 'Really?'

'Yeah. I was hoping you might know somewhere that doesn't only sell bacon rolls or fried chicken.'

The team ran on such food, though Alison in her late thirties was starting to feel it. 'Good luck with that around here, to be honest. I know a place we can try, though.'

'Great.' No mention of why she wanted to meet up, or what she wanted to discuss. 'There's one or two things I want to ask you.'

'Alright.'

Diana left again, without saying anything else, leaving Alison puzzled. But then it wasn't surprising. If you learned anything from this job, it was that everyone had secrets, everyone had something they didn't want the world to know about. Even her. Her eyes were drawn to the only picture she'd been able to find of Nina da Souza, taken by Monica at that barbecue. An attractive, fit-looking woman, tanned, jingling with earrings and bracelets, dusty bare feet, a tattoo on her arm. They knew so little about this woman – they hadn't even found her address so far, which seemed crazy, or if there was any next of kin to let them know her fate. Had she had secrets too? And if so, had one of them led someone to push her off the balcony that day, killing her outright?

The day of – Kelly

She hadn't meant to do it. She'd told herself it was going to be hard, all those babies, but it wasn't the other mums' fault that their babies had been OK and Kelly's wasn't. She would go and smile and be nice to them, act like a normal person, not one leaking crazy all over the place, leaving a trail behind her like a slug.

But seeing the baby, Cathy's baby, so soon, had thrown her off. It was like going into one of those haunted houses that Ryan loved at Halloween, your heart hammering because you knew any second something could jump out at you. His huge wide eyes, his little hands, opening and closing on nothing. Kelly's baby had been a boy too. Tom, she was going to call him, or Charlie. Something simple. Strong. Her dad's name had been Charlie. He'd died of a heart attack when he was fifty-two. Too many fags and cans of Special Brew.

Cathy led her into the kitchen, making a fuss of her, like she was sick or something. She saw Anita in the garden, recognised a look in her, a barren look, a worn-out-with-sadness look, like you were sick of how unhappy you felt all the time, you just wanted to feel normal for a minute. Kelly knew in that moment that Anita's baby had not come from America after all. Someone said something about there being a delay, the due date hadn't been right or something like that, but no, she knew what had happened: the woman in America was going to keep her baby after all. It was hard to even blame her. Her eyes met Anita's – *the two of us, here, we don't have babies* – two people who didn't belong. Monica barely said hello, too busy moaning that Ocado had sent the wrong kind of leaves for the salad or something. Kelly hadn't even known you could get different salad leaves until she was twenty – basically you got iceberg and that was that. What was cavolo nero? It sounded exotic, something from a world Kelly wasn't part of. She pulled at her hoody sleeves, self-conscious. It was hot, she realised. She hadn't thought about the weather when getting dressed. Hadn't been outside in a week. She'd just wanted to swaddle herself up against the world.

Her time at the party was confused, and weeks later she would still be trying to figure it out, work out why she'd done it. In the garden, Hazel was doing the barbecue, shoving Ed out of the way. His face was red. Rahul was near the end of the garden, doing something on his phone like always. Kelly had been a bit afraid of him since that day he'd mashed Ryan's face into the wall. Aaron, the only person near her age, was holding a beer and talking to Jeremy, the two of them awkward. Kelly had no idea what to say to Jeremy. He always looked like he was writing an essay in his head. Then she was back inside, feeling dizzy and too hot. Jax came into the kitchen then, pushing aside the curtain. She had a baby in her arms too, and when she saw Kelly she looked guilty. Before that, she had looked worried. Something wasn't right. 'Oh! Hi, Kelly. Er . . . how are you?'

'Is that your baby?' Kelly looked at her hungrily, the little girl.

'Oh yes. Hadley. Do you want to . . . You want to hold her?' For a moment it seemed like everyone held their breath. But of course she wanted to. She held out her arms and the squashy little body was in them, so warm and soft, her skin like the velvet on a cushion Kelly's mum had on her sofa. *This could be mine*, she thought, as she held the baby asleep against her. It nearly had been. Her baby had been perfectly formed, just not ready to come out. Small, but perfect. He was buried now. Under the ground, soil in his eyes.

Aisha came into the room then, holding her baby. Also a boy. Also beautiful, with a cap of dark hair already. She looked worried too, Kelly thought. It was as if her loss had given her super powers, like she could see what everyone was feeling beneath the surface. 'Kelly, I was looking for you. I'm so sorry for what happened. Did you . . . give him a name?'

The question she wanted people to ask. She opened her mouth, found a sob there, swallowed it. 'Charlie.'

'That's lovely. This is Hari – H-A-R-I, that is.'

Someone else came in then, and Aisha moved to let them past. It was a teenage girl carrying a baby dressed in pink frills. Kelly was confused for a moment, she thought maybe the girl was someone they'd got to replace her in the group, an even younger mum. Then Monica said, 'This is Isabella. Oh, and my other daughter, Chloe.' And just like that there were four babies in the room, Hari draped over Aisha's shoulder, Arthur in a sling on Cathy's front, Isabella being held by the teenage girl, and in Kelly's own arms, Hadley. Not her own. But a baby all the same. Kelly handed her back, before it got too hard.

She hadn't meant to do it. But after an hour or so at the party, drinking pink fizzy wine because she could now and it had been six months since she'd had a drink, and her tolerance was shot but she needed something to get through this, she'd seen Hadley on her own in the garden. She was in a bouncy chair and wearing little jeans and a yellow T-shirt. Kelly liked that. If she'd had a girl she wouldn't have dressed them all in pink. Let them be whoever they wanted, like. No one was with Hadley. Kelly stood and looked around for Jax, for Aaron, but there was no sign of them. The baby was alone. A bee buzzed near her, around the bush of pink flowers. Kelly didn't know what they were called.

'Are you OK, sweetheart?' Hadley looked up at her, eyes unfocussed. She must be scared. Her mummy and daddy had left her. Then Kelly was stooping, picking her up, and no one seemed to notice. 'Let's go and see the roses, baby.' And she just walked down the back of the garden, out the gate and into the park, and it was as easy as that.

Jax – six weeks earlier

I blinked my eyes several times, unsure if what I was seeing was real. But it was. Nina sat at the head of the circle – if a circle can have a head – and brandished the plastic doll-baby with rolling eyes. She was busy shoving its head through what I could only describe as a knitted vagina. I wondered who had knitted it and why, if there was an instruction book of body parts out there waiting to be rendered in wool.

'So you see,' Nina instructed, 'it's a fairly brutal process. Your vagina doesn't have the stretchiness of this wool, mums, so you may get some tearing or rupturing.'

Tearing. Rupturing. Those weren't words I wanted to associate with my most intimate parts. I glanced at Aaron in terror and he stroked my arm without taking his eyes off Nina, like the good student he was determined to be. To protect myself, I drifted off into the same thoughts I'd been having ever since Claudia came to my door. Thoughts about what I'd done back then, and why.

Over the years, I had thought a lot about why Mark paid me that initial burst of attention, which so blinded me, which caused me to behave the way I did, which in turn led to so many other things falling apart. At first, I told myself he did genuinely like me, even when it became clear I was not exactly his type.

Later, I realised it was all calculating, that this kind of person is so very good at what they do, even if they don't consciously think about it. I was a young member of staff, easily led, with no experience of actually applying the safeguarding rules I had been taught. With no knowledge of how you should push back against your own fear, your ingrained politeness, your respect for authority. Your bedazzlement with older men who bought champagne and used fountain pens. It was such things they hid behind. I was naive and I had access to the teenagers who needed our services, children really. That was my appeal for him. It became obvious as soon as I went to his flat that night.

I had extracted and carefully hoarded information about his life, both from Mark and from gossip around the office. I was not the only young woman working there who had looked at him and at Claudia, once beautiful but now ageing, and wondered if there might not be an opening of some kind for me. With the pregnancy, she began staying at their country house, only coming to London for meetings and doctors' appointments. Mark, hard worker that he was, stayed at the 'pied-à-terre', a flat in Belgravia that I now realise must have been worth close to three million even then. Apparently, this kind of arrangement was common. Paying for two homes. A husband in the city four nights a week, a wife alone in the country. It astonished me.

It was easy to find where Mark lived; his address was on the work database, and in any case bandied about the office for whenever we needed to courier papers for his signature. One night, instead of booking a bike messenger as I'd been told to by Veronica, I simply got on the Tube and went there myself. I'd stayed late in the office, knowing that Mark put in long hours and might not be home early. I was the last one sitting at my desk, drawing admiring looks from my boss as she went, and irritated ones from my colleagues. As I strolled down the street to the Tube, it was already cold, a breath of winter in the air. Excitement quickened my steps, and I forced myself to slow down, savour it. I had slept with only two boys before, one a university boyfriend who never cut his toenails, one an internet date so nervous he could barely look me in the face. This would be different. Mark's flat was near the expensive shops of Bond Street, which were still open as I passed, lit up and scented, exuding the promise of a better life, one where I'd wear designer clothes and have opinions about perfume and never set foot in a Primark again. I had put on my best underwear, but even that was only from H & M, cheap nylon lace over turquoise satin.

I rang the brass bell of his block of flats and he buzzed me up without speaking – he must have been expecting a food delivery, or else he got callers so often it meant nothing. When he opened the door I was in the process of arranging myself sexily against the wall; an effect that was something like an ungainly flamingo.

'Jax!'

'I hope you don't mind. I thought I'd bring the documents myself.'

He wore an open shirt and his suit trousers, stockinged feet. I quailed for a minute – he looked old, and tired. Did I really want to do this? 'Usually they bike them.'

This wasn't right. He was meant to be pleased to see me. 'I couldn't get one,' I lied.

'Well, OK, come in. I have a lot on tonight – in fact I thought you were my pad thai.'

'I love Thai,' I said, on the strength of one green curry at college.

Mark was polite. It was another of his defences, his shields, a way to hide who he really was. It took me a long time, too long really, to stop equating good manners with decency. 'Oh. Well, I'm sure we can stretch it out. Do come in for a bit. I must finish off some work later, though.'

I dismissed that. Later we'd be feeding each other strawberries, and I'd be lying against his strong chest in his bed, and he'd be saying, *Claudia, she doesn't understand me, but you* . . . and things like that. I had said them to myself, imagining them, making them real, until I almost felt it was inevitable.

His flat was expensively neutral, little sign of habitation except for his papers and laptop on the coffee table, his shoes on the floor and his tie cast over a cushion. I had a vague idea we could use that. I'd let him tie me up, I'd say I loved it. That was what sexy girls did. 'Sit down if you like. It's rather a mess.' I remember that the TV was off, but the red light on it flashed, as if it was on standby, an angry blinking eye. I remember I had the vague feeling of walking in on something, but I did not have the experience, the instincts, to realise that I should have left then.

'Excuse me a moment,' said Mark. 'I just have to . . . Keep an eye out for the food, will you.' And he went into the next room. I assumed he was making a call, but there was no sound of voices. It was just me, and the switched-off TV, and the pile of boring work documents, and Mark's laptop, left slightly ajar . . .

◆ ◆ ◆

'Babe.' Aaron nudged me, and I saw that Nina was looking at me.

'If we're all listening.' Her blue eyes swept around us. 'Now we're going to learn about labour, your different pain options, all the things that can go wrong.'

I felt myself tense up between the legs. I was desperately worried about labour – after all, whatever I'd done to my mother on the way out, it meant she'd never had another child, and clearly, never forgiven me. What if it was the same for me? I was quite fond of my vagina. What if the baby tore me to shreds, like I'd read about happened to some women, so they never recovered? Aaron definitely wouldn't want to have sex with me then, and my mother's dire predictions might come true after all.

Over the next hour I heard and saw some truly unpleasant things, the likes of which I wished I could wipe from my memory. Aaron had gone white beside me, squeezing my hand, as we watched the video of a birth. So many things could go wrong. Breech, pre-eclampsia, diabetes, haemorrhages, infection, sepsis. Then the baby could get stuck, get the cord wrapped round its neck, lose oxygen. Not for the first time I wondered why having human babies was such a horrendously fraught and complicated process, compared to say, cats, who just went under the stairs and got on with it. That made me think of the still-absent Minou, and I felt a stab of anxiety for her. She'd never disappeared like this before. I needed to nag Aaron about putting up the posters.

Nina turned off the video, staring round at us. 'Don't think women don't die any more in childbirth. They do. You must be extra vigilant about any bleeding or fever, and you, partners, need to look out for Mum when she's not able to care for herself.' That was what I most feared. Losing control, leaving my life in Aaron's hands. He was so young. Was he up to it?

Well, you shouldn't have had a baby with him if you weren't sure, whispered my mother's voice.

Nina landed on me again. 'Jax. Can you remind us of the warning signs for pre-eclampsia?'

Why did I feel like I was back at school, and failing? Wasn't this class supposed to be supportive and friendly? 'Um . . . high temperature, and, uh . . . ?'

Her eyebrows twitched. 'No. Anyone else?'

Monica raised a smug hand, reeled them off. Yes, even her hand was smug. I sank a little in my chair, and felt Aaron's hand in mine, squeezing. I wondered if it was too late to transfer to a different group.

Nina had set down the woolly vagina, the doll's head sticking out of it like a horror film. I was reminded of a production of *Little Shop of Horrors* I'd done the props for in college. *Vagina dentata*. Wasn't that a thing? I felt myself squeezing my thighs together. Around the room, Kelly had gone pale, and Aisha was biting her lip. Cathy raised her eyebrows at me in horror. Monica sat back smugly, as if she already knew her vagina would stretch beautifully. Anita was white too, though she wasn't going to have to do it. I wondered if that was any consolation to her.

Nina was talking. 'Be prepared for serious urine leakage too. Even if you don't have a prolapse it's likely you'll leak for several months after, when you laugh or sneeze or do exercise. If you do have a prolapse, well, you won't pee properly for several years. Especially not if you have another child.'

I clenched my pelvic floor, experiencing deep horror. How did anyone have sex ever again, never mind another child? I remembered a friend joking that her vagina was like Beirut after her birth and wondered how much of a joke it was. Was this the secret horror all mothers lived with? Was that why they sometimes seemed so cross with childless women, so dismissive of what we thought we knew about pain and of love? Oh God. I had a very sensitive bladder; I'd spent most of my twenties a martyr to cystitis. How would it cope? I could hear my breath coming faster, sweat patches spreading under my arms. It was so hot in here. Why was it so hot? By contrast Nina looked beautifully cool, not a bead of sweat on her smooth tanned forehead. Nina must not have children – no one would be so trendy and so slim if they did. How then was she qualified to teach this class? But there I went, putting the divisions up myself, mothers versus non-mothers. I had to be more accepting.

Nina was holding something else now. It looked like a giant hook. 'And this is in case the baby gets stuck in the birth canal. Kind of like what you'd use to reel in a giant fish.' I made an 'o' of horror across the room at Cathy. She was looking like the green-faced sick emoji. Jesus Christ. 'And these are forceps, if you find that you need those.' They were enormous. Like something a vet would use on a cow. Would the doctor stick their arm inside me too? I licked sweat from my upper lip. 'And of course, ventouse.' This looked like an actual Hoover attachment. Oh God.

'Any questions?' Bloody Nina, so composed. She didn't have to go through it in a mere matter of weeks.

Kelly raised a tentative hand. She looked tired and pale, conspicuously alone beside the empty chair. 'What about those epidurals, like? I want one of those.' After the last group session, when Ryan had burst into the room so dramatically, I was relieved to see he hadn't turned up. I wanted to say something to Kelly but didn't know what. *I'm sorry your boyfriend is an arse? You should leave him?* I could only imagine what it would be like to be pregnant and alone. If she didn't want that, I wouldn't judge her. And besides, being with Aaron had taught me that people love to judge other people's relationships. I thought briefly of how he'd slammed the table that time, but pushed the thought away. It was just one time, and he'd been so good ever since. He wasn't like Ryan.

Monica made a little noise, half amusement, half contempt. God, she was awful. 'It is supposed to hurt, you know! Honestly, I don't know why people get pregnant if they're so afraid of a little pain. After all it's a perfectly natural process! Women have been doing it for millennia!'

Cathy, still pale, said, 'I've written into my birth plan that I'll be non-interventionist. I assume they'll respect that? I want everything all natural, no drugs, no implements. Studies show interventions cause a lot of foetal distress.'

Nina blinked slowly. 'I'm afraid you should know, Cathy, birth plans very often go out the window in the heat of the moment.'

Hazel chuntered at this. 'But we wanted a water birth!' I caught Aisha's eye and knew she was thinking, as I was: *sod the water, I'll need heroin to cope with all the tearing and rupturing.*

'That depends if the birthing centre has space, and if nothing occurs to classify the birth as higher risk. In that case you automatically go a surgical/medical route, so it's best you plan for that scenario now.'

'You mean . . . they would give drugs and do surgery when you don't *want* it?' Cathy was horrified.

'To save your life, yes. And the baby's life. They'll ask your permission for a Caesarean, or your partner's if you're out of it. But do you really want to be making those choices while you're haemorrhaging on a table?'

Cathy bit her lip. 'But . . . I'd really rather not have one of those. The scarring alone . . .'

Nina just looked at her. Then, in a quiet, savage voice, she said, 'You should prepare yourself for the alternative then. Your death. Your baby's death.'

Cathy gasped. Hazel put a hand on the bump. 'Now hang on . . .'

Nina went on. 'I just think you should know. Yes, it would be lovely to have a natural birth, but what's natural is often death and pain and suffering. You must do what's best for the baby. Isn't that what you want? That's what any mother should want.'

Cathy was close to tears; I tried to catch her eye to give her a sympathetic smile, but she didn't see. 'Well, of course. I . . . I just . . .'

'You should all get used to that now. From the moment you got pregnant, your life became less important. Frankly, you shouldn't be having a child if you feel differently.'

176

A distressed murmur went round the room. Kelly also looked close to tears. Aisha was frowning hard, rubbing her bump. Monica said, 'I'm not worried. I've always been very healthy, and I'm sure this is no exception.'

For a moment, Nina's mask slipped, and I saw her bare her teeth in anger. 'You might think that now, Monica. But let me tell you, you have no idea what it will be like once you get in there. Things can always go wrong. Always.' Perhaps I was wrong then. Maybe Nina did have kids. But if so why had she never mentioned them?

◆ ◆ ◆

Can worrying make things happen? As we left the meeting, my head full of hooks and blood and torn flesh, and shuffled back to the bus stop, I began to feel a wetness between my legs. *Just a bit of discharge*, I thought. But it grew and grew, and as Aaron turned to me to ask what time the bus left, I saw his eyes travel down, and grow in shock. 'Babe!'

I followed his eyes down, taking in the huge spreading stain at the crotch of my maternity jeans. I was bleeding. A lot.

Alison

Jax Culville answered the door as the other women had, wary and tired, but for once a baby was not attached to her body. She still looked pregnant, in fact, her face pale and puffy, and she was wearing pyjama bottoms and a long cardigan. She was a few years older than Alison, but not that many. 'Ms Culville?'

'Yeah. Come in.'

Inside, the curtains had not been pulled and the house had a sour, disordered air, dirty dishes piled on the table and a basket of washing on the sofa. 'Sorry,' she said. 'I can't seem to keep on top of things, what with . . .' She winced as a squawk came from upstairs. 'Just a second.'

As Jax went upstairs, heaving herself up the bannister, Alison looked around her. It was a nice little house, red-brick, two-up two-down, Victorian, although strewn with dirty clothes and dishes. The kind she'd like to be able to afford with Tom. There must be family money, because she knew Jacqueline worked in the charity sector, and her partner, who was much younger, was only entry-level in his job. There was a laptop open on the table, and Alison was just thinking about maybe taking a very quick peek, only a glance really, when Jax came back down with a howling baby in her arms. Alison actually winced at the sound, which drilled into her ears.

'I'm sorry. She just . . . She won't stop crying. I don't know what to do.' Alison saw tears in the other woman's eyes. 'This isn't me,' she said thickly. 'I don't have a messy house or not get dressed or stay awake all night covered in puke . . . I just, I don't know who I am any more. I feel like I'm changed. Like I don't know myself.'

Alison didn't know what else to do. She held her hands out. 'Let me try.'

The baby was very light in her arms, strangely light somehow. It felt natural to hold her, jiggle her, mutter soothing nonsense. Somehow, she stopped screaming, a terrible noise like police sirens and roaring animals all rolled into one, and went limp against Alison's chest. Alison shifted her in her arms – it was a girl, Hadley, which Alison thought was a cool name, very F. Scott Fitzgerald – as Jax made them coffee. It was cold and the milk was slightly on the turn, but she said nothing. 'Now. I just need to hear from you what your recollections are of the day. So I can piece together what happened.' Assuming she could ever make the disparate facts and stories add up.

Jax ran a hand over her face. 'Oh, I don't know. It seems so muddled. I think I was feverish, you know. I'd had mastitis. You ever have cystitis?'

Alison, floored by the question, just nodded.

'Well. It's hell, isn't it? Like poison in your blood. This was like that, only worse. Like bits of me were raw and just getting rubbed open more every day. And I had to get dressed and go to that stupid bloody barbecue, just to keep up appearances, and everyone else seemed to be coping, Aisha and Cathy, they're tired but they had good births, and they're younger, they bounced back, and as for Monica – well. You've met her?'

Alison admitted that she had.

'Nothing seems to touch that woman. She's like a cockroach in Michael Kors. No puffiness, no leaking, she's not even got a tummy. And she's older than me!'

'Alright. But what do you remember? I heard there was something with the baby, an incident of some kind?'

Jax hesitated. 'It was just a misunderstanding. I just . . . I panicked for a second. But she was fine. Someone had her.'

That chimed with what Alison had heard. 'Alright. Can you tell me where you were when the fall took place?'

Jax fiddled with the milk carton. 'Um . . . I'm not sure exactly. I think Aaron and I were inside, in the living room maybe. I didn't see or hear anything until someone started screaming. We were still kind of reeling from . . . what had happened. I wanted to go home but it takes ages, finding all the baby's bits and pieces. You know.'

Alison didn't know and felt this was a rather vague explanation. 'And about the victim. How well did you know her?'

Was that a slight hesitation again? 'Not well at all. Just from the group, and that was only once a week.'

'You don't know of any tension – anyone in the group who would have wanted to hurt her?'

'No. I mean she had a run-in with Ryan, Kelly's boyfriend . . . but he wasn't there that day. Really, I think it was an accident. The balcony was very slippy, it had just been power-washed apparently.'

'Where is your partner now, Ms Culville?' Alison spoke towards the baby, trying to appear cosy and non-threatening.

'Umm. He's at work, of course.' She reached out for her coffee, and Alison saw that her hands were shaking. She went in for the kill.

'Does the name Mark Jarvis mean anything to you, Jax?'

The cup slipped in Jax's hand, and as the liquid splashed her, she gave a yelp. Alison held the baby back, safe from danger, and waited.

Jax – six weeks earlier

The doctor sighed. He was giving me the strong impression that I was interrupting his morning with my inconvenient health problems. I knew he was incredibly busy – there were twenty people in the hospital waiting room, and my own emergency appointment had run forty minutes past its time. But I was scared. This dingy room, paint peeling off the walls, mouse-brown carpet on the floor, was also not helping. The bleeding had slowed after the first spurt, and I'd been told to come in on Monday, but I'd spent all the rest of Saturday and Sunday leaking. On my way in, doors opened as I passed to show people on beds and in wheelchairs, shrivelled and grey. How strange it was to be pregnant, not sick, not dying, but full of new life, and still coming to this place. And yet this was likely the most my life would ever be in danger, though I wasn't ill.

He blew his nose before speaking. 'So yes, I'm afraid you have developed placenta previa, Jackie. More common in older women.'

'Jax. That's . . . bad, right?'

'It can be very serious, yes. Some women are admitted to hospital for their entire third trimester. I'm surprised this wasn't spotted at your eighteen-week scan.'

I gaped at him. Going into hospital for a month? What the hell would I do? I wouldn't last a day eating that salty tinned soup and instant mash. 'I can't do that.'

'No, we don't think that's required right now. Anyway, we can't spare the bed.' That was less reassuring. 'However, you do need to be on virtual bed-rest. Stay on your back as much as possible, don't do anything.'

'But . . .' I tailed off. There was no good reason why I couldn't lie on my back for the rest of my pregnancy. I wasn't working, I had a partner who was more than willing to run round after me, I had no other children or elderly relatives to care for. The only reason was my life. The only reason was my sanity. But that seemed to have taken a back seat the moment I got pregnant. 'You really think that's necessary?'

Another sigh. 'Let me show you.' He began to draw on a drug-branded legal pad, a rams-head outline of a womb and a baby in it upside down, its head enmeshed in thick lines. 'These are the blood vessels. In your placenta, they're sitting at the bottom at the womb, which is very weak. The bigger the baby grows, the more pressure you put on those vessels. If labour starts, they will rupture, and you may bleed to death, and likely your child will be deprived of oxygen and die too. Is that clear?'

'Yes,' I said, feeling like a knocked-up fourteen-year-old. 'It's serious then.'

'It often resolves itself, but we can't take any chances. Oh, and you should have a C-section at the birth.'

Several thoughts ran through my head. The disapproval among the group for any form of intervention, the comments about being too posh to push. On the other hand, the saving of my vagina from all the rupturing. That word was getting used a bit too often for my liking. 'OK . . .'

'It means we can schedule in the delivery, so you know exactly when it's going to happen.' He flashed me a weary smile. 'Makes the whole thing a bit easier.'

'Right . . .' I was still reeling. Too late, I remembered it was best to have someone with you for significant medical appointments, since shock will send your mind totally blank. I'd urged Aaron to go to work that morning, though he hadn't wanted to leave me.

'Talk it over with your husband,' he said, dismissing me, my five minutes being up. I didn't correct him about the husband. 'And remember – full rest. As much as possible. Every time you stand up you're putting pressure on those vessels, and eventually . . .' He made a gesture with his hands like something exploding. Startled, I just stared. Then of course I had to get up and shuffle out to the bus, and walk the rest of the way home, all the while acutely aware that my womb might rupture and I'd flood the seat of the number 61 with blood and mucus. My poor baby, gasping like a fish out of water. *Stay in there for now, OK?*

As I struggled home, every step a terror, tilting my pelvis against the rigours of gravity, I looked at the outside world like a prisoner being taken to jail. The peeling doors of our street, the dustbin contents a fox had strewn over the road, the diamonds of broken glass where someone's car had been nicked. All of it beautiful since I wasn't going to see it for a while. I was standing with my face upturned to the grey spring sky, breathing in the polluted air of South London, when I heard the phone ringing inside, and hurried to find my key from my bag. I was out of breath already when I reached it. 'Hello?'

''Ello there, Mrs Cole?' I didn't bother to correct him. 'Speedy Garage here. Found the problem with your car, didn't I.'

'Oh yes?' I was only half listening, undoing my coat with my other hand. I hoped it wouldn't be too expensive. Likely it would be something I wouldn't even understand and would just trustingly hand over the cash. I imagined he despised me, clueless middle-class woman that I was.

'Looks like someone's playing silly buggers. You got a rock shoved up your exhaust pipe.'

My heart began to hammer. Dimly, I told myself, *you should be sitting down, this is bad for the baby.* 'What? You mean like it bounced up from the road, or . . . ?'

'Nah, nah. That can't happen. Someone put it there, didn't they? You know anyone got a grudge against you, Mrs Cole?'

Alison

Diana was in the pub when she went in after work, and waved over from a table she'd managed to get, despite the crush at the bar. Alison moved towards her, aware that she had a fixed smile on her face, that this was awkward somehow, like a date almost. 'Well done on getting a table.'

'Oh, I just flashed my badge at them.' Alison knew she was joking. Diana was not the type to break rules, she could already tell. So why then were they meeting out of school?

'You're OK for drinks?'

Diana indicated a bottle of white wine in a cooler. 'I got you a glass. Unless you want something else?'

'Oh no, this is great.' Even though she wasn't supposed to be drinking because of fertility bollocks. Alison worried she didn't have the strength of character to be someone with dietary needs, who didn't drink or eat meat or gluten or anything like that. Even if she had a severe allergy she'd probably just mumble, *oh, it's fine, lovely thanks*, as her mother had taught her, and eat whatever it was, then suffer the consequences. At least if you were pregnant people respected your boundaries.

'Cheers.' Diana had poured her out a glass of wine, and now lifted her own. Alison clinked awkwardly, then let the cold liquid slip down her throat. Ahh. How could she give this up, on top of not having a baby? 'Anything from Jax Culville?'

'Nope. But she's jumpy, that's for sure.' This case was like a hall of mirrors – she'd been excited when they'd uncovered that little nugget about Jax, that she'd been the one to whistle-blow on Mark Jarvis, and she'd testified against him. His wife, who'd had a miscarriage before the verdict, had shown up in court shouting and screaming that it was all Jax's fault, that she'd planted the material because Mark had dumped her after a squalid affair. And sure enough, Jax had been rattled by Alison's knowledge. But not enough to tell her anything she didn't know already. She hadn't seen Jarvis in fifteen years, she claimed, had no intention of contacting him. Why would she? A good point, Alison had to concede. Then there was that thing with the baby at the barbecue.

Was it true? Alison had asked Jax, watching her face. Had she left the baby unattended?

Yes, Jax had admitted. She had perhaps been longer in the kitchen than she realised. What was wrong with these women? Alison had wondered. They went to such lengths to have babies, and then they barely looked after them. She caught herself – she didn't know what it was like. Jax clearly wasn't doing so well, perhaps she even had postnatal depression. And after all, no harm had come to the baby. Just a misunderstanding, poor Kelly deeply upset by it all.

'So what did you want to chat about?' she asked Diana, enjoying the cool feel of the glass in her hand.

Diana sipped for a moment before answering. 'I'll be honest, Alison, I wanted an alliance. Like an old-boys' one. But for women.'

'Hmm?' Alison was puzzled for a moment, because their boss was a woman too, and one you did not want to cross.

'A non-mums one, that is.' Diana flushed slightly, as if embarrassed. She was so young and pretty, with her clear olive skin and dark braided hair. Alison felt old just looking at her. Haggard. 'You know, I'm having a lot of push-back from Colette on this. Like, a *lot*. She seems to think the women from the group are . . . I don't know, like a new mother could never do anything bad to anyone? Are you getting that?'

Alison thought about it, trying to suppress her conflicted feelings about being lumped into the non-mum group. 'I suppose. She did chew me out for upsetting Monica Dunwood.'

'Exactly! I just don't see why squeezing a kid out of you makes you, I don't know, morally better in some way. I mean, you don't think it's an accident, right?'

'No. But I wasn't sure you agreed.'

'I didn't to start with. But they're all lying, right? About something, at least.'

Alison felt a wave of relief that someone else could see it. 'I think so. But how do we prove it? I feel like they've closed ranks, almost. The mums.'

'Oh, there's always cracks,' said Diana, lifting her glass and narrowing her eyes. 'They're hiding something. Don't you think?'

Alison leaned in. She had missed this, dissecting her cases with someone out of the office, now that she didn't work with Tom any more. 'Yeah. But tell me your thoughts.' Diana had been on her own visits to the couples, thorough and meticulous.

'Cathy, she's afraid of her partner, I think. Not in the usual way. But she's definitely afraid, she defers to her in a weird way. I think she'd tell us more if we pushed. Aisha, her and the husband aren't getting on, they don't seem to talk at all. She told me they'd only known each other three months before the wedding. Monica Dunwood is jumpy as hell, and not just because of us, Anita's a basket case, poor woman, and Jax . . .'

'She's interesting.' Alison had not yet got to the bottom of Jax.

'Yeah. Not coping very well, I suspect. Not to mention poor Kelly Anderson. Imagine those women rubbing their babies in her face like that. It'd be easy to snap.'

Alison noted Diana's identification with Kelly, who after all was near her age. She herself identified most with Jax Culville, she thought, in terms of age and background. But the woman was hiding something for sure. As Diana said, they all were. They just had to find out what, if it had any bearing on this murder. Assuming it was a murder.

'Your partner, he's in the job, too?' Diana asked, pouring out more wine. They were getting down the bottle quickly.

'Yeah. Used to be my work partner, but then. You know. He's at Sevenoaks, gutted to be missing out on this.'

'Even more yummy mummies down there.' Diana shuddered. 'So you and him, you didn't want kids?'

It felt like a slap in the face. The sudden question, the past tense of it. Alison floundered for a minute. 'I mean, it's not . . . we still . . . I'm only thirty-six.'

'Oh yeah, yeah, I know that, I just . . . sorry. That was a rude question.'

'No.' It was, kind of, but it was one that people felt perfectly entitled to ask, and it did have a bearing on the case. 'We're trying.' She hated that term; you might as well say, *we're shagging! A lot!* 'But so far . . . it's not happening.'

'I'm sorry.' Did Diana's expression shift, knowing that Alison was only reluctantly in her camp, not willingly a non-mum? 'I just kind of assumed, the way you talked about babies . . .'

'Yeah. It's true, I'm not the biggest fan of other people's kids. I thought it'd be different if it was my own.' But would it? What if all this fertility stuff worked and she didn't even like the baby in the end? 'What about you, you don't want them?' She deflected the question back.

Diana shook her head. 'God no. Actually, I've had my tubes tied.'

Alison was shocked. 'Really?'

'Yeah. It'd ruin my career, ruin my body, my sleep . . . plus, not having kids is the single best thing you can do for climate change . . .' She stopped, realising what she had implied. She bit her lip. 'I'm sorry. You should totally have one if you want, of course.'

'I'm trying,' said Alison, a little tartly. She was slightly reeling from Diana's words. There was truth in them, for sure. But to say it out loud like that . . . Alison had not really thought through the downsides of it, so fixated on the fact that it wasn't happening.

Diana laughed. 'It's so awkward, isn't it? Like you can't make your own choice without seeming like you're judging other people. I'm not, you know. This is just my own.'

'It's OK.' Alison felt a wave of camaraderie with the younger woman. 'You're right, it's a trap, either way.' She drained her glass. 'Since I'm not pregnant, I can at least get smashed. Another bottle?'

Jax – five weeks earlier

It was pretty humiliating to be pushed into the next antenatal group in a wheelchair, but needs must. I'd paid for it, and I didn't want to miss it. After the fiasco with failing to save the fake baby from choking, I felt I needed all the information I could get. And I didn't want Nina and Monica disapproving behind my back. At least we had the car back, though what the mechanic had said about the stone had unsettled me even more. Who would do that? Surely it must have just got wedged in there, a freak accident. The messages had stopped. Things were alright. Weren't they? Aaron, ever the optimist, leaned towards an accident, or the local kids just messing about.

All eyes swivelled round as I was pushed in. Anita gasped. 'Jax! What have you done?'

'Nothing, nothing, it's fine, just a precaution.'

'She has placenta previa,' said Aaron darkly. He didn't think I should move at all. 'It's not nothing.'

Nina looked me over. 'I hope you're being careful, Jax. It can be very serious. Are you on bed-rest?'

'Yeah. So boring.' I'd already binge-watched all of *The Crown*, and wished I had a team of private doctors like the Queen, so I could give birth in my own stateroom.

'Should you be here, hon?' That was Monica, of course, look-ing as healthy as an ox herself, in another maternity smock. 'Is it worth the risk?'

'There's not much risk when I'm pushed from door to door,' I said, trying to sound cheerful. All the same I was scared. Everyone looked so worried for me. Perhaps I should have stayed at home after all. But bed-rest couldn't mean *absolute* bed-rest, could it? They didn't really expect me to lie flat on my back for weeks? I'd go mad.

Nina's eyes rested on me all the same, and I wondered again why they felt so unsettlingly familiar. 'If you're sure, Jax. Please do take the utmost care of yourself. Just watch, don't join in any exercises.'

I nodded meekly. Never mind *The Crown*, I felt like Olivia Colman in *The Favourite*. Old and feeble and pathetic. Acutely aware of the healthy young man beside me, the way his T-shirt rode up to show his flat muscled stomach. Aaron and I had seen that film on a date at the Curzon in Soho, and I'd wondered why he was so quiet after, not realising he'd been horrified at the prices, and hadn't fully understood what period of history he was watching. So many things I took for granted.

'Goodness!' Monica laughed. 'I don't know what it is about this group, we're dropping like flies.' Did she really say this? Yes, she did.

'What do you mean?' At the same time I looked around the room, noticing averted gazes, counting heads. 'Where's Kelly?'

And that's when I heard the terrible news, Kelly's baby lost in the night, that she wouldn't be coming back. 'Oh my God.' Tears pricked my eyes. 'That's terrible. We should send her something. Flowers, or . . .' What could you say when something like this had happened? I almost couldn't get at my sympathy for her, when I was so afraid for myself. Monica's careless comment had made me wonder. Was I next? It didn't work like that, I told myself. But clearly, it could and did happen.

In the break, Nina approached us. Since I couldn't stand up, Aaron had brought me over tea and this week's baked offering, high-protein flapjacks made by Hazel, which had the consistency of lead. 'I wanted a word, if you don't mind.'

I was sure I was going to be told off for something yet again. 'Yes?'

'I heard Aaron was training in accountancy. Well, I could really use someone to help get my taxes in order – you know, being free-lance, nightmare – would you be up for that? I'd pay of course.' She named a sum that was far, far too high for a bit of bookkeeping. Aaron blinked.

'I work in the day, though, in the office.'

'No problem. Evenings are better for me. It should take three or four nights, maybe. What do you reckon?' She was asking him but looking at me. I thought about being alone night after night as well as day after day. I thought how much the money would mean to Aaron, that he could buy the baby a crib or a high chair.

I put on a cheerful tone. 'I think that's a great offer, love, if you're up for it. Go for it.'

Nina nodded, and I couldn't help but feel she looked somehow triumphant, although really it was her doing us a favour.

The day of – Jax

Kelly was gone. The baby was gone. I read something once that said people often die in disaster situations when they could in fact survive, because they don't react fast enough. They don't accept that the plane is on fire or the ship is going down or that they've been shot by a madman. Panic, and denial, those are the things that kill you. It took me several seconds to accept that the baby was gone, standing on Monica's lawn, very aware of my bare feet on the grass. Monica had made us take our shoes off at the door, of course. Aaron was gesturing wildly at me. 'Jax! Where is she?'

'I don't know!' I tried to say, but I wasn't sure if words came out or not.

Voices were overlapping all around me. Anita, Hazel. 'Should we call the police?'

'Let's look first, they can't be far . . .'

'Are we sure she's not upstairs? Anita, go and look.' Hazel, taking charge.

People were scattering, looking for my child. I saw Monica, an irritated look on her face, and Ed, vaguely ashamed. Why? I saw Jeremy, quietly combing through the bushes. I thought how small she was, how easy it would be to hide her. I saw Cathy and Aisha at the kitchen door, their own babies safely in slings. Maybe if I'd had a sling, this wouldn't have happened. Strangely, it was Rahul who came to me, grasped my elbow, spoke in a low and calm voice I had not heard him use before. 'It's OK. She won't have hurt her. They don't, in this kind of case. She'll be fine. She can't have got far.'

This kind of case. It only occurred to me afterwards how quickly we'd all assumed we knew what kind of case this was. That Kelly, who'd lost her child, had taken mine, as if that was something women did all the time. The conclusions we'd leaped to. I had to do something. I began to beat at the bushes with my hands, getting scratched. I lifted up the rug her chair had been on, as if she had somehow crawled under it, when she couldn't even turn over yet by herself. She was simply gone, as if I'd blinked and her tiny body had vaporised. A voice in my head, my mother's voice perhaps, said that I deserved this, that I hadn't loved her enough. That I had complained about this gift, this child at thirty-eight when I'd thought I'd have none. I don't know how long Hadley was even missing. But in those seconds that stretched forever, I had given her up entirely, and accepted a future where I'd had a baby for only two weeks, and then lost her, through my own failure.

It couldn't have been very long. A shout went up from the back of the garden, 'She's here!' Monica's and Ed's house had an unusually large garden, of course, with a gate that backed on to the park behind. That part of the lawn had been allowed to grow slightly wild, in what Monica described as a 'bee meadow', to help 'our little buzzing friends'. Aaron came through the park gate then, Hadley tight in his arms, held like a bag of shopping. Kelly followed, her face red and tear-stained.

She said, 'I took her to see the park! She loved it!'

Everyone stood around gawping, not sure what had really just occurred. Had she taken the baby? Was it just a misunderstanding? Kelly's sobs were harsh and rasping. She wrapped her arms around herself, as if trying to hold her own child, who was gone. 'No one was looking after her,' she cried. 'She was all by herself. She was scared. I just . . . I just took her to see the flowers.'

How quickly it turned. From blaming Kelly, poor unstable Kelly, everyone now turned to look at me. Blaming me, the bad mother. And unlike Kelly, I had no excuse.

Alison

Alison barged into the station with perhaps unnecessary force. She'd rolled in at almost 1 a.m. the night before, half-cut, and had a vague memory of Tom smoothing the duvet over her, placing a pint of water on the nightstand. When she woke up the glass was still full and her head was pounding. This bloody case. Were they all lying, was that it? She couldn't seem to get it straight in her head, who'd been where and when that day, who had seen what. What if it was just an accident, and she'd put these new mums through an interrogation for nothing? Wasted time, budget, energy?

Even the incident of the missing baby appeared to have been resolved easily, all a misunderstanding. Poor Kelly had gone home, weeping. Jeremy had driven her, so he was also off the hook for what had happened next. Which was still not exactly clear.

Everyone had a different story. Anita – that she'd been waiting for her husband in the side garden. Was there any way to prove that? Kelly Anderson had cracked under the pressure of being around all those babies – might Anita have been feeling similarly unbalanced? Then there was Aisha, and the mysterious husband they still had to track down, the tension there which both she and Diana had sensed. Aisha and Rahul had been down at the barbecue with Hazel, which both seemed to corroborate, but there was a strange vagueness in their account all the same, a gap that Alison could sense the edges of. Cathy's story was even vaguer still, and she'd admitted to being in the house, as had Jax. Then there was Aaron, Jax's young partner, who Alison also still needed to interview, and Monica's other daughter, who the group hadn't even known existed, as well as her ex-husband. As for Monica and Ed, there was a lot of tension there, but whether it related to the case or not, who could tell? Several people had vouched for them being in the kitchen at the time of the fall, dealing with some kind of dessert emergency.

Forensics might shed some light, but it was taking ages. If they could match the hairs in the victim's bracelet to anyone at the party, that would help. But she'd have to wait for the results. So she was no closer to knowing the truth. And yet around forty minutes after baby Hadley had been found safe, Nina da Souza had plunged from Monica's glass balcony, hitting the rockery below and dying instantly. In a group with so many secrets and lies, was it possible it really was an accident?

Today she was going to finish her interviews, and hopefully, find something that would lead her to the truth. As soon as Diana got in, anyway. Alison was almost gratified to see the younger woman roll in ten minutes after her, late, pale-faced, and clutching a sausage sandwich.

Jax – five weeks earlier

The days dragged on. Aaron went to work, came home late. My mother called by, a whirl of activity on her way to book group or Zumba or coffee with one of the many friends she unaccountably had. 'Darling! Still lying about like a slug in the bed?' She didn't seem to take in the fact that I was on compulsory bed-rest. When she found me still in bed or on the sofa, she would tut. 'Jacqueline! Slobbing around all day isn't going to help your mood, now is it?'

'Mum, I'm not supposed to be up.' I shouldn't even have been answering the door, and I sank back down again, though she was standing there with her coat on, expectantly. 'What? I can't make you tea. I have to lie down as much as possible, or the placenta will rupture.'

'Goodness, such a fuss! In my day you just got on with it. *I'll* do it then.' She strode into the kitchen, and I heard her sigh. 'Those dishes will be hard to clean, if you leave them like that.' I waited for the offer to wash them, but none came. 'Do you have Earl Grey? No? Well, I suppose a herbal . . .' I could hear her rummaging in my cupboards. 'Really, darling, some of these things are quite out of date. You ought to have a clear-out before the baby comes.'

I took a deep breath. On the muted TV, people argued on a daytime chat show, their faces working with silent rage. 'I would have, if this hadn't happened.'

'You'll never catch up if you don't get on top of it before the birth. I had the whole house cleaned, dinners batch-cooked.'

There was only one thing to do, and so I did it. 'Mum? I know you're right, and I so much wanted to have a clean-out, but the doctor says I can't move. Could you help me?'

A silence. 'If you let me do it how I see fit.'

'Of course.' Let her line the drawers in cloth and arrange the tins by sell-by date. I didn't care any more, if it got her off my back.

Every moment stretched and burned, my own thoughts wrapping around me like sodden sheets. I had ruined the lives of two people, at least one of whom did not deserve what happened. And if it wasn't Claudia or Mark Jarvis, someone was still trying to hurt me. I tried my hardest to think of everyone I'd ever wronged. Colleagues whose jobs I'd taken? Service users with a grudge? Ex-boyfriends, or even an ex of Aaron's I didn't know about, one of those damaged young women from the care system? But I couldn't think of anyone. I became as jumpy as my mother, double-checking the windows and doors.

One morning I had been slumped in bed for some length of time, I couldn't even say, when I heard a scuffle outside. I had slipped into bad habits, lying in bed all day, sometimes transferring to the sofa, clicking on to some mindless TV show. Aaron brought me things, cakes and magazines and books, which he could hardly afford. I pretended to look at them, but really I couldn't take much in. The doctor came to see me, told me I was doing alright but had to keep up the rest. My home had become my prison. Aaron would not even be home at six that night, since he was going to Nina's to help her with her taxes. I couldn't complain, since I really would have liked it if he earned some more money, especially now I might get fired, but how would I cope being alone all day and all night? Alone and not able to move?

When I heard the noise at the front door, it took me a while to realise what it must be – the milk. We had recently switched to a glass-bottle delivery, in an effort to save the world so the baby could grow up in it. It gave me a small boost of normalcy – something different. Perhaps I could catch the milkman, say hello. Although I'd thought they would come earlier in the day, wasn't that what milkmen did? The clock told me it was after twelve. I'd lain there for hours, not sleeping, not engaged with the world either. Elizabeth Barrett Browning of the modern era.

I rushed downstairs much faster than I should and pulled open the door. But there was no one there. No one on the street either. I stepped outside for a moment – and screamed. I looked down. A shard of broken glass had pierced my stockinged foot, and blood was now oozing out into the white pool of milk I stood in.

Alison

'Mrs Dunwood.' Alison let Diana knock on the door, her smile spread wide, while she lurked behind with a bad-cop frown. She didn't care if this over-privileged cow didn't like her, the feeling was mutual. She could see a cleaner's van parked outside, and sure enough a South American-looking woman was in the hallway, polishing a table which held a huge vase of lilies. She flinched when she saw the police officers – possibly she was undocumented. Alison smiled to try and show she was no threat.

Monica Dunwood was wearing another unsuitable outfit, leather trousers and a black silk blouse, which didn't appear to have any spit-up milk on it, Alison noticed. She smelled of some expensive perfume and her hair was once more newly done. 'Not again? Honestly, what do you need now? You've already torn my house apart.'

'We need to talk to Chloe,' Alison glowered.

'What? Why? She's only a child.'

'She was here that day, so she might have seen something. Just a quick word would be appreciated.' Diana was more conciliatory, and so Monica led them into the living room with bad grace.

As they passed the cleaner she barked, 'Not so much polish, Marisol, you'll ruin the wood!'

The woman jumped. '*Sì*, madam, sorry.' Alison's glower deepened.

'I suppose you'll be wanting tea?'

'I'm fine,' said Diana, and Alison reluctantly said she was too.

When Chloe appeared – a dishevelled teenager in a hoody and pyjamas, with unbrushed hair and pale spotty skin – she could not have looked less like her polished mother. She was also, surprisingly, carrying a baby in a frilly white dress. Monica seemed annoyed. 'Why did you get her up from her nap?'

'She was awake, Mum. You can't just leave her there.'

Monica set her jaw. 'Give me her.' She held the baby at arm's length. To the officers: 'Do I need to be here if you're talking to her? She's underage.'

'Yes, if you wouldn't mind.'

She sighed. 'Fine. But if the baby cries, I'm taking her out.'

Alison wished they could chat without Monica; she didn't think Chloe would feel exactly at ease with her mother in the room. 'Hi, Chloe. We just need to talk to everyone who was here that day, who might have seen something.'

Chloe seemed nervous, but it could have just been her age. 'I didn't see anything.'

'OK, but could you just talk us through it? Maybe you'd like to sit down?'

'Sit down,' barked Monica. 'Honestly, don't they teach you any manners at that school?'

Chloe perched on the edge of a plush grey armchair. 'I was in my room most of the day. I don't like the sun and I've been off sick this term. Glandular fever.'

'I'm sorry to hear that, Chloe.' This could explain her pasty and pale appearance. 'Your room is upstairs?' Near the balcony. Maybe she had seen something.

'Yes, but . . . I only went out when I heard the screaming. So I don't know what happened. She fell, I guess.'

'And who was out there?' Diana was taking notes.

Chloe fiddled with the fringe on a cushion. 'Dunno. Lots of people were on the landing. Aaron, Jax, that Cathy woman. Mum came up as well.'

'Cathy? You're sure?' Cathy had said she was downstairs when the fall happened, changing the baby's nappy. Was that a lie? And Jax said they were also downstairs, in the living room. Alison was acutely aware of Monica's stroppy presence, the baby in her arms who seemed half drowsed, barely making a peep.

Chloe shrugged. 'Think so. I don't know all their names.'

'She had her baby with her?' Maybe she'd meant she was changing Arthur upstairs, not downstairs.

'No.' Chloe shook her head.

'You're sure?'

'Yep. That other woman, her wife or whatever, she had their baby when she came up afterwards.'

So Hazel and Cathy had lied about that. Or did they just make a mistake, remember wrong? Diana took over. 'And did you see anything else that day – notice any tensions between the couples, maybe?'

Monica opened her mouth. 'Eh, excuse me . . .'

'Please, Mrs Dunwood. I must ask you only to interrupt if Chloe's at risk in some way, or you think she doesn't understand what she's being asked.'

Monica subsided. 'She's *fifteen*. I don't know why you'd take her word for anything.'

Chloe snorted, ignoring her mother. 'Tension? Er, only loads. All of them were in some kind of fight, I think. The Asian couple, the two women, Jax and her guy – he must be loads younger than her. Only people who weren't were that older posh woman and her husband.'

'Anita and Jeremy?'

'Yeah. They seemed OK. But the rest – drama city.' Chloe's eyes went to her mother. 'And I mean everyone.'

At this Monica sat upright. 'I think that's enough now. I can call your supervisor, you know. Don't think we're not aware of our rights, in this house. My husband plays golf with one of the country's *top* criminal barristers.'

Chloe rolled her eyes dramatically behind her mother's back, and Alison fought a smile. 'One thing, Mrs Dunwood.' She tapped the framed wedding picture, deliberately smearing it. 'Your wedding – this was six months ago, I believe?'

'I suppose. Why?'

'You said it was a year ago before.' Alison heard a small chuckle that she assumed was from Chloe.

Monica frowned harder. 'I believe I said about a year; anyway, a year, six months, what's the difference? It hardly has a bearing on the case.'

But maybe it did. There were so many little lies and omissions here, that Alison didn't know what was important and what wasn't. 'I'm sure it doesn't. Thank you, Chloe, you've been very helpful.' Now Alison knew for sure that several people were lying about where they'd been when the fall happened. She just had to find out why.

Jax – five weeks earlier

'But what can have happened? Who'd do this?' I sounded hysterical, but I couldn't help it.

'No one.' Aaron knelt in front of me, tenderly looking at my foot. The bleeding had stopped but it still throbbed where the glass had gone in. I'd done my best to put a bandage on it, but it was hard when I couldn't bend over, elephant that I was. 'Something just knocked it over, probably. A fox maybe.' It was certainly plausible; we were plagued by foxes screeching at night and getting into our bins. But broken bottles, on top of everything else? The car, Minou, the messages, the mail-out . . .

'Both bottles?'

'I don't know. You said you heard someone outside?'

'Maybe. I'm not sure.' Would someone really do that, come all the way to my house and smash my milk bottles? What a strange combination of pettiness and rage. I realised that I should have told Aaron about the messages before this, and at the very least I should now, but I still found that I couldn't. Things were too unstable, still no more word on his mother, my health issues. And he didn't know that version of me, naive and wilful and destructive, and I didn't want him to. I was a different person now. I wondered if Mark Jarvis would say the same about himself, if that was why he'd gotten out of prison now. He'd said at first he hadn't done anything, that it was just curiosity that had made him download the images. He'd even tried to say it was research, which I suppose was another good explanation for why he gave so much time to the charity: camouflage. Then the truth came out, the picture that showed his face, and he couldn't lie any more.

It wasn't the same. I drew my cardigan around me. 'I'm just worried, you know? It's not nice, being stuck at home all day, afraid I might start bleeding any minute.'

He frowned. 'I wish I could be here with you. And I'm sorry, babe, but Nina wants me to go round again tonight.'

'Again?' I knew we needed the money, but I needed him too.

'Something about VAT.' He sounded so apologetic. 'At least she's paying me.'

Was Nina really making so much from running antenatal groups that she could afford to pay someone for five nights of accountancy support? Perhaps she was just trying to help us. I forced a smile. 'It's OK. I'll watch TV or something.' And wait for whoever had broken my bottles and sabotaged my car to come back.

'Just rest, babe.'

Rest. As if it was easy to lie flat on your back, alone, with nothing but the circulation of your thoughts.

I heard a noise outside, a rap at the door. Aaron's head turned. 'That'll be her now.'

'She's picking you up?'

He shrugged. 'She said it was on her way home anyway, we might as well walk together.' He was putting his jacket on, the muscles of his shoulders twisting beautifully. 'Bye, babe.'

'Wait!' I called him back. 'Did you do those posters?'

He frowned. 'Posters?'

I knew he hadn't. 'For Minou! She's missing, remember?'

He sighed. That enraged me. 'Babe, she's a cat. They do this.'

'And how would you know? Did you ever have a cat?' That was low. Of course he hadn't. Kids in foster care didn't get pets.

'No, but—'

'Please, Aaron. I can't do it myself, I can't even stand up. I ask you to do this one little thing and you still won't!'

'I've been busy!'

'She's my best friend,' I said dramatically. 'I don't know what I'll do if something's happened to her. What if it's the Croydon Cat Killer?'

'I thought they said there wasn't one.'

'Huh. They might have *said* that.'

A look crossed his face, as if upset that I'd said the cat was my best friend rather than him. I saw him force the irritation down. 'I'll do it this weekend, I promise. Love you.' He was gone. As the door slammed I shuffled to the window, in time to see him and Nina walk off. Why hadn't she come in to say hello? It was weird, wasn't it, calling round for him just so they could walk there? Nina wore jeans and a sort of poncho, long silver earrings. She looked slim and stylish, not remotely like an elephant. I watched as the two dark heads disappeared down the street, and for a moment Nina turned to the side and I saw her laughing, glowing face. For some reason, I was stabbed by a shard of fear. *She has him now.* I told myself that was stupid and lumbered back to the sofa to watch something mindless on TV.

Alison

Rahul Farooq was on a break when they arrived at the hospital he worked at – as it happened, the same one where Alison was having her fertility treatment. A sense of doom had fallen over her. In this building her dreams had come to die. But never mind that now.

Rahul was easy to find – lounging against the side of the building smoking. Alison thought of the painfully tidy house she'd met his wife in and wondered if Aisha knew he smoked. Perhaps not, from the guilty way he stubbed it out as they approached. Alison explained who they were.

'Is everything OK?'

'We just need a word. Since you weren't home when we called round.'

He flushed. 'It's work, I can't always get back in time. You know how it is.'

She did but wasn't going to let him see that. Diana said, 'Is there somewhere we can talk, Rahul?'

He sighed, ran his hands over his face. He looked like he hadn't slept in weeks – was it just having a newborn and doing shift work, or something more? 'There's a lawn bit out back.'

It turned out to be a picnic bench and scrappy patch of grass, ambulances coming and going in the background. Alison went first, her usual questions, where were you at the barbecue, did you see anything, did anyone have a reason to hurt Nina. His story was the same as Aisha's – they were in the garden, they didn't see it happen but heard the noise. Yes, Hazel was with them when the fall took place, but then she went inside. No, they had hardly known the other group members, or Nina either.

'You and your wife, you haven't known each other long either?'

He bristled slightly. 'Over a year.'

'But before you got married . . . ?'

'It's not so unusual.'

'Would you say you know each other well?'

Slight pause. 'As well as you can after living together, having a baby.'

'And how are you coping with little Hari?'

'Fine. Well, he cries at night, but that's what they do, isn't it? I'm on shifts so I'm used to not sleeping.' He smiled slightly, and Alison saw how attractive he was, dark hair and eyes, slight stubble. Or at least he would be, if he didn't appear so heavy with worry. 'It's worth it, anyway.' She gave Diana a very slight nod. Diana leaned her elbows on the picnic table.

'Rahul. Does your wife know about your previous conviction?'

There it was. He flinched. 'Oh. I didn't realise . . .'

'We ran all the witnesses through the system. You came up.'

'She doesn't know, no. It . . . I didn't want to worry her.'

Imagine marrying someone and you didn't even know they'd been convicted of a crime. It was one reason to date inside the force – everyone had been thoroughly vetted in advance. 'You got off with a caution, was that right?' said Alison.

'And a fine.' His voice was flat, exhausted. 'And before you go shouting about it, yes, the ambulance lot know. They decided to give me a second chance.' Probably they were so short of staff they were prepared to overlook the odd little slip.

'Want to tell us more about it, maybe?' Alison tried to sound friendly, knowing they had him over a nice little barrel.

She heard a faint buzz, which must be his phone. His hand crept to his pocket but didn't take it out. 'Well, I mean, not much to tell. I made a mistake, that's all.' He had stolen a small amount of cash from a patient's coat when it was left in the ambulance. Twenty quid, that was all.

'You needed money.'

'Doesn't everyone?'

Alison said, 'Rahul, do you have a gambling problem? Because we noticed you liked a lot of online poker sites, that sort of thing.'

He frowned. 'Gambling's not allowed in Islam.'

'Well, yes, doesn't mean it doesn't happen.' Diana gave Alison a look – she had to tread lightly.

He thought about it for a long time. 'Look, I just got into difficulties with debt. Student loans and that. I was stupid and young. I dealt with it, put it behind me. And I saw nothing at the barbecue.'

'You have no idea at all what happened that day? You've got a medical background – do you really think someone could just slip and fall like that?'

His phone buzzed again, she saw his energy shift towards it, itching to pick it up. Typical phone addiction, or something in particular making him nervous? 'Of course they could. I see it all the time. People drink, they act stupid, they fall from high buildings, I have to come and scrape them off the ground.'

'You think she was drunk, then.'

He shrugged. 'I don't know. That's usually the case. There was a lot of booze at the party – hardly anything for Aisha and me to drink. And the balcony had just been cleaned, apparently. She could have slipped.'

'You gave first aid at the scene?' Alison imagined how that would have been, having seen the bloody mess of the body. He had tried to help all the same. He couldn't be a bad person, not deep down. Could he?

'Tried to. I could see it was hopeless. You fall that far on to rocks, there's nothing to do for you.'

'Alright. Thank you for your time, Rahul.'

They got up to leave, and he took his phone out, but then called them back. 'Will you tell Aisha about it – the conviction?' He frowned.

'Not unless it becomes relevant.' A secret, then. Alison understood secrets. Secrets were what made people do very bad things. And she knew for a fact that Nina da Souza had not been drunk that day. In fact, she had drunk nothing at all; there had hardly been time.

Jax – four weeks earlier

It all happened because of Monica. It was break time in the second-to-last group session, and we were standing round the tea urn, except I wasn't standing of course. I had irritably refused the wheelchair this week, but still had to sit down as much as I could, walking only the few steps from the car. Luckily my incapacitation gave me a great excuse not to bake; this week it had been Cathy, something chewy she claimed was 'hydrolase-free'. I didn't even know what that was and was too tired to ask. All of a sudden Monica said, 'You won't believe the email I got from the nursery today. All children must show proof of vaccination before admittance!'

Hazel was dunking a biscuit in herbal tea, which must have been disgusting. 'Fair enough. There was a measles outbreak near us last year, a kiddie nearly died.'

Monica just blinked, as if she hadn't spoken. 'The nerve of them! What business of theirs is it if we don't vaccinate?'

A small silence fell. I saw Nina look over from where she sat outside the circle, checking her notes. Her hair shifted around her face, a ripple of light. Anita was the one who spoke. 'You aren't going to vaccinate, Monica?'

'I don't intend to, no. All these stories – you can't be too careful. After all, who does it benefit? Big Pharma, that's who.' She tapped her head in a worldly-wise gesture. I could not have been more surprised if she'd taken out a tinfoil hat and put it on. But then, it made perfect sense. Monica was a wealthy white woman with little to do all day except get outraged online. Of course she was an anti-vaxxer. Oh God. I moved away slightly, already trying to shield my unborn child from such lunacy.

'That's insane,' said Hazel clearly. 'Kiddies used to die all the time from measles, rubella. Roald Dahl, his little girl did.'

Monica waved a hand. 'Eons ago. Hardly happens at all now.'

'Because they've been vaccinated,' I said, though not as firmly as Hazel.

Monica frowned. 'Ed, you agree with me, don't you? Vaccinations haven't been proven safe?' Ed looked up briefly from his phone, shrugged.

Jeremy said, 'Actually, multiple studies have proven there's no link between autism and vaccines. It was based on junk science from one discredited doctor.'

Monica gave him a look as if she'd expected better. 'Well, I must say, I didn't think I'd be attacked, just for having *opinions*. Aren't I free to manage my own baby's health?'

Hazel crunched her biscuit. 'That's the thing, it's not just your baby. There's such a thing as herd immunity – if it drops too low, everyone's kids are at risk, not just the crazy anti-vaxxers.'

'*Excuse* me?'

Cathy said, tentatively, 'Actually I do have some concerns about what's in them, heavy metals and so on . . .'

'What?' Hazel just stared at her. 'You don't mean that. Of course we're having him done.'

'I . . .' Cathy raised her jaw. 'I'd rather discuss it, is all. I don't trust doctors. They don't always listen. And my cousin's little one, he was never the same after his MMR.'

'Autism?' mouthed Monica.

'Something like that, yeah.'

'See? We just don't know what we're putting in them.' Monica looked round at us all, seeking an ally. Aaron's head was dipped, his eyes clouded. He was too young to have opinions about vaccines. Unless it was the band, The Vaccines. She lit on Aisha, who had not yet spoken – Rahul, like Ed, was on his phone. 'Aisha. You must agree. Don't you have something in your culture that means you can't get it? I don't know, what are they made from? I'm sure I was reading that pigs are involved. I mean think of that! Putting pigs into our children!'

'What the hell do you think pork is?' muttered Jeremy.

Aisha said nothing for a long moment, during which I found I was holding my breath. She said, 'My cousin got rubella when she was pregnant, in Pakistan. Her baby can't see or hear. So. Mine will be getting whatever's on offer, thanks very much.'

Monica blinked several times, then said, 'Well! I see we're not even allowed to have *opinions* now.' She flounced back to the circle, but not before seeking one last-ditch attempt at support. 'Nina. You must agree that parental choice comes first?'

Nina paused for a moment. Then she said, 'I believe the health of the child comes first, Monica. To be a good mother – a fit mother – I think you have to feel the same.'

Monica chuntered. 'Oh. And what qualifications do you have to say this, Nina?'

Oh dear. I would have run from the room if I'd been able to move. So much tension. Nina just glared at her. 'As much as you, Monica, plus years working as a doula.'

'But you're not a mother, are you? If you don't have your own . . .'

Nina stood up suddenly. It was just a small gesture, but there was something so threatening about it I actually gasped. Even Monica took a step back.

At this point, Cathy bravely chipped in. I don't know why. Perhaps she was annoyed at how Hazel had crushed her, or perhaps she really believed it. 'Actually, I think she's right, Nina. We can't blindly trust doctors over our own instincts as mothers.'

Nina gave a short bark of a laugh. 'Oh, Cathy. You think all mothers are good?'

'Well . . .'

'You, for example. Are you going to do everything right for this child? Be a hundred per cent honest with it, about everything?'

'I . . .' Cathy licked her lips, confused and suddenly afraid. 'What do you . . . ?'

The moment stretched. Nina closed her eyes for a second. When she spoke again her tone had softened. 'These are emotive issues. I think we should start back. We're running late as it is.' Just like that, it was smoothed over. Except it wasn't forgotten. Monica would not easily forgive that little moment of humiliation. Towards the end of the class, she struck back. First, I saw her go up to Aisha, press something into her hand. Rahul was standing off to the side, on his phone as always. 'Only if you feel it's appropriate, of course! I mean there'd be alcohol. Don't feel obliged.' I was listening in, half wondering what it was, an invite to something? Would I get one? I simultaneously hated Monica and could not bear to be left out by her.

Aisha blinked at the small piece of card. Of course Monica had printed up invitations for a casual party. She was that sort of person. 'Um, no, we're fine with that, but . . . this is right after the babies are due.'

'Of course! Best time for it.'

'But . . .' I knew what Aisha was thinking. Wasn't that tempting fate? We didn't know they'd all arrive safely – look at poor Kelly.

'And dear, it would be nice if Rahul wasn't on his phone the whole time. I know what it's like, Ed's just as bad! Almost makes you wonder what they're *hiding*!' Monica's jovial stage whisper carried across the room, and I felt my face burn with reflected embarrassment as people looked up, pretended they hadn't heard. Aisha bit her pretty lip, put the invite into her bag.

Monica turned away, her eyes scanning the room for her next victim. 'Hazel, Cathy. This is for you.' Another invite.

'Thanks, Monica. We'd love to,' said Cathy quickly. She had a slight case of Monica-worship.

Nina had been packing up the items we'd used in class (immortal baby, knitted vagina, etc.). Now she said, without looking up, 'Will you bring the baby's father, Cathy?'

There was a short confused silence. Hazel said, 'We aren't in touch with the donor, Nina, I did say that.'

'No? I must have got the wrong end of the stick.'

Cathy laughed nervously, the invite held tight in her hand. 'The baby might not be here by then, of course. We don't know for sure.'

Nina said, 'Oh, I think yours will be here quite soon, Cathy.'

Another silence. Only broken by Monica raising her voice. 'Oh, Anita, don't go without one!' She caught Anita and Jeremy heading to the door. 'Please, you'll be as welcome as anyone, even though it won't be quite . . . the same.'

Anita flushed and took her invite. 'Oh . . . thank you.'

Monica then turned on her FitFlop and stared at me. Oh God. What little jibe had she stored up for me? She really was first class at this; she could give my mother lessons. 'Jax.'

I stood up and began to shuffle to the door without waiting for Aaron's arm. 'Thanks, we'll have to see if everything goes to plan of course, if I feel alright.' I held out my hand for the invite, but Monica didn't give it to me. Instead she leaned in. I could smell her strong perfume.

'Do try and come, Jax. It'll be good for Aaron. He's a young man, you know, he needs a bit of excitement in his life.' And she turned her head slowly, looking over to where Aaron and Nina stood. Talking about something, taxes maybe, though would taxes make you smile so much? Nina with her toned limbs and tanned skin. For a second I could have punched Monica.

I said nothing. Just held out my hand, and she gave me the invite, with a sweet smile. I was almost blind with rage. 'Aaron,' I snapped. 'I need to go, I've been out long enough. I shouldn't be standing.'

'Oh . . . OK, babe.' To Nina he said, 'See you later, then.'

Outside, I gulped in breaths of grey London air. 'What were you talking to Nina about?'

'Nothing. Just this and that.' This and that. What the hell did that mean? I looked down, and saw that Monica's invite was already crumpled and stained from the sweat of my hand. I looked back and saw Nina and Monica in the doorway. Ed had gone a few steps ahead to start the car. They had both been odd today, little jibes, strange comments. What did Nina mean about Cathy's baby coming soon? And she knew the donor wasn't on the scene, we all knew that. And Monica – clearly she'd been riled that we'd stood up to her on the issue of vaccinations, but how did she know exactly what buttons to press to cause pain? Aisha's religion, Anita's adoption, my age-gap relationship. It was a terrible skill to have. As I watched, Nina leaned in and said something to Monica, pressed a hand to her bump, and Monica reared back, red-faced, and almost stumbled away to the car. Good. I hoped Nina had told her off for her behaviour.

It would be wrong of me to blame Monica for everything, I know that. But I wondered afterwards if those little seeds she planted that day – doubt, and resentment, and shame – I wondered just how much they contributed to everything that happened next.

217

Alison

Places like the halfway house had a certain smell that nothing could shift. It was a decade and more past the smoking ban, but the ghost of old cigarettes seemed to rise from the tiled floor as they entered. An institutional smell, of indifference and despair. She'd reminded herself about the case on the way over, although it stuck in the mind, especially when you worked in child protection. Mark Jarvis had been rich, super-rich. The kind with not just a second home but a third and fourth too, a wife who didn't work and got her hair done twice a week, suits from a personal tailor. This shabby building was the last place you'd have expected him to end up. But that was before he'd been caught with a massive trove of child-abuse material (she didn't like to use the word pornography) on his hard drive. And he wasn't the only one. The police had been able to trace a network of paedophiles across the country, swapping and sharing material, and eventually to prove Jarvis had been not just watching, but doing. All thanks to Jax Culville, then twenty-three years old, having the courage to speak out about what she'd seen on his laptop one night at his flat. Mark Jarvis had gone to prison, but not before his wife, Claudia, who was pregnant, had gone into an early labour and lost the baby. Someone like Mark Jarvis might have a grudge against Jax Culville alright. Though she'd no idea how any of this might have led to Nina da Souza being pushed to her death.

Alison sighed as Diana spoke to the receptionist, a young man in a cardigan and earbuds. She longed to yank them from his ears, tell him that he didn't have to be connected every second of the day. That in fact this was making him disconnected. 'I'll get him, if you wait over there,' he said, as if exhausted by the act of speech. Alison and Diana took a seat on hard plastic chairs, looking at a peeling noticeboard of flyers about drink, drugs, curfews, benefits. What a place for a City banker to end up. He'd done a lot for charity too, which was how he'd met Jax. A helpful smokescreen for his interest in children, it turned out. It was all gone now, his houses sold to pay legal fees. Alison hoped the wife had walked away with something, at least.

'How was it?' said Diana, tapping her foot on the ground. 'CEOP.'

'Oh. Grim.'

'You have to look at the images, right? To prosecute?'

'Yes. It's kind of ironic that we're sending people down for looking at them, but we have to look at them ourselves to know what they did. People don't last there long.'

'When you meet men like him – it must be hard.'

'Men like him? Sad fact is, they don't get rehabilitated. We're just waiting for him to do it again. So now he's out, they'll be watching. For him to get careless, to feel safe. Give him a year and I'd say he'll be back on it.' Alison did not want to relive those days working in child protection, the parade of images she'd wanted to believe were fake, but had known were real. Real children, somewhere in this country. A tide of it that rose every day, despite their best efforts. Every night she'd wanted to scrub her eyeballs clean with bleach, and she'd watched her colleagues turn from bantering, larky young officers to quiet, watchful wrecks. The relationship she'd been in then had ended because she couldn't resist going through his computer, because what if? None of these men's wives had known they were with paedophiles either. Or had they? Mark Jarvis's wife had said she didn't, but she was pilloried for it all the same, forced to give up her own life, move away, disappear.

The receptionist was coming back, and following him was a stocky middle-aged man, dressed in a grey T-shirt, with close-cropped hair. It was him. Alison saw a flash of some of the images she'd hoped to forget, and her stomach swooped with nausea. 'He's not aged well,' muttered Diana, and Alison was glad to have her there, to work with a woman, with someone who got it. She stood up.

The first thing that was clear about Mark Jarvis was that he was not remorseful at all. A life sentence with a minimum of fifteen years had done nothing to rehabilitate him. When she mentioned the name Jax Culville, he sighed deeply, throwing himself back in the plastic chair. 'What makes you think I'd want to talk about her? She ruined my life.'

'You don't feel you did that yourself, with all the child abuse?' Alison felt Diana's gaze flick to her but couldn't help herself.

He sighed again. 'I looked at stuff, yes. It was a fair cop as you'd say, no doubt. I've done my time for that.'

Alison had never said *it's a fair cop* in her life. 'So how was it Ms Culville's fault?'

He had aged from the glamorous silver fox she remembered in the dock. Baggy clothes hid a paunch, and his skin was grey and unhealthy, his fingers nicotine yellow. Prison had done its work on his body, if not his spirit. 'You really think she did it out of concern for the children? Wise up. It was a classic case of a woman scorned – she thought because I was nice to her I wanted to get her into bed. When I made clear I was a married man, with a pregnant wife, she went snooping on my computer and caused an almighty shitstorm.'

'You were the chair of a children's charity.'

'So? I never touched any of those kids. Isn't it better this way – I just looked, I didn't do it myself.' He really seemed to believe this. 'I mean, the pictures already existed. I didn't take them.'

'You were convicted of having sexual relations with minors,' said Diana, frosty. Hence his long time in prison.

'Teenagers. Not children.'

'Thirteen-year-olds.'

He glared. 'Is there a point to all this, or is it just harassment?'

Alison breathed in and out twice before speaking. 'That's not why we're here anyway, Mr Jarvis. We need to check on your movements over the last few weeks. Ms Culville has been involved in a crime, and it seems to coincide with you getting out of prison.'

'What's she done now?'

'Nothing.' That they knew of. Funny how he'd assumed Jax was the perpetrator, not the victim.

He leaned back, arms behind his head, still confident and cocky despite being a registered sex offender. 'Good luck with linking me to anything. I get one hour of internet access a week, heavily supervised. I'm not allowed a mobile – and believe me they search us for them. I have a nine p.m. curfew, like a small child. I haven't seen Jax since she sent me down, and have no plans to, the vindictive bitch.'

Wow. Just, wow. This guy. 'We'll check up on all of that, Mr Jarvis.'

'You do that, darling,' he said, almost pleasant. 'Can I go now?'

'You can go,' she said reluctantly, wishing there was something new she could charge him with. Of course, he could have paid someone else to hassle Jax, but she knew he didn't have any money, just a post-prison allowance. The powerful men he'd traded images with were also mostly in jail, their network smashed. His wife was AWOL. Seemed like this was another dead end.

The day of – Monica

2.45 p.m.

It all started to go wrong when Kelly turned up. Monica was cursing herself for her stupidity in not editing the email list when she sent out her party reminder – Kelly didn't belong somewhere like this, and she'd only feel out of place. Probably she'd never even seen orzo before and she'd ask what it was and they'd all feel sorry for her. Even if her baby had been born, Monica wouldn't really have wanted her there, but since she'd shown up – unbelievable really – she would have to be made welcome.

However, Monica had not initially noticed that Kelly was gone, that she'd taken Hadley, because she was too busy being furious with Ed. When he appeared from the shed with Jeremy and Aaron, she had not really noticed what Jax was saying to Aaron, not taken it in, because she'd beckoned Ed into the house with a sharp gesture, like a slap that didn't land. 'Come here.'

He followed her to the kitchen, which was in a shocking state, people's drinks and plates left around the counters and table, wine left out to spoil, beer caps everywhere. Monica itched to sweep it all into a bin bag and put her Marigolds on. 'What the hell were you doing?' she hissed, throwing bottles into the recycling with a crash.

'Showing the boys my shed.' Ed picked up another beer. She'd lost count of how many he'd had.

'Did you have to? In the middle of all this?' Monica knew very well what Ed got up to in the shed, what kind of material he had on his computer and filed neatly away in his shelves and binders. He called it *erotica*, maintained he was a collector. Monica had accepted it, because at least it kept him away from her. But now Aaron would tell Jax, and Jeremy would tell Anita, and people would know about it. That their marriage was not as perfect as she liked to make out. That her husband looked at *porn*.

Ed sighed. Now that the baby was here, Monica had the unsettling impression that the power balance between them had shifted, and she did not like that. She said, modulating her tone, 'Why don't you check on the barbecue? That Hazel's totally monopolising it.' He went, taking a second beer with him.

'What's going on?' Chloe appeared in the doorway, like a wraith in the too-big dress. A wave of irritation swept through Monica. Did she have to look like that? Act like that? Did she have to exist, ruining Monica's life?

'None of your business. Can't you behave normally, go out and talk to our guests, hand round nibbles?'

Chloe watched her very calmly. It was an irritating habit she'd developed since everything that had happened. She didn't cry or look scared when Monica told her off any more; she just peered at her mother like she was an interesting specimen. Sometimes Monica thought she even saw pity there. 'I was watching Issy. No one else was.'

'It's Isabella. And she's asleep. She doesn't need watching every minute of the day.'

'She's been awake for ages. You haven't got the monitor on.'

As if Monica had time to sit by a baby monitor all day. She had people all over her garden, that Aisha had even gone upstairs without Monica there to point out features of the house, and there were babies everywhere, naked breasts all over the place leaking milk. Despite what she'd said in the antenatal group, Monica did not see the need for anyone to breastfeed, not if the baby was looked after in other ways, properly fed. She thrust a platter of padron peppers at Chloe. 'Take these out. Talk to people.'

'What should I talk about?' said Chloe coolly. 'There's so many things I'm not allowed to mention, after all.' And she walked into the garden, without waiting for an answer. That was when Monica became aware of the commotion outside, a vague sense of people moving too fast for the event, of searching. When she heard someone say, *Kelly's taken Hadley*, her first thought was of irritation. This was what came of mixing people who should really stay apart.

When that was all finally sorted out, just a silly misunderstanding, and she'd corralled them all to take the photo of the babies (her heart was not in it, but she couldn't have a party without Instagramming it), Monica went back into the kitchen, and saw that someone had left the fridge door open. Ed, presumably, taking out his beer. Oh God, no! She wrenched it wide, and sure enough, the cream-topped cake was melting, dripping on to the salads below. 'ED!' she shrieked. What more could go wrong?

When she closed the fridge door, she jumped – Nina was standing behind it, her blue eyes judgemental, wearing some hippy skirt and vest top. When did she get here? How annoying – Monica had secretly hoped she wouldn't come to the barbecue, after what she'd said to her at the group meeting (the nerve!). And what a moment to catch her. 'Problems?' said Nina.

'Oh! No, no, everything under control. Do help yourself to a drink there. And if you'd like to peek around the house, of course, you're very welcome.'

Nina did not pour a drink, but she did look around her, eyes taking in the garden, the messy kitchen. 'Thanks. I might just do that.'

Jax – four weeks earlier

I was at home. Of course – I was always at home now. And when the baby came, it would be the same. I'd be tied to the sink, the loo, the need to wash and sluice this small thing intent on puking and pooping itself round the clock. Changing Babygros. Feeding, like a cow at a milking station. For someone who'd been single for so long, able to come and go and stay out all night if I felt like it, answer to no one, this was a big change. Aaron kissed me goodbye in the morning, his shirt collar stiff against my neck, and I was jealous of him, even knowing he was going to a big 1970s office in Croydon to answer phones all day and eat Super Noodles for his lunch. I lay in bed all morning, feeling like an invalid in a children's book, Colin from *The Secret Garden* or Katy from *What Katy Did*. I could smell myself, sour and meaty. I wasn't supposed to shower until Aaron got home and could help me, but God, it was humiliating, like an old woman with a sugar-baby partner. Did people laugh at us, when we went by? Was I like some gross old man bribing his way to young flesh?

Sod it, I was going to get up and wash. I needed the loo anyway. I hated the book I was reading – some detective story where a raped sex worker was described as voluptuous and sensual – and the TV was downstairs. Aaron had forgotten to leave my laptop for me. I slithered out of bed to the floor, and shuffled across the carpet on my bottom to the bathroom. It was surprisingly hard, and I resolved to remember this when my baby was learning to walk, how much effort it requires to pull yourself up, to engage those core muscles. If only I'd stuck with the Pilates class taught by the guy in the man-bun and yoga pants. I felt ridiculous scooting across the hall this way, but soon the cool tiles of the bathroom were under me. The sink was above me – from this angle I could see the inadequacy of our cleaning. Aaron genuinely didn't seem to notice hairs or toothpaste stains, hadn't known that you were supposed to clean your house each week at least. I would have to stand up to do this. What harm could it do, standing for a few minutes to brush my teeth and splash myself with water? I wouldn't attempt the shower in case I slipped getting in – we'd have to buy one of those rubber bathmats old people had. A grab rail. I was ageing decades with every day. I grasped the edge of the bath and hauled myself up. Now I could see my face, pale and cross from days indoors, my disordered greasy hair, spots flaring up on my chin. God. I ran the tap, washed my face and teeth and armpits, realising they needed a shave. I went to turn it off again, and that was when I heard a noise downstairs.

I froze. The postman? No, I'd heard him come earlier. A parcel delivery? Buying things online had replaced a social life for me recently, despite my resolutions about cutting back. But the doorbell hadn't gone. All the same it sounded like someone was down there. How could they be? I hadn't heard any sounds of a break-in. Although a key might have been masked by the water running, but Aaron wasn't due home for hours. It was barely midday. Oh – maybe it was Minou, returned from her wanderings. Aaron had finally put the posters up, but I'd been disappointed not to hear anything as a result.

'Baby?' I called. This could work for the cat or for Aaron. No answer, but the noise stopped. I listened very hard, my breath

226

sounding in my ears. It began again – a rustling, like someone flicking through papers. 'Hello?'

Nothing. Should I go down? I made my way to the stairs, holding on to the banister for support, and looked over. I could see nothing in the triangle of living room visible to me. The inner door to the hallway was ajar, had Aaron left it like that when he went? I usually shut it for draughts but he often forgot.

I stopped. Listened. Listened. Barely a sound, but all the same, my senses were aflame, millions of years of evolution urging me to recognise what my rational brain would not accept – someone was in my house. And I was almost nine months pregnant, and forbidden to move. 'Is anyone there?' I hated the waver of my voice. And if no one was, would I seem crazy? Was I crazy, in fact, from loneliness and worry and stress?

I sat at the top of the stairs, like a toddler, and began to bump my way down. I made as much noise as possible and went as slowly as I could. A vague rustle was all I could hear. When I reached the bottom, I stood up, and moved forward with a few shaky steps. Nothing. There was no one in the house, just the kitchen with Aaron's breakfast bowl left out and the milk not in the fridge. A surge of irritation went through me – couldn't he manage these most simple things? And I was having a baby with this man? When I turned back from the fridge, I noticed something. The door of the little bureau, where I kept my important papers, was open. Maybe Aaron had done it, he was always leaving doors open. Maybe I was imagining things, like James Stewart in *Rear Window*, immobilised. Although actually, hadn't he been right in the end?

I still hadn't been to the loo. I shuffled upstairs again, and when I pulled down my knickers I noticed a splash of red there. Just a tiny drop of blood, but enough to make me crawl back to bed, praying to something I didn't believe in that my impatience hadn't cost me my baby. *Stay in there. Please, stay in there where it's safe.*

In bed, I took out my phone. I couldn't believe I was doing this, but I was. 'Mum?'

She sounded rushed and busy, out somewhere in the world, perhaps at the shops. 'What is it?'

'Nothing. I just . . . Could you come by today? If you're not too busy?'

A short silence. 'Well, of course, Jacqueline, if you feel you need it.'

Too late now for any pride. 'I need it. Thanks, Mum.'

Alison

They had now spoken to all the attendees at the fateful barbecue, except for one: Aaron Cole. Every time she rang Jax Culville, Jax said Aaron was at work, or out with friends. Was that normal, for a man with a new baby to be out so much? 'Dunno,' said Diana, when Alison voiced this question. 'Aren't most of them useless?'

'Not all of them.' Tom would be fine, wouldn't he? Not like these other dads she was encountering. 'We'll have to go to his work, drag him out.'

'After this, then.' They were arriving at Beeches, an exclusive private school near Beckenham, red-brick buildings and emerald-green grass even in this weather. As they parked up, schoolgirls walked past in navy uniforms, glossy hair shining. Alison detected curiosity from them, even disdain, but no fear. Unlike at her own school, where the arrival of the police would have seen every toilet in the place clogged with weed and worse.

They were met in the lobby – light-filled and spacious – by Chloe's form teacher, a Ms Li, small and shiny-haired in a neat suit. 'Oh sorry, it's a bit chaotic here near the end of term.' The lobby was quiet and clean. If this was chaos, Alison would take it. 'You wanted to speak about Chloe Evans?' She led them down a wood-panelled corridor to her office. The whole place had the blond-wood-and-light feel of a Scandinavian hotel. Privilege, eh?

'That's right. There was a suspicious death at her mother's house, perhaps you saw it on the news? The fall?'

'That was Chloe's house? Goodness, I didn't realise.' Her groomed eyebrows went up as she sat down behind a desk. 'Do help yourselves to water, by the way.' A glass jug sat on the side, cucumber floating in it. 'I'm surprised they didn't inform us. But then, we've found Mrs Evans – sorry, she's something else now, isn't she? – she's been rather difficult to contact recently.'

'It's Dunwood now, yes. How do you mean?'

'Well, Chloe's been off sick, as you know. Glandular fever. But we do need a sick note for an absence of this length, and, well, we haven't had one.'

'You haven't?' That seemed odd for someone like Monica, who missed nothing.

'Her mother said the doctor was dragging their heels – especially as I gather they moved house around the same time. Then she said she'd sent it, but it must have got lost, so she had to get another one, and . . . well, it's been several months now, and of course we're almost into the school holidays.'

'And did you notice anything strange about Chloe before she went off?'

'She was quiet, pale – but she's always been that way. Rather in her mother's shadow, I believe.' Alison nodded her understanding.

Diana, who'd been looking round her with an impassive expression, said, 'Who are Chloe's friends, Ms Li? Anyone who might know what was up with her?'

'I can't say she has a lot of girlfriends. But she had a boyfriend, I believe.'

'She did?' That was a surprise to Alison, having met Chloe with her baggy clothes and surly manner.

'A boy named Sam Morris, yes. Scholarship boy.' And there was so much contained in that phrase – their relative socio-economic brackets, how Monica Dunwood might have felt about it. 'I believe there was some . . . family opposition.'

Was it as simple as that – Monica had kept her daughter off school to stop her seeing a boy from a poorer family? On the other hand, Chloe hadn't looked at all well. 'Alright, thank you, Ms Li.' They'd have to find the time to talk to this Sam Morris, but they were stretched as it was, the week's grace Colette had given them almost up. Alison would have to go to her soon and plead for more time. Probably, she wouldn't get it.

'No problem.' The teacher rose. 'If you speak to Mrs Dunwood, perhaps you would remind her about the sick note. Unexcused absence is actually illegal, as you'll know better than anyone.'

'Will do.' She might enjoy reminding Monica Dunwood that she was breaking the law. 'What do you think?' she muttered to Diana, as they were shepherded out, catching glimpses of expensive science labs, a library and theatre, even a swimming pool shining blue in the distance.

'I think I went to the wrong school,' said Diana crisply. 'In my place half the teachers would run if they saw the cops coming, never mind the students.'

Alison smiled. She was beginning to like her new partner. As they reached the car, she decided what to do next. 'What time is it in Hong Kong?'

Diana looked it up on her phone. 'Evening. Half six-ish.'

'Maybe we'll catch Thomas Evans at the office.'

This time, her luck was in – the phone rang a few times, all the way across seas and continents, before it was picked up by a man with a British accent, north-eastern she thought. Alison explained who she was.

'Someone died at the house?' Thomas Evans's voice was incredulous, all that way away.

'You didn't hear?' She'd have thought that, even if it wasn't on the news out there, his daughter would have told him.

'Monica . . . she's not the best at staying in touch. I've been trying to ring Chloe for months now and Monica keeps putting me off, saying she's sick. I email her, but I don't know if kids even use email nowadays. Text her, even. She never replies.'

'You're saying you haven't heard from Chloe in months?' Alison looked up at Diana, eyebrows raised.

'Not a word. I thought maybe she was – well, she took the divorce hard, and my move out here. I wanted to bring her with me, but Monica . . . well.' Having met his ex-wife, Alison understood that *well*. 'God, Chloe must be in a state. Someone getting killed in her house! Poor kid.'

'Is there anything about Monica you could tell us that might be helpful? Anything possibly relevant to the case?'

She could hear his hesitation down the line, over the miles between them. 'Look, I don't want to get involved in anything. And yeah, I'm her ex, of course I'm going to say . . . just, don't believe everything she says, OK? She doesn't always tell the truth.'

Jax – four weeks earlier

The next thing that happened was the row. I called it that to myself to make it seem less what it was – disturbing and frightening. And shameful, of course. Let's not forget that.

I started it. Aaron, because of his upbringing, had deep wells of patience that I did not. Or he was just better at hiding things. It was early morning and I was in bed, feeling sour and fetid, watching him put on his tie for the office. I felt like his invalid mother. 'Can't they give you any time off?'

He grimaced. 'I asked but they really didn't seem keen, sorry babe. I'll get two weeks after the birth.'

'There must be something statutory. I mean, I'm not supposed to stand up for the loo by myself, I need you!'

'I know. But we need the money more.' That was true, which irritated me. If I lost my job over these stupid messages, we might have to live off Aaron's twenty-something salary, or even worse – ask my mother for help.

'It's not my fault. I really think – Aaron, don't you think someone has it in for me? You know Minou's still missing . . .' Voicing my fears made them worse somehow. Was it real? Or could I no longer think clearly? 'What if someone hurt her?'

'Cats do run off, don't they?' He finished the tie and began to apply hair gel. He used cheap stuff, leaving his hair stiff and sticky. I kept buying him expensive clay and wax and he would keep it 'for best', carrying on with his 99p supermarket own brand. A surge of rage went through me. Easy for him to say *cats run off*, he'd never liked her. But she'd been my companion all these years, since my failed engagement, through flings and dates and break-ups.

'What about the milk bottles? My car?'

'That was just foxes I think. And the car – well, it's old, babe.'

Rage bubbled up in me. 'The man said it was tampered with!'

'Kids, probably.'

'Why won't you believe me? I'm so scared, Aaron. It's alright for you, you're not thirty-eight and pregnant and on bed-rest, with someone maybe coming round your house breaking your milk bottles!' It sounded ridiculous, which made me even angrier. I reached for my more extreme weapons. 'Just because no one's being starved or beaten like when you were a kid, it doesn't mean something's not going on, you know.' I should have told him about the emails, but I still couldn't. When it came down to it, I was too ashamed.

He blinked. 'I know you're cross being like this . . .'

'I'm not cross. I'm scared. I'm angry that someone's been able to ruin my life like this.'

Aaron came and sat on the bed, and I smelled his aftershave and saw in the mirror the contrast between us. Him young, handsome, showered and shaved, fresh. Me old, grouchy, rumpled and bed-headed. 'Babe, your life isn't ruined. You're having a baby. I love you, we own the house outright.'

'*I* own it,' I said, needlessly cruel.

'Right. Of course. But that's a lot, isn't it?'

I felt sobs in my throat. 'Don't you care? I'm alone here all day, scared and freaked out, while you get to go to work like everything's fine. Someone was in the house yesterday.'

'What?'

'I heard a noise downstairs.'

'You didn't go down, did you?'

'Just a bit.'

'Jax, you have to be careful! Was there someone?'

'Well, no. They'd gone, maybe. But I heard it! And the bureau was open!'

He sighed. 'Babe, do you think maybe you're just a bit . . .'

'What?'

'I was talking to Nina the other night. She said women can get a bit funny in the last few weeks. Paranoid. It makes sense, when you're so vulnerable.'

'You talked to Nina about me?' I pictured them, her hand on his arm. Her tanned inscrutable face. Claudia Jarvis, pregnant and tired, walking across the pub to find her husband laughing with a young girl. I was her now, except Nina wasn't an idiot like I'd been, she was a grown woman, one with depths and strengths I could only guess at.

He hesitated. 'I was worried. You seem a bit, I don't know . . . not yourself.'

He thought I was losing it. Unstable, confused. For a moment I felt it all, him talking to Nina, what Monica had said about young men needing excitement. My mother's comments that Aaron might not stick around. It built up in me, the anger, the fear, the jealousy. I took a deep breath and went for the jugular. 'Maybe you don't care about the baby. Maybe you'd rather I lost it.'

There was a silence of a few seconds, enough for me to feel the damage I'd wrought. Then Aaron punched the wall, and left the room. I jumped at the noise, the sudden violence of the strike, like a snake. The cheap plasterboard wall had crumbled around the shape of his fist. 'Aaron?' I called, my voice wobbling. 'I'm sorry. I didn't mean it.' I heard the sound of running water. 'Please, Aaron.

Please come back.' I was crying now. 'It's not fair, you know I can't get up . . .'

He didn't come back. I sat in bed, weeping pathetically, while the sounds of water continued next door. I don't know how long it was before the doorbell went. Aaron came back into the room. He was cradling one hand in the other, and I saw that it was bloody, oozing through the plasters he'd inexpertly pasted on to it. We looked at each other with guilt in our eyes. 'Who's that?'

'I don't know. I'm not expecting anyone.' I tried to think if I had a parcel on order, but couldn't remember. I ordered so much out of sheer boredom. 'Well, get it.'

'I . . .' He gestured to the blood.

'I hardly can.'

He sighed, then went downstairs, and I heard the door open. Then the buzz of a radio and I knew something was up. The sound of voices, Aaron's rising in surprise, or anger, then falling. Then footsteps coming upstairs. More than one person. I saw the uniforms. The police were in my house, coming into my bedroom. I pulled the covers around me, shocked.

Aaron said, 'Someone called the police. Said there was a domestic disturbance.'

How did they get here so quickly? Was someone listening to us? I followed the gaze of the police officers to the wall, the dent in it, the plaster crumbled on the carpet, and to Aaron's injured hand. Oh God. How bad this looked. 'We just had a row,' I said weakly. 'It was my fault.'

'You punched the wall, sir?'

Aaron appeared frozen, pale and green. He said nothing.

'Sir?'

I began to panic. Of course this would be traumatic for him, the police coming round, the shaky aftermath of violence. Too much like his past.

I saw the police officers exchange glances, and knew they would arrest him next, given the circumstances. It was two officers, one an older white man, one a younger Asian man.

I began to babble. 'Look, I don't know who called you, but we were just arguing, I was upset because I'm on bed-rest and I was taking it out on him, he didn't do anything, he'd never hurt me, honest . . .'

Still they spoke to him. 'Sir, would you step outside while we talk to your wife?'

I'm not his wife, I thought, but didn't say, as it surely wouldn't be helpful. 'It's fine, really. He hasn't done anything wrong.'

But Aaron was being escorted out into the hallway, letting himself be led. The younger officer stood by my bed, looking down at me. He was tooled up, outdoor gear, armour really, mud dropping from his boots to my carpet, and I was in bed, lying down, a mess. 'Madam, I need to ask you if you're safe? If you're not, we can arrest your partner, get a restraining order against him.'

Oh God. Here they were doing exactly what you'd hope they'd do in a case of domestic violence, except it was wrong, all wrong. 'I'm fine. Honestly. It was just a row.'

'But he punched the wall.'

'I provoked him.' Oh God, that was just what an abused woman would say.

'Has he ever been violent before?'

'No, never. And this wasn't violence.' Or was it? I was panicking, not thinking straight. *But he hit the table that time.* That was nothing, I told myself. A moment's frustration.

'Are you aware late pregnancy is the most risky time for domestic violence?'

'That's not what this is. Aaron's very gentle, very loving. He just . . . I pressed his buttons. It was my fault.'

It took a lot of persuading, and the taking down of statements, before they would leave without arresting him. I knew there'd be a permanent record of the call-out, a stain on both our pasts, the hint of violence, a whiff of danger around Aaron. When the door shut downstairs, I looked across the room, strewn with crumbled plaster and splashed with blood, at Aaron. 'I'm so sorry,' I began.

'I'm late for work,' was all he said, and he left.

Alison

At the local offices of Dependent Insurance, they were met by a grey man (hair, skin, suit) who nervously asked if he could help them. Alison flashed her badge and watched him grow even more nervous. 'Does Aaron Cole work here?' The office was depressing, fraying carpets and flickering fluorescent lights. Not a fun place for a young man to work.

'Well, he did.'

'Did?' said Diana, the most glamorous thing in the entire place.

'I'm afraid we had to . . . let him go. There were some issues with timekeeping and absenteeism, and he lost his temper with a customer on the phone. He was only on a two-week notice period, and opted not to work it, so.' The man shrugged.

'He might be at home,' volunteered a young woman who'd come up, dunking a herbal teabag into a chipped mug. She wore an unflattering grey skirt and a striped blouse, but was pretty underneath it, with a blonde bob. The kind of young woman who might have admired Aaron Cole, and perhaps been admired in return.

The man scowled at her. 'Don't interrupt, Cassie.'

'No, please do, Cassie,' said Alison, pointedly. 'Have you been in touch with Aaron? Only we've not been able to track him down at home.'

'Oh, he moved out,' said Cassie easily, and Alison mentally punched the air. Jackpot. He wasn't living with Jax, and she hadn't told them. She had lied.

'You've got the details?' said Diana.

'He gave me them so we could send on his P45. I can get the address for you.'

'Thank you,' said Diana, flashing a glance at the unhelpful manager. 'That's very kind of you.'

Cassie printed it off for them, an address about ten minutes away. 'Is he alright?' So the contact between her and Aaron wasn't that close then.

'As far as we know he is.' Not that they knew much.

'Only I know it was hard on him, the baby coming and dealing with his girlfriend and that.' There was a definite contemptuous stress on the *girlfriend*.

'Dealing with what?' said Alison casually, taking the address from the printer.

'Oh, you know. She went kind of mental. Postnatal depression, I guess. She's not been right for months, Aaron said.'

Diana was driving today. Something about the way she did it made Alison feel judged, hands perfectly in the ten to two position, performing a smooth mirror/signal/manoeuvre each time, checking her blind spot. She'd pulled the car seat way up so her chest was almost on the wheel, her ponytail swinging. 'Interesting Jax didn't tell us her and her partner are living apart, isn't it?' said Diana.

'It *is* interesting, isn't it?'

Diana parked – again, flawless – and they went into the block of flats, ex council, outdoor stairs that echoed with footsteps and the shouting of children. Aaron was apparently staying in one on the fourth floor. As Diana bounded up, Alison found she had to lean on the handrail and gasp for breath. God. Her body was literally breaking down.

Aaron Cole opened the door with a wary look on his face, dressed in the same grey tracksuit most of the young men round this area liked to sport. He was a handsome lad, his eyes very blue, but he didn't look happy, or healthy. There was an ashy pallor to him, and his eyes jittered everywhere. He didn't offer them a drink or a seat, so Alison plonked herself firmly down at the small Ikea table. There were only two chairs, so Aaron sat on the edge of his bed, which was about two metres from the kitchen.

'So. This is where you're living. Not much space for you, is there?'

He fiddled with his hands. 'All I could afford. Lost my job.' It was clearly a dodgy sub-divide of what had been a council flat, just a strip of kitchen and then a carpeted area to serve as bedroom and living room. Alison looked around but couldn't see a door that might be a bathroom; probably he was sharing. She thought of Monica Dunwood's house, the surplus rooms, the acres of lush carpet.

'Why aren't you living with Jax and the baby, Aaron?'

'Um. We just – it was hard, with the baby coming. We weren't getting on that well.'

Diana glanced at her; Alison caught the flick of shiny hair. He had brought it up – perhaps he would be the weak point in the wall this group had built, the one to finally tell the truth. 'Nina. Were you close to her?'

He stared at the bare floor. 'No. Just knew her from the group, that's all.'

'Aaron. We know the police were called to the house you shared with Jax, a few weeks ago. Can you tell me about that?' This had been Diana's idea – searching not just for previous convictions, but any contact with the police at all.

He dipped his head. 'I lost my temper. Hit the wall. Not her. I'd never hit her, or hurt her in any way. I love her.'

'That's a shame you've split up then. Especially as rent must be tight on two places.'

'Jax owns hers. Her dad left her some money.'

'But the baby – Hadley? Don't you think she needs you around?'

For a moment, she thought he might cry. 'I'm no good for her. I don't know what to do with a kid – I never had my own family.' He'd grown up in care, she was aware. 'I try to help out. It's hard.'

'Tell us about the day of the barbecue,' said Diana.

Aaron recounted a familiar story. Ed had taken him and Jeremy to his shed, and while he was gone, Kelly had lifted Hadley from where she sat in a bouncy chair and taken her to the park behind. Just a misunderstanding, all sorted out quickly. 'What did Ed have in the shed?' Alison asked casually.

Aaron was not a good liar. He flushed. 'Er . . . just stuff.'

She had a strong hunch. 'Porn?'

'Not really. Sort of erotica. Japanese and that. He said it was worth a lot.' Of course he did – Monica and Ed were people who knew the price of everything and the value of nothing, Alison's mum would say. 'It's nothing dodgy,' he said quickly.

'And later? After you got the baby back?'

'Well, it was sort of confused. Jax was upset, and we were going to go home, when we heard a scream and we looked and – Nina – she fell. Off the balcony.' His throat worked. 'It was horrible.'

'Was anyone out there with her?'

'Not that I saw.'

'We heard from Jax you were both downstairs at the time, you see. Where you wouldn't have been able to see the fall.' What he'd said, *we looked*, that sounded like they had witnessed it. Like they'd been upstairs near the balcony, as Chloe Evans had said.

His eyes twitched. 'I don't know. I can't remember every minute of it, like.' He was lying. Bless him, he was very bad at it. The question was why. He was hardly the only person there that day to have misrepresented exactly where they were when Nina died. It was this, the obvious lies, the evasions, that had kept her digging into a case that everyone else thought was an accident. Rahul and his financial problems. Monica and whatever was going on with her daughter. The tension between Cathy and Hazel. Was it possible Nina had found out some of their secrets? Was that the motive Alison had been searching for?

'So you think she just fell?'

'I guess so. She must have gone up to see the rockery from the top, Monica was banging on about it all day. The balcony had just been cleaned, she said. Maybe it was slippy.' The balcony had just been cleaned. It was slippy. Alison had heard some variation on that from several people now. Which was almost more suspicious than everyone having a different story. But how was she ever going to prove they were lying?

Easily, she said, 'You know, Aaron, you were the only one there with any history of violent behaviour.'

He looked up, panicked.

'So if it wasn't an accident, if she was pushed, and we were looking for obvious suspects, that's where we'd start. With you.'

She could almost see his brain working, but the reply it came up with was not the one she'd expected. 'If you arrested me – or someone – for killing her, would you end the investigation?'

Weird question. 'Of course, if we thought we could secure a conviction. What I don't know is why. Why any of you would want to push your antenatal group leader off a balcony? Anything you want to tell me, Aaron?'

A long pause. 'No.' She almost heard the addition – *not yet*. What was he up to? Protecting someone, maybe? Jax, the obvious person? She had seemed a total state, but that could just have been the baby.

Diana stirred, she must have felt they'd pushed him far enough for an interview. 'Thanks for your time, Aaron. We may need to talk to you again, so don't go anywhere, alright?'

Another hesitation. 'Alright.'

They stood up. Alison knew she had set something in motion with her visit here today, but she just wasn't sure what.

The day of – Cathy

'Cathy? Sausage or burger?' Ed was waving a piece of meat at her. Cathy shook her head, distracted. How could she eat when she had that message on her phone, glowing like radiation? She should have just deleted it. She should ignore him, hope he went away. After all, he couldn't prove anything, not without her consent. It was almost worse when she'd forgotten about it for a moment, watching Arthur wave his hands around or successfully grab her finger, because then it all came crashing back. The terror. The guilt. What if she got caught? What if she never did – could she live with herself for the rest of her life?

'Aren't you going to eat?' Hazel was at her elbow, her sharp grey eyes taking in everything. 'You need to keep your strength up, when you're feeding.'

'It's just so hot.' The sun had indeed come out blazing that afternoon, leaving everyone pink-faced and a bit too drunk, as they gulped down their wine to hydrate. Monica had said something about getting a jug of water, but it hadn't appeared. You'd think that, as a breastfeeding mum herself, she'd be more attuned to that. Cathy hadn't touched booze for three months before she got pregnant and of course not since, a whole year now, and was staying off it still because anything she drank went straight into Arthur, and besides, Hazel was always watching. Hazel who was now on her fourth beer and had taken over from Ed in the barbecuing of the meat. Aisha was picking at some peppers, and Cathy realised she likely wouldn't be able to eat any of the pork products on offer, or drink the alcohol. She looked worried too. Her husband, Rahul, was standing at the end of the garden, grim-faced and silent, poking at his phone. She wondered what that was like, a partner who didn't talk at you all the time. Restful, perhaps.

'The baby needs his hat,' said Hazel, turning sausages. 'Where did you leave it?'

'I'll get it.' An excuse to go inside, into the cool marble interior of the house, and answer her message, as she'd been itching to do. Walking in, she saw that Nina had arrived, and an irrational swoop of fear went through her. It was OK. Nina didn't know anything, not for sure. Maybe she'd seen that Cathy was further along than she should have been, a little bigger than would be expected. But nothing could be proved. All the same, as she saw Nina go upstairs, she dived into the living room, heart hammering. She took the phone out of her pocket. *We need to talk*, the message read. Her sweaty fingers slipped on the screen. *OK*, she typed. *When?* Then she immediately deleted both the original message and her reply, feeling like a criminal as she covered her tracks.

She jumped as someone came to the door, but it was only Jax, carrying her own baby. She liked Jax, with whom she'd shared many an eye-roll during group sessions. 'Oh, hi. You OK?'

Jax didn't look so good, pale and exhausted after spending weeks inside on bed-rest. She must be relieved now, to have her baby safely in the world. 'You know how it is. Have you seen Aaron? I think we might go soon.' Cathy wasn't surprised, after the panic about little Hadley, even though she was now safe and sound in Jax's arms.

'No, sorry. Outside, maybe?'

'OK.' Jax went out, and Cathy heard her flip-flops going across the marble floor. Alone, she scanned her phone again, already hungry for a reply.

They'd met Dan and Rachel, his wife, at the fertility clinic where Cathy had her initial tests. They seemed to often have appointments at the same time. They shared their stories, despite knowing nothing else about each other, as you do when you're bonded by some shared trauma.

Dan was fine – all his tests had come back normal, better than normal, excellent. Rachel always said this with a painful little laugh. 'Poor Dan! Stuck with me and my malfunctioning system.' Rachel had a lot wrong with her. Cysts and fibroids and PCOS and scar tissue in her womb. Cathy winced just thinking about it, how naive she'd been to assume it was all simple when you were a male-female couple. All she and Hazel needed was some swimmers, and they were easy enough to get if you had the money. They'd ordered some from Denmark, a thousand pounds, and now they just had to do the insemination and wait to see if it worked. Cathy felt a huge amount of pressure, watched eagle-eyed by Hazel to see she was taking her vitamins and drinking her cough syrup (it was supposed to thin up her mucus), not to mention giving up booze and sugar and caffeine until she was almost climbing the walls. She was scheduled for a home insemination, which was cheaper, and was dreading it. She'd confided this to Dan, who was so nice. Such a good listener. Almost like the brother she'd never had.

Or so she'd thought, to begin with.

Someone had abandoned a bottle of white wine on Monica's glass coffee table, already leaving a ring. Cathy picked it up, and swigged from the neck, the cold sharp liquid making her gasp. Booze, after a year of none. She was going to have one drink today, and Hazel could piss off. As her phone lit up, and she seized on it, running her eyes over and over the message to take it in before she had to delete it, her hands were shaking, her brain firing with dopamine and guilt and excitement.

The message: *I want to see him.*

Jax – three weeks earlier

There were no baked goods at the last group session, and I realised this was because it was my turn, and I felt bad despite all the other much worse stuff that was going on.

'No Cathy today,' said Nina, sweeping in on her usual cloud of essential oils. 'She went into labour last night.'

'Really?' I said. 'The baby came early?'

Nina didn't answer for a moment, and I remembered – she had predicted this, hadn't she? She'd told Cathy her baby would arrive soon. A chill went over me. How did she know these things? What could she see just by looking at me? I had been sunk in embarrassment ever since the police came a few days before. I wasn't that type of person. What must my neighbours think of me? It was a good job I couldn't leave the house, I'd be too ashamed to face them. Aaron and I had not discussed it, of course. It went into the big pile of things we were ignoring, swept under a carpet now so bulging we had to walk around it. He'd been violent, twice now, if I was being strictly honest. I was picking fights, pushing him away. And the baby hadn't even arrived yet. What would we be like after? 'Fingers crossed for her,' I said weakly. If Cathy was already in labour, my own wasn't far off. This was real. It was happening.

This was the last session we'd have. Our due dates had come inexorably closer, and our bodies – me, Aisha, Monica – strained with fullness. Anita, of course, stayed the same, and sometimes I would catch her looking at my belly, a complicated expression on her face. I hoped everything would work out for them.

Nina stood up at the end. 'Well done, everyone. I wish you all the best with your upcoming journey, and what comes next.' She folded her hands in a namaste gesture. That was it. We were on our own now. People were hugging, swapping contact details, Monica reminding everyone about the party in just three weeks' time. By then, everything would have changed. We might all have babies, be parents. Nina stood at the door, seeing us out. She hugged Aisha and Anita, whispering something into their ears, encouraging comments I imagined, but not Jeremy, Rahul, or Ed. Not Monica either, and I saw her frown as Nina turned away, and felt a momentary flicker of sympathy. Aaron and I were the last to go. 'Good luck, Jax.' Nina's cool eyes swept over me. Clearly, I was not getting a hug either, and I felt obscurely hurt by that.

'Thanks. And thank you for the group, it's been . . . I learned a lot.' Enough to know I had no clue what I was doing. I didn't really feel grateful towards her. I felt a lot of things, angry that she'd spent so much time with Aaron, talking about me behind my back, jealous of her strength and beauty and confidence, beholden for the money she'd paid him, which he needed so badly, hurt that she'd been so hard on me in the sessions. But I had been brought up by my mother, so instead of any of this I just said *thank you*.

Nina just nodded, stepped forward to Aaron and enfolded him in a hug. It went on. And on. Just as I was thinking *what the hell*, she stepped back. 'Thank you for all your help, Aaron. You've been amazing.' She turned to me, one hand on his chest. 'You've got a good one here, Jax. I hope you know that.'

'Of course,' I said mechanically. 'We should go.'

Aaron went out into the corridor and Nina put a hand on my arm, pulling me back. 'Just be careful, Jax. I've seen this before.

Young man, older woman, baby coming into the mix . . . it won't be easy.'

I was stunned. 'I know it won't be easy.'

'Do you? Well. Just take care of him.'

On the way home, I kept thinking what an odd thing that was to say. *Take care of him.* Shouldn't he be taking care of me? As I drove, I found myself mulling over Jeremy's question from weeks back, about why I'd not had children sooner. What would my life have been if Aaron hadn't come along when he did? Receding a little each year from the possibility, until I could no longer see it at all? What would I have done with my time? Taken group holidays to learn painting or cooking. Cared for my mother until her death, the only child's burden. Ended up one of those old women who sit in their flats and talk to nobody all week. A shudder ran through me at the idea. This was the trade-off – let something rip you open, your heart and mind and body and life; or die alone. Watching Aaron's profile as he looked out of the window, I wondered if it was different for men. If the decision to have a baby was no more significant than choosing whether to get Sky Sports or not. If he might regret it, even. He was only twenty-four of course. I thought again of Nina's hand resting on his chest, and tried to focus on more immediate worries.

Although I knew the group was a source of tension, I didn't really pay enough attention to it. I was too worried about my mysterious ill-wisher, the oncoming birth, and about me and Aaron. I thought the group people were just minor annoyances, their eccentricities good for dinner-party chat if I ever went to one of those again, or perhaps even with future Mum-friends (Cathy, Aisha maybe). As I left that day, I wasn't sure if I would ever see any of them again. Nina included.

Alison

Every public-sector receptionist she'd ever met was exactly the same. A woman, and determined to keep you from finding out information as though their life depended on it, whether that was the availability of a single doctor's appointment, or the details of who had hired the community hall for the baby group, as this one from the council was trying to do. 'I'm sorry, but I really am too busy for this. And data protection . . .'

'You realise she is dead, yes? Killed? Not coming back? Data protection doesn't apply here.'

A huge sigh ruffled Alison's hair, which today she had worn down, freshly washed, shamed by Diana's shiny mane. 'I'll have a look.'

'That's *so* kind of you.'

There was a silence, filled with the sound of clacking. 'Da Souza, you said?'

'Yes.' Alison spelled it.

'I don't have any more information than that. The hall was hired by a Nina da Souza, yes, for eight weeks every Saturday afternoon. That's all.'

'You didn't take a copy of her ID, or what about bank details?' This was her last-ditch attempt to find Nina's address, since no one else seemed to have any record of her. She must have lived somewhere. What kind of person had no wallet, no phone, no ID of any kind?

'Why would we do that? And she took the money directly from the participants – in cash, I believe. Paid us cash too.'

Alison couldn't believe this. This woman had been running a baby group without bank details, without anyone checking her identity? 'You must have had her DBS checked?'

The receptionist hated Alison, it was clear. 'We're not required to, since it was a private group. She just hired the hall. Anyone can do that.'

'You had someone working with pregnant women and babies, who isn't DBS checked?' Had they learned nothing, after Soham?

The woman scowled. 'No babies. It stopped before they were born. And it's private, like I keep saying, so we aren't liable.'

Alison gave a gusty sigh back. They glared at each other over the desk, public servant to public servant. Several people had gathered behind her in the council offices, clutching letters. 'Can I at least see the booking form for the hall?'

A few more begrudging clicks pulled up a copy of Nina's signature, scrawled on to some scanned sheets of paper. A mobile-phone number, which they already knew had been pay as you go and disconnected. How could a woman leave so little trace on the world? Then Alison spotted one thing – in the address section of the form, something had been scrawled. A postcode only five minutes from the hall. At last, an address! They could search her home and surely find out something about this mysterious dead woman.

'Will that be all, officer? I hate to keep all these taxpayers waiting.'

'Thank you,' she said. 'You've been very helpful.' That was a lie.

Stepping out into the sunshine, she thought again how strange this all was. A woman with no friends, no family, no ties to the world at all. Nothing. If Alison hadn't seen the body herself, the blood spreading out over the rocks, the eyes wide open and staring at the sky, she would have wondered if this woman ever existed at all.

She went to ring Diana, and saw in one of those enjoyable coincidences that Diana was at that precise moment calling her. 'You must be psychic. Guess whose address I finally found?'

'No way!'

'Yup. It was on the form the whole time, they just couldn't be bothered to look properly. I'll text you it, meet me there?'

'Sure thing. Alison, we finally have something! Fucking result!' She was surprised to hear Diana swearing – really, she'd completely misinterpreted the woman.

'Let's hope so, anyway.' As she walked to her car, her steps were heavy with tiredness, with the heat. She just wanted to stand under a cold shower and then eat three Magnums with her feet in an ice bucket. But Diana was right, they finally had something. A clue, in the middle of all this baffling nothing.

Jax – three weeks earlier

Try to keep life stress-free as you approach birth, to ensure baby is born into a welcoming and serene environment.

I almost snarled at the pamphlet Nina had passed out in the last session. Some chance of me creating a stress-free environment. Here was my situation, one week off my scheduled Caesarean. I was on bed-rest, my placenta likely to rupture at any minute. At the slightest hint of bleeding I would be carted off to hospital, there to stay until the baby arrived, at which point either one or both of us might die. I was hardly speaking to my partner, who went to work and came home, leaving me alone during dull daylight hours, while I dozed and moped and was barely awake except in the middle of the night, seized by terror. Aaron had moved into the spare room to 'give me space'. I was possibly going to be suspended from work, my cat was still missing, my car had been damaged, and someone was doing these things to me, I was sure. Someone had sent these messages – I'd deleted that Facebook post myself. Hadn't I? Of course I had. It was just hard to think straight, cooped up like this.

Worst of all, I felt myself changing. I had never been jealous in relationships – on the contrary, I was the one more likely to chafe against the edges of commitment. But now I couldn't stop. Aaron's phone buzzed one morning as he got dressed, and before he'd lifted it from the bedside table I'd seen who was texting – Cassie. The blonde girl from his work, the one who'd put the picture of me on Facebook. 'Why's she texting?' I hated the sound of my voice.

'Just giving me a heads-up. Area manager's in today, I better run.'

'Sure that's all?' And Aaron would give me his bewildered blue-eyed gaze, and I'd feel worse than ever, an angry jealous old woman, and delusional to boot.

Because Aaron was right. A fox could have smashed the milk bottles. My car could just have broken down or been tampered with by the neighbourhood kids I was always chastising for hitting it with footballs. It was very possible no one had been in the house that day, that I just wasn't used to its daytime sounds. And the open door of the cabinet? Aaron could have done that. If that was true, if there was no one malicious, had I imagined the Facebook post? But no, Dorothy and Sharon had seen messages too. Then had the complaint been genuine – someone really thought I was not appropriate with the kids? I wracked my brains to remember. A young boy, fourteen maybe, weeping in my office as he recounted his abuse in care, while I recorded him for a fundraising video. I had put my arm around his shoulders, hadn't I, without thinking? Had someone walked past, Dorothy or Sharon or someone else? I believed now it was nothing to do with the Jarvises – Mark did not have the means to contact me and she didn't have the malice, even though I had in fact ruined her life, not that I'd meant to. That was the worst thought that came to me on those endless, dull days – I did not deserve this baby. I did not know how to be a good mother, since I'd never witnessed one in action. I was going to fail.

One day, one of those other days without end or beginning, I lost it entirely. Aaron was late home. I'd been watching the clock tick past six, up to seven, and after. When had I become the kind of woman who watched clocks? In the past I was usually home after him, often felt guilty about taking work back with me, lying awake finessing presentations and pitches. When he came in, at almost twenty past seven, I was waiting on the sofa. I must have looked a sight, huge in my unwashed dressing gown and unbrushed hair, face like thunder. 'Where were you?'

He stopped, midway through taking his jacket off. I had bought it for him. He never bought himself anything new, even if he could afford it, even if his old ones were full of holes. 'Work, babe.'

'Till this hour?'

'It's getting to quarter-end. Busy time.'

That sounded reasonable, so I changed tack, spoiling for a fight. 'I suppose *Cassie* was working late too.'

'We all were.' He placed his jacket on the sofa, instead of hanging it up like I'd asked him to hundreds of times. 'What'll we have for dinner?'

'How should I know? I've been stuck here all day. I can hardly even go to the loo unless you help me.'

'Well, I'm here now.' Aaron hefted me up the stairs, practically grunting with the effort. As I shut the bathroom door, I caught sight of myself in the mirror. An angry, dishevelled mess of a woman. What must it be like to come home to this? Especially when there was Nina, so slim and glamorous, and Cassie at his office, so pert and young. I had to stop this. I had no evidence at all that Aaron even looked at other women in that way. I took a deep breath and went out, determined yet again to stop sniping, be nice, suggest we order a takeaway. But when I bum-shuffled back down to the living room, Aaron was standing there, all the colour drained from his face.

'What's happened?' He was holding his phone. Or no – he was holding *my* phone. He looked down at it, shocked. A dozen scenarios ran through my mind. Mark – Claudia – Sharon . . .

'It rang. I thought I should answer.'

'What? Why?'

'Who's Denise Edwards?'

Oh God. I never had told him about her. 'Er . . .'

'A detective, right? She said she was calling with news of Georgina Partington-Smith.' Aaron's voice was flat. Not quite calm. Something else.

I held out my hand for the phone. 'I was doing it for you, OK? I'd have told you if she found something. Did she?'

'She traced her to a place in Wales. Some farm, like . . . a commune or something, she said. But she doesn't live there any more. She's gone – no one knows where.'

'Oh.'

'I can't believe you didn't tell me.'

'Aaron, I just—'

'All this time getting on at *me* for hiding things, who's texting me, why am I talking to Nina or Cassie – and you're the one keeping secrets. You didn't tell me about Mark Jarvis either, did you?'

I stood very still. 'How do you know that name?'

'You left your laptop open on the article! I wasn't even snooping, it was right there! I didn't want to bring it up and upset you when you're like this, but Christ, Jax, you were mixed up in a *court* case and you never told me? You basically broke a paedophile ring?'

That wasn't exactly the truth. That left out the real reason it had happened, my stupidity, my selfishness. 'Aaron, give me back my phone. You shouldn't be answering my calls.' As if I still had some claim to the moral high ground.

He slapped it into my hand. 'You don't need to worry. I'm not the one sneaking about.' His eyes when he looked at me were bleak. 'What happened, Jax? We used to be so good. Is it the baby, is that it?'

I didn't know what to say. Maybe it was the baby, revealing the fault lines between us. All the things I hadn't told him. Our age gap, his past. My past. The fact that I had never really trusted him, not entirely, and that this was my fault, not his. He'd never given me a reason not to. Whereas I had given him plenty.

Aaron shook his head. 'I can't do this, Jax.'

'What?' My heart quickened.

'Come home every day, upset you like this . . . It's not good for any of us, you or me or the baby. I'm sorry.'

'What do you mean?'

'I think I should stay somewhere else for a while. I'll still check in of course, help you out when I can . . . or maybe your mum can stay or something . . .'

'Aaron! You can't leave me when I'm about to give birth! Are you mad?'

'*I'm* not.' I caught the stress on the word. Meaning I was. 'But whatever this is, between us – it's not good, Jax. I punched the wall. I haven't done that since I was a kid. I can't be here right now, that's all. I'm afraid of what I'll do.'

He was putting his jacket back on again. This couldn't be happening. 'But where will you go?' It was crazy. Aaron had no money, no place to stay. When I'd met him, he'd lived in a massive house share in town, and had been only too happy to relocate to my place. He couldn't go. What would my mother say? How would I cope? Was this for good? Was I a single mum now, like I'd been afraid of?

'I'll be alright. Please. Try to rest.'

'But where are you . . . ?'

Without looking at me, he went upstairs and I heard the sound of opening drawers. Even if I could have chased after him, I was frozen on the sofa. Was this happening? He was leaving me? Even though I wasn't supposed to move, I dragged myself to the bottom of the stairs, pathetic. 'Aaron. Aaron, please talk to me.' No answer. Just the sound of packing.

After about ten minutes, the doorbell went and I was just getting up when Aaron bounded downstairs. 'Sit down, Jax.'

I saw who it was, who'd come to pick him up. I shouldn't have been surprised, really. She came in. She wore yoga pants and a tight vest top, her hair piled on to her head.

'Nina.'

'Hello, Jax.' Her tone was gentle, as if to an invalid or mental patient.

Aaron said, to her rather than me, 'Sorry. One second,' and went upstairs again, feet thundering in his urge to be away from me.

I spat, 'You're taking him to yours, is that it? How is that appropriate?'

Nina twirled keys. 'I heard about a sublet available, that's all.'

'Why are you doing all this? You don't even know him!'

'I just want to help. It's a stressful time for all of you, and Aaron – he didn't have the easiest start in life.'

'You think I don't know that?' Who was this woman, this stranger, coming into our lives? Under my rage, I felt a terrible helplessness. He was going, with her, and there was nothing I could do to stop him.

She said nothing. Aaron came down carrying a leather holdall – another gift from me. He said, 'Please look after yourself. I'll call you later and we'll . . . we can figure something out.'

'You can't leave me.' I still hadn't taken it in. 'I can hardly move!'

'Your mum can come. I'll call her if you like?'

'Don't you dare. Just go. I don't care what you do.' I turned my face to the wall so I didn't see them leave, just heard the door close and footsteps walk away. When they'd gone, I couldn't believe how silent the house was. Just me, and the tick of the clock, and the gentle movements of the baby inside me.

The day of – Aisha

What was on Rahul's phone? She had been wondering this for some time now. Why did it get so much of his attention, pulling his eyes from her and from the baby, clutched in his hand so the screen was sweaty and smeared? Once or twice he had left it in the room with her, and she'd seen how quickly he reversed, dived back in and scooped it up. She'd seen how he tensed if she idly picked it up to dust underneath or clear space for a cup of tea. In fact, she had noticed all this even before Nina said what she had at the last group session, whispering into Aisha's ear as she hugged her. *Check his phone.*

So yes. He was hiding something. The question was – the obvious or not? It wouldn't be unheard of in these situations. Rahul was good-looking, of course he had probably been tangled up with someone less suitable before he met her. White, maybe, though that might not be a huge problem. Jewish, possibly, based on where he'd been living. That might cause issues with his family. Maybe even married, or older, or uneducated – someone that, for whatever reason, he was not able or not brave enough to be with. Aisha could have accepted that; after all, she was under no illusions that they'd fallen in love. They'd just made a sensible choice, for their lives and their future, and here was the proof of it, a lovely little boy, strong and alert.

After Monica forced them to take the group picture of the babies, Rahul had left his phone on the table. It must have been the commotion about Kelly that made him forget it, the need for the men to surge forward and protect the women, the children. Something primal. She stood there, jiggling the baby. Then she put out a finger, noticing how dry and ragged her hands were from endless nappy-changing, and touched the cloudy dark screen. Like an evil mirror in a fairy tale. It lit up, a passcode. Of course she didn't know it and guessing could only lead to trouble. There was nothing she could do.

But as she stood there, vaguely listening to the hubbub of voices around her, something flashed on to the screen. A text from an unknown number. It said, *You have till the end of today. Then I'm telling her.*

'Ais?' She looked up; Rahul was coming across the garden to her. The message had disappeared already, so quickly she might almost have believed she'd imagined it.

'Everything OK?' She tried to seem normal.

'Yeah, it's just . . . oh.' He'd seen that she had his phone. For a moment she was embarrassed for him, his face so white and sick.

'You left this.' She passed it to him, and watched the colour gradually return to his face. He thought she didn't know. Maybe that was the most disappointing thing – that her husband, the father of her child, thought she was so stupid she hadn't noticed things were terribly, terribly wrong. Suddenly, Aisha couldn't stand it any more. 'Tell me what's going on?' she blurted.

His face paled again. 'What?'

'You know what. The phone. The messages – I saw the last one, it came up.' She shifted the baby, their baby – the one she'd made with this stranger – on her front. 'Is it another woman? I'd just rather know. It makes sense in a way – we rushed into this. What is she, married?'

Carefully, he put the phone down on the table, its bottomless black surface between them. 'It's not another woman.'

A man? That would require some . . . adjustments in her thoughts, but at least it would explain things.

He saw what she was thinking. 'It's not anything like that. It's . . . I have some . . . money problems.'

Her first thought was relief. Didn't everyone have some money problems? But then more fear arrived – how bad would it have to be, to make him like this? 'And?'

'I owe some money. To some people.'

'Bad people.'

'Quite bad, yes.'

'Why?' She couldn't think what he'd need it for; their parents had paid for the wedding. 'The house?'

'No. But . . . it's mortgaged more than you know.'

Vaguely, she was aware of something going on up at the house. Figures on the balcony. She didn't look to see who.

'Just tell me why,' she said, shifting Hari in his sling. She'd move back in with her parents, if they were destitute. 'I need to know what I'm dealing with.'

'Gambling,' he said, surprisingly calm. 'I gamble. Online. Poker mostly.'

Of course. When he said it, it was as if she'd always known. 'And . . . you're not very good at it?'

He looked startled, as if he hadn't considered this. 'Sometimes I am. At the start. I won a lot. But then . . .'

She sighed. Everyone knew that was how gambling worked – how stupid was he, this man she'd married? She'd seen enough films about it. 'How much do you owe?' Was it just him, or was she liable for his debts?

He told her the sum. Aisha swayed on her feet for a moment, thinking – the house, the car, we'll lose it all – then made herself speak. 'First thing tomorrow we'll go to our parents and tell them. Work out what to do.'

'Oh . . . alright.'

'These men, do they know where we live?'

'Yes.'

'Will they come to the house, if you owe them money?'

'It hasn't come to that.'

But it would. She could have been in danger, her and Hari, over a stupid debt, and he'd never have told her. What a stupid cowardly man. 'If you pay them, will they go away?'

'I . . . I mean, probably.'

'So. We'll pay them. That's the first thing to do.' Assuming he could stop running up more debts.

'And then?'

She didn't even know. Could someone be fixed, with a problem like that? But before she could answer, she heard a scream.

Jax – two weeks earlier

It's hard to live permanently in a state of medical emergency. I'd always been so healthy, so strong, that it was difficult to believe the doctor when he said I had to lie flat on my back for at least twenty-three hours a day, or else I'd haemorrhage. Apart from the first short, shocking bleed, I felt fine. Or not fine – bored out of my mind. Lonely, sad, scared. But not sick. Would it really matter if I got up, did a few things? Perhaps it was my mother's recent visit, reminding me that I was slacking. She'd rearranged all the cupboards, decanting the cereals and pulses into Tupperware and throwing away the boxes (she didn't believe in recycling), and cleaned out each of the shelves and lined them with greaseproof cloth she bought from Lakeland. I would never be able to find anything, and Mum did not approve of the contents of my cupboards: 'Whose is this sugary cereal? Not for the baby, I hope?'

So I had to explain that no, the cereal with the cartoon bird on the front belonged to my child's father. Had belonged? Aaron was gone, that was for sure. He was diligent about checking in, visiting every day after work, but wouldn't discuss when he was coming back. I was alone, and days off giving birth. I hadn't told Mum he was actually gone and luckily she hadn't noticed his things weren't there. Probably because she preferred not to think about him at all if possible.

Whatever it was anyway, something compelled me to get up from the sofa that day, and finally go outside, turn my face up to the sky. I felt like a cave dweller at the end of winter, cramped and stale and pale. Outside was a cool but beautiful day, a slight haze of light over South London. Daringly bipedal, I opened the patio doors and stepped into the small garden I'd once nurtured so proudly, with visions of growing tomatoes and cucumbers, pressing them on friends when they came to visit. *I grow them myself you know. Such a glut this year!* As it was, I had a few straggly herb bushes and some wild rambling roses, plus a bird feeder. I'd noticed there weren't so many fluttering round my window of late, keeping me awake at 4 a.m., and I wanted to see why. As I shuffled across the patio in my slippers, I did. The wire feeder had been wrenched apart, the nuts I'd put into it two weeks ago scattered over the ground, no doubt by predatory squirrels. I'd had the feeder since I was twelve – my dad had made it for me in his shed not long before he died – and now it was ruined. I stooped to pick it up from the ground, then realised I couldn't. Worse – as I bent I saw a dead bird under the feeder, its feet curled up and black eyes dull. What would have done this – a cat? Minou was so good about not killing things; perhaps in her absence something else had colonised the space. Or a fox again? They couldn't climb though, could they? I would have liked to bury the poor thing, but I couldn't bend and anyway it probably wasn't a good idea to touch a dead bird. I'd have to ask Aaron, if he ever came round again. I'd have to sort that out too, somehow, persuade him to come home – we couldn't go into labour not getting on. I had to make him see how crazy this was. I sighed, thinking how this time dragged, this waiting, having to follow my body's timetable and not that of work, social life, London.

Then I straightened up and something pinged inside me and a cramp rolled through me and I must have cried out in the empty garden, because Mrs Johnson next door heard me and called the ambulance, otherwise I don't know what would have happened to me, but I tilted slightly and was aware that something had loosened and broken, and that there was red on the patio tiles, that I was bleeding. I don't remember anything after that.

Alison

They said that, after a while, you stopped noticing the smell of your own house. Alison, who was her mother's daughter, did not like the sound of that. What if it stank and she'd just stopped noticing? What she had noticed over the years, however, was that the homes of dead people had a certain smell. Unloved, empty. Stale, no matter how clean. She'd been in plenty that were horrific, hoarders dying under piles of rotting newspaper, or old people who'd stopped being able to clean their home or themselves, and simply sat down to die, sometimes not found for weeks. Suicide victims. Nasty murders.

Nina da Souza's flat wasn't like that. It just smelled empty, unloved somehow, after almost a week unoccupied, since the resident had gone out one Saturday afternoon and not come back. Dust and stale air. 'This all her stuff?' said Diana, standing in the middle of the near-empty living room in her blue gloves. 'It's been cleaned out?'

'Don't think so. She must have just been minimalist.' Alison's mother had briefly got into Marie Kondo, and given away the accumulated family junk of two decades, only to buy it all back again when she came to her senses. Alison still had some boxes crammed into cupboards in her flat.

'Even so, this is extreme.' Diana was right – the place barely looked lived in. There were no pictures on the neutral cream walls, no ornaments or books or CDs on the shelving unit, a basic one from Ikea. A television on another basic unit, some clothes in the wardrobe, toiletries in the bathroom. That was it. 'How long had she been here?'

'Landlord said not long, a few months. He didn't know where she was before that – he seems the kind who wouldn't bother checking the references too closely.' Alison had got the impression Nina was paying over the odds for this place, little bigger than a studio in a shifty part of town. All the same, it was spotless. Some dust had settled on the TV in the days since its owner had been dead. She wanted to wipe it away, a gesture from one obsessive cleaner to another.

Diana was in the kitchen, opening the fridge, which let out a sour smell. Nina had been expecting to return, of course. No one expected to fall over the balcony of a show home and on to a rockery. It was a ridiculous way to die that happened all too often, a momentary slip, a foolish act of bravado. Lads on Spanish balconies was the common occurrence, or teenagers at cliffs, the shared element in all those cases being drink and/or drugs. But Nina hadn't touched a drop of alcohol at the party, the toxicology report proved that. She had eaten only a small quantity of salad leaves that day, which explained how she could be so slim and toned at the age of thirty-eight. They only knew her exact age because she'd given the landlord her date of birth (assuming it was real). That reminded Alison of something. 'Did you get the impression they all thought she was younger than she was?'

'Maybe.' Diana's voice echoed vaguely from the cupboard she was looking in. 'Why?'

'Dunno. Maybe she was lying about her age, or she wanted to seem younger for some particular reason.'

'Hardly unusual.'

Alison had never lied about her age, except to seem older when underage drinking, and felt it was a point of pride. But as it approached – forty – she wondered would she change her mind about that, as she quietly had about Botox; not that she'd had any yet, too expensive. In a sexist, ageist world, was it wrong to give yourself a leg-up? Oh God, she sounded like Carrie Bradshaw. 'Anything in there?' A door shut.

'Rabbit food and beans, essentially.'

'The pathologist said he'd never seen anyone with better muscle tone or less fat.'

Alison wondered what they'd find on her if she died. An empty, scarred womb. Visceral fat around her belly and thighs. The ill-advised tattoo she'd been hiding from her mother since she was eighteen. Bodies said so much, and yet all Nina's had told them was she was older than she'd seemed, and that she'd once given birth. She wondered about that. Where was the child? If they were grown up, wouldn't they have seen their mother's death on the news, come forward? 'No one knew anything about a kid?'

'No, but she might not have told them. Boundaries or whatever.'

'Mm. Is there really nothing else here?' Alison turned in a circle, looking round the small flat.

'Nothing. Here's another thing – there's no ID anywhere. No passport, no driving licence. No birth cert.'

That wasn't as unusual as you'd think in a country with no ID-card requirement, but surely someone like Nina, who everyone described as urbane and knowledgeable, would have at least had a passport. 'Nothing at all? Library card, Blockbuster Video?'

'What's that? Just kidding. No, she had no wallet on her that day, and her bag only had keys for this place and some bits of make-up, Monica's address on a piece of paper. Just an old burner-type phone, unregistered as you know.' It was so strange. Nowadays you had to actually work quite hard to be so off-grid. Question was, why would she?

Alison and Diana looked around the tiny space. The bedroom only had space for the wardrobe, bed, and a nightstand. The drawers of that lay open, empty. No laptop. No iPad, not so much as an MP3 player. 'Internet cafe?' Alison tried.

'What was she, living in the nineties?'

'Maybe she's one of those hippy off-gridders.'

'But still. Try doing anything now without a smartphone or computer. And how did she get a job, if she had no ID? Thought everyone had to show passports now in this dystopian nightmare we call home.'

'She was freelance.' Alison ran her eyes around the room, searching for something, any clue to this woman's life.

'Still. DBS checks, that sort of thing? This baby group can't have been her only income?'

Alison had no answer to that. She had never known so little about a victim.

They stood in the empty flat, dust motes hanging in the air, the fridge full of food that was spoiling, the woman who had bought it never coming back to this small and impersonal space without so much as a cushion. It felt like a furnished apartment, albeit a nasty one. Like the places they put care-leavers or recent offenders.

Diana sighed, batting at an open door. 'I mean, I don't have a lot of stuff, but this – this is pathological, isn't it? She'd no family, no friends even that we could find. The group are the only people we've found who even knew her. Someone with as few ties as possible, like she could leave in the middle of the night.'

Or like someone with things to hide.

'We should try the neighbours. There's nothing here.'

But Alison couldn't leave it. She knew she'd have to face Colette otherwise, with her total lack of evidence. 'One more search. Look behind everything, under the furniture.' And sure enough, she had her gloved hands underneath the fridge when she heard a yelp from the bedroom.

'I found something!' Diana sounded excited, so it must be big. 'Hidden down the back of a drawer. Between it and the frame.'

Alison's heart did a victory lap as she got to her feet. 'Oh?'

'Come see.'

They met in the living room. Diana was holding out a photograph, slightly dog-eared. Alison peered at it. 'A baby?'

'I reckon it's a picture from the nineties, based on the photo stock. Got a sticker from a chemist on the back.'

She scrutinised it. It showed a young woman, in her teens perhaps, dressed in leggings and DM boots (classic nineties look, enjoying a revival right about now). She was smiling, pressing a baby close to her face. A little boy from the clothes he wore, just a few months old. 'Is that her? In her teens?' She peered at it, but she'd never seen Nina alive. It could be her. This could be her child.

'I think so, yeah.'

'So she did have a baby, and had him young. He'd be grown-up now, I suppose.' Alison flipped the photo over, noticing the sticker from the developing lab. A local one, by the looks of it. Maybe they'd still have records.

◆ ◆ ◆

As Alison knocked on the door downstairs, it opened a crack, and a pair of owlish glasses peered out. 'You the police?' said a woman's voice, harsh and complaining.

'Yes. Are you . . .' Alison checked her notebook. 'Ms Conway?' The downstairs neighbour.

'*Mrs* Conway, please,' she sniffed. Alison heard a mewing sound, and a cat emerged, winding round her legs. A pretty one, with grey striped fur and little white socks. Mrs Conway – Celia, Alison knew from her notes – picked the cat up and let it twine round her neck like a stole. 'Oh Bootsy, who's a bad girl, you aren't allowed out!'

'Nice cat,' said Alison, who didn't really trust them.

'She came to me just last week. Mewling around the door upstairs, she was, starving, poor thing.'

Alison's ears pricked up. 'You mean she might belong to the lady upstairs – Ms da Souza?'

'If that's what she calls herself. I don't think she'd even had a cat before – never saw her bring back cat litter, or proper food! No wonder she came to me. That's right, that's right, baby.' The cat was now licking the woman's face, while fixing Alison with an evil green gaze.

Alison was trying to think. There'd been no trace of a cat upstairs, no tell-tale hairs or smell of unchanged litter tray.

'She even locked her in the shed outside half the day, poor baby.' With no trace of irony, the woman said, 'I think they should bring back hanging for people who hurt animals.'

'You know she's dead, your neighbour?'

If she was expecting an expression of sympathy, none came. 'Oh well, got what she deserved, didn't she?' The woman tickled Bootsy under the chin.

'How long had she been upstairs?'

'Three months or so. Not that she was there much – out at all hours, she was, very strange.'

'And did she have any visitors during that time?'

A pained sigh at having to help them. 'Just that boy, the odd time.'

Alison's radar went off. 'Who was that?'

'How should I know? Some lad, twenty-something, I think he was *mixed*, you know. Tall. In a suit, so he wasn't doing DIY or anything like that.'

Interesting. A young mixed-race man had been at Nina's flat. 'How many times was he here?'

'Maybe three or four, I reckon. I did wonder what they were up to up there.' She raised her tufty eyebrows significantly.

'Thank you, Mrs Conway, you've been *very* helpful.' As the door closed, trapping off another mewl from the cat, Alison did wonder if they ever got her sarcasm at moments like this. Most likely not, but it was the only weapon she had.

She went to join Diana, who was by the car, on her phone. 'Any luck?'

'Nobody home in 3b or 3a. You?'

She told her about Celia, an archetypal cat lady if ever there was one. Diana frowned. 'Aaron Cole?'

'Sounds like him, doesn't it? Why did he not mention it when we interviewed him?'

'You would, wouldn't you, if you'd been round to a dead person's flat. In case there's DNA or whatever.'

'A sensible person would.' A person with nothing to hide. Finally, some leads. As they drove off she tried to work out what had bothered her so much about that cat, but couldn't grasp it.

Jax – two weeks earlier

If I'd thought being on home bed-rest was bad, hospital was a hundred times worse. There was rest in the physical sense that I couldn't leave my bed, this time not even to go to the loo by myself, but it was impossible to sleep with the shouting and running feet and bright lights and the other women on their phones all night long. It was a ward of misery, and we swapped tales in the pockets of time when the nurses and doctors weren't moving around us, handling our bodies like machinery they operated. Burst ovarian cysts. Miscarriage. And me – placental abruption. I couldn't quite find out what was wrong with me. I wasn't in labour, not yet, but the longer the placenta wasn't functioning the more danger to the baby. Doctors and nurses came and went, and I told them the same things each time. No, I didn't smoke. Yes, this was my first baby. Yes, I was a first-time mother, yes, I was thirty-eight years old. I don't know why they make you repeat these details so often in hospital, to everyone who comes to see you. Perhaps because it's so easy to lose yourself, your clothes taken away and replaced by soft, well-washed rags, your bag God knows where. Your identity softened by drugs, your free will gone, handed up to the people who wheel you here and there and take your pulse and put needles in you.

Aaron arrived what seemed like hours later – I couldn't see a window so I didn't know what time of day it was. He looked very young, like a teenager on work experience. His tie was off and rolled up in his pocket; he smelled of sweat and Lynx. I had to buy him some decent aftershave. But was that even my role now? Where did we stand with each other? 'I'm sorry. I've been waiting for ages to see you, no one would tell me what was going on.'

I rested my arms on my bump, as if I could keep the baby inside that way. 'Well, I ruptured.'

'Are you OK?'

'Dunno. I think they're trying to work it out.' I looked him over, as if I hadn't seen him in weeks. A young man, with a boy's thinness and sharp, edgy movements. Cheap shirt and tie. How could this be the father of my child? I suddenly imagined the worst, if I lost the baby after all this. Would he leave me for good? I didn't know how we could pick up from where we were now. Suddenly, it was too much, the thought of him hovering over me, only to leave if the worst happened. The baby was the only thing tying him to me now. He'd made that clear by walking out. 'You should go home,' I said, making my voice cold.

His face fell. 'What? Do you not . . . ?'

'I'm alright. There's nothing you can do for me right now. They'll call you if anything happens, I'm sure.'

'But you'll need stuff, won't you?' He hadn't thought to bring anything. Would someone older have known I needed nightclothes, toiletries?

'Mum's getting me things.' I was prepared for frilly nightgowns that did right up to the neck.

'Alright.' He looked miserable. 'You really just want me to go?'

'No sense in both of us being here.' I was being cruel, but I was just so tired. I didn't have it in me to care for myself and the baby and him as well.

Aaron lingered a while longer, his cheap clothes rustling, and then he turned and went away.

◆ ◆ ◆

I had no sense of time in there. People came, introduced themselves as the nurse or the nurse practitioner or the surgeon or the anaesthetist. A variety of accents and coloured scrubs. Someone started coughing in a curtained bed opposite and didn't stop, and there was a vague flurry of rushing feet and a woman was wheeled away. I found I couldn't care much. The clock on the wall ticked around and still I lay there. My mother came, bringing home-decoration magazines and some huge pyjamas. She didn't ask where Aaron was, and I didn't tell her. I had not been allowed to eat or drink in case I needed surgery, but when the clock said eight, someone came and told me it wouldn't be today. They offered me what they said was food and I opted for plain toast and tea and it tasted amazing after a day of fasting. The women on the ward were nearly all pregnant too, and husbands came and went, and other children too, and sometimes you could see other women, the not-pregnant ones, flinch at the sound of the high voices and pattering feet, and I could only guess at why, what horrors they'd been told were happening inside them. My baby was apparently still alive. The heart monitors showed it was clinging on, although as the placenta died it would begin to struggle. I waited. Eventually, though the lights were never turned off, I must have slept.

◆ ◆ ◆

Someone was there. I woke with a start sometime in the night and found I couldn't move. My arms and legs were weighed down and my eyes seemed too heavy to lift. A dark figure stood over me and I couldn't see. I tried to cry out – help. Nothing came out. The figure reached out their hands and put them on my belly, and I tried to wriggle away but I couldn't. I was aware how vulnerable I was, the catheter in my hand, the wires and monitors I was linked to. Why was this happening? Had I been given something, or were the blankets too tight? I couldn't seem to figure it out. My eyes closed again, as if of their own accord, and everything was gone.

◆ ◆ ◆

When I woke up it seemed to be morning, judging by the bustle and terrible noise and searing light. I lifted an arm experimentally, and it seemed fine. A nurse was dispensing little packets of corn-flakes and tea from a big metal pot. There was something comforting about it, the simplicity, and I wondered if I could have some. 'Was something wrong with me last night?' I asked. My voice was croaky in my dry throat. 'I woke up and couldn't move.'

She was busy, bustling about. 'Sometimes people have bad dreams in here.'

'I don't think it was a dream.' But maybe it was. I didn't even know what drugs I'd been given; I could easily have been hallucinating, though I felt fine now. 'Was someone standing over me? Touching me?'

'Night nurse doing the rounds, most likely.'

But it didn't feel like that. Would a nurse not have spoken to me? Would I have felt such dread? I was so vulnerable here, where anyone could walk in and get to me. But I didn't know how to explain this without sounding paranoid.

Alison

'Look at these houses. Mansions! Where do they get the money?'

'Banking. Law.' Jobs that a lot of people in the police could do as well, since they were certainly smart enough, but which paid up to a hundred times what Alison earned in a year. She felt her socialist hackles rising as they drove through the small town of Wilmer's Wood, in Buckinghamshire. On the high street was a Boden, a Waitrose, a branch of De Beers. Not a fried-chicken shop in sight. The chemist that had developed the photo was still there, unbelievably, and had been easily able to identify the family in it: 'Very good customers over the years'. Finally, they were getting somewhere, and not a moment too soon: she'd have to report back to Colette by the end of the day.

'Is this it?' She was driving up to a large house surrounded by high brick walls, the gateposts topped by crouching lions. 'What number is it?'

Diana consulted her phone. 'No number. It's called "The Ridings". What the hell?'

'It's another world here, comrade. Press the button there.'

She pulled into the driveway and Diana leaned out into the light drizzle and buzzed it. After a few moments the gates swung back without a sound and let them in. The car crunched on the gravel as she pulled up beside a Mazda and a BMW. The front door was open, and a woman of about seventy stood there holding a small dog with big ears. A chihuahua? It was panting hard, staring at her with beady eyes. The woman was wearing cream slacks and a cream jumper and a lot of jewellery. 'Are you the police? I expected you some time ago.'

'Traffic,' said Diana as they clattered into the marble entryway.

'Shoes please,' said the woman – Elaine Bracknell – and they obliged, throwing small glances at each other. They'd bitch about this on the way home, Alison knew, and looked forward to it. It wasn't a nice house, despite its opulence. Chilly marble floors and cream carpets, stiff-looking sofa, lots of ugly vases with huge twig-like arrangements in them. The air felt cold. 'I imagine you'd like a coffee or something.'

Just to be annoying, Alison gave a complicated order involving one and a half sugars and non-dairy milk, which was of course available. Diana asked for water. When they were sitting down in the cream wasteland of the lounge, Alison regretted having such a potentially staining drink. She set it down carefully on a coaster on the side table (also cream). Elaine and the dog were opposite. Her hands were bony, weighed down by rings. 'So. This is about Georgina, is it?'

'She was going by Nina, we believe.'

'Her name is Georgina. Was.'

'We're very sorry for your loss,' said Diana, though not as sympathetically as she might have. 'When did you last see your daughter?'

'Not for twenty years. She was very wild you see. Even then. I believe she was overseas, up to all manner of things. It's very difficult, but that's how it was.' Mrs Bracknell, formerly Mrs Partington-Smith – mother of Nina da Souza, as she was calling herself – seemed more upset at her daughter's behaviour than the fact that she was dead, pushed from a balcony.

'Do you know where the da Souza came from, by any chance? Is it just made up?'

'Some marriage I assume. She was in Brazil for a time. That sounds Brazilian.' Her mouth twisted.

'And were there any children that you know of? That is, any other children?'

Further twisting. 'I wouldn't know.'

'And the boy – can you tell us more about him?'

'If I must.' She set down her own cup of coffee with a sharp ting and a sigh. 'We called him Edward at first, after Georgina's grandfather. Of course, it wasn't ideal, a pregnancy at fourteen – but at first we thought we could manage. David – my late husband – he was keen on the idea of a grandson. Take over the family business and so on.'

Because a girl couldn't do that. Alison clenched her fists by her side, tried to nod politely. 'But it didn't work out?'

She hesitated. 'You have to understand we tried. Georgina simply would not tell us who the boy's father was, no matter what we did. At first, we couldn't see it, it wasn't obvious. But as he grew up, and his hair came in – well, he just looked darker and darker, and we couldn't take that. We felt it would be better for the boy to be with people like him.'

'What do you mean?' said Diana coolly, though she must have known very well.

'Well, isn't it obvious? The father was *black*. Goodness knows how she even met a boy like that round here – wild, as I said. Adoption seemed kindest.'

'I see. So your grandson was taken into care at what age?'

Her hands twisted on the dog, who yelped slightly. 'I believe he was two. Almost three.'

Old enough to know his mother, to remember a little of the life he'd had. 'And Georgina?'

'Oh, she wanted to keep him. Ridiculous. She had no money, wasn't even eighteen. She threatened to run away with him, but we just made sure she was gone the day they came. She made quite a fuss when she found out, but it was in everyone's best interests.'

A stunned silence from Diana and Alison. Alison forced herself to keep her voice neutral. 'So – Georgina has a son out there somewhere? He'd be in his twenties now?'

'I suppose so. I try not to think of it – I have real grandchildren now, my son and his wife.' She indicated a huge framed picture of a smiling white couple and angelic, white children.

'Right. Is there anything else you can tell us, anything that might help us find out who killed Nina?'

'*Georgina*. I honestly have no idea what her life was. She chose it, instead of the one we gave her, private school and a pony and everything she asked for. What kind of person turns their back on all that?'

'And the boy's father, he never surfaced?'

'Never. I have no idea who he was and don't wish to think about it.'

There seemed nothing more to say. Alison had not drunk her coffee, which she suddenly couldn't stomach. This period they were discussing had been in the nineties, 1995 to be exact, not the fifties or sixties. This family had brought up a grandson, loved him presumably as much as they knew how to for two years, then abandoned him to care as soon as he started looking a bit too black. Taken him from his mother, who had wanted to keep him. No wonder she'd run wild. Poor Nina – Georgina. She stood, as did Diana. 'One more thing. Would Nina have been trying to find him, do you think? Her son? Edward?'

'I doubt he's still called that,' Elaine said. 'We asked them to change his name. A clean break. But yes, I imagine she wanted to find him.'

Diana was frowning. 'One thing I don't understand – if she wanted him, given the preference of the system for the birth mother, why would she not have got him once she was eighteen? Assuming he wasn't adopted already.'

Another sigh. 'Oh, because she wasn't well. That's where she was when they came for him. She was sectioned – we just wanted to help her, really. She needed to learn that we had her best interests at heart.'

The day of – Chloe

2.59 p.m.

Her mother was the worst. The worst of the worst. She'd been ignoring Isabella all day, leaving her alone in the room, then dressing her up in that horrible frilly pink horror to parade her about these strangers. Who even were they? Why did it matter what they thought? Chloe knew her mother wanted her to stay in her room as well, as helpless as the baby, but after an hour or so listening to the party downstairs, she snapped. She picked Isabella out of her cot and took her downstairs. She loved the feel of the solid, hot little body in her arms. The way the baby's eyes, barely open yet, took everything in. The people actually weren't so bad, kind of nice really. There was a woman in a pretty headscarf, and a young good-looking guy who had a baby with an older woman. There was a woman who didn't have a baby at all but had been at the group, and her baby was supposed to come from America or something but hadn't. There were two gay women even – this was the most interesting group of people the house had ever seen. Much better than Ed's gammon-faced golf buddies and their screechy wives, rattling with jewellery.

Chloe liked carrying the baby. She liked how people smiled at her, how natural it was. Isabella was a good baby, and hardly ever cried, which was lucky because Monica certainly didn't have the time or patience for a difficult one. She wondered how it was all going to work as Isabella got older, when Chloe left school and maybe went to university. Could she abandon the little girl here with Monica and Ed? In the garden, she imagined opening the door and walking down the street, far away. Monica wouldn't even notice for a while, she was too busy wanging on about salad. But what would she live on? Maybe if she could find Sam, they could live there. He'd made his parents sound so nice. But she'd never been to his house and didn't know the address, and Monica had taken her phone away so she was basically a prisoner in this shiny glass palace.

She missed Sam. The shy way he smiled at her in debate club. The way he took off his glasses and rubbed his eyes, the red marks on his nose. Monica tolerated her being at the party for a while – probably because it would look weird if she stayed upstairs – but after that thing happened with the baby and the weird red-eyed woman, who'd lost her own baby or something, Monica's patience had run out. She was mad at Ed for something, so of course she took it out on Chloe. 'What are you doing down here with the baby?' she hissed, as soon as no one was in the kitchen. 'You know the rules. I don't want you around her too much, people will talk.'

'So what if they do? It's hardly the end of the world.'

Monica's eyes bulged. 'This is the only way! You agreed to it, and I've held up my end of the bargain. Just behave yourself for three years and you can be out of this house, we'll give you an allowance and you can live your life. That's what we agreed. Isn't it?'

God, why did money have to be such a powerful thing? Chloe had always had it growing up and knew she couldn't find a job and live in a bedsit all by herself. Or even not by herself, as she some-times dreamed of. 'Yeah.'

'Right. So go upstairs before someone puts two and two together. Take her and put her down.'

Her. Not Isabella. There seemed to be no love between Monica and the baby, just as little as there was between her and Chloe. It wasn't fair, Chloe thought, to put another person through that. But she went upstairs all the same, thinking she'd bring the baby into her own room. Monica wouldn't find out.

As she went up, she saw people on the balcony. A few different people. Talking. Arguing, actually. She could hear the raised voices through the glass, but not the words. She should take the baby away, keep her safe. But something sent Chloe forward, towards the door.

Jax – two weeks earlier

In the middle of the night I broke in two. That was how it felt, anyway. Ripples of fire rolled down my middle, and I was sure I was going to die soon, which was something of a relief, if it would make the pain stop. I tried to call a nurse and found I didn't have a bell; I also couldn't seem to speak. 'Urgggh. Urrgh!'

I had disturbed the woman in the bed next to me. 'What's up with you?'

'Urrrggggh.' I flailed around some more.

'Oi!' She was able to shout, anyway. 'There's something not right with this one.' A bored nurse sauntered over.

'What's the matter?'

I tried again. 'Urggggh.'

'Come on, let's sort you out then.'

I still couldn't speak. Perhaps I had in fact had a stroke, on top of labour. As they wheeled me away, I was thinking of Aaron. How we hadn't chosen the name for the baby. How we hadn't made up yet, and I hadn't told him that none of it was his fault, despite what I'd said. It was mine.

The day of – Jax

I knew that, after this terrible day was over, I would add the events of it to the file of things in my head that I didn't want to think about. Not just Mark. Not just the fact that Aaron and I were still living apart, and we'd come to this party to pretend everything was fine. The endless seconds when Hadley was gone, and I knew it was my fault. Kelly's broken-hearted crying, knowing we'd accused her of child abduction when she'd just taken the baby into the park because no one was looking after her. This was true. Aaron had assumed I was watching her and had felt unable to refuse Ed's invitation to his shed. I had been in a kind of daze. Perhaps Kelly had done me a favour, showing me how bad things were with me. Not long after that, Jeremy had driven Kelly home, still weeping and barely able to walk, collapsed in grief.

As soon as we were alone, Aaron and I turned to each other, in that moment bleak-eyed strangers. 'How did this happen?' I was trying hard not to blame him. I knew it was more my fault than his, but admitting that meant admitting things I had long feared about myself but had been unable to face. 'Where did you go?'

Aaron's arms were locked tight in shock. 'Ed made us – he wanted to show us stuff in his shed.'

'What stuff?' I had been sure I would never feel Hadley in my arms again, and now I had her, light and squashy and radiating heat, I wanted to cry. Without me she would die in days, and I wasn't sure I was up to the task of looking after her. I had taken on too much, that's all there was to it.

Aaron looked around furtively. 'It was . . . He called it erotic art, all this Japanese stuff and that, but Jax, it was porn. He showed us porn.'

I was standing in the middle of a sunny lawn, inside a fenced garden, and I had my baby back in my arms and my partner at my side. I should have felt safe, relieved. Instead I felt a cold trickle down my back, the bad feeling from that morning back again, despite having experienced and averted one near-disaster already that day.

Then Monica came out of the house, clapped her hands like a teacher rounding up pupils. 'Alright, everyone, it's time to do the group photo, before anything else goes wrong! I want all the babies in a circle on the rug, please. Heads in.' She was brandishing her iPhone. The last thing I wanted was to put Hadley in a photo, to have a reminder of this day, or even to let my daughter out of my arms. Aaron seemed to pick up on this.

'Monica, I don't know if we really want . . . We didn't want her in pictures yet.'

'I agree,' said Hazel, who still held barbecue tongs. 'We want Arthur to live a screen-free life until he's at least two.'

Monica gave a merry laugh. 'Well, he doesn't have to *look* at it, Hazel, just be in it! Come on. Who knows when they'll all be together again. It'll be such a lovely memory. Ed, fix the rug.' Already she was managing the scene, pointing where to straighten the mat and directing him to pick some flowers and lay them out between the babies, pouncing on a cute stuffed dog that was Arthur's to add to the general adorableness. 'Where's Isabella?'

Chloe appeared in the doorway, holding the child, who before this had apparently been asleep for much of the day, missing the drama. She was awake now, her eyes half open, but appeared floppy and placid, in a pink dress that must have been terribly impractical to get on and off.

I sighed. I didn't have the energy to fight this. 'Fine. Put her down.' And I handed Hadley to Aaron to carry forward and lay down. Aisha brought Hari over, and Cathy did the same with Arthur, after a defiant glance at Hazel. Immediately he began to cry, his feet up in the air. Isabella lay there, a little doll. Hari clenched and unclenched his fists, as if he might be filling his nappy. Hadley gave a small moan of distress. 'Ready?' Monica raised her phone. The picture was taken. It was 2.35 p.m.

Jax – two weeks earlier

I wasn't dead. I was somehow awake, and I had a baby. A daughter. She lay on my chest, pink and squirming, like the naked mole rats they had at London Zoo. The past few hours – thirty hours, it seemed, a whole day of my life swallowed up by anaesthetic, C-section, and the sheer time-warping properties of a medical emergency – was a blur to me. The contours of my body seemed changed – the bump gone, packing gauze in odd places. But I appeared to be alive.

Aaron was sitting beside me. 'Have you been here the whole time?' I had no memory of him arriving and yet it was a different day, like an especially hellish kind of jet lag.

'Most of it, yeah.'

'I don't remember anything.' I vaguely recalled being told I'd had a Caesarean. I bet Monica would have her baby naturally, with an intact perineum too. In some distant corner of my mind I cared about that, but it was so far away, a different galaxy.

Aaron was pale, like a boy soldier back from the trenches. 'Probably for the best.' I wondered if he'd ever find me sexy again, and reflected that maybe the old-fashioned way was best, whisky and cigars in the waiting room. 'Is she alright?' He nodded to the baby. His daughter.

'I think so.' She looked fine, if alien. She had been inside me, and yet I didn't recognise her at all. I was so tired that if she slipped from my arms and to the ground, I wasn't sure I could bend to pick her up, like I'd once read happened to sloths in the jungle. 'You can hold her, you know.'

Had he been waiting for permission? I passed her over and he held her, looking stunned. 'What's going to happen now?'

'I don't know.' My mother would arrive at some point; I was surprised she wasn't here already. The last few weeks had been a nightmare, reliving everything with Mark and Claudia, convinced someone was stalking me as I silently gestated, flat on my back. Now I had to return to my life and try to live it, raise this baby, fix my relationship if that was even possible, sort my job out, clear my name. It was too much. Part of me wanted to ask for more anaesthetic, and just go to sleep for a week.

The day of – Anita

3.01 p.m.

Jeremy came back from dropping Kelly off about twenty minutes later. She had been counting them down, hovering at the edge of the house, feeling uneasy, while everyone else settled back into gales of relieved laughter and nervous smiles. They had taken a picture of the babies, and of course Anita had none to place in the circle. Disaster had been averted. Nothing bad had happened after all, in this suburban garden on a sunny day. Kelly had not stolen the baby. She saw Ed open another bottle of wine, slosh it into glasses, spilling some on the table. But Anita could not smile or laugh or feel relieved. Because what they thought Kelly had done, picked up an unattended child and spirited her away, hadn't that very thing crossed Anita's mind? She had seen Hadley alone, and worried that she was too hot in the sun. She'd seen a bee crawling on the nearby bush and worried she'd get stung. She'd thought about picking her up, taking her out of danger, and then the thought had progressed. Walking out to the car, taking her home. Holding her on her knee in the nursing chair she'd already bought, not that she would be able to feed Victoria when she came. Kissing the silky-soft top of her head, stroking her tiny fingers and the soft pads of her feet, never walked on yet. She'd understood that impulse and it scared her. She wasn't that woman, the one people were afraid of, desperate for a baby, snatching one from a pram outside a shop. She'd never been desperate – if she had, she wouldn't have waited until thirty-six before even trying. It was simply a madness that had taken over her, the disappointment that came from outside yourself, the smugness of mothers, the clinical way you were herded through the IVF system. A sunk-cost fallacy – we've come this far, we may as well carry on.

Jeremy pulled in at the kerb, and she went to meet him. She saw him take out his phone, and frown at it. He removed his glasses and rubbed his eyes. She thought how tired he looked. She went over.

'Is Kelly alright?'

'I don't know. I asked if I should ring her mother, but she said no.' He was still looking at his phone, frowning.

'News?' she said lightly.

He hesitated. 'I've had an email from Madeleine.' The adoption lawyer.

'Oh?'

'Darling, I . . .'

'She's not coming, is she? Victoria.' It was as if she'd always known it. Strange, how strongly you could picture it, play out scenes in your mind as if they had already happened, and then in a single moment it was all gone. She would never meet that baby from Alabama, if there even was a baby.

'I'm sorry.' Jeremy looked wretched. All that time and money and heartache. 'The mother's gone AWOL. They think she wants to keep the child after all – apparently, she'd been dropping hints about it. They'll try to track her down, but . . . Madeleine thinks we could sue the agency for our costs, at least.'

She found she didn't much care about that. She had brought home almost one million pounds that year. So much money and nothing she really wanted that could be bought. 'So . . . what can we do? If they don't find her?'

'Legally, there's not much to be done, even if we track her down. She still has parental rights. And the cost of a civil case, well . . .'

She took his hand. 'Let's just go home, Jeremy. I don't know why we came here, put ourselves through this.' She had taken a whole antenatal class and had no baby to show for it. She was childless in a house full of babies. Her and poor Kelly. 'It's OK.' Anita felt the small, soothing feeling of giving up. She would not throw herself any more at this barbed-wire fence. 'She was never really ours, you know.'

'I'm so sorry. You wanted this so much.'

'I think I just . . . went a little mad. I did want a baby. But not instead of everything else. Not instead of my life.'

'I just want you to be happy,' he said shyly. 'It's all I ever wanted.'

'I know that. And I will be.' She knew it was true. Perhaps not today, perhaps not for a long time – already she was dreading going home, and looking into the nursery with the beautiful Victorian nursing chair and the frieze of bunnies on the wall, and having to dismantle it – but one day, yes. One day, she would feel happy again.

They turned back towards the house, and so they were perfectly positioned to see what took place on the balcony. It was Jeremy who made the first phone call to the police, at 3.04 p.m.

Jax – one week earlier

The problem with holidays from your life is that your life is still waiting when you get back. After a day I was booted from hospital and sent home to care for the baby they'd saved for me. We had to get a taxi, and I knew Aaron was worried about the cost.

'What's her name, then?' Aaron had asked me again that morning, as I packed up to leave.

'I don't know. What do you like?'

'I don't know. Don't you want to pick it?'

'You're her father. Do you want maybe Georgina?'

He actually flinched. 'I don't . . .'

'Or whatever. Fine.'

And we'd travelled home in silence, the baby squalling in the car seat Aaron had brought for her, the harsh outside air touching her new-minted skin for the first time, so perfect it was an invitation for the world to put its mark on her. When we turned into the street, I thought: fuck it. I gave birth to her, I'll choose her name. 'I want to call her Hadley.'

Aaron jolted out of his gloom. 'Is that a name?'

'Of course it is. Hemingway's first wife was called Hadley.'

His eyes flicked nervously.

'Ernest Hemingway.' Jesus, had I had a baby with someone who didn't know who Hemingway was?

'I know, yeah. Why that name though?'

'I just always thought it was cool.' A Hadley was a smart girl, a posh girl, someone brilliant and confident who the world would not screw over. I decided she needed all the help she could get, with parents like us.

The driver pulled over at the house, and I might have asked Aaron in, might have suggested we start our lives as parents together, put the past behind us, try to heal the wounds, but my mother was standing on the doorstep, holding an enormous pink stuffed rabbit wearing a frilly pink tutu. 'Oh God.'

Aaron cleared his throat. 'I'll get out here. I'll take the bus to the flat.'

'But . . .' Mum had seen him, how would I explain why Aaron was leaving? 'What will I tell her?'

'The truth, I guess.'

I didn't want to ask him what that was.

Alison

Getting a rush DNA result was such a pain in the arse, endless forms to fill in, budget items to shuffle, death stares from Colette. 'You really think this is worth doing?'

'Yes. If I'm right about who Nina was, and I can tie up one or two loose ends, I'm ready to make an arrest.'

'For?'

'Murder.' Not that she entirely had the proof for that yet. If she was right about the DNA, that would be a start.

Colette sighed, weighing it up. Alison looked round at the artwork on her walls, stick figures drawn by her children when they were small. They were now at Oxford and medical school, so they clearly hadn't suffered too much from their mother working all hours. 'Fine,' Colette said eventually. 'Send it off, and tie up whatever loose ends you mentioned. I don't want loose. I want tighter than a nun's chuff, understand? And if this is an accident after all – well, you and me will be having some words.'

◆ ◆ ◆

Later, as they waited for what seemed like hours, Diana sighed and leaned forward on the conference-room table, her dark hair slipping over her shoulder. 'This case. Are we mad to dig into it so much? Maybe she did just fall, like.'

'She didn't.' The temptation to close it was strong. An accident. Not a murder. File it away and move on. But Alison couldn't stop picking at the mystery all the same. Why was everyone in this group hiding something? There was Monica and her daughter. They'd spoken to Sam Morris, a short, sweet-faced boy of fifteen, who'd confirmed that he and Chloe were, 'kind of like, yeah, boyfriend and girlfriend', but that she hadn't so much as texted him since she went off sick, and he hadn't been allowed to see her either. He seemed sad about this.

There was Rahul, with his dodgy past, who clearly had gambling problems. There was Cathy and Hazel, some odd tension between them, and Cathy had perhaps lied about where she was during the fall and who had the baby. And the biggest liars of all, Jax Culville and her young partner, who were living apart but hadn't said. Who hadn't mentioned his visits to Nina da Souza's flat. Who had also lied about where they were when Nina died.

More questions. Why had the dead woman been working under an assumed name? Why had she nothing in her flat, apart from a hidden picture? What had happened to her son?

Alison looked at the clock. 'God, they're taking their time.' Just then, her phone beeped. She scanned it quickly, heart quickening. She'd been right. Of course she'd been right. But did he know? That was what she needed to know. 'It's true. And the hair analysis, they've done that too, about bloody time.' She looked up, a huge smile spreading over her face despite herself. *Bloody yes.* 'It's hers. Like we thought.' There it was, forensics, motive, opportunity. Finally, proof that this must have been a murder.

Diana already had her phone out, nodding. 'Are we going to make the arrest?'

'Not yet. First we're going to visit the others. Tie it all up nice and neatly.'

◆ ◆ ◆

Cathy Hargreaves was at home, of course, and there was no sign of Hazel, which was just as Alison had hoped. 'Oh.' The look of guilt that flashed over her face, it was like crack to Alison. They could never hide it, unless they were psychopaths, and you hardly ever came across those. 'Is something wrong?' She had the baby strapped to her again.

'You tell us, Cathy. I'd like to know why you lied about where you were when the fall took place. You were upstairs, weren't you? You must have been, since no one else mentioned seeing you in the garden or downstairs. And you didn't have Arthur, Hazel had him.'

She nodded slowly. 'Alright. But – it's not what you think. Come in.'

When they were sitting at the table, with some more gross herbal tea, she began to talk, pacing up and down by the kettle.

'The baby,' said Cathy, with the air of someone letting go of a huge breath. 'He's not from a donor. I mean, we were going to try it, but I – around the same time I – there was this man we'd met at the clinic, him and his wife, and he and I . . . we started meeting for coffee.' She saw the officers' eyes widen. 'I used to date men too – I mean, I'm not like Hazel is. Anyway, I was such a mess with all the fertility stuff, I called him just to talk, and. And . . . well. Things happened.'

'Arthur is his son?'

'Yes.'

'And he knows?'

'He worked it out, yes. He's been asking to see Arthur. He and his wife, their treatment didn't work.'

'And what, Hazel found out at the barbecue?'

'Yes. Now we're just . . . well, she's deciding what to do. She's wanted this so long, you see – she tried herself with another partner and it didn't work. And she always knew the baby would be from someone else, of course, that's not the issue. It's the cheating.' She glanced up. 'Will I get into trouble for lying?'

'Depends on how much you cooperate. That's everything, Cathy?'

'That's everything.'

'And you saw who was on the balcony when the fall took place?'

'I – yes, I was coming out of the upstairs bathroom just before it happened and I looked out there. It's just opposite.'

'And who was it?'

Cathy had not wanted to say this. 'I'm not totally sure, you know. I didn't see the actual . . . fall.'

'We'd like to know all the same.'

She sighed. 'Nina, obviously. And Aaron, and Jax and the baby. That's who was out there.'

◆ ◆ ◆

'Who's next?' Diana was smiling, riding on the exhilaration of this moment. It was all coming together, a coherent story finally appearing among all the lies.

Alison started the engine. 'Kelly Anderson, she was already home by the time it happened, and Jeremy drove her there. Anita, I think we can write her off too, she says she was outside waiting for him.'

'And Cathy was lying for another reason.'

'Right. Hazel, we'll check up with her, but she was seen going up the stairs after the fall, and that was confirmed by Monica and also Aisha and Rahul, who were with her at the barbecue just before.'

'We're clearing Aisha and Rahul?'

'I think we can with one more chat, yes.'

When she drove up to the house, it was the same. A woman with a baby in her arms – Aisha. Rahul slumped on the sofa with his phone, off shift. She saw the look that went between them. 'Can we have a word?' *I'm here for the truth, finally.*

Aisha nodded. 'Come in.'

The day of – Cathy

It was a game, really. Until she texted Dan back, she wouldn't get another shot of dopamine, sending her high as a kite. But once she did text him back, she lost the power, handed it back to him. She'd almost forgotten that this was how it was with men, a tug of war, not a sensible choice they made together. But as soon as she saw that Nina had arrived, sending cold blasts of fear down her legs, Cathy lost it – she had to text him. Now. 'I need the loo,' she said to Hazel. 'Will you take him?'

She passed over Arthur in his sling. As she watched his little face, the thought came – *who does he look like?* Would this happen every time she looked at her son, for the rest of his life? Peering for dark eyes and a cowlick of hair? Praying Hazel would not remember the couple they'd chatted to at the IVF unit? Then she remembered her phone was in the sling. 'Oh, wait.' She fumbled it out.

Hazel watched her curiously. 'Why do you need that for the loo?'

'Oh! I said I'd text Mum, forgot.'

She crossed the green lawn, aware that Hazel had noticed some-thing that wasn't right. Hazel was sharp. She had to be careful. She went to the bathroom upstairs, although the downstairs was in fact free, needing some space. She sat on the edge of the claw-foot bath, breathing hard. Was it worth it? Excitement felt so close to terror, like her brain couldn't tell the difference. Why did it matter? Hazel knew Arthur's father was some random man, did it matter which one? Of course it mattered. Her hands were sweaty and left marks on the screen. *I want you to see him*, she replied. *Where and when?*

A delay. She waited, looking round at Monica's pristine bathroom. Not even any toys or nappies or a baby bath. Not to mention the detritus of a teenage girl, spilled make-up and strips of hair-covered waxing paper. Perhaps Chloe had an en suite. As she waited, she let herself remember it, the terrible thing she had done and which, even worse, she couldn't manage to regret. Because there was Arthur, and because it had been so good with Dan, that afternoon at his garden office, when Rachel and Hazel were at work, on an old red sofa with a blanket over it, his books and drawing table all around. It had been chilly in there, and he'd put his hands on her skin to warm her up. She'd been craving it ever since, like just one hit of a dangerous drug.

A buzz. Cathy jumped, her heart rocketing into her chin. *Same place. Tuesday 3pm?*

OK.

I can't wait, he said, and it was everything, everything that he'd said it. *Delete this now.* It was part of the beautiful pain of it, that messages could not be kept. She gorged on it a few times more, those three words. *I can't wait.*

◆ ◆ ◆

The same place meant a coffee shop in the park in Beckenham, where they'd met the first time. It had been casual. *Hey, it's hard going through all this. If you want to get coffee sometime, I'm free during the day a lot.* Dan was a freelance web designer. She said yes.

No reason she couldn't have male friends, Hazel had plenty, guys from work she held pint-drinking competitions with and earnest conversations about macros. But Cathy didn't tell her, and when the day came, she found she was nervous, putting on mascara. They'd talked for four hours, until it grew dark and the cafe staff were putting the chairs on the tables to sweep up. That had been the start of it.

Then of course, Cathy was pregnant, and Rachel, Dan's wife, was not, and that made everything different. Dan had told her he didn't want to try IVF again, that it was destroying their marriage, making sex all about procreation, or the lack of it, about failure, not about love. Cathy wondered if that was true, on some deep level. She'd always known she would need intervention to have a baby with Hazel. The fact that it had happened so easily with Dan, without even trying, seemed like a message.

She needed to go back to the party. Her heart was soaring – she was going to see Dan! This week! Thank God, oh, thank God. Cathy went out, crossed the landing by the balcony. The bathroom was directly opposite the doors to the balcony, doors made of squeaky-clean glass. That meant Cathy saw who was out there. She saw what happened. She knew who did it.

'We need to call an ambulance.' Hazel, who had come up the stairs in response to the screaming, was good at this sort of thing, crises. She'd been in the army as a younger woman and Cathy often thought she would thrive in an apocalypse-type situation. 'My phone's out of battery. Give me yours?' She held out her hand. And Cathy froze. The last message from Dan had not been deleted yet, in all the confusion. But she could not refuse to hand it over, not when she'd gone out on the balcony and seen Nina's arm hanging over the edge of the rockery down below, and a trickle of red blood running down it.

Hazel saw the hesitation, the phone right there in Cathy's hand, and in that split second, everything between them was ruined. She could hardly remember what happened after that. Cathy dialled 999 herself, at 3.07 p.m., and it felt so strange to say the words she'd heard on TV so many times, to explain that someone had fallen from a balcony – she knew she'd put it that way, *fallen*, because the call operator had read it back to her – and she asked Hazel what the address was, and Hazel had told her, and that was the last time she spoke to Cathy all day.

The day of – Jax

I had spent the two weeks since Hadley's birth in the grip of terror – it wasn't supposed to be like this. I wasn't meant to hide in the bathroom for a few seconds longer while she howled in her cot. I wasn't supposed to fantasise about being at work, behind a peaceful desk with a gently ringing phone far in the distance. I was supposed to love every moment of this, a baby at my age. I was supposed to lie adoringly in bed with her, and take artfully arranged Facebook shots declaring how lucky I was to have my beautiful, funny little girl. Could children be funny at two weeks old? Was it normal now to praise your kids publicly? The best my mother had ever said about me was that I wasn't too much trouble. Now it was non-stop boasting, leaving the rest of us feeling crap about our mothering skills. I stood over her cot and watched her move, hands groping blindly, eyes scrunched up as if she hated the world. Did I not love her? I went to pick her up, press her satin skin to mine, and she howled. Did she not love me?

I had no sense of time, falling asleep and waking to a thin grey light, hearing the howls of the baby in my ears even when she wasn't crying, like tinnitus. Aaron had to go back to work after two weeks, so he wouldn't be around during the day to help me.

I was not coping. We both knew it. I hadn't been dressed in days, and I spent most of my waking hours in tears, leaking milk and saltwater and blood and one or two other things as well. At night Aaron went back to his own place, some horrible little studio, to sleep apart from me.

One day – could have been morning, could have been evening – Aaron came into the bedroom. I was wrestling the baby on to my nipple. Wasn't she supposed to want this? Not arch her back and make a noise like a lawnmower? 'Er,' he said. That was how he started talking to me now, with a nervous throat-clear, like I was Alexa or something.

'What?' I raised my voice over her cries.

'This party today.'

'What party?'

'Monica. She's having a barbecue, remember?'

'Oh Jesus, really? That's going ahead?'

'Yeah. To get all the babies together. Everyone's had theirs now.'

The idea of going to a party seemed absurd. So did the idea of getting out of bed, showering, and putting on clothes. 'Are you serious? I can hardly move.'

He hovered there. 'Jax. I'm worried about you.'

Jax, not *babe*. Maybe he'd never call me that again. And using my mother's phrase, *I'm worried about you*. I sniped back, 'Been chatting to Mum, have you?' A pause. He actually had! Things must be bad. 'Maybe if you helped me more, I'd be better.'

'What can I do? I can't feed her. I'm doing her bath, dressing her.'

'Yes, and then she craps herself four more times during the day.'

'I can't help that,' he said quietly.

'You could have not moved out and left me.'

He didn't say anything, just looked at me in a way that took in my milk and snot-encrusted nightie, my wild hair and puffy eyes, the stink of me, of sweat and sour dairy. The way I'd told him to leave the hospital, just when I needed him most. Fine. He had a point. 'Alright, Christ, we'll go to the party if you want, play happy families. It'll just be Monica trying to get one up on us with her home-made tzatziki or whatever.' I bet Monica was busy right now coordinating Instagram shots, not a drop of bodily fluid in sight. But I agreed to it.

Lunchtime came, or so the clocks told me. We went to the barbecue.

The day of – Aisha

Someone had called the police, or maybe more than one person. She hated how confused she felt about what was happening, what to do next. One minute she'd been talking to Rahul, facing ruin, the worst thing she could imagine. Then she'd heard a scream, and a thud, the blur of a falling body, and knew something bad had happened, but she was still standing frozen with Rahul by the smoking barbecue. Rahul was holding his phone, of course, but had not used it to call for an ambulance. Why not? Why had they even come here? She felt a rising anger, or sadness, or panic in her throat. 'Aren't you going to do something?' He was a paramedic, this was his job. 'Go and help, Rahul!'

In the distance, she could hear sirens. The police were coming, or maybe an ambulance, or maybe both. Voices overlapped, panicked:

What happened?

Who was up there?

Oh my God, is she . . . ?

She's dead! Oh my God! In our house!

His eyes snapped open, as if he'd shut down for a minute. People were moving around them – Hazel had gone into the house carrying baby Arthur, and someone was crying, and someone had screamed, 'Oh God! God!' Someone ran across the patio. And she and Rahul were just standing there, doing nothing. Helping no one. 'What should I do?' he asked. Helpless. She wasn't sure if he meant this, or the money, or both.

'Something. Not just . . . nothing. This is your job!'

His hands tightened on the phone. 'What's going to happen? With us?'

The sirens grew louder, and stopped. Someone was dead. Aisha had not even begun to think about who. She was in shock, maybe. 'I don't know,' she said. 'Does it matter?'

He seemed about to answer, then he turned away. 'I better go and help.'

Jax – now (one week after the barbecue)

Perhaps I should have done something, knowing as I did that the police were sniffing around. Run, fled the country. But where would I go? I had a newborn, and precarious control of my pelvic floor. For the week after the barbecue, I concentrated on getting through one hour at a time. Not days, because days had lost their meaning as a morning, afternoon and evening, a night where you slept through and woke up.

Aaron was still living elsewhere, subletting the studio flat of a guy who'd gone travelling for a month. Temporary, we called it, though I knew as well as anyone that temporary separations were just stepping stones to permanent ones. He came by each night to bathe Hadley and avert his eyes as I tried to feed her while she howled and batted my breast away, scratching me with her little sharp nails. We didn't talk about what had happened on the balcony, or about his search for his mother, or the strange events which had now stopped. The things I'd said to him, the hole in the bedroom wall. The visits from the police. Kelly, and the baby. Nina on the balcony. The revelation. The struggle. The push. We didn't talk about anything much, just how to keep Hadley alive when she didn't want to feed and screamed herself hoarse every time I went to bathe or change her, despite covering herself every hour or so with pee and worse. The house stank. I stank. I cried without knowing I was doing it. In the middle of all this, DS Alison Hegarty came around with her questions and her watchful eyes. I didn't have the brain capacity to mount a defence. I just had to wait for her to figure things out, and come for me. And she did. It was three weeks since the birth, and a week since the balcony, when I heard a car draw up outside. It was two in the afternoon, though this meant nothing to me. I had last slept an hour before, for ten minutes on the sofa. I had last showered almost three days before. I had last washed my hair for the barbecue. I heard the car, then the footsteps on the path, and I knew the doorbell would ring, and I waited, and it did. They were here.

Alison

Aisha and Rahul had confirmed what Cathy and Chloe had both said – Nina was on the balcony right before the fall with Aaron and Jax. 'Nina was up there first,' Aisha had volunteered. 'Then Jax and the baby. Then I think Aaron got a text or something – I remember Rahul thought it was his phone, they had the same tone, and he jumped – and then Aaron sort of ran off into the house.'

'Did you see what happened next?'

'No. Rahul and I were talking, we weren't looking – until we heard the scream.'

A significant look passed between them. Rahul cleared his throat. The sound of his voice came as a surprise to Alison – it was much more confident than before. 'I have some gambling issues,' he said. 'Like you guessed. I owe some money. That's why I – what we were talking about. I'd been hiding it from Aisha. I've told her everything now, even about my – about the caution I got. But I promise, neither of us had anything to do with the fall.'

Aisha looked anxious. 'Poor Jax. She won't get in trouble, will she? I always liked her. I'm sure it was just an accident.'

She would get in a lot of trouble if Alison had anything to say about it. 'You should have told me this to start with. It's very serious, withholding evidence.'

Aisha bit her lip. 'I know, but . . . we weren't sure, you know? We only knew they were up there. And she's just had a baby . . .'

'Alright. If you need any resources to help with gambling debts, I can suggest some.'

Rahul's head was bowed, ashamed. 'Thanks,' he mumbled. 'I'll get it sorted.'

Back to the car, closing their doors with pleasing matching clunks. Diana mimed a clipboard. 'Tick and tick.'

◆ ◆ ◆

Next up was Monica Dunwood, who they caught in the middle of doing Pilates in front of the TV, in yoga pants that Alison knew cost a hundred quid. No sign of Chloe or the baby. 'What do you want now? Is it about the rockery clean-up?'

That bloody rockery. 'Just some clarifications.'

They got little more from Monica. Chloe had been sick all term, she maintained, and she'd sent the note but the stupid school had lost it. She was, however, keen to agree that yes, Jax and Aaron had been on the balcony with Nina before the fall. 'I mean, I didn't see for sure, I was in the kitchen, but when I went upstairs they were there, and Cathy.'

'No one else?'

She flexed her hamstring. 'No one else.'

'And why did you not mention this before?'

'Oh, I don't know. Like I said, I didn't *see* anything. And of course one doesn't like to *incriminate* people.' Alison could have said something to her about withholding information, but decided it wasn't worth it. And hopefully, after today, she'd never have to see Monica Dunwood again.

So there it was. Five witnesses had confirmed who was on the balcony. Plus, the DNA results, and the hair analysis, which showed the strands in Nina's bracelet belonged to Jax Culville. More than enough for an arrest, and she couldn't wait to see Colette eat her words about this being a simple accident.

She swung away from the kerb. 'God, I feel like Mulder and Scully today.'

'Who?'

Alison shot Diana a look. 'If you try and tell me you're too young . . .'

'Only kidding. Bags me be Scully though.'

The day of – Jax

The party had felt like a series of shocks, each one worse than the last. I wanted to go, but Aaron had disappeared again, so I had taken Hadley upstairs to cool her down. Guiltily, I saw she did look red. I had left her too long in the sun. My mother had been right – I wasn't coping. I was messing this up.

In Monica's upstairs bathroom, shockingly tidy, I splashed water over the baby at the sink, making her flinch and cry. I was close to crying too. 'I'm sorry, darling. I'm sorry.' Why had I thought I could do this? After thirty-eight years of only thinking about myself? Aaron was trying but he was so young. Hadley cried some more. 'Baby, I'm sorry. I'll take you home.' And when we were there, Aaron and I would have to have a serious conversation. I'd have to go to the doctor and confess I wasn't well. Maybe take medication. If I was lucky, they wouldn't call social services.

I went out on to the landing, and saw someone hovering there, their face in shadow. It was Nina. I hadn't realised she was coming today and couldn't face her. Whether she meant well or not, she'd played a role in tearing Aaron and me apart. Now I just said, 'Hi. I think we need to head off.'

I couldn't read her expression, but no surprise there. 'Already? I was hoping to talk to you.'

'Oh?'

'Why don't we go out on the balcony? There's a nice view over the park.'

I hesitated. Hadley had already had too much sun. But Nina had a pull over me, or rather, my craven need to impress her was strong. I followed her out, and the glass door closed behind us, sealing off sound from the house. In the garden below, I could see Rahul and Aisha, their body language stiff, like people arguing, Hazel turning sausages at the barbecue. I saw Anita head round the side of the house, and the noise of a car drawing up that must be Jeremy, returning from dropping off Kelly. I didn't know where Aaron was. The park spread out below us, and I wondered how much Ed had paid for this house, if we'd ever be able to move from my small one.

Nina said, 'Hadley looks quite red.'

'I know. I didn't quite realise how strong the sun was. I'll take her home and put some cream on her.'

'You shouldn't have left her, you know. Kelly was right to pick her up.'

I bowed my head. 'I know.'

Nina shifted, her shadow falling over me. 'I've always thought it was strange, who gets to be a mother and who doesn't. Take Anita – she'd be a wonderful mum, and she can't make it happen. But here you are, and it's easy, even at your age. *Our* age, I should say.'

I hadn't known we were the same age, but that was hardly the important point to note in what she'd said. 'Hang on . . .'

'My baby was taken from me, you know. Not because I wasn't a good mum. I mean I was young, I was only fourteen, but I loved him. And that's what mattered. I'd never have left him out in the sun, and they took him off me all the same.'

318

What was she talking about? She had a child? 'I don't . . .'

'But I swore I'd find him one day. It took twenty years, but I did. And imagine my surprise to find he's shacked up with someone my age! Literally old enough to be his mother!'

I didn't understand what was happening. My head hurt; maybe I'd had too much sun as well. The baby was heavy in my arms. She started to cry again, the sound ear-splitting. 'Nina, I don't think you should be talking to me like this.' But it was feeble, because I was used to women telling me off, of course.

'Someone needs to, Jax. Before you put this little baby at risk. Before you corrupt my boy.'

'What are you talking about? You have a son? Why did you never . . .' How old would he be now? She said she'd had him at fourteen, and that she was my age. That meant . . .

'Here he is,' she said, her voice glowing with pride and love, and I turned and saw Aaron at the balcony door, and then I understood.

Aaron looked worried. Even more so than usual. 'I got your text.' To Nina. 'Is she OK?' Meaning me. My head was spinning. Did he know? Was Nina really his mother? Georgina was *Nina*? How was it possible?

'Well, not really,' said Nina, looking at him with her head tilted. 'She's no good for you. You know that really, don't you? She's too old for you. Not a good mum to Hadley. You need better, Edward.'

He looked so confused. So he didn't know. I felt frozen to the spot, as I had after the anaesthetic. Nothing made sense. How could she be his mother? Why did she call him Edward? She must be crazy. 'What?'

'Darling, it's me. Don't you know me?' She held her arms wide. 'I'm your mum. They took you away from me, sweetheart, but I found you at last. I didn't even know your new name! I had to pay a detective. But I found you.'

Aaron's frown deepened. 'What are you talking about?'

It was me who spoke. 'Aaron . . . I think Nina's saying she's . . . who you were looking for. Your birth mother.' Nina. Georgina. But how? Could such a coincidence be possible? It was hardly credible.

I found you, she'd said. Not a coincidence. And I remembered how I'd heard about this group, the flyer posted through our door, and I went cold all over. *Move*, my brain was telling me. *Take the baby. Get out now.* But I couldn't.

Nina stepped towards him, her hand outstretched to his face. 'And look at you. You've grown up so handsome, so kind. I'm proud of you. We've found each other at last, Edward.'

'That's not my name,' he tried. He was as white as the paintwork.

'It used to be.' She smiled, wide and happy. 'When you were mine. You're my son, sweetheart. I've found you at last.'

Jax – now

I felt my life had taken a nightmare turn and I couldn't seem to get it back on track. How far back could I trace the misstep? Meeting Aaron? Getting pregnant? Or further back – did I sow the seeds of this, waiting to grow up around me like a thicket, the moment I met Mark Jarvis?

The detective, Alison, she was someone I might have been friends with in other circumstances. I could see us moaning about our jobs and men over a bottle of white wine. She'd be direct but kind – *he's not good enough for you, love, move on. You deserve better.* That sort of friend, who buoys you up but doesn't flatter.

But we weren't friends. Instead, she had come to my house and arrested me. I had been sitting in a cell for an indeterminate amount of time when she finally came in to get me. Blue mattress, cold walls, high dirty window. No doubt that was part of their strategy, to disorient you so you'd be more willing to confess. I wanted to say I didn't know what I should confess to. But I did. The guilt was scrawled across my face like lipstick on a mirror. She knew it and I knew it.

'Jax.' She looked as tired as me, her hair frizzy under the fluorescent lights. 'Come with me, please.'

'Where's my baby?' I said, as we went down the corridor.

'With your mother.'

'Not Aaron?'

'We've arrested him too.'

I digested this. I almost said, *he didn't do anything*, but had the sense not to, not until I knew what was going on, what evidence they had. 'I'll need to feed her you know. How long have I been here?'

'Forty minutes or so.'

It had felt longer. 'Well . . . she'll need a feed in an hour or so.'

'Alright. Noted.' She sat down opposite me, fixed me with some intense eye contact. She said some things about being under caution and having a lawyer if I wanted, and switched on a tape machine and it was all so much like the TV that I could hardly take it in. 'Do you know why you're here, Jax?'

I thought about blustering it out, but I knew I wouldn't be here unless she had some pretty compelling evidence. 'I imagine because I was on the balcony when Nina . . . fell.'

'Which you didn't mention when I questioned you. In fact, you lied about where you were.'

'I didn't want you to get the wrong idea.'

'Which would be?' She put her elbows on the table, leaned forward. *Careful, careful.*

'I didn't push her.'

'So we can agree she was pushed.'

Careful! 'No. She fell.'

She sighed, and again I imagined her as my supportive but honest friend. 'Jax. We know she couldn't have fallen. We also know she was Aaron's mother.'

Oh God. I paused. 'We only found that out right before. She'd been looking for him – stalking him, really. She'd even set up the baby group just to get to him! I mean, it's crazy!' Maybe I was making things worse. Maybe I should have had a lawyer after all, as they'd offered, but I'd only thought about our bank balance, or rather lack of it. Stupid.

'So what happened – she told him who he was, and he pushed her off?'

'No! Christ, no, he didn't do anything. He'd been wanting to find her.'

'I imagine he was pretty angry though – the woman who abandoned him, pretending to be someone else, infiltrating his life.'

'It wasn't her fault. She was made to give him up.' I had believed Nina – I'd heard the cloying love in her voice.

'So what happened, Jax?' She sat back. 'You have to tell me, you know. I have enough to charge you both with murder. Your hair was tangled in Nina's bracelet, did you know? Imagine that – little Hadley left with no parents. I imagine she'd go to live with your mother.'

Damn it, Alison, I thought we were imaginary friends. 'Neither of us pushed her. She – she tried to push me.'

She nodded, as if she finally believed me. 'Go on.'

And so I did.

The day of – Jax

Aaron was frozen, staring at his mother. Because I could see it, now they were side by side. The blue eyes, the shape of the face. Oh my God. All this time, his mother had been right under our noses. 'How . . . I don't understand,' he managed.

'I've been looking for you. And you've been looking for me, haven't you? Of course, I've changed my name, so I couldn't do it through official channels. But I found you – a little note on Facebook of all places, just the tiniest reference to you in among all that rubbish! – and imagine my shock – you're about to be a dad yourself. With a woman my age. She's *my* age, Edward!'

He couldn't have known, but the thought did blaze across my mind like a comet. Mother issues. The Oedipus complex, wasn't that what they called it? Aaron had been two when he went into care; old enough to have bonded with her, to have a memory of some kind. I was the same age as my partner's mother. And here we were, trapped on this balcony with her. I began to edge back towards the door. Aaron said, 'I . . . Jesus, I didn't know.'

'You must have, on some level.' She took another step towards him, which meant that, on the small balcony, she was very close indeed. I was pressed against the glass wall, Hadley squirming against me. 'It's OK, darling. You don't need her any more. I'm here. I'll look after you, and Hadley too. We can start again – a family!'

Something at the back of my neck was screaming *run, run, this is bad*, but my brain was trying to rationalise it. She wanted me to break up with Aaron? Well, we were well on our way to that without her help. Or . . .

'My cat,' I blurted out. 'The milk, the car . . . Christ, the emails! The *mailing*. Was that you?'

Aaron looked confused. Nina tilted her head in my direction, irritated. 'Imagine how you'd feel, if you found your son and he was shacked up with someone your age. Naturally I was a little . . . angry. Your office, they're quite lax, aren't they? It was easy to walk right in. You'd left your computer on, the spreadsheet open. It was too simple, really. You should talk to them about that.'

I couldn't believe this. 'You took my cat! God, is she alright? You told people I was a paedophile!'

'You may as well be. And of course she's alright, I wouldn't hurt an animal.' She turned around, and I saw the blazing of her eyes – Aaron's eyes – the wiry strength of her yoga-honed body. 'Give me the baby, Jax. You don't want her anyway. You're not coping, are you? I know. I saw you in hospital.' The figure standing over me in the dark. The feeling that I couldn't move. Nina held her arms out. 'I've been watching you for a long time, Jax, seeing what kind of mother you'd be. And today just proves it. You left her alone, in the sun, and someone took her. Give her to me. I'll look after her, and Aaron.' For a terrible moment, I was tempted. She would leave me alone, she would shoulder my burdens. I could go back to the Jax of two years ago, an independent woman with control of her bladder. 'Give me her.' Nina's strong hands went around Hadley's soft body. And I held on. Something primal had kicked in. *My baby.*

'No! Get off me.'

'You're hurting her!' Aaron shouted, and I didn't know if he meant me or the baby. 'Let me take her.' His voice was shaking but I saw he was trying to sound calm.

'I won't hurt her, darling.' Nina's eyes were fixed on me. 'I just want rid of this . . . pervert. I'd never hurt a little baby.'

'Then let me take her.' She hesitated, then let him take the baby, and his eyes met mine, trying to telegraph something, but I didn't know what. I could no longer read him. Aaron took Hadley a few paces away, further from the edge of the balcony.

My voice shook. Part of me still couldn't process this, was insisting it was all a misunderstanding. People didn't *do* things like this. 'Nina, this is crazy. I'm not giving up my baby. You must know that.'

'She'd be better off without you,' said Nina easily. 'They both would.' And then she seized my upper arms and tried to force me over the edge.

Jax – now

'So she pushed you?' asked Alison.

'She tried to, yes. She thought – well, I think she was unhinged by losing Aaron all those years ago. I'm the same age as her. I think she thought – I don't know, if she got rid of me she could have him back, and the baby too. A chance to start over.'

Alison was nodding as if she was on my side. Was this a trap though? 'So you fought back. Pushed her over.'

'I . . .' The moment went on and on. 'No. I didn't.' But she had me. Someone must have done it. I weighed up all my bad options. Take the blame myself, go to prison for the rest of Hadley's child-hood. Or drop someone else in it. What was the right thing to do? I was a mother now, it wasn't just about me. But was I a good one? Did I know how to soothe her, care for her, make things better? Not leave her in harm's way? Was it true, what Nina had said, in that terrible moment under the blazing sun – would Hadley and Aaron be better off without me after all?

'Well?' she said. 'What's it going to be, Jax?'

Alison

'She confessed.' Alison couldn't help smiling as she bounded into the office.

Diana's groomed eyebrows shot up. 'To the push?'

'To everything.'

'What did the boyfriend say? He backed it up?'

'Nothing, so far. Want to come in with me?' The feeling had begun to break over Alison, her favourite in the world – when the case was almost wrapped up, when the loose ends were all tied off for one glorious day – sometimes less, sometimes an hour was all you got – and the mystery was solved, justice would be done. Before the next murder or rape or burglary came in and it all started again.

Colette was standing outside the other interview room, leaning back on her high heels, which Alison knew were Manolo Blahnik and not even bought in the sale. 'Jax Culville confessed,' Alison couldn't help but boast.

'Oh?'

'I was going to talk to the boyfriend, see if he corroborates.'

'Well, there's a slight problem with that, Alison. He's confessed too – says it was him that did it, not Jax.'

◆ ◆ ◆

After days of lies and obfuscations, here she was with two confessions on her hands. Alison slumped against the wall in the corridor, with its peeling paint and smell of old dust. Aaron Cole in one room, maintaining he had pushed Nina da Souza, aka Georgina Partington-Smith, aka his mother, in order to protect Jax and the baby. Jax Culville in the other, insisting she had struggled with Nina in self-defence, and Nina had gone over. Just when she thought she'd wrangled the case into submission, it had come back and knocked the legs from under her. 'How can we break them?'

'Send them both down,' Diana shrugged. 'Joint enterprise.'

'They have a baby.' She was inclined to save Jax – surely a woman with no history of violence would not have done this. Whereas Aaron had punched a wall, and learned moments before the fall that his long-lost mother was stalking him. But was she just biased, thinking of Jax having to give up her newborn, see her once a week at most, depending on what prison she ended up in?

'Murder's murder.' Diana was not sympathetic. It wouldn't be murder now, most likely – there was evidence of self-defence, of provocation. All the same, time would have to be served. She honestly didn't know what to do, and so when the desk sergeant bustled up and said there was someone in reception for her, she was pleased. Put the decision off for a few minutes.

Under the harsh lights of reception was a girl in school uniform, along with a noisy drunk singing a Katy Perry song. It was Chloe Evans, Monica Dunwood's daughter.

What the hell was she doing here? 'Are you alright, Chloe?'

'You have Jax and Aaron here, right – you arrested them?'

'I can't discuss that with you.'

'Well, you have to.' Chloe laid her hands, with bitten nails, on the counter. 'They didn't push her off, you see. It was me. I did it.'

The day of – Chloe

Chloe couldn't stop crying. Someone was trying to take Isabella from her – Cathy, she saw. A group of people had gathered on the landing. Jax was staring at her, her own baby pressed tight to her chest. Aaron was staring over the balcony, where Nina had just fallen, plunging over as if into a swimming pool. Hazel had just come up the stairs, holding Arthur in a sling.

'She fell! She . . . She fell!'

'I know,' said Cathy soothingly. 'But won't you give me the baby, sweetheart? Look, she's frightened.'

Chloe held Isabella tighter. 'She's fine!'

Her mother was coming up the stairs now, eyes flashing. *You stupid girl.* 'Chloe! What have you done?'

Always assuming it was Chloe's fault, everything that went wrong. Cathy said, 'Chloe, won't you give your sister to your mum?'

Chloe couldn't bear it any more. Monica didn't even love Isabella. She'd locked her up in her room most of the day, and Chloe had seen the bottle of baby Calpol on the side and knew what that meant. She wasn't stupid. She'd noticed that every other baby at this party had been crying and fussing and Isabella was quiet and floppy. 'She's not my sister!' she burst out. '*She* didn't give birth two weeks ago. Look at her! Can't you see?'

All eyes swivelled to Monica. Her stomach flat. Her body toned. 'Chloe, you stupid girl, shut up!' Monica shouted.

'I won't shut up.' She held the baby close to her face, breathing her in. 'She's my baby. I had her, and Mum made me stay off school so she could pretend it was her. She put a pillow up her jumper! Look!' And Chloe lifted her own baggy dress so they could see what was underneath, the scarring, the stretch marks, and the women there understood what it meant, because they had them too.

All hell erupted then. But holding her daughter in her arms, being acknowledged as her mother at last, Chloe found that she didn't even care. She'd move out, she'd manage somehow. She never had to see her mother again. And, oh, the freedom of finally knowing that.

Finally, she allowed herself to think about what had just taken place on the balcony, a few minutes before. She had seen the three people out there – Nina, the instructor woman, had hold of Jax by the shoulders. Chloe wasn't sure what she was seeing – was she trying to help her, stop her falling? – but then she saw that no, Nina was trying to force Jax over the edge. The young hot guy was holding their baby close to his chest and trying to get his arm in between them. He saw Chloe standing there and shouted, 'Help. Help me, she's gone mad!' So Chloe did. With Isabella pressed tight to her body, making two babies and four people on the small balcony space, she charged out and tried to help Aaron pull Nina's hands off Jax. They only had one free arm each what with holding the babies, and Nina was strong, so strong, bracing her legs against the small ledge around the bottom of the balcony, where Monica kept pot plants and tea lights. Finally, Aaron managed to get her hands off Jax, and Jax slumped down, white and winded, but Nina was free, her hair blowing in a faint breeze, her eyes wild. Her gaze flicked to Aaron's arms. *She's going for the baby!* Chloe was never sure if she'd said it out loud or not, but she had seen what was going to happen, just like she was watching a film, and it wasn't right, it wasn't fair that people kept taking babies that weren't theirs, like her mother coming into the hospital that day and taking Isabella and saying she was hers, and no one had even noticed or cared. It was all too much, and she hadn't thought, she'd lunged forward at Nina, and . . . that was that.

Alison

'Chloe – you need to wait. We can't talk to you like this.' Alison was staring at the slight teenage girl in front of her, trembling in the cold air of the interview room. How old was she even? Fifteen? They hadn't had time to find an appropriate adult or contact her mother, as she'd walked right up to them and started blurting out her story. Likely none of this would be admissible.

'But I pushed Nina. I could see she was trying to take the baby or hurt the baby and she already tried to push Jax. I didn't mean to do it, not really. I was just sick of people taking babies.'

'What?' Was she talking about Kelly and Hadley?

'Like my mum. I mean my mum, taking Isabella.'

Again, what? 'Um . . . you'll have to explain more about that, Chloe, but could you just wait until . . .'

Chloe sat back in her chair. She seemed tired, but not afraid, just adrenalised, as people often are when the truth finally tears its way out of them. 'Isabella. She isn't my mum's – I mean, come on, she's forty-four and weighs eight stone, like she really just had a baby? She's mine. Mum made me pretend, and to be honest I'm sick of it. I just pushed Nina, to save the baby.' She looked at Alison, who was totally lost for words, eyes clear with youth. 'So what happens now, do I, like, go to prison?'

The day of – Monica

Everything was ruined. Not only had her party been disrupted by that chavvy Kelly, taking a baby that wasn't hers, for goodness' sake, but she was enraged with Ed for showing people his disgusting collection. But even worse than that, she herself had been exposed as a liar and a fraud. As the mother of a slutty teenager, who'd got herself knocked up by some boy from a council estate.

When Monica had first found out – too late to do anything about it, since Chloe had hidden her bump for months under those awful baggy jumpers she liked – she'd been thrown into turmoil. What would Ed say – he'd been reluctant enough to take on a stepdaughter, let alone a stepgrandchild. She'd had to use every trick in the book to get him to commit and he still wasn't there. Adventurous sex, helping with his career, and above all, appearing perfect at all times. Having a pregnant teenage daughter was not perfect. If only *she'd* been the one who was pregnant, Ed would have had to marry her, and it would all have been ideal.

That was what gave her the idea. Then it was just a matter of convincing Chloe, who was scared out of her wits anyway, and telling the school she had glandular fever and needed several months off. They'd asked for a doctor's note, but Monica had stalled and stalled, claiming she'd posted it and it must have got lost, that the doctor hadn't sent it. She'd move Chloe to a different school if she had to. It would be worth it, to be married again, and to a much richer man than Thomas, her ex. She'd told Chloe that Ed would put them out if he knew the truth. And with her feckless dad refusing to pay child support, what else could they do? No matter that Thomas was doing his best to support his daughter. Served him right for leaving and knocking up a twenty-something.

Amazingly, Ed had not noticed. Monica had never let him see her naked in the light anyway, and the stuffing she wore around her waist was simply kept on at night. She'd slept in another room for most of the pregnancy, saying she was hot and uncomfortable. They had plenty of rooms. He'd been so proud of himself, knocking her up when she was forty-four and he was older. *Strong lead in the pencil, eh?* She'd had to pretend it was a surprise to her too, that she hadn't noticed she was pregnant for a while – she'd hinted delicately that things were not as regular as they could be – and made sure he wasn't at any medical appointments or the birth itself, which wasn't hard since he was squeamish about women's bodies and worked non-stop. It had gone perfectly. She had a pretty little girl to dress up and parade, and Chloe would be away to university in a few years anyway. Monica was even toying with making some new friends and knocking a few years off her age, since she had a little baby to back up her claims. The only difficult moment had been when Nina seemed to know. She'd leaned into Monica in that group session where they'd all been so rude about vaccines, touching her bump, and told her to be careful. That not everyone was so easily fooled.

Now, standing at the top of her stairs, her hands sticky from cleaning up the melted cake (because stupid Ed had left the bloody fridge open!) she realised it was all ruined. These people she had met and brought to her home to be dazzled by her success, they would see her for what she was. Worse – Ed was coming up the stairs. 'What the hell happened?' He sounded stunned.

It was only when Cathy said she had called an ambulance, that Monica remembered she had an even more pressing problem. Someone was dead in her garden, and pretty soon her entire life would be under scrutiny. She'd had a reason to get rid of Nina herself, hadn't she?

It was Hazel who spoke, quickly taking in the whole situation, that Chloe had pushed Nina over the balcony. 'She was going to hurt Jax,' Chloe kept saying. 'She wanted to take the baby. I couldn't let her do that.'

Hazel said, 'We need to decide what happened here. Cathy's already called an ambulance, the police will come too.'

Monica didn't understand for a moment. Then she did, and she was surprised, because she hadn't realised Hazel was also someone who understood the importance of how things looked. And, looking about her at the pale and shaken faces of her guests, she had a feeling she wasn't the only one here with something to hide.

Alison

Alison and Diana sat in an empty interview room, across the table from each other. Neither spoke for a long moment, and then Diana flopped on to the table and let out a howl of frustration. 'We were so close!'

'I don't know what to do. What do we do?' Chloe Evans was claiming Isabella was actually her child – this would explain her absence from school, and Monica's lie about her wedding date, why she'd gone to such a downmarket antenatal group, where she wouldn't see anyone she knew. It could easily be proven with a DNA test. Chloe had confessed to the push, but maintained it was done to protect baby Hadley and Jax, so she might get off with any charge. How to prove any of it? Only the people on the balcony could say what had happened, and they'd all lied to her already. And Chloe was a child, with rich parents, who could afford the lawyers. By the time Alison got a proper, admissible interview set up, she might have clammed up again.

'Only thing we can do,' said Diana. 'Question them again. All of them. Tell them what Chloe's said. Ask if it's true.'

Alison thought about dragging herself up from the chair, and walking out of the room, and starting all over again. 'Would they really all do that though? Lie, cover it up just to protect Chloe? None of them had even met her before.'

Diana thought about it. 'They would, maybe, if they wanted to cover something up themselves. And to be fair, it was very convincing. Everyone thought it was just an accident.'

Alison pushed herself to stand. 'True. But they didn't reckon on us.'

Diana mustered up a smile. 'That is very true. They didn't.'

One day later

AISHA

'That was the police on the phone. They're closing the case.' Aisha stood in the living room, watching Rahul as he held Hari, feeding him from a bottle. 'Apparently there won't be any charges brought.' So maybe it was just a fall? Aisha had told the police everything she knew, that Jax and Aaron were on the balcony, and that was all she'd seen. The death had always seemed abstract to her, which she was vaguely ashamed of.

'Oh? That's . . . good.'

'Yes.'

It was over a week since the barbecue. Since then, she had been holding her breath. Waiting for a knock on the door, for bailiffs, for strangers to come and take her things. Afraid to go out in case she came back and the locks had been changed. She had considered moving back in with her parents every day for a week, but was still here. Rahul assured her that between their families, the debts were paid off to a manageable level, at least for now. He'd promised to go to Gamblers Anonymous, however much shame it brought. She knew she would always be watching him, wondering when he'd slip up. That kind of problem was like a sickness, it didn't just go away. But for now, they'd witnessed a murder and not been involved, they'd swerved away from danger at the last minute, and Rahul had been leaving his phone in the other room for most of the day.

She held out her arms. 'I'll take him.' How funny it was, to look at this virtual stranger holding their baby in his arms. Maybe they hadn't known each other very well to begin with, but they had this little boy now, and that meant they were locked together forever. That meant she had to find a way to make it work, for the rest of their lives.

CATHY

When Cathy's mobile buzzed, Hazel gave her a quick look, and Cathy was reminded of what she'd forfeited – the right to ever hide her phone, to casually receive messages, to keep secrets, perhaps forever. Cathy was washing the dishes after their dinner of couscous and tofu, and had to take off her rubber gloves to read the text. 'It's the police,' she said quickly. 'Jax and Aaron are cleared. They're not going to charge Chloe, in the circumstances.' The day before, she'd finally told the entire truth, what she saw happen on the balcony, the decision to protect Chloe – protect them all, really – by saying it was an accident. After all, Cathy had a motive to kill Nina too, didn't she? Nina had guessed her pregnancy was more advanced than she claimed, and one word to Hazel would have been enough to bring her life crashing down. Of course, that had happened anyway.

'Wow. I hoped that'd be the case, but you never know.' Cathy wasn't sure why Hazel had so readily agreed to lie about what happened on that balcony, pretend they hadn't seen who'd pushed Nina. For her, it was self-preservation. But Hazel? Perhaps it was just kindness, to save ruining the life of a teenage girl. Hazel was a kind person, under all the bluster. Cathy had to remember that, and hope she'd be forgiven one day.

'It's over then, I guess.'

Hazel reached past her to take an apple from the fruit bowl. 'I suppose.' The murder enquiry was over. But was it over for them? Would the lie she'd told be between them always?

'So . . . that's good.'

Hazel weighed the apple in her hand, then half turned away towards the living room. 'Just one thing I want to know,' she said.

Cathy's heart quickened. 'Oh?'

'Will you ask Dan about his medical history, his family and so on? Same as we did with the donor?'

She had already promised she would never speak to Dan again, had deleted his number while Hazel stood over her. Dan might protest, but what could he do without blowing his life up, his marriage? It was harsh – Cathy felt the loss as a constant ache in her chest – but it was the only way. And she understood what Hazel was saying with this question – *I will accept what you did, I will fold it into the dough of our relationship. I will think of him as a donor only, not as your lover.* 'I'll have to talk to him to do that,' she ventured.

Hazel nodded. 'Just the once, and no more.'

'Of course.'

Hazel moved towards the door. 'That Scandi drama's on tonight.'

'Great. I'll just finish these and we can watch it?'

'OK.'

And that, it seemed, was that.

KELLY

She was grateful that someone at the police had taken the time to tell her the investigation was over, but it still meant she somehow had to get on and live the rest of her life with no baby and no boyfriend. Funny. Just two months ago she'd felt weighted down by her life, stable and secure for the first time ever. Now she was single, alone, not a mum. Now she could do whatever she wanted. She'd already been looking into courses at the local uni; she kind of fancied doing something like what Nina had done (not that Nina actually had any qualifications, or was even using her real name). Counselling. Listening to people when they were desperate. Helping women who'd lost babies, and still had to go out and about in the world haunted by the ghost of someone who didn't officially exist.

Kelly was thinking about all this as she got home to the little flat, with the empty spaces where Ryan had taken his stuff. She knew she couldn't really afford it on her own, especially if she went to uni. She was vaguely thinking she might leave London, go somewhere cheaper. She'd be far from her mum and family, but on the other hand, she'd be far from her mum and family.

As she got to her door, it was already dark, and she was taking her keys out. When she saw the shape detach itself from the shadows and move towards her, her heart was in her mouth for a second, and it was a shock to realise she could feel something other than sad. Even fear made a change. 'Ryan?'

'Sorry, didn't mean to scare you.' He was wearing his Sainsbury's uniform, his shoulders hunched. Her heart gradually slowed to normal.

'What are you doing here?'

'Got a text off the police – case is closed.'

'Yeah, I know.'

'Just wanted to check you was alright.'

Was she alright? Would she ever be alright again? Her baby was gone, and she knew she and Ryan were done as well. She was on the verge of a whole new life, one that didn't include him. It was strange now, to look at him and think how close they'd been, how she'd carried a child that was half him and half her. 'I will be. Will you?'

He shrugged. 'I'm sorry for what I did. Losing my temper. I just – I wasn't ready for a kid. Doesn't mean I'm not sad about him.'

'I know.' The sadness would always be there, the imagined feel of a small hand in hers as she walked down the street. But she was only twenty-two – to the women in her group, that was nothing. There was ten years, fifteen years, to think of having kids. There was a whole life to live in between.

Kelly took out her keys. 'Come in for a cup of tea,' she said, and she knew it was the last time she'd ever see him.

ANITA

She and Jeremy got the text at the same time, as they sat on the sofa watching the latest BBC crime drama. Now that she'd been up close to a murder herself, she'd seen how silly it all was. How much of police work was mundane, or just sad rather than mysterious. '*Chloe* did it! Goodness me, she's only a child. Pushed her right over, apparently.'

'I did wonder how she'd managed to fall like that.' Strange how little attention she'd paid to the murder that had taken place in front of them, so consumed had she been with the loss of Victoria. There had never been a Victoria, she knew now – there was a baby, yes, but she would be called something different, be brought up in a trailer in Alabama instead of in their nursery. And after all, Nina had been rather unkind to Anita, with her comments about adoption. It was sad, of course, that she'd died, but . . . it wasn't all that sad.

'So what now?' said Jeremy, his finger hovering over the remote control's play button. 'Do we . . . I mean, would you want to try local adoption?'

She thought about what they'd been told. Only older children, only damaged ones. Behavioural issues. Trauma. She looked around their lovely cosy house, the well-chosen pictures, the vinyl stack, the hand-woven blankets on the sofa. 'Oh, Jeremy, I just don't know. Life's not so bad, is it? Without a baby?' She thought of what she'd seen in the group. Monica's manic perfectionism, Jax's postnatal misery. Kelly's terrible loss. The tension between Cathy and Hazel and Rahul and Aisha, the unequal division of labour. The loss of sleep, loss of bladder control. She looked down at her flat stomach and shiny-clean house.

'So what will we do?' said Jeremy.

She took his hand. 'How about we take some time off. A holiday, maybe, just for us. Somewhere kids aren't allowed.' They could drink cocktails and sleep late and do all the things you couldn't with a newborn. And think. And see how they were after that.

Jeremy said, 'Alright. Why don't we shelve it for now?' As if it was an academic meeting.

'Right. Just a bit of time to think. See how we feel.'

'Fine by me.' His arm went round her, solid and sure, and after a few more moments, he pressed the remote and the TV show began to play again.

CHLOE

'Will you be OK in here, love?'

Sam's mum was so sweet. Sure, they only had a small house, so Chloe and the baby would be sharing a box room, but they were kind to her. They cared. And she was allowed to have Isabella – Issy, she'd decided to call her – with her. That was all that mattered really.

The police had been nice to her, considering she'd confessed to pushing a woman off a balcony. There'd been a lawyer, paid for by

Ed, she assumed. The police had asked a lot of questions. Had her mother pressured her to pretend Isabella wasn't hers? Yes. Had she felt Isabella and Hadley were in danger from what was taking place on the balcony? Yes, probably? She didn't entirely know what she'd felt, it had all happened so fast. Had she thought Nina was a danger? She hadn't even known who Nina was before that day, but she'd seen her pushing Jax then going for the baby, and she had acted. She hadn't known Jax either. Just that she was a woman with a baby, and in that way they were alike. The police had allowed her to go home after that, except not to her actual home. She wasn't sure she'd ever go there again.

'I'm fine, thank you.' She smiled at Sam's mum, snuggling into the double bed that filled the small room. Sam was in the bathroom, cleaning his teeth, and soon he would come to say goodnight. Since they were only fifteen, the social-services people said they couldn't share a room, but that was OK. She didn't know what would happen to them in the future, but for now at least she had her baby. Issy's warm scented head was under her chin. Chloe had claimed her now as her daughter, and the social worker had said she never had to see her mum again if she didn't want to. Her dad was flying over from Hong Kong to look after her, and apparently he hadn't abandoned her all this time, it was just her mum running interference as usual. Chloe couldn't wait to see him, and hear about the new baby brother or sister her stepmum was expecting. It was OK. It would all be fine.

MONICA

'Do you really have to?'

Ed was looking around the kitchen, vaguely patting the overnight bag on his shoulder (Louis Vuitton, £1,958). 'I can't imagine a way back from this, no.' She had lied to him about being a dad at his age – that was what seemed to sting the most. Not cheating her daughter out of a baby and tricking him into marriage. The affront to his manhood. 'Have you seen my iPad charger?'

'In the kitchen.' She'd like to see him last five minutes without her subtle organisation of his life.

'I'll be in touch about . . . the legal side, and so on.' Meaning he'd made his mind up, and it would be divorce rather than reconciliation.

'I'll get the house, you know.'

Ed shrugged. In his income bracket, you didn't let petty worries like that hold you back from doing whatever you wanted. He was still supporting his wife and children from his first marriage, after all. 'Get yourself a lawyer, Monica.'

'Oh, I will. Don't you worry about that.'

He bowed his head slightly, and with one journey back because he'd picked up the wrong set of car keys, he was gone. Monica stood alone in a five-bedroom house that had recently held her daughter, her husband, and her granddaughter, who she had almost convinced herself was her daughter too. Now she had no one. A brief pang went through her – she'd staked everything to get Ed, and lost. How humiliating, that everyone, and especially Thomas, would know she'd had to lie her way to a proposal. At least the police had stopped their irritating investigation, and Chloe wasn't going to be charged. And Nina . . . well, when it came down to it, she hadn't been a very nice person, had she?

She spotted a fragment of grass on the marble floor, and stooped to pick it up. Her eagle eye scanned over every surface, but could find nothing amiss. Her new cleaner was good, and of course Chloe wasn't here with her endless mess, not to mention the baby dribbling and throwing food. Perhaps some time apart would do them good, make Chloe realise Monica had only ever tried to help her, give her a better life. Monica sighed, and put her shoulders back. At least now her house would actually be perfect, and if the rest of her life wasn't, well, there were always ways to cover that up.

JAX

Turns out there is very little ceremony to being cleared of a crime. They come in and unlock your cell, give you back your clothes, then you sign a form and you can walk free. Free. Somehow, I had been so close to a murder I wasn't actually sure if I was guilty of it or not, and still walked free.

Aaron was standing in the car park, Hadley in his arms. They'd let him go before me, since his DNA had not been on Nina's body. I shuffled towards him. A night in a cell coming after birth, and two weeks of hellish motherhood, had just about done me in. For a moment I thought about running away from both of them, these dependents I'd strangely acquired. Get back poor Minou, who'd apparently been living with Nina's neighbour under the humiliating name 'Bootsy', and pretend none of this had ever happened. 'Are you OK?' he said.

'I'll live. Here.' I took the baby, because I felt better with her in my arms. She might have been a tiny millstone, but she anchored me down, at least. 'She'll need feeding.'

Aaron burst out, 'Jax . . . can I come home with you? I hate being in the studio. Not just because it's small, because I miss you. Both of you.' He looked so miserable, I felt an answering sadness in my chest. 'Also – I lost my job. I'm so sorry. I was just a mess.'

So I'd be responsible for supporting us all, assuming I wouldn't get fired myself. 'Aaron, I don't know. After all this . . .' His mother had been stalking us, had infiltrated our lives so thoroughly we hadn't even noticed. We had watched as she died, and not saved her. I might have killed her myself if I'd had the strength.

'Please. She was my mum, you know? No matter what she did. All these years I hoped I'd find her, and then I did and . . . she's gone.'

I couldn't bring myself to think of Nina – not her real name – with much sympathy, remembering the moment she'd pressed me back against the balcony edge, my feet lifting off the ground with her strength. 'I know she was your mum. I'm sorry for what happened.'

'They've said I can bury her now. If I want. My grandma's still alive but . . . well. She doesn't want to know, apparently.'

Poor Aaron. He'd found the long-lost family he craved, only to end up with nothing after all. Except for Hadley, the little girl squirming in my arms. His daughter. Could I really take that away from him, the chance to see her every day? 'You didn't believe me that something was going on all that time.'

'I know, I'm sorry, it was just – you seemed so kind of . . . crazy. I'm sorry. I thought you weren't well. And Nina said . . . well. And you didn't tell me all of it, did you? The emails. Jarvis.'

It was true, I hadn't been well. What now? The threat was gone, we weren't going to prison, but where did we go from here? I eyed Hadley, this tiny little being who had hijacked my life. She was three weeks old. None of this was her fault. Something pattered on to her head, making her blink – I was crying. 'Aaron, I don't know what's wrong with me. I'm so scared and so . . . I can't seem to bond with her. What's the matter with me?' My shoulders heaved as I stood hunched over the baby, but then I felt someone's arm round me. A smell of Anais Anais released complicated feelings – love, resentment. 'Mum?' Of course, she had driven Aaron over.

'Come on, Jax, we can't have you crying in the car park, can we. Let's go.' She began to lead me towards the car. She'd called me Jax, for once.

I was still crying. 'Mum, I can't do this. You were right. I was too old to have her, I, I, I just didn't know how it would be.'

'Nonsense.' She opened the door. 'I never said you couldn't cope, did I? Go on, get in.' She took Hadley from me and put her in the car seat, with efficient movements. I got into the front as I was told, blubbering pathetically.

'Honestly, I can't. I feel . . . Oh, I'm just not managing. I'm not, Mum.'

Mum met my eyes in the mirror. 'Are you scared all the time? You sometimes feel like Hadley's judging you, she doesn't like you very much, that maybe she's even plotting against you? The world seems suddenly full of darkness and horrors and nothing else?'

'I . . . How did you know?'

She fastened the baby's seat belt. 'That's how it was for me.'

Oh my God. After me, my mother never had another child. 'Mum . . .'

Briskly, she said, 'It's alright, darling. They have good drugs now. We'll take you to the doctor tomorrow, make them help you. It does pass, you know. The hormones.'

'But I felt like this *before* she was born. It can't be postnatal—'

'Nonsense, it can start before birth, did you not know that? Didn't you read the baby books at all, darling?'

I could hardly believe it, this new light opening up through the fog. That maybe the crushing fear I'd felt since she was born – before, even – wasn't just something I had to deal with. That maybe something was actually chemically wrong and could be fixed. That maybe there was a way out of this.

Aaron was hovering outside, as if he didn't know if he was welcome in the car. I wound down my window. 'Come on, get in the back with her.' I heard Mum sniff, but didn't care.

'Really?' The haunted look on his face lifted slightly, and I wondered if I looked the same. Like someone given a last-minute reprieve. Like someone getting a second chance, and didn't I know how that felt?

'Yes. Come on, we're going home.'

ALISON

'OK?'

It was a different way of looking at the world, flat on your back. Alison felt pleasantly helpless, her clothes left back in the ward with her purse and ID and phone and bag. She was wearing surgical stockings and mesh pants, a gown of much-washed cotton with a gaping back, a hairnet. The anaesthetist asked her the same questions she'd been asked a dozen times – her name and date of birth. If she had any loose teeth or crowns. If she had allergies. Someone was fiddling with her hand, attempting to get in a cannula; she knew she'd have bruises when she woke up. This was it. Like taking a deep breath and diving in, unsure if you'd surface. Such an act of trust, giving herself up to the doctors and nurses, the unseen hands that would touch her and undress her and open her up to the air, the secret parts of her.

'OK, Alison. Start counting down from five.'

The bed was moving, and she had the impression of dazzling overhead lights. When she woke up, with her laparoscopy done, she might be able to have a baby. Or it might be bad news, it might never happen, an abrupt end to a road that had already been so much longer than she'd thought. Tom would be there to take her home. Her life would be waiting for her, but at least she had solved the case. At least she knew now what had happened on the balcony on that hot summer's day, though there would be no charges brought. Chloe Evans would get off, given her youth and the circumstances, the two small babies present, the fact that Nina had tried to kill Jax. Most of the crimes of the group had, it turned out, not been illegal ones, just ones of the heart, which are so often harder to forgive. But at least she had . . .

By the count of three, she was unconscious.

BOOK GROUP QUESTIONS

1. *The Push* is about a group of new parents who meet at an antenatal group and are quite competitive with each other. Have you ever experienced rivalry like this within a group of friends?
2. Alison feels as if women without kids are being pitted against those who have them – would you agree this is sometimes an issue?
3. Jax's partner, Aaron, is considerably younger than her. Do you think an age gap is more of an issue when the woman is older than the man?
4. Kelly sadly loses her baby before the end of the group. What do you think the other mums should have done in this situation? Was she right to go to the party anyway?
5. Did Nina have the right to interfere in the lives of the group members, if she thought it was for their own good?
6. Monica is obsessed with her image and will do anything to protect it. Do you think that Instagram and social media make this attitude more common?

7. Is Jax right to feel some guilt about what happened with Mark and Claudia Jarvis? Should she have told Aaron about it?

8. Most members of the baby group are hiding something. Which of the group members do you think has the worst secret?

9. Who did you find to be the most sympathetic character in the book? And the least?

10. Who is really to blame for the death?

ACKNOWLEDGMENTS

Many thanks to everyone who shared their stories, good and bad, about antenatal groups. Thanks to everyone involved in the making of this book, especially my amazing agent Diana Beaumont and brilliant editor Jack Butler. Thanks to Graham Bartlett for checking the police bits and to all my writing friends for continuous support, encouragement and gifs. And finally, thanks to everyone who's read my previous books – I hope you enjoy this one! If you'd like to get in touch with me, do drop me a line on my website, www.ink-stains.co.uk, on Facebook or on Twitter @inkstainsclaire. I promise I'll reply.

ABOUT THE AUTHOR

Photo © 2017 Jamie Drew

Claire McGowan was born in 1981 in a small Irish village where the most exciting thing that ever happened was some cows getting loose on the road. She is the author of *The Fall*, *What You Did*, *The Other Wife* and the acclaimed Paula Maguire crime series. She also writes women's fiction under the name Eva Woods.